Roberta Latow has .... Springfield, Massac.................... ...... York City. She has also been an international interior designer in the USA, Europe, Africa and the Middle East, travelling extensively to acquire arts, artefacts and handicrafts. Her sense of adventure and her experiences on her travels have enriched her writing; her fascination with heroic men and women; how and why they create the lives they do for themselves; the romantic and erotic core within – all these themes are endlessly interesting to her, and form the subjects and backgrounds of her novels.

'Her books are solidly about sex . . . it adds a frisson. It sets a hell of a standard'   *The Sunday Times*

Love Chooses

Roberta Latow

HEADLINE

First published in 1993
by HEADLINE BOOK PUBLISHING
First published in paperback in 1994
by HEADLINE BOOK PUBLISHING
10 9 8 7 6 5 4 3 2

The poem on page vii is taken from *The Collected Poems of C.P. Cavafy*, edited
by George Savidis, translated by Edmund Keeley and Philip Sherrard, and
reprinted by kind permission of Chatto & Windus and The Hogarth Press and
The Estate of C.P. Cavafy.

All characters in this publication are fictitious
and any resemblance to real persons, living or dead,
is purely coincidental.

ISBN 0 7472 4225 9

Typeset by CBS, Felixstowe, Suffolk

Printed and bound in Great Britain by
HarperCollins Manufacturing, Glasgow

HEADLINE BOOK PUBLISHING
A division of Hodder Headline PLC
Headline House, 79 Great Titchfield Street, London W1P 7FN

For Don Munson

Who always inspires in one
the rage to live

Loved, idealized voices
of those who have died, or of those
lost for us like the dead.

Sometimes they speak to us in dreams;
Sometimes deep in thought the mind bears them.

C.P. Cavafy

LONDON,
GLOUCESTERSHIRE

Chapter 1

The train pulled out of Paddington Station, swaying lazily from side to side on the tracks. How grey, how grim London looked. No distinction by colour between pavements, buildings, sky, nor the atmosphere in between. Arianne closed her eyes. She could feel the train pick up speed and shoot forward as if at a target. 'Away Day' was the name fancifully conferred on a simple journey by the publicity department of British Rail. 'Let the train take the strain', cooed the advertisements. It was her own purse that took the strain, mused Arianne before relaxing into her seat, her eyes still closed. She liked the motion of the train. She found it somehow inviting. Maybe even anaesthetising. Once a week for an hour and a half she went under. The journey acted on her like some psychedelic drug; her mind seemed to turn to mush, all memory and thought dissolved. In a half-sleep she floated in space and time. Today, her last thought, before she slipped into the mental limbo of a passenger on British Rail, was, Maybe the sun will be shining in Gloucestershire. An hour later she opened her eyes. The sun was not shining in Gloucestershire.

The fields, broken by hedgerows and clumps of elm and beech of considerable age and girth, in the low chilly mist made of the countryside flashing past the train window a manicured landscape, a neat quilt of arable affluence. Today, here in Gloucestershire, all was monochrome too. It was as if the whole world had been painted battleship-grey.

Mesmerised by the greyness flashing past the window, Arianne saw herself and Jason emerging from the swirling mist, hand in hand. They were happy and very much in love. He stopped and took Arianne in his arms and kissed her. A carnal kiss. All their kisses were bodily, intensely intimate. It had always been like that right from their beginnings.

The beginning. That had been at a crowded house party at

3

Tanglewood, the summer home of the Boston Symphony Orchestra, in the beautiful Massachusetts Berkshires. She had been one of a hundred guests, mostly musicians, friends and patrons of the open air concerts that Tanglewood had become legendary for.

People spilled out of the old wooden house set among birch trees and on to the verandah, down the steps. Arianne felt somehow lost in the crush of summer people, all with glass in hand, full of chatter and laughter. A word here, there, was all she could muster with the friendly revellers. She was never very good at large parties, they intimidated her. Jostled into the far corner of the verandah, she loitered on the fringes of a small group of people making an effort at polite conversation, which no one paid much attention to, except for one man. Every time she opened her mouth he topped up her glass. A summer punch, pink, potent.

A sultry, sunny, summer day in the country. Heat, humidity, too many people and too much gin, a tipsy-making combination that sidetracked Arianne's sense of isolation. She was feeling no pain, just euphoria, and a certain recklessness that caused her to scan the verandah in search of she knew not what.

Arianne's first sight of Jason was through the throngs of people. He was flanked by two long-legged beauties, a blonde and a brunette, so young, so glamorous. His virile handsomeness, the mischievous light in his eyes, something wicked, dangerous even, in his face when he laughed, his lusty manner with the girls – all held her attention. She was captivated. Staring across the open verandah at him, time, place, vanished. She lost her heart. At one moment their gaze locked, and his smile was there for her and no one else. Embarrassment at being caught out caused her to look away at once.

Her first inclination was to flee from the party. But her host waved at her from across the lawn and she knew that was not an option. Someone spoke to her, someone else refilled her now empty glass. She was grateful for the distraction. It helped her to compose herself.

Late afternoon. Several barbecue pits with whole lambs skewered on spits were rotating over fiercely hot charcoal. From her perch on the verandah, Arianne watched a cellist and a violinist arrange themselves under one of the birch trees, pick up their instruments and begin to play. Neither heat nor humidity had abated, and Arianne was definitely under their influence: languid, voluptuous. A swim in the lake came to mind, a nap under a tree somewhere away from the party, to revive herself. But she seemed unable to move.

Arianne felt someone tug at the hem of her skirt. She looked down. He was standing below her on the grass. His smile disarmed her. He reached up and swung her by the waist down off the verandah, removing her glass from her hand.

'My name is Jason Honey. You can think of me as Prince Charming come to rescue you or the wolf who might just gobble you up.'

'Do I look like I need rescuing?'

'Yes,' he told her, slipping his arm through hers.

'Oh. And are you so hungry as to want to devour me?' she teased. 'How about just a little nibble? Would that not be enough for you.'

'No. No more than it would be for you.'

He had not taken his eyes from hers and now she looked directly at him and asked, 'Now how could you possibly know that?'

'By the way you looked at me earlier.' Arianne was feeling too aroused by his attentions to be embarrassed at being caught out this time.

Together they walked among the other guests away from the house and down the path that led through the wood. The scent of roasting lamb and rosemary filled the air and billows of white smoke rose from the pits to drift among the white birch trees. There was a special kind of gaiety enhanced by the music: jazz. The classical violinist and the cellist were jamming for fun, and the party shifted into overdrive. Arianne felt that at last she was one of the revellers.

They walked through the birch trees for several minutes in silence, leaving the party behind them. A couple leaning against a tree, kissing, and another pair of lovers walking arm in arm fondling each other were inspirations. Jason drew her closer in to him, and kissed her on the cheek. She felt herself giving in to him, wanting him, much more of him than she had ever wanted

5

of any other man. It was thrilling yet frightening.

The birch trees thinned out and soon they were walking under the still bright late afternoon sun through high grass and a field of wild flowers in full bloom that sloped down to the lake. She hesitated. 'Where are we going?'

He laughed and pulled her along, answering, 'To meet our destiny.'

She broke away from him and dashed ahead, parting the near shoulder-high grass and flowers as she ran. Jason caught up with Arianne and, grabbing her by the arm, turned her around to pull her into his arms. He held her bare shoulders in a tight grip and looked at her as no other man before him had ever done. He emanated lust, lasciviousness, all things sexual, and she wanted it all.

He pulled her close and rubbed her breasts up against his chest. He placed his lips upon hers and licked them and kissed them, nibbled at them with erotic hunger until she parted them. Then he was where he wanted to be and kissed her with passion, licked the inside of her mouth, sucked on her tongue. She was dizzy with desire for more, wanting only to give herself body and soul. Sensing her pleasure, he smiled and stroked her hair.

'Why me?' she asked him in a near whisper quivering with passion. 'Why me?'

The kiss he placed on her cheek was sensitive, loving, as he used his hands to undo the buttons at the back of her neck. The white silk halter of her dress slipped down off her breasts to her waist. 'Oh, perfect!' he exclaimed at the sight of her nakedness.

Arianne's breasts *were* lovely. Full, high, a voluptuous shape, and raunchy with their already erect nipples, large and dark aureoles around them. He cupped her breasts in his hands, caressed them and felt her tremble. Her pleasure in his caresses delighted him, brought a smile to his lips. 'Why you? Because you love me. You need me. And at the party you stood out among the crowd as no other woman there did. Because you are beautiful, quiet, serene even, honest and true, and behind that façade I see a fascinating and very sexy lady. You appear to me unique, something special that I can love. And because you've fallen in love with me, even though you know romantic love is a totally irrational and unpredictable thing.'

6

'Have I?' she asked, astonished at his self-confidence.

'Of course, otherwise what would you be doing here.' He placed a finger across her lips as if to silence her. 'No. Don't try and explain it away.'

He kissed her again, only this time his kisses were for her breasts. His mouth sucked fiercely on her nipples, his tongue licked them, and he bit into the soft flesh. He left her with a trail of kisses between them and one on the side of her neck before he placed his lips upon hers once again.

Arianne told herself, 'This is romantic infatuation, that mysterious process that is making me believe Jason is the only person like him in the whole world. If that's what it is then so be it. I can live with that.' It was an easy decision to make because Arianne believed this stranger loved her. His next words confirmed that.

'I don't know why I love you, but I do. I see you as special and I've marked you for my own.'

She watched him lower his braces off his shoulders, unbutton his shirt and fling it to the ground. His trousers swiftly dispensed with, he placed one of Arianne's hands around his ample, erect penis and formed the other into a cup and placed it under his large and voluptuous scrotum. Then he eased Arianne's dress down off her hips and watched it slip to the ground.

'Whoever lov'd that lov'd not at first sight?' A great poet's words said it all for Arianne. She dropped to her knees and without thought and driven by desire, she opened her lips and licked the knob of his penis, sucked it slowly into her mouth and savoured the taste of him. She moved on it with exquisite kisses and imbibed Jason deeply, to the very base of his penis, until her lips were caressed by the rough curls of his pubic hair. With pointed tongue, she licked the underpart of the pulsating organ and thrilled at the life force she felt throbbing in its veins. She sucked, ever so gently, his scrotum into her mouth and licked it, caressed the balls within the sac with pointed tongue and passionate kisses.

'You're wonderful,' he told her repeatedly, and she marvelled at the sexual power she had over him. Marvelled because this was something new for Arianne, making love to a man, all inhibitions cast off under the summer sunshine. From the very moment she had seen him across the verandah she had been behaving out of character. She sensed that nothing would ever again be the same for her after this encounter with Jason Honey.

'More sublime even than I imagined,' was what he told her as he laid her down in the grass between uncontrolled kisses, a fiery passion. He was rough with her when he tore the cream satin and ecru lace French knickers apart at her hips and pulled them from between her legs.

For a moment Arianne came to her senses and protested, 'Please, Jason, someone will see us,' as he moved his lips from her breasts down her body, to bury his face in her silky pubic hair, to lick it, and to bite, passionately, the mound beneath. He raised his eyes to look into hers and tell her, 'So what? I wish the whole world could see us and all the erotic and depraved fun we're going to have together.' And with that he spread her legs far apart and licked in between her cunt lips.

Jason was delighted that Arianne was already moist with come from several timid orgasms which even she had not been aware of. All she had sensed was ecstasy and had given no thought as to where it had come from. He felt the silky smoothness first on his caressing fingers and then on his tongue. He adored the taste of her, it was like an aphrodisiac. Now her come glistened on the knob of his penis as he moved it back and forth across her slit and probed gently the place he was about to enter.

She was tight; it excited him that she would clench him so well. What further thrilled him was the realisation that she was quite innocent, inexperienced in the ways of hard core lust. She would be a delight to corrupt. And he fell in love with her that little bit more.

He gripped her hard by the shoulders. She very nearly called out in pain but forgot about pain when he fed one of her breasts into his mouth. He sucked hard on it, and bit deeply and she squirmed with pleasure and felt her body tense as a powerful orgasm began to build. He took Arianne with one powerful and deep thrust, calling out, 'You are magnificent, so luscious to be inside of.'

She grasped his arms, and called out, again and again as he mastered her with his prowess as a lover, thrusting in and out of her with changing rhythm: fast, slow, gentle, with a certain

8

roughness, 'Yes, yes. How beautiful. What bliss.'

And Jason, out of control, confessed, 'I love you. You're mine, mine.'

He wrung orgasm after orgasm from her. She came and each time her comings were stronger, more powerful: she drenched his penis with the warm satiny flow. He adored her for her sexuality. Her lust for him. The way she gave herself to him so completely. She was his, she could be no one else's. He had indeed fallen in love. He came, after a long and exquisite period of fucking, in a gigantic orgasm that seemed to go on forever. Quite exhausted by Arianne, he lay his body full on top of her and, wrapping his arms around her, rolled them both on to their sides. He kissed her, first on her eyes then her lips, and he recited, '"When love speaks, the voice of all the gods makes heaven drowsy with harmony." I'm going to marry you and never let you go.'

An express train on its way to London flashed by in a thundering sound that broke into Arianne's vision of the past and brought her instantly back to reality. She smiled. How nice it was to come, even if it was alone and on a train. Arianne invariably thought about sex during that intermittent period between waking from a sensuous, drowsy half-sleep and reality.

Few people stepped from the train onto the covered platform of Chipping Wynchwood station. The prettified Edwardian rural railway station – all cast-iron columns and hanging flower baskets, dressed for winter: trails of ivy, holly, the odd alpine plant – looked deserted and chilled. The station-master, under a worn, comfortable cap, stood leaning on the handle of an empty railway freight-cart near the large wooden doors, one of which was open to let the passengers through into the car park.

Station-master Pike took the tickets without a smile, greeting those he recognised with a grunt. The mist had a decided chill: it wrapped itself around Arianne. A shiver, less from cold than from dampness, the sheer absence of sunshine and blue sky, snapped Arianne to attention. Back to reality. She searched the sky for a glimmer of light trying to break through. Nothing. Think sunshine, she told herself. This is England. It is autumn.

Arianne placed the cake-box and the black alligator shoulder-bag she was carrying on the wooden bench set against the station wall. She reached into the pockets of her jacket, a torso of sable with a cowl neck and sleeves of thick cashmere yarn knitted on fat wooden needles in some Paris couture house. She withdrew a pair of black gloves and buckled them across her wrists. Fine, soft and supple leather pampered her hands. She tugged at the knitted waist-band of her jacket and settled it just above her slender hips. For her to wear a jacket such as this now was an extravagance far beyond her present means. There had been a time for such luxuries as the cognac-coloured knit and sable jacket, her black Ralph Lauren suede skirt and Maude Frizon black-and-tan walking shoes. Jason adored spoiling her with luxurious gifts to match a hedonistic and always challenging erotic life behind closed doors, an adventurous and unpredictable one up-front and out in the open.

A reflected glimpse of herself in the station-house window. She wore no hat and her long, silky-smooth, chestnut-coloured hair looked very smart: elegant and cool, cut in its shoulder-length bob. It was not often Arianne pondered her looks. When she did it was usually at a time such as this when she was en route to meet her mother. Artemis would be pleased with her daughter's appearance today. Lady Hardcastle accorded scant approval to either her daughter or the man she had married. Her daughter was dull, her husband vulgar, a child pretending to be a man. The only good thing about Jason was that he dressed his wife well. At least he had been able to bring out of her daughter a sensuous beauty that seemed to have eluded the girl until he had married her.

The fact of the matter was that Artemis Hardcastle didn't much care for her daughter. Dull was how she had always described Arianne, beautiful but dull – the reincarnation of her father. Dull was marginally worse than ugly. She had, for that unpardonable sin, abandoned them both when Arianne was five. She divorced them for it, and had moved on twice more before she met Lord Hardcastle, apparent answer to all Artemis's needs and dreams.

Arianne studied her reflection. She had always been pleased enough with her looks on these intermittent inspections of them. Vanity was no more a part of her psyche than jealousy or self-centredness. But, for her mother's sake, she wished that she had the exciting, provocative beauty that Artemis had had, and still, in old age, to some extent retained. The sort of seductive looks, that, combined with a cunning love for men, created the *femme fatale*: a certain female type that stirred men, made them prisoners of the heart, and was capable of destroying them at will. Dangerous beauty. How her mother would have relished that in Arianne. Artemis would have seen that quality in her daughter as an asset, part of 'getting on'.

'We both have to live with what we are' had eventually become Arianne's attitude to her mother's constant criticism of her. Arianne was content with herself. That had always been the barrier between mother and daughter. Arianne did have her strengths, enough to accept Artemis at face value and love her for what she was or was not in herself, had been or had never been to her daughter. Arianne managed always to be her own woman, however much she appeared to be submitting to others. It was more than just playing the role of dutiful daughter and making the effort to please Artemis. It was Arianne's nature to please and it came easy to her. It gave her a certain power all of her own. Combined with her passivity, her quiet beauty, this could be enchanting, attractive, even mysterious. 'In certain lighting, there is about you a madonna-quality, Arianne. I find it particularly irritating. Not at all sensuous to men. You should try *not* to cultivate that.' Part of the small-arms fire of Artemis's lifelong bombardment of her daughter's self-esteem.

Arianne smiled at the image in the window. She had always been, since a child, secure in herself, in spite of having a mother who was a bolter. She had always been – still was – happy enough being who and what she was. That quality must have come from her mother.

She picked up the cake-box and her handbag and slung its strap over her shoulder. She walked swiftly towards station-master Pike, smiled and handed him her ticket. Glancing through the station window into the deserted waiting-room and out again through another window, she glimpsed Mr Pike's rose garden. All pruned back and stumpy, it was as barren as a rose garden could look in autumn. She turned back to the station-master. 'I do miss your rose garden, Mr Pike. And the colourful flowers in your hanging baskets. Especially on a day like this.'

He scratched behind his ear. Embarrassment, but the faint

smile showed pride. 'Anybody from the house picking you up, Miss?'

'No. I ordered a taxi.'

The two stepped into the car park together just as Webb's taxi pulled in. A new driver, one Arianne didn't know. She told him, 'Chessington House, please,' and sat back. The driver pulled out of the car park, leaving the station-master drawing the freight doors closed. Arianne enjoyed the ride from the station through the countryside even in the dull greyness of the day. The taxi passed through a hamlet and then several villages, carefully unspoilt, balanced between the charm of a thriving rural life and the chocolate-box-pretty English village. No billboards yet, or the vulgar drive-ins one saw everywhere in her own country.

Vulgar bits and all, there were times, many, when she did miss the States, the best parts of being American, just living in your own country. The years of residing and travelling in Europe with Jason were the happiest years of her life. But then, too, so had been those spent living with him in America. The best part of agreeing on a two-year transfer from the New York to the London branch of Christie's was that she and Artemis were managing to have rather a good time on these weekly visits.

The taxi approached the dry-stone walls circling the fifteen hundred acres that was Chessington Park. Aged trees rose majestically behind the high walls. Arianne thought how clever her stepfather, Gerald, had been to purchase the ten-room apartment for Artemis and himself as a haven for their dotage, those infirm times that were inevitably to come. At Chessington House they would live in comfort and with minimal anxiety over maintaining a life-style to which they were accustomed.

When the hundred and ten rooms of the magnificent Tudor house had been converted into flats of various sizes, Gerald and Artemis had acquired the best of the Georgian wing along with one Tudor tower. The large and sumptuous reception room of a stately house suited their furnishings and art objects, their paintings. With a place for their hunters in the stables, some wonderfully beautiful parkland to ride in, a private nine-hole golf-course to play, and the comforting spectacle of acquaintances more anxiously maintaining their own grand houses nearby, the move had been all he and her mother had hoped for. The house even boasted an excellent restaurant for the residents, where they could dine, or whence they could obtain house-service so as to eat and entertain in their own dining-rooms. Chessington House gardens were beautifully cared for by the house gardeners, as was their own large, separate garden with its eighteenth-century folly, a place for lively luncheon-parties or tea on a summer afternoon. Perfection. Paradise.

Only the people were wrong. Wrong for each other simply by being there. It was the old story, lived out anew in every condominium.

How had Andrew Marvell, poet and masterly dissector of the pursuit of the earthly paradise in the great age of stately homes, expressed the malaise?

> 'Two paradises 'twere in one
> To live in paradise alone.'

To each other they all appeared unbearably tedious. And what depths of pettiness were plumbed, what heights of aggression attained, in the miniature power struggles for illusory control over areas of the life of the building! The petty and the banal were elevated to forms of art in bickering over the direction of a 'community' that nobody had ever wanted to bring into existence.

Three weeks in the spring at the Ritz in Paris. A month in Barbados in March. August in Cap Ferrat, for as long as health and old age could manage. That had been their plan. And it had worked and life had been just fine. Only poor Gerald had too short a time to enjoy it. Quite suddenly he was gravely ill. With the help of their long-serving staff, Artemis sustained Gerald for nearly a year before he died.

Artemis at her very best. She kept Gerald's spirits up by looking ravishingly beautiful, flirting with him as if he were still the handsome, dashing man she had fallen in love with, running the house as if his illness was not there, giving him, as she had all her life, the best possible time. Small parties, scheduling visits of old friends to keep him amused, bridge games, walks when possible, a wheelchair when not. And when he could no longer go to see his horses, they were brought to him. She kept him surrounded by beauty and laughter, and her love, to the very end, when he closed his eyes and told her she had been his great love and would remain so beyond life itself, and took his last breath.

But once he was gone, Artemis changed radically. She rarely left the park. Became, at times, reclusive almost to the extreme, and somewhat erratic in her behaviour. And when she did periodically come out of her shell she appeared to be as vivacious and full of charm as ever, surrounding herself with much younger people who were amusing, old roués and gigolos who fell under her spell, only to be rejected by her.

The taxi left the main road to pass through an impressive entrance. A pair of open iron gates hung on pillars of stone fifteen feet high and topped by a pair of seventeenth-century bronze lions. The mist appeared to cling to the tree trunks and grass and to rise in lazy swirls towards a blanket of low grey cloud pressing down on the parkland. All seemed so quiet. The drive wound up a gentle slope for nearly a mile before the park flattened out. All the time Arianne caught glimpses of the house with its four Tudor towers and lead-domed roofs. Behind them they had left the wood and now were driving through an arboretum dotted with rare trees and shrubs. Two cock pheasants in their bright plumage suddenly burst from some tall grass, and at about a quarter of a mile from the house a fox nonchalantly crossed in front of the taxi. The arboretum thinned out to well-clipped lawns and the house rose into view. They circled the stone fountain and drew up at the front door.

Arianne rang the bell. Several minutes passed before the caretaker, a pensioner called Clive, opened it and greeted her enthusiastically. He escorted her across the domed hall, a Georgian splendour of fine plasterwork and marble boasting a gallery and a grand staircase. Clive rang the bell to Artemis's flat.

Arianne found her mother sitting in a Georgian wing chair in front of a blazing fire in the drawing room: an impressive double-cube room of egg-yolk yellow silk-damask walls and an ornate plaster ceiling, made more so by the Impressionist paintings in carved and gilded frames. The floors were of rich parquet covered with fine oriental carpets and the windows were hung with French seventeenth-century draperies of ivory silk embroidered with small flowers exquisitely designed and executed. In places they hung in ribbons and were faded, but that only enhanced their elegance. They were another work of art. The room had the scent of woodsmoke and beeswax, and fresh flowers from the many sumptuous blossoms arranged casually in Ming, Tang and Chien Lung vases placed around the room. It was a far cry from the tacky bed-sit accommodation in Belsize Park where Arianne lived.

Arianne liked this room. The furniture, English and eighteenth century, mixed well with some French pieces of the same period, and yet, for all its formal elegance, there was about the room a sense of homeliness and comfort. The books lying about everywhere, the many silver-framed photos, and Aubusson cushions flung about casually added to this impression, as did the dogs: two West Highland terriers, and a mastiff, dozing, or stretching lazily at Artemis's feet. And a black and white Great Dane, which, on seeing Arianne, bounded from his place on one of the several sofas in the room. In a great bound that nearly felled her, he had his front paws on her shoulders and was licking her face. The cake-box was saved by Hadley, once Gerald's valet, now Artemis's butler-chauffeur.

Artemis had been staring out of the window. She rose from her chair to greet Arianne. 'Not a very pretty day. But I do rather like it, all this grey. It bodes something mysterious. Like a great dark figure riding out of the mist. Mr Rochester, and wimpy Jane Eyre.' Artemis began to laugh. 'I once hated wimpy women; now I am beginning to appreciate they have a way of getting what they want. When I was younger a dull day such as this would have driven me mad. Cake for tea? Or croissants for coffee now?' she asked as she walked over to her daughter and affectionately pulled on the dog Ralph's ear.

'Your favourite, croissants.'

'Oh, good. Coffee, then, Hadley. In front of the fire, I think. And call the dining room and tell them we will be having a late lunch, my usual table.' Ralph released Arianne and she gave him a hard spank of affection, and mother and daughter watched him lope away and climb once more on to the sofa.

Arianne smiled to herself, pleased that she had made the effort to dress for her mother. The look of approval in Artemis's eyes told her it was worth it. 'Have you had a good week, Mother?' she asked.

'I never know what that question means, Arianne. You always ask it the minute you arrive. It irritates me. You seem to use it as a greeting, or an introduction to a day of small talk. And, oh, how I hate small talk.'

Her words, sharp and hurtful, were too full of truth and they silenced Arianne. True, she never did know how to greet her mother, nor in fact how to have a conversation with her that was other than small talk. The attack told her that Artemis was, at the very least, tetchy today; at worst she was going to be downright difficult. Arianne thought, I'll settle for erratic.

She watched her mother walk to one of the two concert grand pianos nestled together in the clutch of windows overlooking the garden. Artemis sat down and looking briefly across the room at her daughter said, 'You look really attractive when you are dressed well, Arianne. I'll lend you a hat and we can go for a long walk before lunch.' Then she placed her fingers on the keyboard and sat very still meditating for several seconds before beginning to play Chopin Mazurkas, until Hadley set in front of the fire a small table already laid with a crisp, white linen cloth embroidered in small white chrysanthemums; Limoges coffee cups and plates and Queen Anne silver; the croissants, on a pedestal dish; and pots of apricot and plum jam.

Arianne removed her handbag from her shoulder, her gloves from her hands, opened her jacket, removed it and placed her things on a bench covered with a twelfth-century tapestry. She sat down in the wing chair where her mother had been sitting and listened to the piano. Artemis played well. Arianne studied her mother at the instrument. Artemis looked really beautiful. That she had a certain charisma was unquestionable. Today, she was dressed in a white satin shirt worn over wide cream flannel trousers; a belt of silver and gold mesh links hung loosely around her waist and rested on her slender hips. Wide antique ivory bracelets separated by slim Cartier diamond bangles had been removed from her wrists and placed on the bench next to her while she played. Artemis had style and incredible chic. It had after all been her whole life. She was not the sort to let it slip away in old age. Like the Duchess of Argyll, Lady Diana Cooper, Babe

Paley in the States, old acquaintances, she would be as admired in old age as she had been in middle age and in her youth. That she had been a rotten wife to three husbands, an indifferent mother at best to a daughter she had abandoned, seemed hardly to have shadowed her life.

There had never been anything maternal about Artemis. When after years of separation she and Arianne renewed their relationship to more than the basis of a holiday two weeks a year, and a present every Christmas, miraculously neither of them dwelt on the past. They stepped into their mother-daughter roles as if the relationship had begun with Arianne already a married adult. Arianne, not ungraciously, had always accepted Artemis's self-centredness, her inability to love Arianne in the normal way of mother-daughter associations. And now the two women were, for the time that was left them, respectfully forging a bond that they could both comfortably live with.

Artemis was aware of her erratic behaviour. She preferred to think of it as eccentric, but in her heart she knew better. She was slipping away from the real world, and strangely she didn't mind all that much. She had enough wealth to be cared for in the style she craved, and a doctor who was sympathetic to her wishes to ensure that, before she slipped over the edge into senility, she went to sleep with the angels. Of this Arianne was unaware. Artemis insisted upon that. She did not want to be a burden to her daughter any more than she wanted Arianne to be a burden to her. Strangely, Arianne sensed that it was the obvious cut-off points in their relationship that allowed them to love each other as best they could.

Artemis dunked the corner of her buttered croissant in the hot black coffee and neatly popped it in her mouth. 'Delicious,' she announced. The taste of almonds brought delight to her eyes. 'And my favourite, these with the almond paste.' She placed a thin slab of butter on another corner and a dollop of apricot jam on top of that. Looking across at her daughter, she said, 'I've been meaning to tell you: about these weekly visits of yours, much as I appreciate them, I would rather you didn't make them if they are some sort of duty-call.' She broke off the piece of dressed croissant and handed it across the table to Arianne.

'They aren't.'

'Oh, good. Then you will feel free not to come, and I will feel free to tell you when I'd prefer you didn't.'

'I enjoy these outings. It gets me out of London.'

'I don't want to be merely an escape route for you, Arianne. There must be other people to see, places to go. Time to create a new life for yourself. And I do have a life beyond your weekly visits.'

Arianne said nothing. She was neither peeved nor disturbed by Artemis's comments. It was quite remarkable how little effect mother and daughter had on each other. Duty? No, these visits had little to do with any sense of duty a mother and daughter might have towards one another. Their years of estrangement had killed that, and, if anything, facilitated these visits. Mother and daughter came together without family angst or the burden of duty and forced feelings, or any moral obligation. But blood is a tie, and so is love in any form. That, perhaps, was what these visits were about. The two women enjoyed their coffee and croissants in silence.

In the boot room just off the entrance hall to the flat, Artemis found a tweed shooting-jacket that had seen better days, but was still handsome and warm with its quilted lining. She handed it to Arianne. She wrapped herself up in an old and worn, belted tweed coat, and Hadley helped her on with her favourite black leather walking-shoes. She gave him a fierce look when he handed her a sturdy walking-stick. The two women chose stylish felt hats from the many hanging on pegs in the boot room. With the dogs leaping around their legs in anticipation, they set out from the Hardcastle flat across the great hall.

The walking party was nearly at the front door when they were confronted by a tall, slim woman dressed in smart trousers and a turtle-neck sweater. She still had vestiges of a beauty that must have been considerable in her youth some fifty years before. Now she seemed all wrinkles and old eyes with unimaginably slim lips. Arianne had met her several times before. Always she had reminded Arianne of bitter almonds, arsenic and old lace. She was forever playing the role of the châtelaine of Chessington House, the headmistress to her neighbours, the missionary to their social and spiritual conscience, believing that if they had any it was tainted, too weak, less worthy than her own. In fact she

18

was merely a resident widow with a control problem. A busybody, a snoop, sniffing out minute flaws in the running of the co-operative residence. Any detail to agonise over and torture her neighbours with seemed to give her something special to live for: a woman who chose, with her now-deceased husband, who had had his own control problems which he had mercilessly vented on his neighbours, to live in a small section of one of the grand Tudor houses of England. Her object in life now seemed to be to reduce the house to her middle-class taste, mentality and morality. Curious, since she professed to adore Chessington House for its beauty, its history, neither of which were middle-class.

Her opening volley, was, 'Artemis, could I have a word, just a minute of your time?' With it came a slick, false smile.

'No,' answered Artemis.

The meaning of that monosyllable is not widely disputed, but Beryl Quilty did not understand no. No, to her, was merely the opening of a dialogue. She stepped directly in Artemis's path. The smile was even more intense now, and the stubbornness in it fierce. 'I am getting up a work party to polish the furniture in the great hall. Another to sweep the drive, a cleaning party. We will serve hot tea and biscuits in one of the empty garages. Ginger biscuits. Can I put you down?'

'Certainly not,' was Artemis's reply. Disdain blazed in her gaze at Beryl Quilty. Mrs Quilty's appearance seemed to act as a tranquilliser to the dogs. All joy went out of their leaps and dashes through the hall. They gathered round Artemis and Beryl Quilty, wriggling and wagging and panting. Mrs Quilty was barely visible now. 'I never eat ginger. Not in biscuit-form, certainly.'

Mrs Quilty dug her heels in. With her missionary zeal on maximum, she pressed on, 'Thursday the fifteenth. Eight o'clock in the morning for sweeping the drive. The furniture-polishing is the following Wednesday at eleven in the morning. Coffee first in my flat.' The lips had nearly vanished into Mrs Quilty's mouth. Her eyes were like cold, dead steel.

'Beryl Quilty, I have never polished my own furniture. Why would I want to polish the house's? Most especially when we pay a resident cleaning-staff to do it?'

'It would be good for the house if we could all make the chores here a communal thing, a rewarding exercise.'

Artemis looked fixedly at Beryl Quilty. 'I am not looking for exercise, Mrs Quilty.' Arianne could feel the tension between the two women, energised by the determination behind those slim lips to enlist Artemis in her current projects. Artemis grabbed the mastiff Hubert's thick leather collar and made him sit down. Then she turned back to Beryl Quilty and said, 'That drive is three quarters of a mile long. It is also twenty-five feet wide. Worthy as your plan may be, it is unthinkable for a houseful of semi-geriatrics like me. It is neither sensible nor practical. Come, dogs.' At that they sprang up as a quivering mass of wagging tails, slithers and slides on the polished marble floor. The hall resounded with barks and howls of joy as Artemis and her adored pets side-stepped Beryl Quilty and aimed once again for the front door. Looking over her shoulder, she snapped at her daughter, 'Arianne.' Arianne followed her mother, relieved that Artemis had not raised a hand and belted Mrs Quilty across the mouth, which, Artemis had often intimated to her daughter, women like herself were often tempted to do.

Chapter 2

The two women pushed open the door to the courtyard. The dogs all but bounded out into the still very grey day. 'A bitch in nun's clothing. A missionary who destroys the spirit. A woman determined to bring everyone down to her level. She's a vulture for God and charity, and her will to control. And she's made of cast iron and will outlive us all. But she doesn't fool me one bit, she's evil. Evil is trying to bend people to your will, making them miserable in their own homes. I can promise you this, if there is a God he will be smart enough not to let her through those pearly gates. Have you any idea how many people have left their homes to get away from her and her brimstone? Well, she'll . . .' At this point Arianne could hold back no longer. She burst into laughter at her mother's tirade. Artemis turned to face her daughter. Much as she tried, she couldn't stop bursting into laughter as well.

'I never stop about her, do I?'

Arianne confirmed with a nod of her head and a smile on her lips.

The two women, still laughing and playing with the dogs, rounded the fountain to walk down the drive towards the stables.

'There is something just a little bit mad about this place.' And just to prove the point another neighbour greeted them as he pushed a motor-driven lawn-mower over the gravel. 'There he goes, walking his lawn-mower instead of a dog. Mad, crazy with old age, no matter how we fight it,' she said, smiling up at her daughter and linking an arm through Arianne's.

Artemis was on her best form. Lucid, wickedly witty about her fellow residents, intelligent in her proposition that Chessington House was a microcosm of the world, and, that being the case, she was ready to get off. That she had thought herself shock-proof until she saw what appeared to be good, sane people sharing a residence behave with such self-serving, unbelievable pettiness,

21

such utter disregard for their neighbours.

Artemis's detestation of Beryl Quilty set her off, and the two women continued their walk in the dull grey day brightening it up with laughter about the house, its beauty and the joy of living there except for the spectre of the Residents' Committee, the AGMs and her *bête noire*, Beryl Quilty.

'Why do you hate her so?' asked Arianne. 'All she did was ask you to take part in another of her insignificant projects.'

'Because living here has brought out the worst in me, and she is directly responsible. I am made to defend myself against the petty bourgeois life Beryl tries to drag me into. Real beauty, laughter, the *joie de vivre* that is part of us all: I have seen her exercise her obsessive need to put a damper on those things. Not only in me, but in everyone and everything. And, what is worse, she does it in the name of the have-nots. Any have-not – Cancer Research, the children of Ethiopia, the Red Cross – she rattles her charity boxes in our faces. And when she hasn't any, she rattles herself in our faces.

'One gives a concert in the hall, she polices it. Give a party, she's there directing the parking of the cars. Christmas: she goes particularly mad to take over and decorate the public rooms of Chessington House in the manner she approves of. And as for the forced bonhomie among the residents in the name of the birth of Christ – it's best not even to speak of that. Her interference is odious, and her need to enslave us to the way of life she approves of, contemptible. It's not just me; I have fared well against her, but others have not. They just upped and ran in the face of her policing their lives. Can you imagine: strong, tough men that because they could not bear the atmosphere she created, breathed sighs of relief as the removal-vans containing their households disappeared down the drive? Why ever did Beryl Quilty leave her homeland? New Zealand's loss is our misery.'

Artemis picked up a stick and threw it. The dogs went bounding after it. She turned her collar up and looked at Arianne. 'I think that should about answer your question.' They continued walking down the drive with Artemis in full flood continuing to amuse.

Whatever dark depressions or silent driftings away from reality had begun to affect Artemis's life were for the moment

22

dormant. Even in childhood during those brief visits they had together, Arianne had always been aware of her mother's serious mood-swings. This was one of her upper ones and the two women were making the most of it.

A vintage Mercedes Benz touring car with its drop head and massive headlamps rolled into sight. The women were now completely preoccupied with playing 'retrieving sticks' with the dogs and laughing for the silliness, the barking and the competing for Artemis's attentions. 'Oh, here comes Anson, in his Nazimobile,' she told Arianne.

The Mercedes, its drop head down, purred up to Artemis and stopped. The man at the wheel, Sir Anson Bathurst Belleville, looked much younger than his seventy-nine years. He had a shock of white hair and notable remnants of handsomeness. A broad smile for Artemis, who went to lean on the car door. Smiling at the man at the wheel, and with a comfortable calm in her voice, a sure sign that Sir Anson was the acceptable face of Chessington House, she told him, 'My husband and I were chased through France in his Bugatti right into Portugal by a car exactly like this, Anson.'

'So you tell me every time you see it, Artemis.'

'Well, it's such a terrible reminder of the horrors perpetrated by men who rode in cars like this during the Second World War. The model still offends me. Can't you get him to trade it in, Ben?' she asked the younger man sitting at Sir Anson's side.

Ben Johnson, his nephew, was a strikingly pleasant-looking man with the dashing good looks of a scallywag: a man in his early thirties, with a warmth and charm and openness about him. He smiled at Artemis, 'Not unless he traded it to me, Lady Hardcastle.'

'You're both as bad as each other,' she told them, and then asked, 'are you in the dining room for luncheon, Anson?'

'Yes.'

'Then we'll meet up again there.' With that she smacked the side of the car as if giving permission for them to drive on and turned her attention back to the dogs and her daughter.

They visited the stables and then circled back to the house, where they freshened up before going in to the dining room: a lovely Georgian room whose decorative plaster work was as

23

magnificent as it was delicate, the ceiling a triumph of design. Its buttercup-yellow plaster walls were sensitively picked out in a deep terracotta colour. With its dark-stained and polished oak boards on the floor, and silk damask draperies of deep apricot held back with eighteenth-century cords and tassels of faded dark purple, black, coral and silver at the windows, it was grand chic. And looked every bit what it was: an exclusive dining room for members, and their guests.

There were several tables: round, oblong, square, two with decorative gilded bases and marble tops, the others of walnut, or cherrywood. Round them were small settees, wing chairs, and comfortable straight-back armchairs covered in eighteenth-century Aubusson tapestry. The furniture and decorative objects, though a mélange of periods and styles, worked together and made the room, with its fresh flowers and potted palms of considerable height, enchanting, an inviting atmosphere to dine in. Especially so with the Capability Brown views of the park through the six dining-room windows: thoroughbred horses running wild in the fields or being ridden across parkland still magnificent with many three-hundred-year-old trees, a seventeenth-century folly reminiscent of a miniature Palladio villa in the far distance. It was a Stubbs painting come alive. The dining room was splendour in the country seat, as it had always been for the stately homes of England, except that in the seventeenth century one family would have had the privilege of living with their household in all of the more than one hundred rooms of this stately home.

Artemis used the dining room a great deal with or without guests. She never minded dining alone there, having always been partial to a bit of splendour. She treated it as an English gentleman treats the dining room at White's, Brooks's, or Boodle's. She expected, as those clubbable gentlemen did, to have the service, silence and privacy such places afforded them. Only with better food. She had her favourite table, and the food *was* very much better. It suited her palate.

There had been times on Arianne's visits to Chessington House when she would have preferred to dine in the flat alone with her mother, but she never made that suggestion. Arianne had learned from childhood it was better never to ask her mother for anything. It was more advisable for their relationship if Artemis gave of her own free will. Not to be imposed upon, was her mother's nature. Arianne's was to ask for nothing, expect nothing. Hers was a passive nature, though without weakness. It made for an interesting character, one that ambitious, aggressive people found attractive. An exception had always been her mother.

Artemis was excellent with staff, and though she could drive them into the ground with work and her demands for perfection, she could also be possessive of them, considerate of their needs, as long as it suited the household. Hence the dining room today instead of her cook, the taxis instead of her car and chauffeur being brought out to ferry Arianne to and from the station. Just like any other guest, her daughter was slotted into the steady ticking-over of Artemis's life, which she rarely allowed to be disrupted by outside factors: a selfish character-trait that all who crossed her path accepted because that was Artemis. Those who didn't fell by the wayside; those who did were friends, who, like her daughter, were able to find in her something special, something admirable. Her unswerving belief in man's right to live free, in truth, and with spirit, was what she practised, and she felt every man was duty-bound to do so. Next to taking another man's life, she considered not to go out into the world with what God gave you and make the most of it to be the second greatest sin. She had good friends, but many more admirers, although her selfishness, her egocentricity, the cultured, cultivated life she had lived with Gerald, and now on her own, raised envy, disapproval in some.

Artemis looked across the table at the serene beauty sitting opposite her. Her daughter? It was not often that she thought of Arianne as a daughter. More a child she had given birth to and released into the world with its first breath of life. She pondered for a few seconds on what a pleasant woman she had turned out to be, how easy she was to be with. One of those people in life who is *there* but not there. 'Easy-peasy.'

Arianne looked up from the small white menu of the day written by hand. 'Easy-peasy?' she questioned, a smile for the odd expression her mother used.

'Yes, easy-peasy, that's what you are. What your visits here are. Don't ever think that I don't appreciate that.' Then Artemis took from the pocket of her trousers a small, cleverly folded gold lorgnette. She snapped the catch and it sprang open. She raised it to her eyes and scanned the menu.

A sign of approval of her visits? Arianne knew that was the closest she would come to getting a compliment from her mother. She was giving Artemis some pleasure. That was a nice surprise.

There were several other Chessington House tenants dining in the room. Arianne was aware of the occasional glance from them. Any recognition from Artemis provoked an instant smile. 'Cheshire cats,' was her comment, and they were instantly disregarded as if they did not bother Artemis in the way Beryl Quilty did. In fact nothing seemed to be disturbing Artemis. This was a relief.

Arianne found it heart-breaking when her mother had what they now referred to as one of her off-periods. 'Just pretend I am becoming more eccentric with age. It sounds better than the beginnings of senility – the unattractive label, "Alzheimer's disease". I insist upon that.' Her off-periods or 'eccentricities' when in full flood could linger for several days, a week or more. But then again she could go weeks, months, without a sign of them. She insisted she be treated as normal. Her wish was Arianne's and the staff's command. And as usual Artemis was right because when lucid, and her old self, as she was today, much of what happened and was said did reach her and was remembered.

Mother and daughter hardly spoke while dining. They seemed to be content to sit quietly and gaze out of the window. First they dined on fresh oysters on the half shell, and with that they drank a chilled Chablis. They were just spooning into a hot, creamy vichyssoise, served with a scattering of fresh-snipped chives floating on the steaming white surface, when Sir Anson Bathurst Belleville and his nephew Ben entered the dining room.

Arianne was quite taken with the sight of the two men. The younger one had his arm round his uncle's shoulder, and the look of affection the nephew had for his uncle carried such warmth and charm it declared a lovingness that was extremely appealing and rare across such a gap of generations. The two men went directly to their table, some distance from Artemis's, and the nephew sat down. Sir Anson hesitated before he took his chair and, after excusing himself to his nephew, walked across the room to stop at their table. 'Just to wish you *bon appetit*, Artemis.' She offered him her hand and he placed a perfect continental kiss upon it. Then turning to Arianne he smiled and walked back to his table and his nephew.

'There is something to be said for old-fashioned charm and good manners,' remarked Artemis, and went directly back to her soup.

Arianne looked at her mother, still so very beautiful in her old age. The hair: a dark blonde nearly the colour of amber threaded with silver grey; the eyes still with a glimmer of brightness in their cornflower-blue colour. The strong and seductive bone-structure still there, but softened now by an aged, though well-preserved skin, the wrinkles of time and a rich and full life. Arianne could see why men were still attracted to her mother: she was formidable even now, and still commanded a fatal attraction. As one of her victims, Arianne was a fair witness.

Both women had ordered roast woodcock with all the trimmings: game chips, bread sauce, crisp bacon, small rondels of fried bread spread with liver pâté placed under the birds, redcurrant jelly. The vegetables: purée of celeriac, baby green beans. A most acceptable claret was poured. But it was certainly not one of Gerald's best from his wine cellar. Artemis could be, if not stingy, as penny-pinching as she could be extravagant and generous.

'The wine could be better for such a fine meal. But you will have to put that down to my meanness.' There was about her statement a hint of pride.

Arianne smiled. She was not going to fall into one of Artemis's traps. She had been through tortuous conversations about money with her mother often enough in her life. The latest had been a dissertation about how it was cheaper for Arianne to take taxis on her visits rather than disturbing Hadley to bring out the Bentley. They both knew that most of the time these discussions were designed to make the point that Artemis was wealthy but frugal for all her wealth, and that she was not there to pick up the tab for Arianne or anyone else unless she so chose.

Arianne had learned to side-step any talk of money with Artemis. As she cut into the breast of the little bird on her plate she could only think of how horrible it would be if her mother were to find out that she was nearly penniless, barely able to make ends meet with the salary she earned from Christie's. How appalled she would be to see Arianne's bed-sit in Belsize Park, to know that Arianne was left debt-ridden, homeless. How unacceptable that would be for Artemis. How shocked, distressed she would be, and yet scathing and unsympathetic that Arianne should have allowed that to happen to her. Arianne put from her mind any thought of Artemis finding out, if for no other reason than that she could not bear to upset her mother. She never could.

By the time the waiter removed the dinner plates the ladies had chosen their pudding: lemon mousse in a vanilla wafer cup for Artemis, a hot gooseberry soufflé dusted with powdered sugar for Arianne. Artemis was feeling quite mellow. She liked her wine, and wine liked her. It was good to her. It enhanced the good and the generous in her spirit rather than bringing out, as it did in some people, the mawkish. She plucked a cushion from the end of the settee and, plumping it up, placed it behind her back and leaned into it.

Arianne watched her mother. She seemed to be taking every nuance of the room into account, the people still dining, a couple who were just leaving. An ever vigilant waiter was quick to refill her glass and pad away silently. She smiled at him, at Arianne. 'The secret, I think, is not to have any regrets. I have none. I hope you have none.' She sipped her wine. 'I think that's what makes me unafraid of death and gives me such a disdain for old age. The body goes, the mind loses ground, but it can remain young like the heart if you will let it. That's what I do. It is after all not a bad way to live, don't you agree?'

'Yes, I do,' answered Arianne.

Although some distance away from Artemis's table, Ben Johnson was sitting at an angle that gave him a clear view of the two women dining together. There was about them something very attractive, very appealing. Their presence in the dining room was seductive but subtle, not unlike the scent of a fine French perfume. He liked their being there. The room and lunch with his uncle was somehow enhanced by their femininity. When they left the room Artemis led the way. She stopped only briefly to smile at Ben and place a lovely, long, slender-fingered hand on his uncle's shoulder and was gone, had passed by them before they had a chance to rise from their chairs. Arianne was just a few paces behind her.

It was only dusk and now drizzly, but on such a dull grey day it appeared much later than it actually was, as if night had descended on Chessington Park. Ben Johnson and his uncle were standing next to Ben's thirty-year-old 356B cream-coloured Porsche, its door open. The two men were having a last word before Ben headed back to London, when Artemis and Arianne walked into the courtyard just as Arianne's taxi rounded the fountain and pulled up to the front door. They caught the men's attention for a brief moment, and once more, something positive about the women registered with Ben.

Mother's and daughter's goodbyes were no better than their hellos, always just a little bit awkward. There was no kiss, no hug of farewell, not even a shake of a hand. Just, 'Thanks for a lovely day.' And an appreciative smile from Arianne.

'You could do much more with yourself, you know. Have a better life. Be happy. If you were, I would sense it. And I don't.'

A nod from Arianne, confirming that that was true. But she remained silent. Mother and daughter knew that what had been said and acknowledged was personal enough. To stop was easy; getting too deeply involved with each other's lives difficult, something that held no interest for either woman. Arianne quickly ducked down and slid across the rear seat of the taxi. Artemis closed the door and waved briefly before turning back to the house even before the car spluttered back into life.

The taxi driver turned on his headlights and the last thing Arianne saw as the Ford Consort rounded the fountain was the sight of Beryl Quilty striding past her mother and making a beeline for Sir Anson. Arianne could not but smile.

The train ride back to London sent Arianne once again into that seductive British Rail limbo. It seemed almost a culture shock when she had to step into Paddington station and the real world again. She found, as she always did, taking the bus back to Belsize Park just a little depressing.

Arianne placed the key in the lock and turned it. She stepped into the bed-sit. It faced the street and the light from the streetlamp was sufficient for her to find her way in the dark. She didn't bother to remove her jacket, but sat down on the Empire day-bed and looked around the room. The bed was hers, a table, a chair; nothing else, except her clothes in the closet, some jewellery. It was a charmless room. She had taken it because it did at least have high ceilings and a large bay window, and the street was tree-lined, each a greater plus than anything else she had seen for the money she could afford. But, six months on, the shabbiness of the place – those dreadful cheap, slapdash repairs that landlords are so fond of, the damp patches, the dry rot, the foul-smelling drains, bathroom tiles that insisted on coming unstuck and plopping into the bath-water – was becoming more difficult to ignore.

Arianne removed her jacket but remained sitting in the dark for some time. She thought about her day with Artemis and Chessington House, that lovely meal in the dining room. She smiled to herself. There was no better company than Artemis, when on form. Arianne rose from the day-bed and switched on a lamp. The soft warm light was kind to the room. She was just drawing the curtains when the phone began to ring: a friend, a colleague who wanted to be more than a colleague. She declined his invitation for a late supper at his place. She looked at her watch. It had just gone eight o'clock. The cinema? No. A long warm bath, an omelette and a French film on video. That would do her just fine. She was just walking to the wire cage screwed to the back of the door to her flat, the cage that caught the post when it was pushed through the letter-box every day by Mr Kelly, the house caretaker who lived in the basement below her, when the phone began once again to ring.

The moment she heard his voice her heart began to race. It was always like that when he rang. She was instantly happy, wanting him, excited, feeling sensuous and sexy, and so very much alive. Part of the excitement was that she knew he was feeling exactly the same way. But they had only to say a few words to each other and then those feelings dissolved. The pain of being together without Jason was too great; it separated them. The occasional telephone call, his generous gifts, that was the only way they seemed able to be together now. Theirs had been a sexual *ménage à trois* that worked for three, but was impossible for two.

'Are you well?' he asked.

'Yes, very well.'

'I want you. I am always wanting you,' he told her.

She could tell by the tremor of emotion in his voice that he meant it. She closed her eyes and felt the tears moistening her lashes. The sigh that escaped her lips was deep, and she forced back the tears. 'Me too,' she whispered huskily into the telephone.

There were several moments of silence before he cleared his throat and asked her, 'Do you need anything?'

'No, nothing.'

'The job?'

'Fine.'

'The rest of it?'

'My life, you mean? I'm doing the best I can.'

Again there was a lapse in their conversation and then he told her, 'One can't ask for more than that.'

She smiled to herself and felt considerably better. It was good to know that he understood.

'Did you receive a small parcel from me?' he asked.

She looked across the room at the wire post-basket hanging on the door, yet another bit of added ugliness in the flat. She could see a long, slim parcel wrapped in brown paper. 'Hold on,' she told him. She retrieved her post and parcel and then returned to sit on the bed.

'I have now,' she told him. 'You don't have to do this, Ahmad. Keep spoiling me with lovely, extravagant gifts.'

'I know that. Would you deprive me of that pleasure?'

'No.'

'Little gestures to give you some joy, to remind you that we are still together, even if it is not the way we would like it to be.'

She felt that same old tremor of excitement she could get from his voice when there was sexual innuendo in it. A pause for some seconds, just long enough for her to get herself under control. When she did speak, there was a lilt in her voice. One he knew and loved. He was well pleased when she told him, 'Hardly little gestures. Extravagant gifts that I adore receiving. Reminders of our times together. Thanks, Ahmad.' She felt cheered talking to him now. It was in her voice when she asked, 'And what excuse did you conjure up this time?'

'Merry Christmas. Will that do?'

'In November?'

'Why not?'

'You're quite right. Why not?'

Ahmad heard her fussing with the wrapping. 'I have to go, Arianne.'

'But I want to open my present and tell you how much I like it.'

'Not now. Open the parcel. And call me in a few days' time if you don't like it. If I don't hear from you, I'll know it was the right thing to choose. I'll call you from the New Year.'

Before she could respond she was left with nothing but the droning tone of a disconnected telephone line. One minute he was there on the other end of a telephone, the next he was gone. It happened five or six times a year. A birthday, some holiday, sometimes just because he was thinking of her. That was the only relationship they seemed able to have now. She never called him, though she had a number in Paris and another in Cairo where he could be reached if ever she needed him.

Arianne had needed him. But she never used the number. Once, several months after Jason vanished from their lives, she thought that they might be together, but it had been a disaster for them both. Jason came between them. He had been an integral part of what they were together. Now that he was gone, so was the erotic world they had dwelt in. They settled for distance and memories.

Arianne felt uplifted, not at all sad. They had come to terms with the way they were. She hung up the telephone. His gift. She concentrated on undoing the knot of brown cord, and then removed very carefully the brown paper. Exposed now: a long, slender box covered in silver wrapping with an all-over pattern of tiny red apples, each with a short, bright green stem and a single minute leaf. A bow of narrow silk ribbons: silver and gold, and red and bright green with long streamers. Arianne sat with it in her hand, enjoying the sheer prettiness of the gift-wrapping. To guess its contents was impossible. The wrong shape for a bracelet, too wide. A necklace? Too narrow. 'Everyone loves a present,' mused Arianne, aloud to the empty and dismal room, and then carefully unwrapped her gift. Inside, resting on a long, slender white envelope, a red Cartier box. She opened it, and lying on white velvet was a beautiful key. Quite large, probably from an eighteenth-century box lock, of iron with a decorative oval filigree bow. The key to a handsome front door, or a garden gate.

Could it be? No, impossible, she told herself. But her heart was racing at the very thought that he might have found her a house. That she would once more have a home of her own. The possibility that she might get out of the depressing room she was living in caused her to realise what she had refused to admit to herself. She had not been living but merely existing in her bed-sit. Without Jason she had only been going through the motions of living these last years. A shiver racked her body and she felt suddenly more alive and eager to unravel the mystery of the key.

She tore open the long white envelope and removed the contents. She recognised Ahmad's handwriting. The note was brief.

Arianne,
Number 12, Three Kings Yard. A cul de sac just off Davies Street, near the corner of Brook Street. Opposite the side entrance of Claridge's. A bijou of a house. Eighteenth century, a small piece of London's Mayfair. Just pick up your toothbrush and something to sleep in, and go right now to see your pied à terre. It's from me to you, because I know you will be happy there.
Ahmad

Arianne could hardly contain her excitement. She had felt a rush of blood, and placed the back of her hand to her cheek. She felt the heat, as if she had suddenly raised an instant fever. How had he known how unhappy she was living in this room? But he did know, she was certain of that. She was quite used to his extravagant gifts, his overwhelming generosity. It had been so much a part of her life these last five years that she had learned to accept it graciously. It was that generosity that had not allowed her to go to him with her financial difficulties. That and not wanting Ahmad to know the extent of the business disaster Jason had left her with.

The house in Cuernavaca and all its contents had been the first thing to go. It had made hardly a dent in her financial troubles. The New York residence and two vintage aircraft had been the next things sold. There was a glimmer of hope that Jason's creditors would wait, that the business could be saved. Or so she had thought, for a week, until the next writ had been served upon her. Her jewellery, then the rare books went under the hammer. They paid the firm's employees who, having seen what she could not, accepted the money and walked away. What had kept her going was her imaginings: that one day Jason would return to her and make things all right again. She had put up a courageous fight, but in vain.

The creditors closed in. Bankruptcy. Shame. Degradation. Months of depression and loneliness and nothing else in her life but fighting to save Jason's name. To lose everything was one thing, for her husband to be declared a fraud was another. She would not have it. By the time a clear discharge in bankruptcy for Jason's company, and no criminal charges for him had been declared, there was nothing left for Arianne. She had gone from riches to rags, had walked away with nothing but two pieces of Louis Vuitton luggage filled with designer-label clothes Jason and Ahmad had bought for her, and nothing to fall back on. Not a roof over her head, not a penny in her pocket. To think about that horrible year without Jason sent a shiver down her spine, even now.

There was, too, another reason why Arianne could not bear to take advantage of Ahmad. She feared that to burden him with her problems might somehow change their friendship. That was all they had left. And Arianne needed that for the memories she could not bear to let go. Memories of her love for Jason.

Chapter 3

Jason and Ahmad had always given the orders. She had enjoyed the way they controlled her, never had any reason not to. From them she had derived pleasures she had never dreamed could exist for a woman. Thus it never entered her mind not to go to Number 12, Three Kings Yard.

She gathered her toothbrush, other toiletries, a nightdress and robe into a piece of canvas and leather hand-luggage, slipped back into the same jacket she had worn to Chessington House and left the bed-sit. As soon as she turned around to double-lock the door to her flat she knew she would never enter that room again. That would suit her fine. She rushed from the building into the street, close, luckily, to a main thoroughfare where there was a chance of finding a taxi. She had hardly gone a hundred yards when she saw one pass her. It pulled up several houses from where she was standing. She broke into a run. 'Taxi, taxi!' A breathless smile at the passenger collecting his change from the driver. She dashed through the still-open door.

'In a rush, are we?' asked the driver, peering over his shoulder at her.

'Yes, we certainly are.' Silly question.

The former passenger standing in the street pulled a face at Arianne and closed the door of the taxi.

'Where to, then?' asked the driver.

'Mayfair, Three Kings Yard. Do you know it?'

'Yeah, off Davies Street. You got it.' Morty Silverman from Hackney looked at her through the rear-view mirror of his taxi as they passed under a streetlight. He did that several times. He liked to guess about his passengers. When, that is, he wasn't harrying them with talk, those that would converse. One look at this woman said she wouldn't. He was going to have to figure her out on his own. It kept him amused while they progressed towards the West End. Something funny about her accent. Foreign, but where from? Was she what she appeared to be, a quiet beauty going to stay the night with her date? Or was she one of those thousand-pound all-night hookers on a call to the West End? It was getting harder and harder to tell who was on the game these days. The night-case was a giveaway. But the face and the quiet about her, a kind of laid-back innocence. No, she wasn't on the game. He began to laugh at himself and could bear it no longer. 'Rushing to see a sick mother?'

Arianne had become accustomed to garrulous London taxi drivers. By New York standards they were subtle. She was too excited to be annoyed, but she wasn't going to give anything away either. 'No.'

The tone in her voice and glimpses of her face in the rear-view mirror, lit for a second by the streetlamps, silenced him. Pretty but dull, too passive to be amusing, too soft to be a hooker. Maybe a deep lady who never gave anything away. The kind that married the boy next door. He nearly tried once more to make conversation, but thought better of it. And then he forgot about his passenger because he became preoccupied with the West End traffic. He hated Saturday nights in the West End. The whole world was on the streets. Jams everywhere. But the work was there, the money was good.

Only when the taxi pulled into Three Kings Yard and she stepped out of his cab and paid him, her smile at him made Morty Silverman momentarily sorry he hadn't made a greater effort. She looked now to him like one of those blue-stocking intellectuals, bright and interesting. Oxford, Cambridge, but then again maybe not. Oxford and Cambridge girls didn't wear high-fashion sable jackets. She was a hard one to pin down. She told him, 'I'm so sorry, I have nothing but a twenty-pound note.'

Blimey, she's American. He gave her her change. Unable to resist it, he leaned out his window and said with great authority, 'California, LA.' Now he had her pinned down.

'Connecticut, New Canaan.'

He pulled up the window, manoeuvred the taxi around, and drove from the yard without another word.

Arianne stood in the cobblestone yard facing Number 12. It was as Ahmad had written, a *bijou* of a house: two storeys and quite wide so that it looked rather square. There were four windows set in the façade and the window-boxes were planted. They made her think of the hanging baskets at Chipping Wynchwood she had seen that morning. The entrance was handsome, with its wide door painted black and bearing heavy brass door-furniture that included a huge lion door-knocker.

Arianne looked around the yard. Quite a large square, wide enough for parked cars on either side of it and a taxi to turn around. Its entrance off Davies Street was of the same width. It gave the yard an open feeling. The other houses and the archway opposite the entrance to the yard led through to a second courtyard that Arianne would later find belonged to the Italian Embassy. Over the stone arch, there were rooms that connected two small houses, as charming as Number 12. The two houses opposite Number 12 had less charm. They had been converted with plate glass to some sort of commercial property, she guessed, with flats above. But somehow it didn't matter. It was a courtyard reminiscent of those in Paris whose attraction lay in being both commercial and residential. The French did that sort of thing so well. Whoever had control of Three Kings Yard had made it work there. The other houses had attractive window-boxes. There were gas lights from tall posts to give it all a mellow light.

The place charmed her, and the mere idea that she might be a part of it was enormously uplifting for Arianne. It was only when she had passed between two parked cars and stood at the front door of Number 12, the beautiful old key in her hand, that she registered that lights were on in the house. For a moment she didn't know whether to knock or use the key. She used the key.

The entrance hall had a very worn but well-polished stone floor, and a pretty staircase of dark oak with a threadbare oriental runner laid on the stairs and held in place by brass rods that gleamed. It wasn't a large hall, the staircase more charming than impressive. Like the linen-fold, oak-panelled walls, it seemed slightly askew. From the ceiling hung a small crystal chandelier. It hung plumb, but the ceiling had a distinct wave in it.

Just two steps to the right to open the natural waxed, knotted-pine door, a handsome affair with antique brass box locks and an oval knob and decorative finger-plates. She passed into a sitting room: a twenty-foot square room simply chock-full of English country-house charm. It might as well have had a brass plaque on the wall saying Colefax and Fowler, those designers so famous for that English flowered-chintz look, with its elegant stripes, soft furnishings, wing chairs and comfortable Georgian furniture. Sporting pictures, charming oils, portraits, scenic wonders of the English countryside, shared walls covered in a navy blue wallpaper patterned with minute *fleurs de lys* with Picasso drawings, small Morandi still-lifes of the bottles he was so famous for, and lesser-known contemporary paintings, in handsome carved frames, some wooden, some gilded. A soft glow came from the ivory silk lampshades and a fire was crackling in the fireplace. There were pots of red and white azaleas, and small Chinese pedestal dishes proffering white Belgian chocolates on tables with magazines, books. It was a home.

She was Alice stepping through the looking-glass. She walked around the room. Warmed her hands by the fire. She still carried her handbag and overnight case. She dropped them on the Queen Anne settee near the fire and walked back into the hall. The door opposite the sitting room was closed. She opened it and switched on a light, a crystal chandelier over an oval cherrywood dining table. She stepped into the dining room and the perfume of a bowl of white lilies in the centre of the table made her close her eyes and breathe deeply. He had thought of everything. How had he accomplished it all? The yellow walls were glazed and held black-and-white etchings. Architectural scenes of Rome. Masterly Piranesi. A small table set against one wall had crystal glasses and decanters containing whisky, sherry, vodka, set on a silver tray. A narrow marble-topped and silver-gilt console served as a sideboard at the other wall. A very pretty Queen Anne mirror above it reflected the charm of the room.

Walking from the room down the hall took very few steps. Arianne reflected that Number 12 with its wonky walls, low ceilings, small jewel-like rooms, was like a very large doll's house with everything absolutely in proportion. It amused her to think of herself living in a doll's house. There was something very cosy about that. It was like stepping into Queen Mary's doll's house or one of those that museums were so fond of exhibiting as works of art encapsulating a way of life.

She found the kitchen behind the dining room. Neat, with a shining new black Aga, the ultimate in English cookers, black slate tops on the work-surfaces and antique glass-fronted cupboards painted and dragged in shades of rust and yellow that matched what little wall-space there was. In between the cupboards, practically wall-to-wall, was a framed Victorian collection of rare butterflies. Arianne opened several drawers and cupboards. She could see it was newly fitted out to delight a gourmet. There was a butcher's block in the middle of the room and a high, antique stick chair; from hooks on the ceiling copper pots and pans dangled decoratively. The single window was large, but faced a blank brick wall only a foot from the house, and that was covered in lattice-work and masses of ivy.

Arianne knew before she opened the fridge that it would be chock-full of lovely fresh food. She opened the door and was not disappointed. Upstairs she found two large bedrooms and a spacious, truly handsome bathroom. Every room, including the bathroom, had a fireplace. She stood at the foot of a French, Louis XIV four-poster bed draped in the prettiest way imaginable. The fabric was a cream-coloured silk taffeta with narrow stripes of embroidered flowers repeated every few inches. The bed-linen was also cream-coloured and edged in heavy white lace. She had no idea how long she had been admiring it when she heard someone calling, 'Hello. Hello. Are you here?'

Arianne went immediately to the head of the stairs and looked down. Standing there was a woman in a bulky tweed coat and a rather old-fashioned hat that had seen better days. She was in her late middle age, not unhandsome. She had a loaded, heavy-duty black plastic shopping-bag in each hand, and carried her handbag over her wrist like the Queen. 'Yes, I'm here,' Arianne called down.

'Oh, good. I was worried you hadn't arrived. I would have had to put out the fire.'

Arianne walked down the stairs. She didn't miss the look of surprise on the woman's face. 'Is something wrong?' asked Arianne.

'You're not what I expected,' said the woman quite matter-of-factly. She deposited her shopping-bags on the floor.

It was obvious that the woman had something to do with this amazing gift, and very likely with Ahmad. So the woman might have expected one of Ahmad's beautiful model girls or an aspiring actress, even some amazingly expensive and chic call-girl. The sort of women he favoured. Although the woman was out of line to have said anything, Arianne did not care to pursue her remark, but merely told her, 'My name is Arianne Honey.'

'And I'm Ida, your cleaner.'

Arianne began to laugh. It was a nervous laugh, and she raised her arms and held her hands out as if to encompass the house, and told the woman, 'Ida, I can't afford a cleaner any more than I can afford this house.'

Ida unbuttoned her coat, bent down and reached into one of her shopping-bags and produced a brown manilla envelope with a white envelope paperclipped to it and handed it to Arianne. 'Why don't you go into the sitting room and read this? I'll go and make us a cup of tea.'

Before Arianne could answer, Ida had her coat off and had picked up her shopping-bags and was already on her way to the kitchen. Arianne took a chair by the fire and opened the envelope. She read Ahmad's letter twice and had time to dry her tears before Ida appeared in the room, carrying a silver tray and the tea-service from the dining room, two pretty china cups and saucers, and a plate of biscuits.

Arianne's tears had been provoked by Ahmad's kindness, but they were for Jason. Because she loved him so very much and missed him every minute of every day. Because she knew that Ahmad missed him too, missed them both. Ahmad loved Jason still, as one loves a brother, the closest man-friend a man can have. That he had bought this house as much for Jason as for her was quite clear. The gift was the result of his love, not for her but for them. Because he had somehow found out that Jason had left her destitute, and he could not allow her to live like that. Or Jason to have been dishonoured by not having provided for her. All this she read between the lines of his letter.

Always the diplomat, he had been clever about giving her Ida. 'She's a treasure, an excellent cleaner, and will take very good care of you. Please do me the favour of accepting her. You see I would not want to lose her, but for the moment I have no work for her in London since I have given up my flat there. I mean to stay at Claridge's when I am in England. You need pay her nothing, in fact I insist you pay her nothing, I don't want to spoil her and she is paid more than adequately by me. When I need her, rest assured that I will take her from you.'

Arianne watched Ida pour the tea. She was rather grand-looking, with just a touch of the eccentric. Her dark blonde hair was done into a magnificent beehive hairdo *à la* sixties. She had harlequin eyeglass frames, and a hint of Cockney in her voice. The authority with which she made it abundantly clear that she was in service to Arianne and was most definitely not going to be deflected from cleaning Number 12, swiftly added up to her being 'a treasure'. But, 'treasure' or not, Arianne was much relieved when she was told that she was not Ida's only job. Ida looked after her 'gentlemen' as well. They lived in two other houses in the yard. Exactly what hours this 'treasure' would work was settled between them, and after showing Arianne the basics of living in the house, she hid her beehive under her hat and left, double-locking the door behind her.

Arianne returned to the sitting room and sat in a different chair, one that gave her a new perspective on the room and its contents. She took up Ahmad's letter, read it once more and then placed it in her lap, feeling more calm, able to take note of the many beautiful things someone had chosen for it. The little things that make a home. Now she saw for the first time the silver-framed photographs on a handsome, Tudor oak bible-box in a far corner of the room. There was also a lamp on the box, eighteenth-century Italian, in ornately carved wood, still with remnants of gold leaf, candle-stick-based with a pleated ivory silk shade.

Arianne recognised the photos at once. She was immediately drawn to them. From the lamp warm light spilled over the pictures. The silver frames gleamed, and the photos seemed to come alive. In one, Arianne flanked by Jason and Ahmad in front of the Tiger Moth, the day Jason bought the plane. Smiles. The three seemed to be bursting with happiness. And in another, the trio lying on silk brocade cushions, sunlight filtering through the wooden Arab screens, mushrabiya, to make an exotic pattern over Jason looking down at Arianne, love for her emanating from his eyes. Ahmad, her hand in his, with his head slightly bowed

41

kissing it. 'Our first Christmas together in Cairo,' she said aloud to the empty, silent room.

She picked up yet another of the silver-framed photographs. A white sand beach fringed with coconut palms leaning lazily over it. Emerald and sapphire blue water lapped over the three of them wrapped in the other's arms. Ahmad's magnificent sailing yacht was anchored far out in the lagoon. The laughter and fun they were having together showed clearly in postures fixed by the camera. She announced to the room, 'And the first time the three of us made love together.'

Arianne sat down on the sofa. Placing a cushion behind her head, she slipped out of her shoes, swung her feet up and stretched out. Still the picture was in her hands: she seemed mesmerised by it. She studied the snapshot that had been blown up to a four-by-eight. It had lost some of its sharpness, become grainy, had the sheen of the soft focus. She so concentrated on the photo that she could almost hear the Indian Ocean rolling on to that shore, feel the heat of the sun.

So often she relived the complete happiness of her life with Jason, and the magnificent erotic nights and days with her husband and his best friend. Rich memories. Those erotic threesomes had become so much a part of her and Jason's happiness together that she had almost forgotten the first sexual encounter on that deserted island in the Indian Ocean.

Arianne closed her eyes for a minute and she drifted back in time. She had always had a timid soul. Courage, taking chances, allowing passion to run away with her, the big adventure: that had never been Arianne. But that was Jason, the very heart of him, his soul, the way he lived. She knew what she was taking on when she had married him. And he had enriched her life.

Memories revived, and once again she was contemplating the wavy white line of foam that trailed along the beach as far as the eye could see. The three of them balancing themselves on the rail of the sloop, she in the centre and the two men on either side holding her hands. She was trembling with excitement and fear at the prospect: to dive from such a height into the sea and swim for the shore. It seemed to her too far, but Jason and Ahmad were so certain she could make it. A dingy had been launched with Ahmad's manservant and a picnic. She watched it head for the beach as she tried to calm herself. Certain she was steady on her feet, Jason gently removed his hand from hers; Ahmad did the same a few seconds later. She gathered courage from their macho energy, the power of their strong personalities. The three of them extended their arms, preparing themselves for the dive. Jason called out 'Let's hit that shore'. They looked at each other. In unison the three of them dived off the sloop. The crew had lined the deck to watch the stunt.

Arianne hit the water. Her dive was deep, but she swam smoothly back up to the surface, breaking the water some distance behind the men. They waited for her to swim up to them. Clearly thrilled with their performance, Jason pulled her into his arms and kissed her deeply. Then he turned her around to Ahmad, who did the same. Ahmad had never kissed her like that before. The way he ran his hands over her body, caressed her face with his hands: it felt so good. The water was cold and they set out for shore swimming three-abreast.

It was a marvellous swim. The waves were high, exhilarating to swim through. They paused several times to float on their backs under the tropical sun. The men were happy, playful in the water. Like porpoises they dived around Arianne, sometimes to scoop her up in their arms as they sprang from the deep and then pull her under with them. Other times they would in turn take her in their arms and swim with her, or carry her on their backs. Together they raced the last three hundred yards to the beach. The undertow was stronger than they had expected, but they worked through it to be washed up on the beach, tired but adrenaline-high, enamoured with the swim, the beach, and each other. They crawled away from the grasp of the undertow and lay there on the sand. Waves, their power now spent, rolled lazily over them to the steady rhythm of the push and pull of the sea.

It was as if they never wanted that swim to stop. They were lying on their backs, the men on either side of Arianne, wallowing in the sensuous sensations of the hot sun caressing their bodies, then the lap of the ocean washing over them, over and over again.

It was Jason who first rolled on to his side and pulled himself closer to her, until their bodies touched. Jason who leaned over her and placed a kiss on her lips, caressed her face and then her breasts, and then kissed her deeply while his hand slipped between her legs and under her swimsuit to caress her mound. A wave rolled over them right up to their necks and slipped away again to return to the ocean. The lust was brimming in his eyes, stronger and more provocative than she had ever seen it before. Again a wave broke over them. She felt a passion that became uncontainable.

He slipped the straps of her suit off her shoulders and pulled it down around her waist. Cupping a breast in his hands, he licked the salt water from the dark nimbus puckered from the cold water and the touch of his tongue upon it. Her nipples, slender and erect, felt the suck of his mouth, his teasing teeth. Her cunt felt searching fingers. She was giving way to his lust for her. Now his mouth was upon hers again. They kissed deeply and she felt him roll her gently on to her hip and into Ahmad's arms. Ahmad caressed her wet hair and kissed her with great tenderness, then searched out her tongue and kissed her with ever greater passion. She felt so good in his arms. It wasn't merely male animal lust in those kisses, there was more, something indefinable that took possession of her. The pressure of his hands caressing her back, her breasts, his muscular body pressed tight against hers. And when his hands slipped under her suit to caress her hips, the flat of her stomach, and he ran his fingers through her wet pubic hair, she wanted him no less than she wanted her husband.

He returned her into Jason's arms. Fired by seeing Arianne being made love to by Ahmad, Jason seized her and bit into her lips. His kisses were wild with desire for more of her. When Jason passed her back it was to a now-naked Ahmad, beautiful and erect, who placed kisses all over Arianne's nude body while the water rushed over them. The two men, both now naked and erect, wrapped themselves around her. Hands went everywhere, and kisses. She was tantalised by each of their penises rubbing against her, the feel of them in her hands, grazing her lips. She was crazed by so much male lust for her. Their tongues licked, their mouths devoured. Now erotically out of control, she begged them to take her. She heard herself begging to be fucked by them, to feel their sperm flowing into her as the ocean relentlessly swept over her. Arianne was amazed by her own lust, by her freedom to express her own needs and desires.

All three were lost in an erotic world the men had drawn

Arianne into. Masters of the erotic, of all things sexual, they were enamoured of Arianne for giving herself up to them so willingly. It was her, her sweetness, passivity, her willingness to surrender to them body and soul that sharpened their sexual appetites. Together they took possession of her. They made love to her, fucked her in turn. If one was fondling her breasts, kissing her in a frenzy of passion, he was also guiding the other's rigid member into Arianne's willing cunt. There were whispers of love and passion for her from Jason, gratitude for her willingness to give herself up to his every sexual whim, to form a sexual triangle with Ahmad. And Ahmad, when he entered her for the first time, was magnificent, as exciting a lover as Jason but very different. And the first time they all three came together in the most intense orgasm she had ever had, it was with Jason deep in her mouth, her tongue hungrily in unison with Ahmad's thrusts, and Jason's fingers manipulating her clitoris, the waves of satin-smooth water rushing up over their interlocked bodies and then rolling back into the Indian Ocean.

The ocean washing over them, a womb? Why not? They were indeed born together and anew. Arianne lost herself; the ego and the id died. She sensed a new self born to them when the two men merged as one inside her. And that was their beginning. She felt at that moment they would be together all their lives. She wept with joy at a new sexual freedom that allowed her to take over and become the aggressor in their erotic games. It was all so fluent, so easy, natural even, when in their lust for each other she would pair off with one to give the greatest pleasure to the other. With every orgasm they became closer, more entwined in the other's lives.

Arianne ran her fingers over the glass enshrining the pictured memory of that time. She felt pure joy in the memories the photograph conjured up for her. They had been like carefree, happy children, thinking it would never change for them. They had felt like golden children of gods who smiled upon them, for whom it would never end.

What made the picture even more poignant was that Ahmad's man had snapped the photograph when they still had their swimsuits on, in those first moments when the men had passed her between them, and lust became their body language. It was the inception of an intense sexual *ménage à trois* that was to be theirs for so many years, until fate snatched it away from them.

'Jason. Jason,' Arianne murmured. She often called his name. For her he remained the most important man in her life.

Chapter 4

It should have felt odd to Arianne to wake up in that glamorously draped bed, one she had never slept in before. But it didn't. Nor did it feel strange to her to be luxuriating in the deep, old-fashioned bath, in a room with luscious white terrycloth bath-sheets, with her name discreetly monogrammed in coral satin appliqué, warming on a heated towel-rack mounted to a mahogany-panelled wall.

Sitting in her robe on the stick chair in the kitchen drinking black coffee, eating toast and marmalade while looking at Victorian butterflies, was certainly not the norm for Arianne either, but it felt as though it was. She had no sense at all of being a stranger in Number 12, Three Kings Yard. Quite the contrary. A deep awareness of place and comfort would have described better her feelings on her first morning in her *bijou* gift-house.

It was her nature to be, if not content with her lot in life, at least receptive to it, no matter how good or bad, exciting or dull. Quick and unexpected changes were always taken in her stride. She had, since a child, always lived in the moment, rarely looking back, hardly forward. Having Artemis for a mother; a quiet, passive, fatalistic doctor for a father; and Jason for a husband, had been good training for that.

Arianne was living a solitary life; she had done so since Jason's death. It had not been intentional; that way of life had simply come upon her. Although she lived it from day to day and did not dwell on the past, nor wallow in that never-never land of 'what might have been', it did still include a strong love for a dead husband, and an indefinable relationship with Ahmad that allowed her to accept his overwhelming generosity with a grateful heart.

She expected the knock at the door. Ahmad had told her ten o'clock in his letter. And the man who was to return to the bed-sit in Belsize Park to remove her things was on time. Arianne picked up the list she had written out of the belongings she wanted brought to Three Kings Yard and went to open the door.

He was casually leaning against the stone architrave surrounding the front door. From a clear cellophane florist's box the stems of three dozen white roses poked out. A large white satin bow and long streamers glistened in tne autumn sunshine. They gazed into each other's eyes. Her heart missed a beat. It always did, every time she saw him after a long absence. In earlier days, when Jason was alive, that look in Ahmad's dark, almond-shaped eyes had set her aflame. Now it flared up for a second and then, like a candle in the wind, was snuffed out.

She watched him raise a hand and run his fingers through his silky black hair: a sexy habit he had that drew attention to the decadent, clever eyes, the sensuous bone-structure of his face, the voluptuous lips. Whenever she saw him she was surprised at how tall he was, how handsome and well turned-out. So urbane. But, more than anything, she never ceased to be amazed at how beautiful a man he was. A strange term, but beautiful and erotic, that was Ahmad Salah Ali. He had a beauty reminiscent of the marble statues one sees in the Cairo museum, a Pharaonic prince, a great lord descending thousands of years to the present – only alive, so very much alive.

Without clothes he was unimaginably erotic, the wide shoulders and narrow hips, the hardness of his body . . . Ahmad's skin was smooth, satin to the touch, the colour of dark honey. To caress him was enough to sense a lust unhindered by morality or inhibition, to have all fear of losing one's self in him vanish. He wore his masculinity with a sureness that made not only Arianne but all his women tremble with excitement for more, always much more of him. A libertine who seduced, corrupted if given the chance, he was still the handsomest, most sensual man she had ever seen. One look at him and she was instantly aroused, her body yearning for sexual pleasure with him. Was it possible, she had often asked Jason, for a man to be voluptuous? He had laughed and had always answered her, 'Yes, and Ahmad is the living proof.'

Ahmad's smile warmed her, and she bent forward and placed

a tender kiss on each cheek. And then she told him, 'You're a lovely surprise.'

He removed the slip of paper from her hand and replaced it with the box of roses. Then, without detaching his gaze from her eyes, he called over his shoulder to someone and waved the piece of paper in his hand, while he told her, 'I made a change of plan.'

'The house. It's perfect. I love it.'

'Good.'

She wanted to thank him, but it seemed so trite. She could see how pleased he was that she was there and had accepted his gift. Instead she reached out her hand and took his, then led him into the house. She handed back the flowers. 'Please – for a moment, while I discuss a few things with the mover.'

Ahmad walked into the sitting room and placed the box on a chair. He opened his coat and went to stand by the fireplace. Arianne liked the house. He felt happy about that. He had enjoyed buying it for her, had known exactly how he wanted it done up – what would make her comfortable and what would be merely fussy.

He missed her and Jason. Their deep abiding friendship. Their sexual *ménage à trois*. He listened to her giving instructions to the mover: the sound of her voice held his attention, not her words. Still young, fresh, very American, still capable of hiding within it the fire and passion, the sexual hunger he knew she was capable of. In the sexual life she lived with him and Jason, Arianne had found a way of reaching beyond the limits without succumbing to depravity. She was a very sexy lady in love, not a true decadent like himself and Jason. He had always suspected that when Jason was alive, but had never wanted to believe it. But, after Jason's death, when they spent their first night together imagining that they could pick up the overwhelmingly erotic and passionate life they had once shared so happily, he was forced to accept the truth. It simply did not work for them without Jason. He was Arianne's love, her decadent soul, and now it was gone. Ahmad could not help but hope that one day she would find another man to love as she had loved Jason. Not for Ahmad's sake but for hers. So that she could enjoy again the erotic world she had once embraced with him and Jason. Ahmad knew how much she missed it, yearned for it. She deserved that and love and

49

much more. Arianne and Ahmad? Without her spontaneous, decadent sexuality, Ahmad had no sexual desire for Arianne, merely a deep abiding affection.

It had always been a miracle to him that Arianne's and Jason's marriage had been so happy, so complete. He loved Jason, and knew him down to the marrow of his bones – how wild, compulsive and passionate, what a natural decadent, he was. The charm and cad in him. Once Ahmad had met Arianne he had understood how she was able to tame Jason. She did it with love. Giving him everything, denying him nothing, not a fraction of her heart, no morsel of her soul. And he loved her and was devoted to her for her selflessness. Soon after their marriage when he gave her to Ahmad, she gave those same things sexually to him. Ahmad had always known that he was an intricate part of Arianne's and Jason's marriage, that the attraction of their sexual *ménage à trois* was so powerful it cut off all other avenues that Jason might have wandered down.

As for Ahmad, he had never stopped enjoying the corruption of Arianne. He and Jason had been masters at drawing her into an erotic world that could still excite the three of them after years of being together. It came as no surprise to him that he should fall in love with her and their sexual arrangement. The shock had been that without Jason it was over.

Arianne entered the room and went directly to the box of flowers. She pulled at the bow; it dissolved in her hands. She removed the lid. She could feel his eyes on her. 'How are you doing?' he asked.

'A great deal better than yesterday. But you must know that, since this house and you are responsible for that.'

He went to her and raised her hand and placed the palm over his lips and kissed it. He closed his eyes. Another time, another place, she would have bent forward and kissed his eyes, teased the closed lids with the point of her tongue. She used to tremble with excitement to kiss and caress his beautiful, decadent face, sometimes even to tame his wild, erotic soul. Now she could only admire that face, and remember. A part of him would always be there with Jason lingering in the past. The feel of his soft, voluptuous lips against the palm of her hand, the tip of his tongue licking it, was a sexy gesture. They both savoured it for a few seconds before he opened his eyes again and placed an arm around her shoulder. Together they went to the kitchen to arrange the roses in a Lalique glass vase. Then he carried them to the sitting room for her. They hardly spoke to each other. Their togetherness seemed to be doing the speaking for them.

Finally he asked, 'Have breakfast with me, across the road at Claridge's.'

It had been a long time since she had seen him, nearly a year. And now all this: the house, his visit and a few hours to hear all his news; to bask once again in the charm of his personality. She hurried as she dressed in the same clothes she had worn to Chessington House the morning before. It was quite shattering to think how one's life could change so radically from one day to another. Arianne took a final look in the mirror, 'Well, you'll just have to do,' she said aloud, and slipped into the sable jacket from the dressing room down the stairs. She found him waiting for her in the hall by the front door.

As they crossed Davies Street and walked arm in arm around the corner on to Brook Street to enter Claridge's Hotel by the main entrance, Arianne felt suddenly different. As if some fairy godmother had touched her shoulder with a magic wand, and had chased a darkness away that had been hovering over her life since Jason's death. It was simply one of those inexplicable feelings when you know a space in your life has opened.

Walking through the vast dining room of Claridge's, so handsome in its classic coolness reminiscent of the Art Deco period of the nineteen-twenties, Arianne wanted to giggle. She always did whenever she entered that room. Her imagination was not prone to fantasy, but it was overworked in Claridge's. She had only to walk through the lobby and the salon where the musicians played at tea and drinks-time, then through the decorative iron and glass fret-work doors into the dining room to sense the illusion that she was on one of the grand Cunard ocean liners like the *Queen Mary*, that had made regular Atlantic crossings from Southampton to New York before the airplane took the leisure and elegance out of crossing the ocean. Of course she did not giggle, merely smiled and followed behind the maître d' to a select table where a bevy of black-suited waiters hovered to draw out chairs and fuss over the table and guests.

She could not help noticing the heads of well-dressed, affluent diners turn to look at them as they wove their way between tables. Arianne had learned to enjoy admiring looks from strangers whenever she was with Ahmad. He gave off an erotic essence that signalled sensuality. When she had been with both Jason and Ahmad, as a threesome, they had invariably created an atmosphere that was electric.

Seated across from each other, once breakfast had been ordered and crystal flutes filled with tiny white peaches covered with champagne had been served to them, and the waiters had buzzed off to hover at some other table, Arianne told Ahmad, 'I always feel like the duckling that turns into a swan, the timid mouse who can roar like a lion, the *femme fatale* who rises like a phoenix from the ashes of a plain Jane when I walk across a room with you.' This time she did give a charming giggle, and reaching out she touched the rim of her glass to his and made a toast, 'I miss you. I miss us. The three of us.'

There was no sadness in her voice, merely a truth. Ahmad smiled back at her and suggested, 'Don't.'

'Don't?' Arianne felt hurt by the tone in his voice. It was emphatic, nearly an order.

He was not unaware of her feelings: they showed in her eyes. Her hand was lying on the crisp white damask cloth covering the table. He took it in his and held it. 'There is no point. It's counter-productive to waste your life missing something. Especially something as special as what the three of us had together.' There was tenderness in his voice. He continued, 'That was unique. With Jason gone, it will never happen again; it's irreplaceable. That should have been obvious to you when we tried to create a sexual life for ourselves without him. Remember, oh yes. But miss, no. I don't want you to miss love and great sex. They are too much a part of your life now. Go and grab that lust for love and sex I know you thrive on. Or at least make a space in your life so it can find you. Begin again. Find a new love. It's love that works for you. Love that sets your libido free. A deep, abiding and sincere love. We don't have that with each other. That's why it couldn't work for just the two of us. Jason and you had that. He loved you more than I could have imagined he was capable of loving. But that did not hinder him from taking advantage of

52

you, just as I did. You were vulnerable and we manipulated you sexually. You were lucky. It could have been destructive for you, but it wasn't. It worked for all three of us. We turned you into a sexually liberated lady and watched you enjoy every nuance of every bizarre sexual act we drew you into.' Ahmad, still holding her hand, was speaking low, cautious that no one in the dining room should overhear him. 'Your utter disregard for yourself, your love for Jason and later for me – think what harm you could have come to!'

'But I didn't.'

They were silent for several seconds, simply gazing into each other's eyes. Ahmad saw it for the first time. He was surprised. He had never even suspected in all the years the three of them had been together, through all their amazing sexual excesses, not once had he guessed. 'You knew. You have always known the rotten side of Jason. That touch of evil he could twist around us, and excite us with. His lust for depravity, and my enjoyment of everything erotic. You were never blinded by love for the charming cad you married, were you?'

The colour rose to her face and she lowered her gaze from his eyes. He gave her time to compose herself, then he squeezed her hand. She raised her eyes to meet his again. There was no point in keeping her secret any longer. 'No,' she told him. 'Oh, maybe I did put the blinkers on in those first few days after I met him and he swept me off my feet. But the truth is, I was never blinded by love. Rather, I accepted everything in the name of love. You see, I was very innocent and inexperienced when I met Jason. But not so innocent that I didn't know he was a corrupting influence, that you both were. He was the most exciting thing that had ever happened to me. And then, when I met you, right from the first time we were introduced, I knew you were the second most thrilling man I would ever know.

'When we were together on that beach when he gave me to you, I had no chance. He had been priming me to want more, always more, sexually. And I did. I had already been longing to know what it would be like to be made love to by you. I succumbed to that Ahmad Salah Ali charm, the exotic life you led. I was tantalised by the erotic world you played in. Jason saw to it that I knew a great deal about your fame as lover and libertine. He teased me with you, until I could barely look at you without desire. Every time you touched me, or kissed me, no matter how innocently, the perfume of your skin excited me. It had not occurred to me that you had both planned it, were driving me to a fever-pitch to have sex with you, until the moment he rolled me over into your arms. And then it didn't matter, because I was at last where I wanted to be. Although, as those waves rolled over us, I was for an instant frightened to be made love to by two men at the same time.

'Later on, just how far would such lust as ours take us, was the question that niggled in the back of my mind. But I loved Jason unconditionally. For that very reason I was so happy in our unusual arrangement. Another factor? I knew instinctively that my life was safe in yours and Jason's hands. It was so easy to give myself up to you and a *ménage à trois*. It made the three of us so happy, so much closer, and that was what we all yearned for. It was at first frightening when you and Jason reached down to the dark side of my nature and brought it into the light. But the rewards, ah, yes, the rewards. I revelled in my own sexual lust for the first time in my life. Not yours, Ahmad, not Jason's, but my own, and I loved myself for it as I had never done before.'

Here Arianne stopped and drank from her glass. She could see the excitement in his eyes, could sense his erotic thoughts. He had been her devil in sex. And they loved each other for it. It was what still bound them together. That and their mutual love for Jason.

Ahmad raised his glass and drank, plucked a small white peach from the champagne flute and fed it to her across the table. The flesh tasted sweet, quintessentially peachy. A waiter arrived to refill their glasses, and on his heels two more to serve them Eggs Benedict, of which they were both so fond, and a platter of tiny sausages and strips of bacon done to a crisp. A silver salver draped in a white damask napkin edged in lace proffered hot brioche and croissants. Crystal bowls of apricot and strawberry preserve and golden honey were placed on the table.

It all happened at just the right time, giving them a chance to recover from Arianne's confession. The hot black coffee was poured and after a waiter had added hot milk to it and three teaspoons of sugar to Ahmad's cup, they at last retreated to leave their charges to their morning feast. Ahmad studied Arianne's face for several seconds. She had always retained that cool, natural beauty. It still had a sweetness to it, and innocence. Who in that dining room would ever guess the fire and passion, the depths to which she could go in her sexual lust? Her hunger to experience all things erotic? That she could hold two debauched and depraved libertines in check with her sexual acumen, her will to please them and herself?

He chose a sausage and found it spicy and delicious. Before he raised his fork he smiled at her. With a slight gesture, a movement of his head that indicated wonderment, he broke the silence, 'How is it we never had this conversation before?'

Arianne, who had been admiring the succulent breakfast laid out for her, picked up a fork and looked at him. She sighed. Ahmad and she gazed across the table at each other, both aware that quite unexpectedly some deep emotional problems had surfaced and sorted themselves out. 'We didn't because we couldn't. We weren't ready.'

'Ready truly to let go of Jason?'

'Maybe,' she answered, surprised that the thought should suddenly no longer give her any pain.

'Dead is dead, Arianne.'

'I tell that to myself a lot, Ahmad.'

'Telling is one thing, believing is another. Believe, dear heart. Believe it.'

'I'm trying. And I am getting better at it.'

'Good.'

Ahmad wanted to say more, but thought better of it. Instead he gave her one of his warm and endearing smiles – the sort that made women comfortable, made them feel loved and admired by the handsome charmer who seduced them with no more than that, or with a certain look, full of yearning for them. He buttered the corner of a croissant, broke it off, stood up, went to Arianne and fed it to her. He kissed her affectionately on the lips, and squeezed her shoulder. Several women in the room, having seen the kiss, watched with envy as he returned to his seat to drape the napkin over his knees. Hovering waiters fluttered even more around the table.

Breakfast was delicious, but also fun. Ahmad amused her with tales of his life, and gossip about people whom she had met through him. He was an intelligent and witty man, good company. The love and affection of a man, a happy sexual life: she had been depriving herself of these things far too long. It was only here with Ahmad over breakfast that she realised how much she had stopped living, how empty and lonely her life had been without Jason and him there. Twenty-four hours ago she could not see that. The longer breakfast went on the further she seemed to be drifting from her years of mourning. Although she had thought her time of grieving had come to an end months after Jason's death, she could now see that it had not. The world without Jason was coming back into focus for her in Claridge's dining room on a Sunday morning in November.

Even as she and Ahmad walked from the dining room and through the hotel she sensed subtle changes in herself. It was as if for the first time in years she was seeing things with her own eyes, not through Jason's. She felt as if she were suddenly stepping back in time, to the time before meeting him had changed her life, before she had become obsessed with being the woman in the centre of a sexual love-triangle. It was a strange sensation, looking at a world without them in it. They were there, firmly set in the background of her life, and yet they were the past. It seemed doubly strange because Ahmad was right there on her arm, and Jason somehow still very much alive for them in spirit if not in body.

On the doorstep to Number 12, Three Kings Yard, Ahmad took both her hands in his and kissed them in turn. He gazed into her eyes, then lowered his lips to her hands and repeated his kisses. Then he touched her cheek with the back of his hand, traced her lips with the pad of a finger. A most poignant goodbye. '*A tout à l'heure.*' A smile, he turned away from her and was gone.

'See you sometime', she paraphrased for herself. The perfect goodbye for them, she thought. And suddenly life was an adventure again as it had not been since Jason's death. How different her life might have been these last years had he not so abruptly vanished, had there been a body to bury after the accident, something tangible to mourn.

She sighed and placed the key in the lock of her new home, entered the hall and enjoyed the warmth and comfort of being whole again and in her own surroundings. She felt very safe. She lit a fire and after removing her jacket lay down on the deep, comfortable sofa in front of it. She drew over herself an ivory-coloured cashmere car-rug lined in a dark shirred beaver and relived some of the hours she had just spent with Ahmad. But not many. More emotionally drained than she realised, her eyelids heavy, she fell into a sleep too deep for dreaming.

Chapter 5

Arianne's life, her character, her basic personality with all its needs and desires, and their fluctuations, did not change because she had moved house. Nor because she had suddenly become aware that she was still living in the shadows of in-loveness with Jason. Only the circumstances of her life had changed.

It was the same Arianne who awakened in the pretty four-poster bed on Monday morning. For so many years, her thoughts upon awakening had been of Jason. Her obsessive love for him had been the adrenaline of her life. She had bathed and was having coffee in the kitchen thinking of nothing more than the various routes by which she could walk to work from Three Kings Yard to Christie's on King Street in St James's, when she realised something was missing. Jason. The realisation that he had receded from the forefront of her mind appalled her. She gasped.

Arianne covered her face with her hands, closed her eyes and tried to conjure him up. For a moment, she became frightened because it was difficult, very difficult. That had never happened before. He was there, but less vividly. She began to cry because she understood she was letting him go. Ever since his death, she had been able, by sheer will, to keep him alive as her companion, pretending to herself that he was more absent than dead, even though she accepted that he was, in truth, the ghost she chose to share her life with rather than any living, flesh-and-blood man.

Tears stained her cheeks and she wiped them away. She tried to control her emotions, the sobbing. It took some time. She sat there in the kitchen looking through the window at the ivy-covered brick wall. He was gone, never to return, gone. She understood that now he was the past. From this time onwards they would only ever be a love that had been. Her memories. Her entire body trembled with one last deep sigh. And then she could feel her sadness seeping away. For some minutes, she sat on the high chair next to the chopping-block, quite dry-eyed now, and calm, still staring at the ivy-covered wall.

She roused herself to make a fresh cup of coffee and brought it up to the bedroom. She drank it while arranging her things in the drawers of the painted green, French eighteenth-century dressing-table, the last of her belongings from Belsize Park to be put away. Arianne looked through the bedroom window on to Three Kings Yard to check the weather before she dressed. Cars were being shunted back and forth; someone was entering one of the commercial properties in the yard; and there was Ida walking through the arch to a courtyard beyond. One of her gentleman's flats, thought Arianne, and smiled. The yard in Mayfair was a chic address, and looked frightfully smart, but was somehow homey, cosy even. She felt happy.

The sun was out when she locked the front door and left the yard. The route she had chosen today was down Davies Street to Berkeley Square, then from there to Piccadilly as far as Fortnum & Mason's, and from there down King Street to Christie's. What a joy it was to walk through Mayfair to work. No having to ride the buses. No being trapped with strangers in the traffic going into the West End. She sensed a new spring in her step. Her eyes were feasting on every sight, her ears listening to every sound: London coming alive for another day.

Christie's was an exciting place to work, a crossroads of humanity and works of art, some high, some low. People in droves, from all over the world, passed through the portals of the famous auction house. Buying and selling. Looking and dreaming. It was a place of treasures found and treasures lost. A sort of art stock market that fluctuated, made and broke records and fortunes. A barometer of the art world. The world's furniture and paintings and books, *objets d'art*, were on view to be sold to the highest bidder, by the third stroke of the wooden mallet. The famous formula could still electrify a saleroom tense with expectation: 'Going, going', a bang of the hammer, 'gone'. A place where discriminating buyers and sellers met, collectors and dealers, scholars and critics, along with the Mr and Mrs Joe Public domiciled anywhere from New York to Timbuctoo, from Tokyo to Manchester, who were into the commodity of 'art' to embellish their egos and often their homes too.

For Arianne that part of Christie's had always been exciting, but something she really did not quite know how to deal with. She was part of the 'behind-the-scenes' Christie's. It was there that she felt more comfortable. She was very good at her job as a researcher in the rare books, manuscripts and antique maps department. It suited her temperament. And she was emerging as an authority on travel books of the eighteenth century, more especially those covering the Ottoman Empire. It was a solitary sort of job most of the time, except when she was reporting her findings to an associate or a client.

It had been Ahmad's collection and passion for rare books, and his great-grandfather's library in Cairo that had inspired her to do something with her own knowledge and love of rare books. She had always had an interest in them. Like her father, she had collected all sorts of books printed in the seventeenth and eighteenth centuries. It had been a hobby that the good doctor and his little girl had shared. She had grown up with books and a father, instead of a mother and father. It had been a tremendous blow to her when, after Jason's death, she had had to sell her library to cover some of Jason's business debts. That experience had driven from her the desire ever to collect anything again.

Arianne enjoyed her job, for the books, for the book collectors, and the colleagues in her department. People were somehow different when involved with books, and most especially rare books. It was difficult to explain why, but Arianne thought it had something to do with their being a work of art that was simultaneously tactile, visual and cerebral. They were a written record of the past, history, that was made to come alive in the present. Moreover, once Arianne had stepped into her tiny work area at Christie's, she left all else behind. It was escape into a refined and protected world where she could lose herself. That too suited Arianne and her character.

Several days after she had moved into Three Kings Yard, Arianne became aware of how much time she had on her hands without Jason in the forefront of her thoughts. It was a strange sensation, being suddenly aware again of the time and freedom that had always been there since Jason's death. She was enjoying her aloneness, the aloneness that came with letting Jason go along with the *ménage à trois* whose continued presence she had willed as a secondary ghost to haunt her life. In the days that followed she would have the occasional twitch of guilt because she was feeling so happy without them, but that soon passed, never to return.

On the Thursday of that first week in her new home, a colleague at work asked her out to dinner and was pleasantly surprised when she accepted. On the Saturday she agreed to have lunch at the Ritz with a bookseller from New York. And now it was Sunday and she was once again in a state of British Rail nirvana on the train to Chipping Wynchwood to visit Chessington Park and Artemis.

Bright sunshine and a nip in the air, the scent of autumn, as she stepped on to the station platform. Several people: an elderly pair, three young boys looking scruffy, two attractive young girls, a middle-aged man with a very heavy piece of luggage, a couple, attractive and well dressed, arms around each other, emerged from the railway carriages to rush down the platform to the exit and the waiting station-master. Arianne was the last to hand in her ticket. This time he was smiling. She greeted him with, 'What a glorious morning, Mr Pike.'

'Certainly is,' he confirmed. 'Could you spare me a minute, Miss?'

'Yes, of course.'

'Follow me then, Miss. I've something to show you.'

They walked through the station-house into the small rose garden he tended so lovingly. Prepared now for winter, it was far from attractive. In the midst of the small walled-in garden bloomed what must be the last rose of summer. It was breathtakingly beautiful. Full-blown and white, its petals without a blemish of rust, it had a fragile, serene beauty.

'I was hoping you would come this week, Miss. Lady Camilla Palmer is at her peak. She'll go over soon. Covered her every night so old Mr Frost wouldn't get her. I reckon she heard you remarking last week as how you misses my roses, so she decided to bloom for you.'

'She is truly lovely, Mr Pike.' Arianne bent down to take in the heavy scent of the rose.

* * *

When Arianne stepped from the taxi on to the gravel courtyard of Chessington House she had pinned on to the lapel of her belted tweed jacket the rose called Lady Camilla Palmer. The taxi was just pulling away when she saw Ben Johnson and his uncle emerge from the house. Arianne liked the warmth in the smile Ben Johnson gave her as he and his uncle greeted her. She liked too the way he admired her rose.

Smiling back, she offered, 'Lovely, isn't it?' looking from him to the rose and back again into his eyes. For a second their gaze locked. And with that gaze there passed between them that invisible something that can happen between two people. A spark of life that can inspire instant liking. A flicker that, duly fanned, could flare up into a friendship.

'The last garden rose of summer?' asked Sir Anson.

Sir Anson Belleville's words broke her gaze, but not before she registered the beauty lurking in the dark blue eyes of Ben Johnson. Sensuous, maybe, under that twinkle of charm, and the kindness she saw in them. Deep, mysterious sapphires, she thought, before she forgot about Ben Johnson's eyes and answered 'Yes'. Impulsively she removed the flower from her jacket and, holding it in the palm of her hand, offered it to Sir Anson, for him to catch the scent. 'A perfume not to be missed, Sir Anson.'

Lowering his head to take in the sweet odour of rose, he corrected her, 'Anson, just Anson will do, Arianne. It's no breach of good manners to call me Anson. I have, after all, known your stepfather and mother for years, and your mother even before that. What a perfect rose.'

There was something about the way he delivered that hitherto-unknown piece of information, that made Arianne curious. What was the present relationship between Artemis and Sir Anson Bathurst Belleville? She offered the rose to Ben for a sniff of its perfume and smiled at him.

Something enigmatic about Arianne Honey, thought Ben Johnson as he placed a hand under hers and another at her wrist. He guided her open palm as it proffered the rose to his face. Looking over it at her, he was once more, as in the dining room the week before, attracted to the natural, serene beauty she possessed. That and her vulnerable femininity. He sensed a certain stability of character, which meant a great deal to him. More durable, he concluded, but otherwise not unlike the rose she was offering him. But what kind of woman really stirred beneath that lovely façade? His curiosity was aroused.

He nearly intoned 'A rose by any other name . . .', but suppressed the predictable Shakespeare. He was not looking to play Romeo to her Juliet. His smile broadened and he told her, 'The last rose of summer. What a lucky lady you are to have been given such a jewel.' The two men then walked on.

At the front door, Arianne felt inclined to turn round to watch them circle the fountain and go down the drive. There was something about Ben Johnson, something beyond the sexiness she saw in his eyes. Perhaps a hint of pathos in them? She heard the two men's laughter, and watched Ben dash a few steps in front of his uncle and turn around to face him while continuing to walk backwards down the drive. He was quite animated and waved his arms about several times, presumably to make a further point to his uncle. Not for the first time did she admire the apparent closeness between the two men. She saw Ben use his fingers to comb back his light brown hair. It was straight, worn slightly on the long side. It helped preserve in him an appealing boyishness. She noted that he was an attractive man.

Still walking backwards he suddenly broke into some fancy footwork, dancing like a boxer and punching the air, ducking and diving before some imaginary opponent. His antics made Arianne aware of how good a body he had. He moved like an athlete: the same wide shoulders and strong torso, narrow hips. He stopped and when his uncle caught up the few paces that had separated them he turned around and fell into step with the older man. Still talking, he placed an arm through his uncle's and they proceeded towards the garages. Arianne caught herself admiring the rear view of Ben Johnson. Most especially his round, firm bottom in the tight-fitting jeans. Ben's jacket fitted closely around his narrow waist: it was of chocolate-coloured glove-leather, aged and well worn. There was something rakish about the white silk scarf slung casually over one shoulder, like those that men usually wear with a velvet-collared, black cashmere coat to evenings at the opera. The slanted heels of his black cowboy boots looked well used.

It came as something of a surprise to her to find herself taking so much notice of Ben Johnson. And then, without any sadness, she thought of Jason, and his many pairs of cowboy boots. But Jason and his boots seemed a long time ago. A far-off memory. Arianne rang the bell to Artemis's flat.

On the train returning to London that evening, Arianne did not abandon herself to the mental limbo characteristic of most of her journeys. Instead she stared into the darkness and watched the occasional light flashing from some window in the distance. She recalled her day at Chessington Park. Artemis had been at her best. She was as oblivious as ever of her daughter's arrival; but she had obviously taken pains to see that Arianne was included in her day.

Artemis had invited three men to lunch and an afternoon of bridge. Nothing unusual about that. Artemis was that *femme fatale* sort of woman who has little time for other women. She did have one or two 'best girlfriends', but they were women like herself, who even in their old age spent more time with men than women. She had explained to Arianne that it was a casual, country Sunday-lunch party in the flat: cook would be producing a succulent rib of beef, Yorkshire pudding, roast potatoes, candied carrots, creamed spinach, and a crême brulée for pudding. No starter, because they would have champagne and bite-size smoked salmon sandwiches first in the drawing room. And if Arianne was bored while they played bridge after lunch, Artemis had arranged for her to ride Chattanooga, a white hunter, or find something to amuse herself with.

Life with Artemis was always easier when other people were around, and that was just the way the day went. Easy. Arianne listened to Artemis play the piano while relaxing in front of the open fire in the drawing room, the dogs lying at her feet. The men were charming and amusing: they brought out the best of fun in Artemis. She was clever and flirtatious with them. Lunch had been English Sunday lunch at its finest. And after lunch, when Artemis and her guests retreated to the bridge table, Arianne did go down to the stables and take Chattanooga out for a ride through the park with the two larger dogs, the mastiff and the black-and-white Great Dane running behind.

The ride had been exhilarating, and life somehow seemed richer to Arianne on that Sunday afternoon. When the bridge party broke up, there had been tea and scones, cucumber, egg and cress sandwiches, a rich sand-torte, and tiny chocolate éclairs. After tea there was a ride to the station with one of the bridge guests while the remaining three decided to play one more rubber with a dummy hand. As she left the flat Arianne had laid a note on the table for her mother. Her new telephone number.

Arianne watched the suburbs of London flash by. And when she stepped from the train into the bustle of Paddington Station, she was reminded of the sheer variety of worlds to be experienced that a day in her present life would offer her. Arianne Honey was enjoying her life again. She was gratefully aware of it.

Chapter 6

The following week Arianne did not visit Artemis. Artemis had other plans. But the week after that she did go to Chessington Park. She found Artemis restless, and somewhat vague – terribly preoccupied with plans to go sailing in the Caribbean with a friend, evasive about the friend; planning her wardrobe for a stay with another friend, who had a house on one of the Windward Islands. But of which island or of its owner there was no hint. Artemis never travelled alone; the faithful butler-chauffeur Hadley was to accompany her. Little had changed since Gerald and she had travelled.

For most of the day Artemis was offhand with Arianne. At tea-time she seemed to calm down, and mother and daughter enjoyed their tea, sandwiches and cakes in front of the fire in the drawing room. At one point she smiled at Arianne, and said most charmingly, 'No Christmas or New Year together this year. You have a good heart, Arianne, like your father. The same generous spirit. It is remarkably good of you to love me. After all, I have rarely failed to put myself before you from the day you were born.'

'Was my birth such a trauma?' Arianne asked, trying to make light of that rather heavy truth. The lightness was in her eye.

Artemis was quick to understand. She had always appreciated Arianne and Arianne's father continuing to love her in spite of her evident indifference to them. The morsel of love she was able to feel for Arianne had always sufficed the girl. Artemis had found that clever in Arianne. It had bound them together and yet allowed them freedom from excessive family closeness. That would only have bred contempt.

Mother gave daughter a wry smile. 'I have always thought of any birth as rather more a miracle. A baby, a pup, a foal.'

That triggered a conversation about all the animals Artemis

67

had nurtured in her lifetime, which led her into remarking, 'Yes, I always did have a way with animals and lovers. Still do.' Did that imply that she might at present have a lover? She simply rambled on about the animals, eventually changing the subject. 'You will be doing something nice over Christmas, I am sure.'

So typical of Artemis. Not asking but telling Arianne. That way Artemis need not get involved. She was notoriously good at not getting involved in other people's affairs.

Artemis became very good company as Arianne's visit was coming to an end. At last, Arianne had to make a dash for the train, but, fast as the taxi travelled, she missed it. There seemed little to do but return to Chessington Park and an Artemis who would not be pleased. Sudden reappearances do not fit into a mother's organised life.

When the taxi rounded the fountain, its lights picked out Artemis returning from a walk with the dogs. At the sight of Arianne in the taxi, Artemis's face looked more displeased than surprised. She pointed to the entrance and proceeded there on foot while the taxi followed. Arianne stepped out of the taxi.

'You've missed your train.'

'Yes, I'm afraid so.'

'There's not another from our station.'

'No.'

'Well then, what to do? Go on to a larger station where the trains are more frequent? Stay . . .'

The conversation was interrupted by the arrival of Ben Johnson returning his uncle from a day out. Sir Anson emerged from the car and greeted Artemis and Arianne. The Porsche's motor was still running while Ben greeted them from the driver's seat, and Artemis, the dogs scrambling around her feet, bent down to ask Ben, 'Back to London now, Ben?'

'Yes.'

'Arianne has missed her train. It makes her return quite complicated. Taxi to Swindon or Chippenham or Oxford – who knows where? Sunday timetable and all that. A lift would be very helpful.'

Arianne felt terribly foolish. All she had done was miss a train. Artemis was working it up into a drama. It was not so much her words as the inflection in them, the body language. Pleading, seductive. Several sentences later Arianne was feeling like a fragile package that needed careful delivery. She half wanted to protest. But the alternative on a Sunday really was a long detour by road in pursuit of a train that ran into London.

Ben looked past Artemis to Arianne. He smiled at her. 'But of course. With pleasure,' he told her.

'Oh, good, Ben.' No one standing there could have missed the relief in Artemis's voice. Ben bent across the brown leather seat to open the door for Arianne. Artemis, still organising Arianne's departure, saw her daughter hesitate, then fumble in her handbag in an attempt to settle her bill with the waiting taxi-driver. Artemis took over, saying, 'No, don't bother about the taxi, Arianne. Anson will take care of that, won't you?'

Without a word of protest, the tall, elegant diplomat removed his wallet from his pocket and strolled over to pay for the taxi. He seemed both amused and delighted to do Artemis's bidding. Arianne had no time to think that an odd thing for Artemis to do: she was being rushed into the Porsche by her mother. 'Now, do hurry, dear, it's very kind of Ben to play rescue.'

To protest at being taken over and organised because it suited her mother that she be gone? Impossible. That had always been Artemis's way. As Arianne walked around the smart-looking sports car with its black duck soft top and elegant, cream-coloured body, she could not but admire Artemis. Artemis had them all doing her bidding in a matter of minutes.

Ben watched Arianne slip elegantly into the seat next to him. Her legs caught his attention. They were long and shapely, very sexy legs encased in sheer, sand-coloured nylon stockings. The skirt she was wearing, a rich, deep, coral-coloured suede, rose up past her knees when she sat down. He was very much aware of her body as she hoicked herself up off the seat to pull the skirt back down over her knees.

Once settled and comfortable she sat quite still, clutching the small leather shoulder-bag in her lap and looking straight ahead into the darkness of early nightfall. Ben revved the motor and, putting the Porsche in gear, rolled it slowly forward. He reached through the open window next to him and touched his uncle's arm, 'Thanks, Anson, for a great day. I'll call you about next week.' Then they sped around the fountain and off down the avenue of trees. Halfway down the drive he realised that Arianne had made no attempt to buckle herself into the seat. He stopped the car, and she turned to look at him for the first time since she had taken the seat next to him. It was dark and they could only just make out the details of each other's face.

Ben could sense more of Arianne than he could see. He was aware of a certain tranquillity, and a quiet female sensuality. He liked what he sensed in her. He flicked a switch on the dashboard. A light went on inside the car. She turned her head to look at him. They gazed at each other. He was surprised at how pleased he was to have her there. His first words to Arianne were spoken as he bent across her and found the end of the seat belt, stretched it out and buckled her in. Something about her made him smile, made him want her to be pleased to be next to him. 'You forgot to buckle up.'

'Oh.' She seemed embarrassed. He clicked the lock closed. Slipping his hand under the belt he slid it along the angle of strap crossing her body to make certain it was straight and she was comfortable. Then he switched off the light and they were once more off down the drive.

They had driven more than ten miles to the motorway and about the same distance on the M4 racing towards London and still they had not struck up a conversation. It was not a matter of uncomfortable feelings. Quite the contrary.

Arianne felt comfortable in the sports car and in Ben Johnson's company. She snuggled into her waist-length denim jacket trimmed in the same coral-coloured suede as her skirt. Lined in black knitted cashmere, it felt warm and cosy. She liked sitting in the dark, the scent of the leather seats, the feel of the sports car racing over the tarmac, a man physically so close to her. And she liked Ben's silence, the not having to make small talk. It had been so long since she enjoyed that particular sensation, the company of an attractive, sexy man, in the real world. It was a new and tempting perception for Arianne. She had been reliving her intimate life with Jason for so long that she had forgotten about other men, and that they might interest her again as they had before she had met her husband. At fleeting moments when she had been with Ahmad that morning at breakfast in Claridge's, she had sensed that special kind of pleasure. But they had been just that: fleeting moments that vanished as quickly as they had been sensed. Possibly because she had not, at that point, let Jason go. Had not been free to live and love again.

Ben Johnson flicked the indicator rod on the steering wheel, changed gears, and pressed down on the accelerator, as soon as there was a clear stretch of road. The 356B Porsche pulled out from behind a Rover and shot forward with speed and assurance, remaining for some time in the fast lane. The M4 was swarming with weekenders returning to London.

Ben had not been too thrilled when Artemis Hardcastle had all but shoved her daughter in the car for a ride back to London. She had been too quick for him to concoct an excuse to drop the daughter off at the nearest railway station with a through-train to the city. Not that he didn't find Arianne attractive and pleasant. But he owned a fast car: he liked to make the run into London alone. Driving fast and smoothly, with all his concentration on the road, was always one of the pleasures of going to see his uncle. Ben had a passion for cars and driving. His father had had it, his uncle did still. In their younger days, they had raced in some of the more famous rallies around the world. That was now left to Ben, who had been a winner more times than not.

He felt Arianne's presence, without it being thrust upon him. And that was what attracted him to her. Arianne Honey's stillness was a luxury he had not experienced before in the many women he had known. Everything about her was calm and pleasant and beautiful. A presence he could enjoy. She cost little effort. No banal chit-chat, no having to play the Don Juan. Time off for a practised charmer with the ladies. He thought of her silence as a gift, or a thank-you note for the ride.

Ben liked the scent of her perfume – it provoked thoughts of other women and their Paris perfumes. It was nothing like Clarissa's. She had worn Saint Laurent's Rive Gauche until he had bought her a bottle of Cartier's Panther, and then she never wore any other perfume. He tried to place Arianne's perfume, because he did recognise it. Beautiful women he had known and their scent drifted in and out of his mind, but he could not focus the scent Arianne was wearing. They were now in the middle lane of the motorway. A huge lorry was overtaking them and they had a stream of traffic next to them rolling along on the inside lane.

Truckers fancy taking on a Porsche. The lorry's headlights illuminated the interior of the car for a few seconds as it trundled past them, way over the speed limit. The articulated lorry stirred up a colossal slipstream that trapped the low sports car and made it shimmy and shake. But it was no threat; Ben had the car well under control even at the high speeds at which car and lorry were travelling. He stole a glance at Arianne and she turned her head to face him. The corners of her lips turned up in a polite smile, showing him there would be no hysterics about being sucked under the lorry. Then they were cast once again in the dark night.

Several miles on, Ben, not for the first time since Arianne had sat down in the car, stole a glance at her shapely legs when she changed position in her seat. He amused himself by trying to decide whether it was her sexy legs, a certain look in her eye, the way she walked, her body language the few times he had seen her, or something in her face, that told him that beneath that cool façade there burned a sensuous soul. He liked that, and thought how much fun it would be to uncover it. Ben Johnson loved women: revealing them to himself was the highlight of any chase. He liked to peel back their defences against men and love, to slide into their lives and make love to them. He had always had a penchant for illicit love affairs before he had married Clarissa Carr. He had seen it as his right as a carefree bachelor famed as a fast-living polo player and racing driver, and as a successful voice in the wine world, where his own vineyards in France were renowned, while those in California were respected. His enjoyment of illicit love affairs had enabled him to flee from encounters that might have flowered into commitment or marriage, until Clarissa had trapped him. His playboy reputation worked for and against him. It shadowed his marriage, with tragic consequences. He entered marriage without wanting it or the commitment entailed in it. He had been a selfish man, who had changed under the trial of his wife's neurosis and the challenges he had accepted in the hope of making her happy. But she could never see or accept the changes in him. And in the end it was that blindness that killed her.

Why, he wondered, was he thinking about that while riding into London with a quiet, beautiful stranger? He didn't often think about Clarissa and the miserable time he had had when married to her. She had put them both through hell. Now that she was gone, he liked to remember her as she was when he first met her, a glossy beauty on magazine covers whom women wanted to emulate and men to possess. Anything else was too painful, and Ben was not one to suffer needlessly. That was what he liked about Simone Carrier – she was not into suffering. Not for herself, nor for inflicting it on others. Theirs was a happy-go-lucky love affair, a transient romance that suited them both. They respected each other's infidelities, their selfishness, their fear of being trapped in a relationship they could not easily walk away from. They had fun and great sex together, and they told themselves that was all they wanted from each other. It had worked for them for nearly a year now.

Arianne pulled up the collar of her jacket and thrust her hand into its slanted pockets. Aware of her movements, Ben asked, 'Are you cold?'

She shook her head, wanting to assure him that to be in a Porsche was comfort enough. 'There is a heater,' he told her.

'Really, you don't mind? Just a little to take the chill out of the air might be nice, but don't even think about it if you're warm enough. I am not uncomfortable.'

Ben was touched by her consideration. He switched the heater on low. 'And music?'

He could feel her smile in the dark. It was warming, friendly. Ben switched on the radio before she could answer. It was already tuned into the classical wave-length – the Brahms violin concerto. He fussed with the tone and the volume until he had it perfect. The exquisite sound enveloped them, music that propelled them back into the past, each into their own private thoughts as the car pierced the night.

His were of his wife, Clarissa Carr.

'Your mother is very American,' Clarissa had told Ben. He did not miss the edge in her voice. It was always there when she was setting them up for a fight. How many times had he promised himself he would walk away before she provoked him into willing participation in one of their pitched battles, but never did? That was their life now, what their marriage had come to. That and violent, unloving sex: what she demanded and he had been driven to. That and abject apologies, false declarations of love. They were trapped by her fragility, her neurosis, her eye-catching beauty: looks that could chase a Jerry Hall or any other top mannequin off the fashion-show runways and magazine covers of the world.

'*You're* very American. You can't get more American than North Dakota, Clarissa. I'm very American – well, half of me is, anyway. So what?'

'I hate the way she looks at me. So puritanical. So superior. "Not nearly good enough for my son" looks that she jabs at me like daggers.'

'None of that's true. And you know it. If anything, she is in awe of you. How many times have I told you how she whispers to me whenever we are with her that you are the most beautiful woman she has ever seen, and how lucky I am to have you for a wife?'

'And you? Do you feel lucky to have me for a wife? No, don't bother to answer that. We both know the answer. Your cheating heart, the other women you fuck . . . I smell them on you. I always know when you have had another woman.'

Ben walked towards the dressing-table in the bathroom of their Paris *pied-à-terre* on the Avénue Montaigne. He pulled her up from the chair where she had been sitting looking into the mirror, addressing his reflection. He spun her around to face him. She looked incredibly beautiful with her long, blonde highlighted hair, the perfect face that needed only a trace of make-up to enhance it, setting her among the top beauties of the world. She was standing in a white satin, all-in-one chemise trimmed in écru lace with three tiny mother of pearl buttons across the crotch – one of those splendid pieces of lingerie the French conjure so surely into being. That and bone-coloured stockings held in place with frilly white garters high up on her thighs. Her stunning good looks could tame his growing anger. Nearly in a whisper he told her, 'You know that's not true. That I have never had another woman since I married you.'

She began to laugh, and wrenched her arm from his grip. 'Liar. My God, what a bad liar you are.'

'If that's what you think, then divorce me, name me as an adulterer. Give up pretending to the world that you are happier married to me than posing in front of the cameras.' He hadn't meant to say so much, but the words simply slipped out uncontrolled. His anger at Clarissa for provoking yet another scene had made him careless. The last thing he had wanted to be.

The look in her eyes was wild with rage and frustration: rage because she knew he meant it and she had no intention of divorcing Ben Johnson; frustration because no matter how much he showed her he loved her, nor how many protestations of love he made her, she could not believe him.

She lunged for him. Quick enough to avoid being fended off, she grabbed his hand and bit into it as hard as she could. The pain took him by surprise. He was too strong for her. He tore himself free and raised his hand. The slap hung in the air. She was so wild and beautiful, inhibitingly sexy. He hesitated, because he knew that was what she wanted: for him to lose control and beat her. Violence was a sexual turn-on for Clarissa.

'That's what you'd like. Me to divorce you. Set you free to whore around. Hit me, that's what you want to do. To give me some of the pain I cause you.' She lunged at him again, this time with her hand upheld to slap him hard across the face. Ben caught her by the wrist before her blow landed. He twisted it hard and her knees buckled from the pain. She tried kicking him, but he swept her off her feet by an arm around her waist. She wriggled in his arms, and he applied more pressure to her wrist, until she begged him to stop. He bore her struggling to the bed. Roughly he threw her down and pinned her there with one arm across her shoulders. Then he slapped her across her face several times. He tore open the satin confection that scantily covered her body right down to the tiny pearl buttons. The slim straps that held the chemise on her shoulders snapped. He fought her roughly to spread her legs wide, then knelt between them.

Slapping Clarissa around was unbearable to Ben, out of character, but it did shock her out of her violent attack on him. It was the beginning of the end of her rage against him. She had possession of Ben. That was what all her scenes were about: taking possession of her husband, having power over him, creating in him a sexual lust more exciting than he could have with any other woman. She could see in his face that she had won. She had him where she wanted him, wanting her more than she wanted him. She was excited by the conquest. The sequel was to torture him with her frigidity. And this was truly how she held Ben captive. She pitted her frigidity and beauty against the lust and love he felt for her – those things he prayed she would one day feel for him.

'Why do you do this to us, Clarissa? None of it is necessary. For better or worse, we love each other and you know that as well as I do.' They were lies, he knew that, and so did she. But when she drove them both into a pitched sexual frenzy as now, those were the words she wanted to hear and he wished were true.

'Liar. Prove it to me. I love you totally and you give crumbs of love. All I get are your sexual leftovers.'

How could he tell her that believing her when she told him she loved him had been his great mistake, the wrecking of their two lives? What did she know of love, for herself, for him, for anyone? He had tried to tell her, by god, how he had tried. Trying to help Clarissa to be happy with herself, and in their marriage, to truly love, had become a full-time job. But Clarissa was a woman of the kind that only hears what she wants to hear, sees what she wants to see. So he gave up trying to teach love to the emotionally deaf and blind Clarissa. Now they just used each other and tried to postpone the inevitable. 'Stop trying to destroy us, Clarissa, or I *will* walk out on you. That's a promise.'

He had, once again, said too much. But he had had enough, and it was getting ever more difficult to tolerate her tantrums. The sexual games she played were of late getting too violent. He sensed danger. She seemed to him to be presenting greater emotional problems than they could deal with.

He was handling it badly. That had been a wrong thing he had said to Clarissa. She had nothing but her looks and him to keep her, if not happy, at least centred. They were her life. To take them away would be more dangerous than to remain and make the best of a bad marriage. That had been the verdict of two psychiatrists, who believed that, in time and with Ben, Clarissa could work through her emotional instability. Then he could leave her.

The hatred Clarissa felt at that moment gazed out at him from her eyes. He felt sick at his words. He was too quick for her this time. Before she could strike at him, he tied her hands together at the wrists with the remnants of her silk chemise, and knotted one end of it to the bedpost.

'I hate you,' she hissed.

'I know. But I wonder if you truly know how much you do hate me, and all the men who have made love to you, taken you sexually.'

She struggled against the bonds that held her tight. Ben scrambled off the bed and began undressing, never taking his eyes from the magnificent body lying on the midnight blue quilted bed-cover. No wonder all men and many women craved her, wanted to be where he was now. Once naked, he sat on the bed next to her. She tried to kick him. He grabbed her ankle and held her leg high while he removed the garter and slowly, seductively rolled her stocking down and dropped it on the floor. He kissed her foot, licked the instep with pointed tongue, his gaze fixed on her face.

'Stop looking at me like that,' she demanded.

'Like what?'

'Like you want to devour me.'

'But I do. And I will,' he told her. She trembled at the lust she heard in his voice, and because she knew he would make a meal of her sexually.

'Please, Ben. I don't want to come. You can come. I'll take you in my mouth. Use my hands. Anything you want, but please don't do it, don't make me come.'

It was all part of the game. All a way for her to defrost, to allow herself to have orgasms. That was what the entire tantrum was about. She wanted sex, but could not accept that she was hungry for it. Nor that it was Ben and only Ben who was able to bring her to orgasm. Nor that after several orgasms with him she was insatiable, and no sexual act was too refined or too depraved for her to participate in.

Ben reached out and removed a strand of hair from her face. He lay down next to her and stroked her hair. Then he took her chin in his hand and tilted it towards the light. Her beauty was an aphrodisiac for him. His love for her shone in his eyes. His passion to give her sexual pleasure was boundless. Unable to deny her her game, he carried on playing it. He climbed on top of her and straddled her shoulders, taunted her with his plentiful, erect penis by stroking her eyelids with it, the bridge of her nose, her cheeks, grazing her lips with it. He throbbed with lust for her. And that drew a shiver of pleasure from her. She parted her lips, wanting to take him in her mouth, to feel him tight in her throat, only to have him remove it from her lips to caress the underpart of her chin, her neck with it. She felt cheated. He wasn't listening. She wanted him that way and no other way. She tried again to control their sex.

'Do you love me?' she asked.

'You know I do.'

'Then tell me.'

'I love you, Clarissa.'

'Then come in my mouth. And let's be done with *your* lust.'

'*Our* lust. I'm not alone here, Clarissa.'

'I thought you said you loved me.'

'I do.'

'More than life itself?'

His answer was to place his lips upon hers, to kiss her with passion, to nibble her lips open and then to kiss her deeply. She lay there as if made of ice. He didn't care; he knew that would change soon enough. He placed a kiss on her shoulder and when he removed his lips she shrugged as if she were trying to dislodge it. But her erect nipples, the occasional squirm of her body, the way she tugged at the bonds that strapped her to the bedpost, contradicted her determination to remain icy cool under his sensuous kissing. They were signals that the game was very much on. They excited his desire for her, made him more determined that she should have the orgasms she secretly yearned for and enjoy sex with him. He could make Clarissa come, again and again, and together with him. Nothing in their disturbed relationship was more thrilling for him than when she lay in an erotic exhaustion in his arms, near to fainting, telling him how she didn't want to live without his love-making, that he was indeed her world, her very life, and she loved him. His lust for his wife was rising and he was about to tell her, 'Clarissa, love me, just love me.' But it was Clarissa who spoke.

'You say you love me, then give me what I want.'

'I intend to.'

'Untie my hands,' she ordered.

He ignored her. Instead, he moved down her body with his

lips. Cupping a breast in his hands, he caressed it, sucked deeply on her nipple. She writhed under the sensation. He knew how responsive her breasts were, that it was an erogenous zone that drove her into an erotic frenzy. She began to fight against her desire for more. More heightened passion, more of his love-making.

He nibbled at her flesh. To her his searching tongue was like a whip. She reached fever pitch and began to lose herself. Her body arched and she came in a long, convulsive orgasm. 'I hate you for this. Despise you for possessing me, for reducing me to just a cunt.' She ground the words through gritted teeth, avoiding his eyes.

He ignored her protestations. His lust left no time for them. Ben loved women, adored making love to them in or out of bed. He was a romantic man who believed in romance and sex, and that they went together. Clarissa's words meant one thing, but the intense orgasms she achieved with him, her sighs of pleasure when he was moving with long, leisurely strokes in and out of her, the way her cunt gorged on his penis meant something quite other.

It was true, he did force her to submit, again and again. Not to his lust alone but to her own as well. And he took great pleasure in doing it. He did to her what she most feared, reducing her to little more than a hungry cunt, making her dissolve in their come, until little was left of Clarissa Carr, magazine icon of the eighties. From there she rose and took another form, that of an erotic beauty claiming in full his sexual attention. He gave it willingly. His reward was how happy and fulfilled she was to be in that place she so feared.

The morning started off well enough. Ben woke Clarissa with tender kisses. She responded with passion in hers. He stroked her hair, covered her face with yet more kisses and told her how beautiful she was, how much he loved her. When he slid on top of her and between her long, shapely legs which he had kissed and placed high on his shoulders, and then entered her, it was to a woman playing the role of the dutiful wife tolerating a morning fuck. She had reverted to character, the role player. The real Clarissa Carr, the woman he loved, was not there. He felt sick with despair when she wrapped her arms around him and told him, 'Faster, deeper. Faster, come now, I am.'

She was faking sex. After the night of real lust and erotic fantasies played out to excite them further, until they had been both lost in sexual oblivion, this was unbearable. He knew at that moment that he was finished with Clarissa. If he needed further proof, it appeared when he lay down next to her and saw a faint bruise on her cheek where he had slapped her about the night before. She was turning him into a monster. It was in fact she who had taken possession of him; he who was losing his real identity to give her one. That was all over, right then and there. No words, no actions. Just over. He needed time and a plan to get away from her without causing her too much grief. He left for Lyons after breakfast.

Ben looked across at Arianne. How still she had been all the way to London! Had it been that natural quiet of hers that by contrast had made him recall the life he had once lived with Clarissa? They were off the motorway now, approaching the Natural History Museum in Kensington, the traffic hardly impinging. 'Where do you live?'

Arianne turned to smile at him. 'Just drop me off anywhere convenient. I can catch a taxi.'

'I wouldn't dream of it. Unless you live somewhere outside central London. If that's the case, I might just beg off.'

'Mayfair. But honestly I can get a taxi.'

'No taxi necessary. We're neighbours. I live in Mayfair too. I'm your taxi, ma'am. Address please?'

'Three Kings Yard, off Davies Street.'

'Oh, so we really are neighbours. I keep a small penthouse flat on Piccadilly, overlooking Green Park, the Ritz Hotel end of Piccadilly. I bought it for the underground parking, would you believe?'

There their conversation ended. He turned left into Exhibition Row, at the top of which he entered Hyde Park. He drove the Porsche past Hyde Park Corner and took the exit from the park at the Dorchester. Several smart turns and they were on Davies Street at the top of Berkeley Square. Minutes later he opened the car door for Arianne in front of Number 12, Three Kings Yard.

'I really am immensely grateful for this ride,' she told him as she stepped out of the Porsche. 'But for you, I would probably still be waiting for a train somewhere in the country. But I am sorry that Artemis foisted me upon you. I'm afraid you had little choice but to take me to London.'

Ben laughed. 'She is a formidable lady, your mother. But, have no fear, if I had not wanted to give you a lift, Lady Hardcastle or not, I would have left you there. But for future reference you could have stayed the night at Chessington Park with your mother and taken the early train to London. You would have been here by eight.'

There was something in Arianne's eyes, part amusement, part disbelief. 'Ah. Lady Hardcastle does not like unexpected house guests,' he suggested.

'Good guess, Ben. Ten out of ten.'

That was the first time she had used his name. 'Ben'. It rolled off her tongue pleasingly, lightly.

NEW YORK,
CUERNAVACA,
LONDON

Chapter 7

Arianne closed the front door and leaned against it. She stood in the dark for several minutes before she switched on the hall light. She liked Ben Johnson. She felt good in his company. He was so easy to be with.

She draped her jacket over the banister and walked into the sitting room, where she went directly to the fireplace and put a lighted taper to the tissue paper and kindling. It flared into life. Orange flames licked the blackened bricks. The logs had caught and the fire was blazing when she returned to sit on the settee with a Kir Royale. Champagne and cassis. She closed her eyes to savour the delicious drink. Only then did she realise that she had poured it without thinking. It had been their drink. Hers and Jason's. She did a double-take at her own extravagance in opening even the half bottle for herself. She reminded herself that she was living on a shoestring, no matter how it looked to the outside world.

The ride home had been an unexpected pleasant interlude. She had felt good while in close contact with Ben Johnson in his smart Porsche, not unlike the well-being she had always felt in the presence of Jason. There were similarities between Jason and Ben. They both liked fast cars and drove well. They were attractive men with adventure built into their psyche. Although she didn't know that for sure about Ben Johnson, she sensed it, enough to make a bet with herself that it was so.

Several times she had wanted to speak to Ben, to know more about him than his name and how attached he was to his uncle. But caught in hesitation, she had remained silent and simply enjoyed being with him. It had felt good to have a man in control, someone to care for her once again, even if it was only to get her to London. While she and Ben had been whizzing down the motorway, memories of other times and other places with another man had preoccupied her. She had yielded to the rhythm of the road, the scent of leather seats, the thrill of a fast car, the dark night and the sound of the violin and Brahms to lull her into a half-sleep where she flashed back in time and to another place where she had also been happy. Cuernavaca.

'I love you,' he whispered in her ear.

Arianne turned away from the bookshelf where she was browsing to look at him. She smiled at Jason. 'I know.'

He took her hand in his and squeezed it, raised it to his lips and kissed it before letting it go and walking a few paces from her to a table laden with books on travel. She had hardly returned to her book-hunting when she felt his lips on her bare shoulder, his hand pushing her hair and sensuous kisses being planted on the nape of her neck, the lobe of her ear, his body rubbing up against her back, then an arm encircling her waist.

She blushed, and went all warm and tingly, and was completely distracted by him. She closed her eyes for a minute to savour his advances and tried to compose herself. They were in a busy bookshop in Mexico City.

'The people,' she told him as she turned around in his arms.

'Who cares?' He slipped an arm around her shoulders and kissed her again, this time on her lips. Their gaze into each other's eyes made him smile, and he let her go.

'You're right, of course. But it suddenly came over me. How much I love you. How lovely you are, how happy I am to have you for my wife. It's still a miracle to me how much I love you.'

She placed an arm around his waist, reached up and kissed him on the cheek. Together they walked from the shop, looking at each other with utter devotion. They had purchased nothing. A cab had been parked at the kerb waiting for them. Jason opened the door for Arianne and was about to get in when a flower vendor approached him. He bought an armful of bright blossoms for Arianne and then got into the car to place them in her arms.

'The airport,' he told the taxi driver, and then snuggled up close to Arianne.

'They're lovely. Lunch was lovely. You're lovely,' she told him.

He laughed aloud. 'I don't think anyone has ever called me

lovely before. Are you sure about that?' he teased.

'Quite sure.'

He stroked her hair, and in his eyes she saw his happiness. She had never seen that look of love in any other person's eyes, not for her, surely. But neither had she seen it between any other two people either. Sometimes it made her want to weep with joy; at other times it frightened her, made her wonder that so much love between two people might be tempting fate.

'Having a good time?' he asked her. Her answer was to kiss him and lean in against him. He placed the occasional kiss upon her naked arm, her cheek, in the palm of her hand, and they rode thus in silence back to the four-seater jet, freshly fuelled and waiting on a runway at the far end of the airport, away from the commercial flights.

Jason's inimitable charm, and his familiarity with Mexico City airport cut through the red tape. They were quickly airborne and he was piloting Arianne to the final lap of his mystery anniversary present to her. It had been breakfast at dawn in Long Island, a romantic lunch in Mexico City. Dinner? Where next? she wondered. She looked over her shoulder at the cream-coloured canvas luggage trimmed in brown saddle-leather, and wondered what the cases contained.

When he had awakened her that morning with a kiss it had been still black as night outside the window, and all he had said to her was, 'Happy anniversary. Put on something for very hot and humid weather. That's all I'm going to tell you.'

'Sunglasses?'

'Yes,' he laughed and chided her, 'and no more questions.'

They had showered together, soaping each other with a bath gel of almonds. He tore off her shower cap and dropped it on the tiled shower tray. Then, turning the several jets up to full power, he pulled her into his arms and kissed her deeply. With needles of water vibrating against their skin and cascading over their bodies, and the steam swirling around them, he lifted her by her bottom, to impale her, in one swift and powerful thrust, upon his erect and eager penis. She wrapped her legs around him. Arianne threw her head back and the water poured over her face and streamed through her hair. He adored watching her face as he made love to her with slow, deep penetrations, moving her on and off his penis with a firm grip on her hips. Water, steamy heat, the powerful jet sprays like so many tiny hands sensuously playing on their skin . . . so many erotic sensations at the same time. They found their rhythm together, and they came in a long, flowing orgasm.

The entire day, from that first kiss upon her awakening, had been filled with sensuous, loving sensations and togetherness. What, she wondered as they flew low over the verdant countryside, was to come next?

They were flying through some turbulence, but Arianne felt no fear when flying with her husband – one of the best pilots, or so the small industry of international private air services told each other. Flying, planes, adventurous travel, vintage aircraft, and Arianne, were his passions, his life. And Arianne didn't mind one bit being at the bottom of the list. She knew that it was not a matter of priorities, but of passions, deep and long-standing passions that would never change.

She watched Jason, so handsome and sexy. She had got quite used to the other women who flirted with him, the look of surprise on their faces when she had been presented to them. It amused rather than annoyed her that they should think she was not glamorous enough for him, a man with such a Don Juan reputation. The reaction of his wealthy, and usually fascinating male acquaintances on first meeting Arianne amused them both as well: that look of surprise followed by curiosity about the woman who had captured Jason's heart. The unsubtle sexual sizing-up process, no doubt precipitated by astonishment that he loved her, had married her, and was remaining faithful to his vows.

He had never lied to Arianne. Before he married her he had made it clear that his libido was voracious, that they would have to satisfy it together or, in spite of himself and what he wanted, he might revert to being the philanderer he had been all his life. She had loved him too much not to take up the challenge. Arianne had come a long way sexually to keep her husband, and they both loved her for rising to his needs. Time and sex had done their work well. He had led her down erotic paths that she did not have to learn to enjoy. It came naturally to her, once he had shown her the polymorphous excitements of sexual pleasure. Now they had become smouldering sexual needs of her own, the more powerful because they were governed by love for her husband and his needs and erotic desires, his restlessness and extravagant nature.

She was overwhelmed by his devotion to her. She never questioned her fidelity to him. Only one thing surprised her in her constant love for Jason: that she could so happily ignore the dark side of his nature. There had been unmistakable glimpses of it.

For no reason at all she bent close to him and kissed him lovingly on the cheek. He turned to face her for only a second. 'Again, please,' he asked her with a smile. She did kiss him again and they rode out the turbulence with her hand held lightly on his arm.

Shortly after that they landed on a private grass air-strip cut from an opulent, jungle-like landscape. Parked in bays just off the runway were several vintage aircraft. That they had landed on a friend's or a client's estate was Arianne's guess.

It turned out to be a friend, whom Arianne met when, with a pile of people, children and dogs spilling out of his Second World War, US army Jeep, he drove across the grass airfield to greet Arianne and Jason as they alighted from the Gulfstream. Behind it was a second Jeep empty except for its driver. Effusive greetings and introductions. Instructions about the plane and several bottles of champagne drunk while standing out of the sun and under its wing. Chatter about their flight, excitement at meeting Jason's wife. And quite suddenly it was over. It seemed to Arianne that before she had hardly had time to talk to anyone, their driver had loaded the luggage into the Jeep and they were settled in it and off, waving goodbye to their host, his companions and his hospitality.

It was unbearably hot and humid still, though it was late in the day and the sky had turned a deep, hot pink-orange and was streaked with strips of pale blue pretending to be clouds. The sun, a deep, golden yellow, seemed to shimmer in its own heat. The luggage was piled in the front seat next to Juan Pedro, whom Jason seemed to know very well. Arianne and Jason, dripping with perspiration, clung to each other as they bounced over a dirt track for several miles before turning on to a paved secondary road. Forty-five minutes later they were driving through the centre of Cuernavaca, and Arianne had fallen instantly in love with Mexico.

Wherever they went, people waved, called out Jason's name and shouted greetings in Spanish. Flowers were thrown into the car: someone even ran after it to hand Jason a basket of grapes. Jason, laughing and happy, kept turning back to Arianne to tell her, 'That's my favourite restaurant. The best bread is baked there. Our wine shop. The grocer. The best cantina. Look at the church. That's Oscar, English. Narita, the best party-giver, Spanish from Spain. A fellow American, Abe Scott, painter.' He stood up in the Jeep and waved and shouted something in Spanish that made everyone in earshot laugh. Taking his seat again, he placed an arm around Arianne and they gazed into each other's eyes.

'Is there a poet, a candlestick-maker?' she asked jokingly.

He kissed her, smiled down at her and, removing the cotton scarf from his neck, lovingly wiped the beads of perspiration from her face. Then he pointed down a side-street: 'The candlestick-maker. I don't see the resident poet, nor the writer. Too early for them to be in town. Oh, and that's the local whore-house. The prettiest, cleanest, sweetest and sexiest ladies of the night you will ever meet.'

'And you would know,' she teased.

'They miss me,' he told her, with a very serious face. And now on their way out of the pretty and colourful town, he took her in his arms and caressed her while kissing her affectionately. Love for her seemed suddenly to be bursting from him.

Several miles from town they turned off the road and down a gravel drive lined with the tropical vegetation of Mexico. Yucca ran wild with enormous pandanus and banana trees and several different species of palms, and undergrowth of green that mixed with brightly coloured flowers of which Arianne recognised only a few: hibiscus in abundance, red and white and even a pink; purple and red and orange bougainvillaea running wild as a creeper, wrapping itself around everything. Exotic flowers, with long stamens more like exotic tongues, added floral drama. Jason and Arianne had to shield themselves from the branches that whipped into the Jeep as it sped along the drive to the sound of crunching stones and birdsong.

The house was a hundred-and-fifty-year-old farmhouse, long and low with huge, elegant arches along a deep, open verandah, with five-foot high, wide clay pots in lovely shapes set in the centre of each. They proffered flowering shrubs in a riot of colour. The pitched roof was covered with antique clay tiles.

'Jason,' she exclaimed. 'What a romantic setting, a glorious house.'

'You ain't seen nothing yet, kid.'

He hopped from the Jeep, and then, grabbing Arianne by the waist, he swung her from it to set her on the ground, but not before he crushed her to him and covered her face with a rapid succession of kisses. Her feet barely touched the gravel before he swept her up once more in his arms and, carrying her towards the house, said, 'I believe this is the way it's done.'

Juan Pedro rushed ahead of them to open the large, arch-shaped screen doors. Jason stepped through them. 'It's ours. I bought it for us. Happy anniversary.' He placed her gently on her feet.

Lost for words, Arianne could do little but take his hand and walk with him through the huge living room. Jason took great pleasure in watching her take it all in. It was simplicity itself, all large, deep and low-slung, with white Haitian cotton-covered sofas and chairs, and Spanish antiques of high quality. Mexican painters: Diego Rivera, Tomayo, hung with Georgia O'Keefes, Miros, a Salvador Dali, Tapies, on the white lime-washed walls with lesser-known Spanish and Mexican artists. She stood before the only American painter represented on the walls, completely enchanted by O'Keefe's orchid, a portrait rather than an oil-painting of a flower, where she captured its personality as if it were a person.

Large, colourful hand-blown glass bowls, works of art in themselves, held bouquets of exotic flowers. Books and magazines littered table-tops. It was all there, carefully planned and executed, a room that had taken more than taste and time. Money. A great deal of money. So many questions might have run through Arianne's mind. The how, when and wherefore of Jason's managing it all. But they didn't. Thankfulness for Jason's love and a marriage that could induce such a gift blocked any notion of questions.

She turned from the O'Keefe painting to gaze at her husband. They embraced, were lost for a few minutes in each other's arms. Emotions were running high for both Arianne and Jason. The one thing they never did was to take for granted how they felt about each other. It humbled them, made them aware that they lived in two worlds: their own very private one and the world outside.

'You love it.'

'Yes, I adore it. I can't believe it's ours.'

'Go on, believe it,' he told her, relinquishing her from their embrace, but only to place an arm round her and walk her through the house to the open verandah overlooking the garden. Some twenty feet below them, it was lush with terraces that kept dropping away at various levels, where fountains played. The sounds of a tropical paradise and running water enveloped them. The scent of flowers hung in the heat.

'The bedrooms are on the lower level underneath us, and they open on to the gardens. Come on.'

'Not yet,' she pleaded. And kissed him many times with the urgency he knew so well.

'Wait here,' he ordered, and vanished. Arianne leaned over the balcony and studied the vista before her, the endless glories of a tropical garden that melted away into jungle. She lost herself in paradise. Her mind emptied of everything but what she could see. She didn't hear Jason walk up behind her. He was naked. She straightened up, the better to feel all of him against her.

'Happy?' he asked.

'Gloriously happy.'

'There is a staff of four to run this place for us. But I have sent them away. Juan Pedro has put our luggage in our room, and I have sent him away too. They'll come back in four days' time. I want you all to myself; us to have the house to enjoy selfishly. I don't want to share you or it with even a servant. A world of just you and me for a few days. How does that appeal to you, my love?'

It was difficult to answer, choked as she was with love and happiness. Now, as he undid the halter of her dress and slid it down from her breasts and over her hips to let it drop on to the floor, erotic desire was engulfing her. She trembled with anticipation. She leaned her back into him, her hands still gripping the edge of the waist-high balcony wall.

'I love you,' he whispered in her ear as he reached around her to take her breasts in his hands. His caresses only excited her for more. She wanted only to be taken by him, to feel his passion for her explode inside her. Jason's caresses grew more needy. His lust for Arianne took them over, transported them into an erotic world where they could do and be all things to one another. It was thrilling to feel such powerful desires while in the midst of paradise, in a place where their eyes were feasting on a real garden of Eden.

'I want to take you, right here, lose myself in you, slip out of control. I've a sexual madness I want to share with you.'

His voice was husky with passion. She knew that voice and what would follow. He had taught her to go with it and enjoy it as much as he did. She wanted him in all the ways he would take possession of her. Without a word she leaned over the balcony wall, resting her arms on it. He caressed her bottom, teased the crack between its cheeks with probing fingers, and, when he reached underneath her, found her hungry, yielding slit. She was already on the edge of her first orgasm. She felt the knob of his penis parting her cunt lips. She closed her eyes, surrendering to mere sensation as he slowly sunk himself into her. She came and the moist silkiness of come eased his way. She heard him sigh with the sheer pleasure of her. He placed his hands on her hips and leaned over her bent back. And that was how he took her the first time in their new house, both of them lost in lust while they looked out into their garden. He had indeed created an Eden for Arianne.

But that was not enough for him. He was gentle but determined to open her in that more secret and tight place. He was a master at fucking. He moved between both orifices until Arianne had slipped into her own sexual madness, had come so many times she begged him to stop. That was their signal. Holding hands tightly, he kissing the back of her neck, biting into the flesh on her back, they came together in a crescendo of orgasm where all control was abandoned and they called out in a paroxysm of lust that echoed through the verandah and was swallowed into the jungle that enclosed their hideaway.

Their orgy of sex and togetherness lasted two days. Just as

Arianne expected it would. That was Jason: things to see, places to go, people to party with, and of course planes to fly. Arianne never minded. She was used to sharing him with work and play. She went along. It was her nature to go along. But it was more than that: following made her happy.

They borrowed a friend's two-seater bi-plane and flew to the coast. There they swam in the huge waves of the Pacific Ocean and picnicked on a deserted white-sand beach that stretched either way for as far as they could see. They had their sex naked under the sun. From there they flew on to join several of his friends who had flown vintage aircraft to a meet. Arianne watched from the ground as they played aerobatics in the sky. When he landed she rushed towards the plane as he hopped down and sped past admirers to her. He wrapped her in his arms and kissed her as if he were happy to be grounded with her and nothing else in the world mattered.

Arianne lost all track of time. Mexico and Jason had done their work well; they captured her heart, and had blocked out the outside world. So it came as a surprise to her when, after their return to the house, he told her, 'Ahmad is in LA. I told him we would meet him there in time for dinner tomorrow night.'

Ahmad. She felt a tremor of excitement. She always did when Jason mentioned the three of them were to be together again. She loved Ahmad. But in a different and very special way than she loved Jason. Maybe she loved him because of Jason? It didn't matter to her why. What counted was that the three of them did love each other and were together, firmly in each other's lives.

She had been admiring one of the elegant and expensive dresses Jason had bought her; part of her surprise anniversary gift, a wardrobe for Mexico, that had emerged from the suitcases he had so lovingly presented to her on their arrival at the house. Arianne slipped on the exquisitely tailored, emerald-green, silk-satin jacket. She held the white chiffon strapless dress with its open lattice-work bodice – crisscrossing cords of the same white chiffon – up against her breasts and viewed her reflection. How chic, seductive; a sensuous St Laurent. She swung away from the full-length mirror to face Jason. She could see it in his eyes. He knew that she wanted to stay on. That he was waiting for her to ask him. That he would have granted her wish, if he could. He couldn't. She knew that by the matter-of-fact coldness in his eyes, and a certain restlessness. He was easing her away from this dream-world he had created for her, with something he knew she never tired of: Arianne, Jason and Ahmad together.

She walked towards the bed where he was stretched out, propped against the pillows, and from where he had been watching her dress. He was dressed and ready to go out for the evening, except for his dinner jacket, which was laid out neatly at the foot of the bed. 'Ahmad would love this house and Cuernavaca. I don't suppose he could join us here?' she asked.

'You don't want to leave. That's wonderful. It means you love it here. We'll fly down whenever we can, even if it's only for a few days. We'll plan longer times here, and when we're old and grey it's here that we'll settle. And until then, when I'm away on long jaunts and can't take you with me, you can come here if you like. It's our home away from home.'

'But now, we have to leave?'

'Afraid so.' There was a certain hardness in his voice.

She took his hand in hers. And she stood there for several seconds before he could bring himself to react to her. This was a side of Jason she understood. He was always indifferent to her when he couldn't give her something she wanted. It was a sort of defence against the pain it caused him to deny her anything.

He swung his legs down off the bed and, still holding her hand, told her, 'I have some business to attend to in LA. Just a few hours, but really an important meeting that could pay for this house. Ahmad needs to be there as well.'

She raised his hand to her lips and kissed it. 'Do you prefer this dress or the red one I had on earlier?' she asked with a smile.

They stood silent for several seconds just gazing into each other's eyes. Finally, a softness for her took him over. 'You mean the one before the black one, and the one before that, the white one.' He teased, and the coldness disappeared from his eyes. Still holding her hand, he stepped back a few paces and studied her seriously.

'You prefer the white one?'

He said nothing. She began to feel uncomfortable, thinking the dress she had on was much too glamorous for her looks. 'I want to look right for your friends. So if you think this is wrong, do just say so, Jason.'

'You're perfect, just perfect. I don't deserve you, you know.' And with that he pulled her into his arms and hugged her to him.

She stroked his hair, placed a hand at the back of his neck and caressed him. 'Really perfect?' she asked.

'You'll knock 'em dead. Perfect.'

They were the guests of honour at the dinner party. From there they and their friends went from cantina to cantina where they drank and danced and listened to Mexican music, wild and gay, and in the early hours of the morning, some Spanish guitar music that plucked at the heart and reached down to the soul.

They were happy and gay and in love. He clung to her and she slipped into the happy, decorous and quiet mode he so loved her for. The party did not end, it just seemed to dissolve, and when they returned to the house the sun was just coming up. They lay down on the bed wrapped in each other's arms and watched another glorious dawn.

The maid served their breakfast: mangoes and hot corn-bread with butter and honey and strong, hot black coffee, followed by sausages grilled on charcoal and eggs taken warm from the hens, fried to perfection. Afterwards they said tearful goodbyes to the gardener, the maid and the cook, and Juan Pedro drove them at breakneck speed through town and back to the airfield.

The warmth of the fire felt so good. The Kir, extravagant or not, had been delicious and Arianne felt wonderful. She thought of Ben Johnson again, how pleasant it had been to be in his company. She spoke to the empty room. 'He was probably bored, found you dull. You might have at least tried to strike up a conversation with him. You could have, at the very least, asked him in for a drink. Mere politeness should have dictated that.' She had a little giggle and then added, 'You sound like Artemis.'

I might have done all those things, she thought, had I not been inspired by his presence to remember how wonderful it is to be in love with a man, to be loved by one. For two people to be everything to each other, partners whose trust in their love can banish loneliness forever.

Arianne felt suddenly close to Ben, a near stranger. It was

inexplicable, but that was nevertheless how she felt at that moment. She did not try to explain her feelings away. Instead she delighted in the very idea that she could feel close to a man again. That was somehow where she belonged, in a relationship such as she had had with her husband: the kind of one-to-one love that transcends all the other people and places that one relates to.

Chapter 8

A knock at the bedroom door startled Arianne from the half-sleep in which she had been indulging. 'Who is it?' she asked nervously.

'Ida.'

Arianne nearly asked, 'Ida who?' but remembered just in time that Ida was the treasure who cleaned the house and was invisible. Well, almost. Arianne's and Ida's schedules usually kept them apart. Arianne had been grateful for that. She disliked having people cleaning around her. Their relationship seemed perfect to Arianne: the occasional cup of tea when Ida dropped in for instructions, or declarations of discontent about some household problem that generally had nothing to do with Arianne's house, or just to pass on the Three Kings Yard gossip, on her way home to a cat, two dogs and a parrot called Angel. In the few weeks since Arianne had taken up residence in the yard this was how she had come to know her neighbours, through Ida. She was dazzled by the cleaner's perspective on high life in the West End.

Relieved that it was not a suave burglar, or some stranger with a key to the house, she called out, 'Come in, Ida.'

The familiar beehive seemed especially high and well lacquered this morning as it entered the mistress's bedroom. Ida, smiling beneath it, was carrying a tray in one hand laden with a cup and saucer, a china teapot, some cutlery, a crisp white damask napkin, and a plate. A large carrier bag apparently stuffed to near bursting was in her other hand.

Arianne watched Ida, in the semi-darkness of the room, place the tray at the foot of her bed, the shopping bag on the floor, and walk to the window where she flung back the draperies. A dull morning light flowed into the room. Arianne reached out and switched on the bedside lamp. This cheered the room. Arianne looked at the bedside clock. She picked it up to make sure she was right. Then she placed it back on the table and said, 'Ida, it's seven in the morning. Happy as I am to see you, what are you doing here at this hour?'

'I came to talk to you about Christmas.'

'Christmas?' Arianne was genuinely perplexed. It had been happening all around her, Christmas and its approach, for weeks, but she had managed to ignore it. Not deliberately but because she had got out of the habit of Christmas since Jason's death. She had simply lost her enthusiasm for it and all the compulsory bonhomie.

'Yes, Christmas. The days I'll be here and the days I won't. Holiday time. Going somewhere nice?'

Arianne propped herself up against the pillows, thinking she could really do with that pot of morning tea. First Artemis and now Ida pushing Christmas at her. She poured the tea and wondered what she *was* going to do about it. In another time and another place she would not have had to think about it. Jason and she would have been travelling to some remote part of the world to elude the commercialisation of a holiday that they thought deserved more reverence than shopping conferred on it. Or spending it in the house near Cuernavaca, or staying with Ahmad in Cairo. Even in childhood Christmas had posed a problem for Arianne. It had meant being sent to Artemis, wherever she was, and leaving her father. She thought, nothing ever really changes. Well, this was another time and another place, and, although she didn't dwell on it, she recognised Christmas as another thing she had to sort out without Jason.

She took a sip of her tea and watched, as one would a magician, Ida with her bag of tricks. She listened, enthralled by her patter as she performed her conjuring act. With a prestidigitator's flair, Ida made magic with her shopping bag. First she produced one of the Baccarat crystal goblets from the dining room and placed it on the tray. Then, hey presto, an ugly luminescent orange plastic thermos with a screw-on lid for a cup, patterned in some unauthentic clan tartan, appeared.

'Fresh orange and pineapple juice. I squeezed it at home this morning.'

'Thanks, Ida, but I'm just fine with the tea.'

Her words were wasted. As if by a touch of the wand the glass was full, and in Arianne's hand. Watching Ida perform was riveting. To hear her was to succumb to her every wish. Strong men bent to the will of her shopping bag.

'The croissants are still warm. They were on the trays hot from the oven when I picked them up at the Patisserie Valerie over in Soho. Just smell this brioche. Or would you prefer a jam doughnut? Myself, I can't resist a fresh jam doughnut.' A box of six was produced. A lump of butter was unwrapped from its tinfoil and placed on the tray after a deeper rummage in the bag. A small jar of peach preserve 'with extra fruit' and a Fortnum & Mason label on it came next.

Ida was always smartly dressed, with a touch of the trendy from each of several periods of fashion from the fifties on. One might imagine her house to be a treasure trove of 'things' emptied every night from her shopping bags. Today she was dressed in a purple tweed skirt and a black twinset with a double strand of pearls. Over that was a pink mohair cardigan. Her boots were very new, quite à la mode. The harlequin glasses and an expensive underwater diver's watch did not look out of place on her. Ida has to be the smartest, most interesting-looking cleaner in the West End, thought Arianne. Was she a reincarnated Sybil Thorndike playing a West End charlady? she wondered. That brought a smile to Arianne's lips and she buttered a piece of the brioche, thankful for the luxury of breakfast in bed and Ida.

'About the shopping.'

'What shopping, Ida?'

'Your shopping. Food for Christmas shopping. You know you don't have a thing in the house. Not even a pound of butter.' She pointed to the butter still on its bit of crunched foil on Arianne's plate. 'You do keep the cupboard pretty bare. I never saw such a mean house for food as this one. I know you're busy. If you would just leave a note I could fill the fridge once a week, get the staples in. That's what I'll do after Christmas. But what about now?'

Indeed, what about now? 'No need to shop, Ida. I haven't made up my mind what to do about Christmas.'

'You won't find anything in the shops if you leave it too late.'

'I won't leave it too late.'

'Can you cook?'

'I think I can cook, Ida. I was married, you know, had a house to run and a man to cook for. I am a very good cook, as a matter of fact.' Then she began to laugh. 'Admittedly, because my husband sent me to a *cordon bleu* cookery school for a year. He loved good food.'

Ida looked both amazed and pleased. 'I'll buy you a small goose from Allen's and some sausage meat before they run out. If you go away you can put it in the freezer.'

'That seems a bit extravagant,' she told Ida somewhat feebly. That was about as far as she could go. What could she tell her daily: 'I can't afford a goose for Christmas'? But it was true.

'Christmas is extravagant. I'll tell them to put it on your account.'

Arianne wanted to tell her that she did not have a charge account at Allen's or Bailey's or Hannell's, or anywhere in the neighbourhood, but kept silent. It was easier for Ida to find out for herself and that would be the end of the goose. That bit of Christmas drama over, Arianne went back to her breakfast, thinking that buying a goose would mollify Ida. Fat chance.

'A fancy cook, you must like fancy food. Mind if I sit on the end of the bed for a minute?'

Now there was some serious rummaging through the shopping bag. 'It just so happens I have a few things here. I had a food hamper from Harrods given me for Christmas by one of my gentlemen. They'll start off your larder nicely. I don't much care for caviar.' A large tin of the best beluga surfaced, then crocks of fresh Strasbourg *pâté de foie gras*, one *en croute*, a jar of fat white asparagus, half a smoked salmon sealed in air-tight clear packaging. This was strapped to a walnut cutting-board with a slender, pearl-handled, serrated knife lying across it under a red satin bow and a sprig of plastic holly, berries and all. Now the ensemble was slapped down on the bed among the other delicacies.

'But, Ida, I can't possibly accept all this.'

'Of course you can. I know what they cost, and if you cook fancy you must like this sort of nosh.'

102

'Well, I'll choose one.'

'That's silly. I'd rather they stayed in this house. My friend on the door at Claridge's will get plenty of this top-store stuff. As if he needed it.'

Arianne had visions of Ida making her rounds of the neighbourhood, spreading her largesse to the staff of the best addresses, the most influential tradesmen and their employees, even her *gentlemen*. She knew when she was beaten and accepted graciously after one more protest. 'But, Ida, what will you give the doorman at Claridge's?'

Ida lifted the still half-full shopping bag off the floor so Arianne could see it. 'And the doorman at the Connaught. No problem, I still have bits and pieces and another shopping bag in the kitchen. Untouched,' she told Arianne proudly. Then, having announced when she would and wouldn't be working, she vanished, leaving Arianne with Christmas all over her bed whether she liked it or not.

Arianne had splurged and bought a bicycle a week after she had moved into the house. Often as not she liked to ride to work. She kept it out of the way in the cupboard under the stairs. She manoeuvred it through the hall and out into the yard. Bond Street was her route to work this morning. As she passed the doorman at Claridge's, he tipped his hat. She waved and pedalled on. Further on, a commissionaire in full uniform, who tended the door at one of the exclusive jeweller's shops on Old Bond Street, stopped sweeping the pavement to wave to her. Arianne was fast becoming one of the familiar Mayfair faces. She was enjoying a sensation of belonging that she had not felt for a very long time. At first she had been amazed at how like a small village Mayfair was, with everyone knowing everyone else through a network of gossip among the staff that ran the lives of the residents. Unsurprised now, she was beginning to understand that was the norm for the many different areas that made up the sprawling capital. She had no doubt that, had she lived in Knightsbridge or Chelsea, Belgravia or Kensington, it would be the same. It was not just the residents and their staff who were involved in the neighbourhood, but the shopkeepers and their employees as well.

Mayfair had nob and snob appeal that danced easily with

pride and upper-class homeliness, that was all part of living or working there. Amazingly, even with the most chic of tourists and visitors from all around the world hungrily enjoying it, it could still retain its village atmosphere in the heart of London. And yet, come Friday afternoon, when most of its residents decamped for the country, and the business offices closed (Mayfair had come to be largely offices and the classiest shops the city had to offer, with few residents) it was a very lonely, unloving, empty sort of place. Especially if you lived around the Berkeley or Grosvenor Square, South Audley Street, Shepherd's Market, area.

Waiting to cross Piccadilly, Arianne realised that she had succumbed; she was feeling Christmassy. She now felt quite jolly about the Christmas and New Year season being nearly upon them. Arianne was experiencing something she had not for years, thinking what *she* alone would like to do for Christmas. Whom *she* would like to see, to be with.

Only when she was at her desk and hot coffee had warmed her from her ride in the crisp December morning did the reality of Christmas hit her. Money. There were cards to buy, a few presents, token gifts, stocking-presents really. She had left it all too late. It was with some relief to her that Artemis had made a point of telling her 'No exchange of presents this year. We'll double up next year and I'll make Christmas here at Chessington House.' Nervously, she opened her cheque-book to look at the balance. Three hundred and thirty-three pounds seventy-four pence. And her Christmas salary had been paid. She had a Coutts gold card, which she never used because she was terrified of debt. She had been put through that pulveriser with Jason's affairs after his death. The card was kept as a line of credit for emergencies only. Christmas did not constitute an emergency.

The Christmas buzz seemed everywhere except in Arianne's office. There it was more quiet than usual. This year's main rare book sale had come and gone only a week before. Arianne's department was almost dormant. The next sale was far enough away to give ample time for preparation without pressure on her and her colleagues. She made her Christmas list: cards, token gifts, telephone calls, a small tree for the house. She felt quite happy and incredibly lucky that she had Number 12, Three Kings Yard to spend Christmas in. To hear her colleagues talk about their Christmas plans was to make her realise how very isolated she had become since Jason's death, how much she had abandoned friends so as to remain cocooned against life. She felt like the pupa that had transformed itself into the butterfly. She was splitting her wrapping and making ready to fly.

Fly to where? She was daydreaming about herself as a beautiful velvety yellow and silver butterfly flapping her fragile, elegant wings through the air, discovering life, the whole world. How fanciful, she thought. Even smiled to herself about it. And since Arianne was neither a fanciful nor an adventurous person on her own, she found the prospect of being like that butterfly very exciting. It inspired her to take a couple of hours off and go shopping.

Neither the crowds of people in the shops nor the commercialisation of Christmas seemed to bother her as they had so often before. But she was quite shocked at the cost of Christmas – she could not afford it, not even in the token form she was attempting. Money, or her lack of it, could have been depressing, but she refused to allow that. She was too grateful for what she had; too busy counting her blessings, the least of which was that she was no longer a chrysalis. She had got past that torpid stage of passive development, the form insects that turn into butterflies take. Only Ida buying the goose worried her.

The goose. She had returned to her desk just before lunch and was thinking about that goose. Whom would she have liked to cook a Christmas lunch for? She imagined the menu: the goose with a prawn, crab and mushroom stuffing; red cabbage; candied sweet potatoes; cranberry sauce; a salad of endive and watercress. Ben Johnson was the first face she visualised at her table. The idea appealed, and she admitted to herself that she liked him, the way he made her feel. Ahmad. Oh, yes. It would be wonderful to spend Christmas alone with Ahmad in the little house he had given her. It quite surprised her that she was thinking of him rather differently since they had had that breakfast together at Claridge's. The frank talk, had that changed her feelings about him? So much so that she could only think of him in the present, for himself alone, and how attracted she was to him, without their earlier sexual life dominating her feelings for him. She wondered if they didn't after all have something for each other to build on, that they could create a new sexual life together governed by love. She felt moved even by the thought of it.

The ringing of the telephone broke into her thoughts. Arianne answered it. 'Good afternoon, can I help you?'

'No,' said the voice quite emphatically. 'Old books have never been my particular thing. How would you like to join me here at the Connaught for lunch, a little Christmas lunch, just you and I? If you have a previous engagement, not to worry.'

'Artemis, I thought you were winging your way to the Caribbean today.'

'I am. After lunch. Can you make lunch with me?'

'I'd be delighted.'

'Now.'

'Yes, Mother, right now.'

'I'll send the Bentley round for you.'

'No, don't do that. The traffic. I'll get there much faster on my bike.'

'Bike! Motor-bike?'

'Bike, as in two-wheeler, Mother.'

'I'll time you.' Artemis hung up the telephone, but not before the lilt of laughter in her voice was caught by Arianne. It seemed that Arianne pedalling to the Connaught amused her.

Artemis was on her third martini when she saw her daughter cross the dining room of the Connaught Hotel. Artemis was well known there and it remained one of her favourite places to dine when she was up from the country. She liked the solid elegance of the room, the service and most especially the food. They all went together in perfection. Nor was she averse to the handsome, well-dressed men dining there in their pin-stripe suits and Turnbull and Asser shirts. Those smart silk ties . . . they inspired her to flirt. Only rarely when she had been alone had some man not been smitten enough to send over at least a bottle of champagne with his note. The women were mostly attractive enough and well dressed, even the American ones. She always put it down to their coming from Boston or Philadelphia, despite the Texas twangs or the New Yorkers' far from dulcet tones audible in the ladies' room.

She thought that Arianne was looking just right for lunch there. She was wearing a steel-blue, two-piece suede dress. The top had a curved neckline that showed off her slender neck and the shoulders, though padded, were round looking, the sleeves long and loose. It was cut short to hang loosely just below the waistband of the skirt, which was long and flared slightly away from the hip. It covered the tops of her black leather boots. What was particularly pretty was that the leather had appliquéd on it several flowers of the same coloured suede, their petals slightly raised. Around her neck she wore a leather thong and one of the suede flowers.

Artemis's first reaction to the outfit was that Arianne had not bought it. She still found it strange that Jason had always dressed his wife, having the taste and money to do it in style. Jason had always been a puzzle to Artemis, his love for Arianne even more a mystery, for she had always considered him a cad, someone not quite honest. Yet her feelings had little to go on. Accordingly she had had almost no contact with him. And Jason? She had been well aware that he had been content never to see her. She reckoned he sensed she was on to him.

There was something quite attractive about Arianne today, she told herself, and saw it confirmed in the attention several of the men gave her daughter as she passed their tables. Well, thought Artemis, I do have to give that devil Jason his due. Arianne may have been blind to what I saw in him, but he did make her happy. Grudgingly she had to admit that her daughter might not have been as dull as she had thought her. The quiet ones . . . She pondered. But not enough to become more embroiled in her daughter's life than she already was.

'Old habits die hard,' she said aloud as the maître d' drew back the chair at Artemis's table and a smiling Arianne sat down.

'What?' Arianne asked, puzzled.

'Old habits die hard. That's a good thing to remember when judging people.'

'Who's judging, Artemis? Me or you? I don't quite get what you're on about. Shall we start again? Hi, Mother, really nice of you to ask me to lunch.'

Artemis felt really pleased, even a little proud to have Arianne there dining with her. She actually reached across the table to pat her hand.

'You've turned out quite a nice woman, Arianne.'

Arianne could make no sense of what Artemis was saying. Was she being cryptic about something or just slipping into one of her vague periods? A waiter placed a Kir Royale in front of Arianne. She raised her glass and smiled at her mother. 'Christmas.' Her toast. It seemed to please Artemis.

'Ah, yes. Christmas.' She in turn raised her glass and the two women drank. Artemis replaced her glass on the table and told Arianne, 'I'm really looking forward to this holiday. I don't know how long I'll be away. You know what I'm like, you may or may not get a card from me.'

'You don't have my address.'

'Quite right. I don't.' Arianne made an attempt to take her small shoulder-bag from the banquette where Artemis sat and where she had placed it next to her. Artemis stopped her. 'Not now, later. We must order.' Discreetly she summoned the maître d' to take their order. She waved the menu away. 'Oysters, nine, I think. And wild duck for me.'

'Mange-touts, and purée of celeriac?' the maître d' asked, familiar as he was with her preferences in vegetables.

A nod of her head, and she asked, 'Arianne?'

'The same,' Arianne told the frock-coated man poised with a smile, pad and pen in hand.

'You don't have to have what I'm having, Arianne.' Why must her daughter decline to make a different choice from her own?

'Duck and oysters. It can't be bad, Artemis.'

'Well, as long as it's what you want.' She took a long swallow of champagne and then said, 'Hadley is travelling with me. The flat at Chessington Park is closed, and the key is with Clive, the housekeeper there. I've left instructions with him that you are allowed to come and go in the flat as you like while I am away. I've given the staff a month's holiday, so there will be no one there to cook or clean for you. You may sleep over in the guest room if you like.'

'That's very generous of you, Artemis.'

'Generous? Hell, it's Christmas.'

'But still, I didn't expect the invitation.'

'Well, it's possible because I'm not there. You do understand.'

Oh yes, Arianne did understand. It was not to be expected when her mother was in residence. Mother and daughter understood very well the ground rules of their relationship and just how closely it was allowed to develop.

It turned out to be a pleasant lunch. Artemis was looking quite vivacious in her sable hat and a chocolate-brown silk-jersey dress made for her by Givenchy. She wore her fabled pearls, and jewels on her fingers. Not for the first time did Arianne think that Artemis had missed her vocation. An actress – she could have been a brilliant one. A spy – they'd have had to do a film. She never spilled a secret worth the telling. Where might Artemis be going? With whom? Hadley might have been accompanying her. She certainly wouldn't limit herself to the butler for company. One thing for sure: Arianne would never know who the man was.

Arianne was looking the dessert trolley over. To reach a decision from among the toothsome array of cakes and puddings, each more luscious and tempting than the last, seemed impossible. Torn between the *milles feuilles* and the trifle, she turned from studying the trolley to ask Artemis what she was going to have. But her mother was putting on her gloves. Now what? Before she could say anything, Artemis looked at her and said, 'There really is no contest here, Arianne. It has to be the trifle. The best trifle you will ever eat. I adore it, but, alas, no time. One more sip of wine, and I'm off. But you stay and have the trifle and finish the bubbly. It is Christmas, after all.'

The maître d' arrived with Artemis's sable coat over his arm and held it out ready for her to slip into. She slid over the banquette, and the table was pulled away by a waiter. As she passed by Arianne she leaned over and pressed her cheek briefly against Arianne's. This served as a mother-daughter kiss. It was what a best girlfriend would have received. 'Merry Christmas.' She was gone.

Arianne stood up to watch Artemis leave the room. That was lunch, then. It took a few seconds for Arianne to realise that her mother had indeed gone. The maître d' suggested that Arianne take the seat on the banquette where Artemis had been sitting.

This she did, and in a flash waiters had cleared and rearranged the table. The trifle was served and her glass recharged with vintage Bollinger.

Long after Artemis had gone, when Arianne had finished her pudding, and was sipping the strong black *demi tasse* of aromatic coffee, she realised how very much alone in the world she would be without Artemis – Artemis who was always there in her life, but not there. Arianne sighed. She marvelled at the degree of their attachment. Each had made the best of a relationship that neither had ever excelled in.

Arianne's Christmas lunch had come to its second ending. She looked at her wristwatch. It had been a long and delectable lunch. It left her disinclined to pedal back to Christie's. But she picked up her handbag, and lo! – a long white envelope had been slipped beneath it. She read her name and recognised the hand. Artemis's. How had she missed seeing her mother place it there? Arianne opened the envelope. Inside: a cheque for two thousand pounds and a card with a very jolly Santa Claus on it. She opened the card and read:

I hope you will use this Christmas money on a travel extravagance. Somewhere exotic, warm and romantic.
Artemis

That was Artemis, always catching her off-guard. 'No presents this Christmas,' she had said. Indifference to Arianne's holiday plans, and now, this. Arianne's world seemed to be getting bigger every day. Well, at least a chance of it expanding by the day existed. Options loomed suddenly in her life. She considered that on the way to the ladies' cloakroom. She gave the elderly attendant, smart in her black silk dress and white-lace collar and cuffs, a pound piece by placing it in the saucer on the marble-topped dressing-table. She slipped into her black and tan herringbone cashmere wrap-around jacket and tied the soft belt, adjusting the wide revers. From its large patch-pocket she withdrew a black beret. Outside the doorman accepted his tip with a smile and wheeled her bike out. 'I don't get much of a chance to park one of these, madam. Merry Christmas!' – accompanied by a broad smile.

He held the bike while Arianne put her hat and gloves on. She smiled back, 'Merry Christmas.' She mounted the bike and rode off round Carlos Place towards Berkeley Square. Where, she wondered, should she go for Christmas?

LONDON,
GLOUCESTERSHIRE,
EGYPT

Chapter 9

Women sometimes do that. Play little games with themselves to muster the courage to step out of themselves and into the unknown. At such times, real desires sometimes get confused with the game and what they think they *should* want. Arianne's game was to keep asking herself: Where would you most like to go over Christmas? For days, she mentally ranged the world with that question and arrived nowhere. Finally, she realised why. It was the wrong question. She changed the game. Who would I like to be with this Christmas? It came as something of a shock to Arianne that Jason no longer sprang immediately to mind. Instead, Ben Johnson. When she thought of him, she thought of love: the caring way he had with his uncle; his silence, and the solicitude shown during that ride to London. She had appreciated his avoiding mere small talk. She liked his sureness of self; the way they had become friends without much effort by either of them. Had it been an imaginary closeness or real togetherness she had sensed between them?

Ahmad. He was someone she would like to be with. Since their breakfast together at Claridge's, she had been thinking of him on and off in a rather different way. Without Jason. When he had been among her thoughts she had quickly banished them from her mind. But today it no longer seemed an act of betrayal to want him, to love him without Jason. She sensed that talk at Claridge's had changed their relationship – on her side, anyway. Yes, to see and be with Ahmad was a real possibility. And she knew where he would be; that he would welcome her, if not as a lover then assuredly as a close friend. A half dozen other people drifted in and out of her thoughts – friends, for she had never had a lover other than Jason and Ahmad. But they could not match the interest that Ben and Ahmad had.

It was easy for her to figure out that she was looking for a man in her life. And that she had little idea how to go about finding one. For nearly three years she had forgotten about getting involved sexually with someone. It had hardly entered her mind. She had lost interest in the sexual act. The erotic Arianne had died with Jason. But now suddenly that appeared not to be true. Desire for sex with an exciting man, the love and passion, the hot lust men can have for women, was what she wanted for Christmas. Romance.

How had Artemis known? Somewhere in her strange and remote relationship with her daughter Artemis did understand and appreciate that Arianne was more than she appeared to be. Beneath the calm and quiet there was another woman striving to get out, a woman unable to do so alone. Jason had recognised that in her, and had rejoiced in being the man to release her. Ahmad? Was he the man to take on that sort of commitment? He had been happy enough to participate in a lustful *ménage à trois*. But as one of a couple in love, without Jason? Too many questions, she told herself. The more she thought about Ahmad, the more she wanted to be with him, the more she wanted to try to enter his erotic world again.

She booked the only flight she could get to Cairo. Christmas day. While waiting for her ticket to be processed she thought about Ben Johnson. Would he be at Chessington Park with his uncle for the holidays?

Jim O'Connor was not happy to be in Cairo. Nor was Ahmad any too thrilled to have him there. It was an unpleasant business for both men. What made things even more uncomfortable for O'Connor was that he had never been able to figure out the man he was working for, still less his motives. There was something else – he liked the man, and he wasn't so sure that he should. Jim O'Connor was one of the south Boston Irish. He had punched his way out of the bars and docks of Boston and New York, footballed his way through Notre Dame, and fought his way out of a Korean war, with a medal of honour to prove it. Now, as owner of the hottest and most respected detective and security agency in the States, he found himself almost charmed by this urbane, handsome, international playboy-millionaire into overseeing the investigation himself.

O'Connor had done some investigating of his own. On Ahmad Salah Ali. He turned out to be the genuine thing, all that he had a reputation of being and more. Something else. He was a nice guy, even though a Harvard man. And that was what bothered Jim O'Connor. For a nice guy, he had a helluva lot of wealth and a great many serious connections. Princes, and yes, even kings, had dined at his table. He was on intimate terms with a variety of prominent men. Here was a guy with a great deal of power. Yet he acted like he didn't have any. He claimed he was just a dilettante, an amateur geo-politician, and a friend. Enough there for a full-time job.

Jim knew more. The women. The many women. The debauched and depraved sexual life he led *and* that he took enormous pains to keep secret. Even the names of the few men he shared his erotic games with. Important names. Sure of making the headlines on two continents if a scandal blew up in their faces. He knew about Ahmad's wife, whom he almost never saw and who was settled in LA. His three teenage sons, whom he was very close to. And his best friends, Jason and Arianne Honey. By all accounts they were like real family to him. They went everywhere together, were everything to each other. So why was there no report of a sexual relationship between them? Jim O'Connor didn't believe that, not for a minute. That twitchy nose of his told him differently. Until he was introduced to Arianne Honey. Then he believed it. She was not the type for a sexual threesome. Too quiet, refined, pretty. And there was a subtle sexiness about her. Too subtle, surely, for a man like Ahmad. He liked them wilder than Arianne Honey. And besides, by all accounts, the Honeys had been mad about each other. Crazy in love, neither of them had wandered. They were each other's lives, and both loved Ahmad.

When Jim had his findings on Ahmad, Jason had already died. That was why Ahmad had hired Jim O'Connor: Jason was dead, and Ahmad wanted to know why. How it could have happened to an experienced pilot such as Jason. What Jason had been doing flying the red, single-seater, supersonic jet over the Himalayas. His own pet plane. Was he test-flying it? If so, why in a place so remote from his bases in England and the States? Ahmad had been a man distraught at the loss of his best friend in a hideous accident when he called in Jim O'Connor to investigate. That was nearly three years ago. Now here was Jim, the day before Christmas, in Cairo, summoned by Ahmad and even flown out on a chartered private jet.

Any one of numerous good operatives could have been there in his place. But when the call came from Ahmad, Jim, without hesitation, had agreed to be there. Over the years, Jim had been in contact with Ahmad Salah Ali no more than three or four times. That had been enough to see and dislike the way the man worked. It was his generosity, the way he gave and stayed in the background of things, minded his own business and did not get involved. The way he put people together and stood in the wings watching, waiting to see how they were going to act out the scenario he created. Jim O'Connor didn't care to be a puppet on anybody's string, but that was how he felt when he was in the presence of Ahmad Salah Ali. That was bad. But, worse, the man had never given him any real justification for those feelings. Justified or not, Jim felt he was being used. This Mr Good-guy was not all good. He was corrupt, that was his kick, being corrupt and corrupting others. Jim's professional nose detected the whiff of a minor genius at it.

Jim liked to know where he was with people. With Salah Ali, he never knew. He got to think of him as an Arab Mafia Don, just waiting for that moment to call in a favour, a debt that had to be paid. And Jim *was* in Ahmad's debt. The O'Connor Agency had picked up, on a direct recommendation from Ahmad, the security consultancy and control of several heads of state and consequently fat contracts in their countries. Massive and powerful jobs that propelled him and his company into a position of power no private company in their line of work had ever had before. The CIA watched with interest and respect bordering on envy, and bought him expensive lunches. And Ahmad? Not once had he put himself forward as the man in the middle. Not once did he acknowledge Jim's notes of thanks. Was this summons on the day before Christmas the pay-off at last? He hoped so. It made him uneasy to be indebted to Ahmad. Jim always liked to know what a thing cost. Then he could pay on delivery.

It was a smiling Ahmad who walked across the room to greet Jim. 'It's really good of you to come at such short notice, Jim.'

'Ahmad.' They had been on first-name terms since they had

met. Ahmad's insistence. The two men shook hands. Ahmad placed an arm around Jim's shoulders. Anyone seeing them would have thought they were old friends.

'Good flight, Jim?'

'Very comfortable. I travelled with two of my men. Do you want them in on this?'

'Not for the moment. I'll let you deal with them. I don't think there's any need for me to see them. Can I offer you a drink?'

Three fingers of malt whisky and a lump of ice. Ahmad had a flattering memory for Jim's favourite drink. Jim took the Lalique crystal tumbler in his hand and watched Ahmad open the clear bottle of champagne, Louis Roederer Crystal. Ahmad's favourite drink, registered Jim's computer mind. Watching Ahmad, Jim had to admit to himself that the man held a kind of fascination for him. Was it the hedonistic style? In matters of pleasure Ahmad was certainly a front runner. His success with women? His erudition? An urbanity rare in macho men like Ahmad? Or was it the polish laid on so thick that Jim doubted his own intuition of Ahmad's corrupt soul searching out people's weaknesses, working on them for his own amusement? Well, it had not been *all* intuitive. Hints had emerged from his discreet digging into what went on in Ahmad's life behind the baize door.

Jim took a long swallow of the amber liquid in his glass. The bite of the whisky was an instant pick-up. Yes, the man before him remained, even with all he knew about him, an enigma. An enigma, OK, *but*, he told himself: You've been around too long, seen too much, Jim O'Connor, to be fooled by Ahmad Salah Ali. There's something not quite kosher going on here. He took another large swallow. Suddenly he felt better about being in Cairo with Ahmad. He had made up his mind to crack the mystery of his fascinating client. Simply for his own satisfaction.

The two men walked together towards the impressive Boule desk, set in front of three twenty-foot-high windows. Arched at the top, they were French windows that opened as twelve-foot-high doors on to a wide terrace of white marble softened in colour to a mellow whitish-beige by a century of sun, heat and the mist that rose intermittently from the Nile. The silk taffeta draperies, a faded burnt orange draped voluptuously, were tied back with thick ropes of entwined silk in luscious colours: plum, and coral, aubergine, and emerald green. Huge pairs of tassels hung from them. A choice frame for the unobstructed romantic view of the Nile flowing past the windows, the feluccas – the working lateen sail-boats of Egypt – plying the river. And on the opposite shore, tall, rich green palm trees, an impressive open eighteenth-century pavilion in the Ottoman style, and a closed building of the same period and style: the Cairo boathouse of Salah Ali. At a dock with several feluccas tied up, white turbaned and robed men, several women covered from head to foot in black, and children, all busily running about, brought life to the scene.

The winter sun cast a warm light into the two-storey library of cherrywood, splendid for its books and the gracious curve of a staircase leading to the narrow gallery that encircled the room. There the shelves lined the walls and reached to the ceiling with a fine collection of rare books. The library, with its reading tables and comfortable tapestry-covered, eighteenth-century high-backed chairs, its worn leather sofas and priceless Persian rugs, the large Chien Lung, Han and Tang vases with lids topped with golden dogs, again impressed Jim O'Connor, as it had the first time he had seen it.

Then he had become acutely aware of time stood still, history, ancestry, incredible power and stability, beauty and class. The kind of rank that comes with hundreds of years of privilege, power meted out in just the right proportions, and a cultured life that had been nurtured for centuries. He had been cynical then and was no less so now, still believing there were plenty of skeletons dangling in this family's closets. The mere fact of having survived into the nineteen-nineties guaranteed that. As head of the family, Ahmad, he was certain, had plenty of his own messy secrets. On top of the depraved and debauched sexual life that Jim knew about. He smiled to himself, having to admire the man. He mused: You bury your skeletons deep, Ahmad, but not deep enough. My curiosity feels as if it's just about to conquer my discretion.

He stood for several minutes at the window watching the scene outside. The room smelled of beeswax polish and jasmine, sandalwood. The scent drew him back into the room and he turned to walk past one of a pair of huge antique globes, spun it with his hand, and continued on towards a mahogany curved-back chair that boasted a pair of superbly elegant and sensuous swans for arms. Covered in an eighteenth-century Persian embroidered cloth of pomegranates, it was a thing of both beauty and comfort. It was placed in front of the desk behind which Ahmad sat watching Jim O'Connor. Jim stroked the mahogany swan's head, the curve that imitated a neck. He gazed from it to Ahmad. 'Very Leda and the Swanish.' He was quite proud of his cultured hint that he was on to Ahmad's appetite for 'anything-goes' sex. He had even given an indication that he was no slouch himself in the sexual arena. Not very professional, maybe, but promoted by a sense that Ahmad was somehow using him, pulling the wool over his eyes about something.

The smile at the corner of Ahmad's lips irritated Jim; his remark even more. 'A large, beautiful white swan, huge downy wings spread wide to embrace a lovely, voluptuous and naked lady. His long, sensuous neck wrapped around hers, ecstasy in her limbs and on her face. The human aspect of the bird, an erotic expression in his eyes that suggests to the viewer a man.' Here Ahmad hesitated for a moment, giving Jim a look behind which lurked a sly smile. 'I have a small oil painting of Leda and her swan. You must allow me to make a gift of it to you.' The offer seemed much more than just a generous act.

Now why did he have to try to be a smart-ass with Ahmad? It had backfired on him. It only proved his point, that Ahmad dwelt on the dark side of others. What did the bastard expect him to say – 'Keep the painting, how about delivering me the real thing? A little bestiality is a turn-on'? Jim finessed his way out of the tight spot he was in by raising an eyebrow and saying nothing. He merely held up his glass as in a toast, and took another swallow of his drink.

Ahmad picked up a silver casket from his desk and raised the lid. Standing up, he bent across the desk and offered Jim a cigar from the humidor, then a silver cigar-clipper. Ahmad watched Jim light the cigar. He took a Gauloise and placed it in an amber cigarette holder, wet his lips with the point of his tongue and then ran the bit of the holder sensually over his lower lip, before clamping it between his teeth. A long-time habit, natural to him, but to women provocative and very sexy. It irritated Jim.

Ahmad took a gold Cartier lighter from his pocket, flicked the switch. As the flame touched the tip of the cigarette he looked over it and thought, If Jim O'Connor comes through for me with the sort of news I am looking for, I will send him a bonus. Two Nubian girls. Very talented – they could make him sexually crazy. If Ahmad knew anything about men and their sexual appetites, and clearly he did, Jim O'Connor would devour Ahmad's two black goddesses. All that good Irish Catholic sexual guilt would be out the window for ever – or the man would shoot himself. Ahmad banked on 'out the window'. He smiled at Jim. 'I have a delicate job for you, Jim.'

'More delicate than usual?' asked Jim half facetiously. Jim saw a hardness come into Ahmad's face. He had seen that look several times before. It told him that this business was serious stuff and meant a great deal to Ahmad Salah Ali.

'Yes.'

'How so?'

'The last time I asked you to do an investigation for me, it was out in the open and I didn't care how public you were when going about your business. This time round, I very much do mind if your investigation is discovered. I don't care how you do it or what it costs, but no one is to know your firm is on this case. Or even that there is a case to investigate.'

'That's what you want, that's what you'll get.'

'Fine, I knew I could count on you.' Ahmad took a key from one drawer to open another. He placed two brown envelopes on his desk, and locked the drawer again, replacing the key where he had found it. Then he handed one envelope to Jim. 'There is a hundred thousand dollars in this envelope, a deposit. If you need more before the case is closed and we do a final accounting, just call me. You still have the numbers where you can reach me?'

'Yes, I do. But hold on, Ahmad. There's no need for money.' Jim was thinking to make this his pay-off to Ahmad for all the business Ahmad had sent his way. But he realised Ahmad wasn't just picking up on favours when Ahmad told him:

'I think there is. I want no records in your office of our transaction. Strictly cash, and no book-keeping. Agreed?'

Jim was having strong feelings about this job, chiefly a rich curiosity as to what it was and just how dirty Ahmad was willing

122

to play to get the answers he wanted. 'Agreed,' Jim told him after a moment's hesitation.

Ahmad picked up the second envelope and rose from his chair. 'A little fresh air, I think.'

He pushed a pair of the French windows open and the two men stepped into the afternoon sunshine. It was warm and felt good. Jim leaned against the balustrade. The house was nearly at the water's edge. Below, Jim could see a large felucca being loaded with supplies. Paranoia was something he had not figured on in Ahmad. But Jim and Ahmad were there on the balcony: Ahmad was afraid of being overheard. Did he think the library was bugged? Who, he wondered, would be bugging it? And why?

Ahmad liked Jim O'Connor. For a man in the business he was in, he had a certain amount of class, a subtlety Ahmad appreciated. He knew when to push it, when to retreat, when to wait. He must have been a terrific commander, thought Ahmad. And then stopped thinking about the man he was dealing with and presented him with the second envelope. 'Here's your brief. Read it. If you have any questions or decide not to take the job, now is the time to speak up.'

Jim opened the envelope. There were only two pages. One was a letter of instruction, the second, the copy of an official document. Jim slipped the papers back into the envelope. 'That document is a tissue of lies. How did you manage it?'

'I managed it. May I have the envelope back?'

Jim handed it to Ahmad. 'It's contrary to what our investigation revealed.'

'That's true.'

'Why did you bother to hire us?' Jim felt peeved.

'I wanted to know the facts. Which does not, however, mean that I wanted the world to know what I do. You have my word that you have no need to worry. Neither you nor your company is compromised.'

Reluctantly Jim began to believe that Ahmad was telling the truth. Angry though he was, he decided that he would say no more about the fraudulent document. 'Got a light?'

Ahmad handed his lighter over to Jim and watched while the man relit his cigar. 'Time is a factor, Jim.'

'What does that mean?'

'It means I want you to produce concrete evidence as soon as possible.'

'This job is complex. Could run a long time. And there's no guarantee that I can come up with the goods. You've waited too long. The trail – if there ever was one – is cold.'

'I won't be satisfied until you bring me something absolute. Move on it, Jim.'

'Why?'

'I don't think that's really your business.'

'What if I told you I'm making it my business?'

'I would say we have a problem.'

Ahmad placed his hand over his chin, and rubbed it pensively. He looked away from Jim. The two men remained silent. Then Ahmad went through his ritual of lighting a cigarette. He turned back to look at Jim. 'Why must you know, Jim?'

'Because it's a weird brief. Because I can't figure out what's behind this. Look, Ahmad, this is the third time we've taken on a job for you. You're a good customer. Anyway, the customer is always right – all that shit. Normally, I may feel curiosity, but don't really care about the whys and wherefores of my clients. But then none of them, after taking our findings on board as acceptable, has ordered a second investigation years later. I suspect my company is being used to discover secrets: drugs, arms deals, money-laundering. Some kinda murky stuff. I came up with info that was suspect the last time. OK, it wasn't linked to you, but . . .'

'Well, I am glad you recognised that.'

'Look, Ahmad, you can't blame me for thinking you're not levelling with me. That document shows you used us once and twisted our findings to what you wanted the world to know. I don't much like that. My clients don't have to be clean as Little Red Riding Hood. But they gotta be up front with us, so I know what we're in for.'

Ahmad was struggling with a smile. That irritated Jim. What the fuck am I doing here, anyway? he asked himself. The pompous prick, laughing at me. Why don't I walk out of here?

'A pretty good analogy, as it happens, Jim. Only I'm the wolf. Tamed. Will it satisfy you to know, this is personal, strictly personal?'

124

It was evident that Jim had not worked it out, or if he had he was not convinced. 'It has to do with ego and the id.' The jargon cleared up nothing for Jim. Ahmad tried again. 'I'm not going to go into it any more than this. It's an affair of the heart. It has to do with obsessive love, passion, sex and jealousy. My own. That's my final word on the matter, and more than you really have to know.'

Ahmad liked the embarrassed look on Jim O'Connor's face. The man deserved to be embarrassed. Ahmad preferred having him at a disadvantage. He also liked the idea that Jim could not put the brief Ahmad had requested he take alongside Ahmad's motives and then make sense out of them. He tapped him on the shoulder and told him, 'Don't look so confused. Love, sex, they're serious business. Very powerful motives. All sorts of acts are carried out in their name. Kings have lost thrones for them. Men have killed for them. Princes and paupers alike can be victim of them. The wisest of men and women have been enslaved. People who thought they could control their desires. But could they, hell! I know that passion – the desire of unfathomableness.' Ahmad hesitated for a few seconds, then asked, 'Will you take the case or not?'

The two men gazed at each other. Jim O'Connor thrust out his hand to shake Ahmad's.

'What has been said here will remain strictly between us?' questioned Ahmad.

'How else?'

'Good. Then we have no need of this.' And he tore the manila envelope into quarters and then eighths. The two men re-entered the library and Ahmad closed the doors. Glasses were refilled. Jim, watching Ahmad, had no doubt that what Ahmad had told him was true. But *all* the truth? It seemed no longer to matter to Jim. He had indicated to Ahmad that he did not want to be used to promote any sort of underhand dealings. One thing was for sure, he felt sorry for Ahmad's Little Red Riding Hood. She had every chance of being devoured by him. He would manage it, and she would never know what had gobbled her up. He would be that smooth about it. Had it already happened? he wondered.

'I'll walk you to the car.' That was it. Dismissed. It was abrupt. But that was how Ahmad always worked. Once he had what he wanted, *finito*. Jim O'Connor could identify with that. It was his way too.

The two men joined Jim O'Connor's two detectives. Introductions made, the four men walked to the waiting Rolls-Royce. Ahmad closed the car door. 'I have a bonus in mind for you.'

'And it doesn't fit in a bank book?'

The two men smiled knowingly at one another. 'I'm glad we understand each other, Jim.'

'Yeah.'

Ahmad signalled to the chauffeur to drive off.

Chapter 10

It seemed an odd thing to do: rent a car and load it with Ida's shopping, which did indeed include a goose – thank goodness, the smallest goose Arianne had ever seen. But then again everything Arianne found herself doing since she had had Christmas thrust upon her, first by Ida and then by Artemis, seemed strange to her.

Several days before Christmas, Mayfair seemed to be emptying out. The foreign visitors were vanishing from the streets. The residents were loading cars for the airport or the country. All that was left were frantic last-minute shoppers and a kind of Christmas panic to get it all together before the event. Arianne got swept up by the buzz of an exodus. It made her not want to be alone in London with nothing but the past for company. That had been all right for the last two Christmases. She had wanted to be alone with the ghost of love. Not now.

Now there was something else. Although Jason was these days somewhere back in the recesses of her mind, she did occasionally feel his spirit reaching out to her. It was different from how it had ever been since his death. Now it was as if he was watching her and cheering her on. Go out into the world and have a good time. As if he were sanctioning her every move. Arianne was not insensitive to such apparent approval from him, but it meant little. She was gathering strength from herself now. This approval certainly did not govern what she was doing, as it had done all of their married life. She felt a pang of sadness about that. Like the prisoner who is set free after a near lifetime in chains, locked to a fellow inmate – prisoners of love, broken free from each other for ever. That image as it passed fleetingly through her mind was to give her strength to push forward. She pedalled her bike faster down King Street towards Christie's.

No one was more surprised than she when she went to work

as usual, and an hour later announced to her boss that she was taking a few days off to get away for Christmas. Minutes later, with his approval, she walked out.

And now here she was, thanks to Artemis's generosity, in a stream of traffic going over the Hammersmith flyover on her way to Chessington Park where she would stay until Christmas morning. Then she would drive back down the motorway to Heathrow airport, turn the car in to Avis and board a plane for Cairo. She would arrive just in time.

Ahmad kept open house on Christmas day. People drifted in and out from early morning until the last guest was gone – usually sometime the following day. Guests from various parts of the world arrived in Cairo for the much sought-after invitation. Christmas day at the Salah Ali house on the Nile was a spectacle to be part of: an impressive collection of people assembled to dine on an exquisite buffet that ran all day and into the night and to drink his vintage Margaux, and Roederer Crystal champagne.

Then there was the annual Ahmad Salah Ali boat race. Hundreds of people congregated on the dock on the opposite side of the Nile from the house. A small cannon was fired to send the entrants up the Nile to Luxor and the Winter Palace Hotel. In Cairo that day the banks of the Nile would be lined with thousands of people waving and cheering on the many dozens of feluccas, the largest number ever sailing together up the Nile. The crowds would peter out to a trickle as the population dwindled and the days went by, but they would be there nevertheless, all the way to Upper Egypt and the finish-line. The race was something unique that the average man in the street and the poor peasant could be part of. It was an excitement for them that they could afford – unless they chose to gamble money on it. But as well as being risk-free, there was something else for all who watched: it was probably the most beautiful boat race in the world.

The felucca – a wooden boat with a sail, triangular on a long yard at an angle of 45 degrees rigged to the mast of the boat – was almost unaltered since the time of the Pharaohs of Egypt, three thousand years before. To see them in full sail under a clear blue sky or a hot pink sun or a spectacular sunset of pinks and mauves, oranges and deep purples, with the tall, voluptuous palm trees, the spires of the mosques as black silhouettes, and the sound of the muezzin's call to prayer for background, as they laboriously sailed their way up the Nile in the heat, was a sight never to be forgotten.

The men in their turbans and galabiyahs scampered over the feluccas to get the best of a current, to exploit the least breeze. It was a race out of time. The backdrop was the palms and flowering trees, the verdant banks of the river, period houseboats, and a transition from a capital city teeming with people to a narrow band of green dissolving into desert and crumbling remnants of civilisations thousands of years old the further up the Nile one went. Beautiful seemed a hardly adequate description for such splendour; such romantic history, of time frozen and waiting like a sleeping princess to be awakened from the deep, mysterious sleep of the past. Was it any wonder that the whole country seemed to take pride in Ahmad's favourite event?

It was a race for the working man on the river as well as for the upper-class Egyptians who sponsored those men who could not afford to enter the race, and those other men who could, but had no skill to sail the Nile, and therefore manned the boats as recruits alongside simple hard-working boatmen, those masters of the Nile. The prize was a fortune to most of the men in the race. And every year Ahmad sailed as master with his crew on one of the several feluccas he owned. If he won – as rarely happened – he divided his prize money among the losers.

Arianne had sailed with Ahmad and Jason in the race several times. All three had taken it seriously, but for Arianne there had always been another dimension to the race. Romance. The romance of time and place and the two men she loved and craved sexual intimacy with. During those sailing days, going south into Africa with the other boats on the river, time had stood still for them, the outside world had vanished, their hearts had beat as one and they had sailed together as one body and one soul.

The traffic on the M4 was steady and heavy but it did roll along after Heathrow airport. It had been maybe somewhat less painful getting out of London for Arianne than some of the other travellers. She had been lost in her memories of the race with

Ahmad. She had sent a fax announcing her arrival. Now that it was done, the ticket for the plane in her purse, the fax issued, the memory of the excitement of being in such a race and with Ahmad stirred new sensations in Arianne. New and different. Different because she was stepping into Ahmad's world, a single woman, free, looking, seeing, experiencing everything with an altered perception.

She left the motorway and passed through several villages. Then the high, dry-stone walls surrounding Chessington Park came into view. She found herself thinking about Ben Johnson. Would he be staying with his uncle at Chessington House for Christmas? Would she see him? To think so gave her a warm feeling. She conjured up a picture of Ben when she had said goodbye to him in Three Kings Yard. She liked his smile, his handsomeness, that something special that seemed to be in his eyes – the way he looked at her as if he understood her instinctively and accepted fully who and what she was.

She turned the car into the drive, through the gates and along the avenue of trees. How strange was the feeling of being there alone without Artemis. The house loomed into view. Under the late morning sun of winter it looked incredibly stately and beautiful. As she rounded the fountain and pulled the rented red BMW up to the front door she did feel suddenly a stranger, an intruder even. Inhospitable as Artemis could be at times, she had, at least, never made Arianne feel like that on her visits to Chessington House. Arianne shrugged off the sensation. About to leave the car to ring the housekeeper's bell for entry to Artemis's flat, she was surprised by a knock at the window next to her. She jumped. Her hand went to her heart. She had been caught off-guard.

Whose was that face under the woolly bubble-hat with knitted flaps over the ears? The matching woollen gloves continued to knock at the car window. Arianne sighed with some relief. Just Beryl Quilty in a pink puffy, eiderdown-like jacket. For a moment she was mesmerised by the face and its pinched disapproval. The continued rapping sound, muffled by the woolly glove, was rapidly becoming an irritant to Arianne. It only stopped when Arianne had wound the glass down away from Beryl's fist.

'Mrs Quilty.'

'You can't park here, you know.'

'I know.'

'No one is allowed to park in front of the entrance. Not the residents or their guests.'

'I know. This is not parking. It is lingering for a minute to call Clive on the intercom and to unload my things.'

'Oh. Then you are here for Christmas?'

'Yes.'

'I didn't know that. No one told me.'

'No one told anyone, Mrs Quilty.'

'But the flat is closed. Staff gone. Artemis away. If you were to be allowed in the flat the house should have been told. We have to think of security.'

'Mrs Quilty, if you don't mind.' Arianne attempted to push the door open against Beryl Quilty. The woman stepped aside. 'Are you asking whether I have permission to enter my mother's flat?'

Mrs Quilty managed an approximation to sheepishness in the face of this question. Her lips slimmed out in silence. Arianne could barely detach her gaze from them. Could it be her tongue Beryl was biting? 'Put your mind at rest, Mrs Quilty. I do have permission. What is more, the custodian of the house knows it.'

'Well, he should have told me.'

Arianne suddenly felt much like Artemis did about Beryl Quilty. In a matter of seconds she had put a damper on Arianne's joy at doing just what she wanted for her Christmas. But Arianne was having none of that. She quickly quelled that feeling, got out of the car, and moved away from Beryl Quilty to ring the housekeeper's bell.

'You needn't do that. Don't disturb him. I can let you in.'

'You can, but you won't.' Arianne rang the bell.

'That was not necessary.' Now Beryl Quilty was very annoyed. It showed, along with an anxiety not to lose control of herself and the drama she was conjuring from nothing. As if to prove her point, Beryl placed a key in the front door lock and opened it.

'You see,' she said, rather smugly.

'Perhaps you have the key to my mother's flat? Maybe you can turn off the alarm-system? May I expect you to let me in whenever

131

I come to Chessington House? And to give me a key?'

The irritation now showed not only on Beryl Quilty's lips but in her eyes as well. Arianne was relieved to hear Clive's voice.

'You've not been sent an invitation for mulled wine and minced pies on Christmas Eve,' Beryl Quilty continued regardless. 'It's for the residents and their guests. Everyone in the house will be there. I hope you will too. We like everyone to be a part of the evening. It makes for a good community spirit. If you had told me you were coming you might have had a proper invitation. Never mind. Mulled wine between six and seven-thirty.'

The slim lips curled up into a smile: a façade of sweetness. The good samaritan face was now displayed to Arianne, supposedly an incentive for her to obey the call to mulled wine and Beryl's directive that the house should band together in the spirit of Christmas and goodwill to all men. No wonder Artemis had done a runner from home for Christmas.

In London, spending a few days in the country at Chessington House had seemed a good idea. Now the whole great production of getting into Artemis's flat and the prospect of being regimented into Beryl Quilty's Christmas Eve plans were making Arianne wonder. There were worse fates than being stranded in a near-deserted Mayfair. Clive, though helpful and kind enough, was behaving like an old woman. He fussed far too much about her arrival, with too many instructions on what to do and not do in the flat. At last she was given a key and he was gone.

She made a journey across the hall to her car to unload her things and overheard bickering: two women, obviously residents in the building, were working with some dreary plastic Christmas decorations in an attempt to render down the arrogant splendour of the ancient hall to the cosy comfort of a bourgeois Christmas. The arrival of Beryl Quilty was to add weight to the tug of war on taste. Beryl shot a smile across the cavernous hall to Arianne. 'I hope we have moved our car by now. Rules. House rules, you know.' We hadn't.

Once the car had been moved, Arianne was at last able to enter Artemis's flat alone and to close the door behind her. She leaned against it, and sighed with relief. She could at last get on with her own Christmas.

She strode into the sun-filled drawing room and felt the

132

pleasure she always did at being in that room. There was something uplifting about it. She *was* happy she had made the effort to be there. She picked up the shopping and brought it into the kitchen, a room she was a stranger to: it was Artemis's cook's domain. She located a kettle and was filling it when there came a tapping at the window. A spurt of anger kept her from looking up. Clive or Beryl Quilty: she could hardly bear it. Again, the rap at the window. She turned off the water and put the lid on the kettle. Feeling a bit like Artemis about the people in the building, she whirled around to confront the intruder, thinking, Why is Artemis always right?

She began to laugh. Happiness. The sheer pleasure of seeing not Beryl but Ben Johnson peering in at her. She placed the kettle on the counter-top and went directly to the window, unfastened it and lifted the bottom half up.

'Am I that funny-looking?' Her laughter was infectious and it brought a broad smile to his face.

'No. That was laughter that came from joy.'

'Oh.' The smile broadened even more in surprise to her admission. 'At seeing me?'

'More, at not seeing Mrs Quilty.' Then she quickly added, 'And at seeing you.'

'You're being polite?'

'No, it's not just good manners, I am pleased to see you. But what are you doing in the shrubbery?'

'I thought I saw you walking up from the garages, but the truth of the matter is that I chose the window to avoid a brush with those women in the hall.'

'Would you like to come in?'

'I'd rather take you out to lunch. Would you consider that?' He sensed her hesitation. 'Nothing serious. A pub lunch. I was going anyway.'

'Well then, yes, I'd like that.'

'Great. Come through the window – I have the car at the back drive.' He extended a hand.

'Do you know how pathetic this is? Two adults sneaking out of the house through a kitchen window because we're too wimpish to ignore those busybodies?'

'Pathetic in the extreme. Give me your hand. "*Là ci darem la mano*",' he intoned from Mozart as their hands joined to pull her through the large Georgian window, which came nearly to the floor, and into his arms. Her hair caught on a branch of one of the shrubs. He carefully disentangled it. She felt good in his arms. He sensed it. Their eyes locked on each other's for several seconds. The attraction was there between them but there was something else too in her eyes. Hesitation? Apprehension? He was quick to place her on her feet. The last thing he wanted was for her to feel those things about him. He went first, to hold the branches of box hedge apart so she could pass easily. Together, they walked to his car.

There was once again between them that same comfort, a certain ease that he had experienced with her when they had shared the ride to London. Just being together, walking in silence with the occasional look at each other, a smile, seemed to draw them together. Words? The chat? The charm? They were redundant. It was as if each of them was savouring an inexplicable pleasure in simply being together.

Was he, she wondered, really the reason she had wanted to come these few days to Chessington House? To experience just what she was feeling now – the pleasure, the stirrings of excitement over a man again? He walked with a long stride and seemed to be always just that little bit ahead of her, enough to permit her to steal a glance at him every now and again. He was wearing clothes similar to those she had seen him in the last time they had been together. This time she found him that little bit more attractive. Everything about him seemed to suit her. She took pleasure even in the sound of his boots on the gravel, the firmness of his step, the way his body moved with every stride.

Ben had thought Arianne beautiful from the first time he had seen her, with a quiet, almost still kind of beauty as against the ravishing looks he usually went for in women. The kind of dramatically perfect looks his wife had had, that his present lover Simone had, was what had always excited his lust, and generated his love for a woman. It surprised him how much more beautiful and provocative Arianne seemed to him than he had remembered. She was exciting something more in him than he had expected when he had tapped on Artemis's kitchen window.

When he had seen Arianne walking from the garage, it had

134

registered with him what a good body she had, in her tight jeans, body-hugging polo neck jumper, and denim jacket thrown over her shoulders. There had been something about the way she moved – a certain sureness of herself that he had not seen in her before. There was a sexiness in the way she moved her shoulders when she broke into a little run every few steps, presumably to keep the jacket from slipping off. Or was it? He had after all imagined that there was a sexy lady under that still and quiet beauty she carried so well. Now, riding the few miles to the pub, he was amazed at how happy he was that she was there beside him. He nearly reached out to touch her. What stopped him? He sensed that, if he did, there might be no turning back.

It had been an impulse, asking her to lunch. And now, sitting in front of the open fire, warming themselves, bottle of claret on the table, he wondered if he hadn't wanted to see her all along. Ever since he had given her that ride to London.

'Lunch,' he announced as a waitress appeared with the menu written out in chalk on a small blackboard framed in wood. He rose from the bench where he was sitting opposite Arianne and slid in next to her. She made room for him and together they scanned the offerings of the day.

'How about cottage pie?' Ben suggested.

'Sounds fine to me.'

'There are other things. I don't mean to push the cottage pie at you.'

He seemed anxious to please her, concerned that he might be taking over, leaving her without choice. She sensed he wanted reassurance that that was not the case. 'I would have chosen it myself.'

'Honestly?'

She nodded. 'I nearly always order cottage pie for a pub lunch.' And, gazing at each other, they left it at that. There was silence between them. Less of a smile than a quiet pleasure shone in their faces, as it sometimes does when two people are pleased to be where they are simply with each other.

Ben wanted to touch her, to bend in close to her and graze her cheek with the back of his hand. It seemed such a natural thing to do. But there was something vulnerable about her that spelled caution. It made him hold back. It did, in fact, make him retreat.

135

He returned to his place opposite her and raised his glass: 'Have a happy Christmas.'

'Happy Christmas to you too, Ben.' She touched the rim of her glass to his and drank. Then, replacing the glass on the table, she unbuttoned her jacket, removed it, and placed it on the bench next to her.

Once again he was aware of her body, and of how much he was attracted to it. Carnal feelings were taking over. He liked the way the cashmere jumper she was wearing hugged her, accentuating her long neck, the wide shoulders and slender arms. The hint of nipple he could see through the soft knit of the jumper suggested that she wore no bra. Her breasts were unexpectedly large and there was something extraordinarily erotic about them and the narrow waist. They seemed a contradiction to the seemingly shy person with such an understated kind of beauty sitting opposite him. She excited his interest more than ever. But . . .

'We have things in common,' he told her.

'Oh?'

'We both have one parent that's English, the other American.' He seemed very proud of that. And she thought, We have *that* in common too.

'I didn't know that, Ben. And?'

'And what?'

'The other things we have in common. What are they?'

'I don't know yet. But I'm sure we do have other things in common. They'll reveal themselves to us, in time.'

'Chessington House. Are you as attracted to the place as I am?' she asked. 'I mean, your uncle notwithstanding.'

'Yes. But in my case I am not so sure that's a good thing.'

Arianne wanted to pursue that question, but she felt it was too personal. It did, however, make her wonder how much of a good thing her own attachment to the place was.

The waitress arrived with their cottage pie.

Arianne sensed that Ben was just as relieved as she was by the interruption of food. Their mutual attraction and attachment to the Tudor house and its parkland seemed suddenly fraught with all sorts of emotional traps that gave them reason to be there, issues too personal to be readily revealed to each other. Arianne had already admitted to herself that it was not just for Artemis that she made the trip to Gloucestershire every week. Not Artemis, nor simply the beauty of the place drew her to it as often as possible. It was certainly not the astonishingly unattractive atmosphere that the residents created from their rootless notions of how to live up to the place in which their money had landed them. Nor their downright silliness, though that now brought the hint of a smile to her lips, not missed by Ben.

'A penny. Will that buy your thoughts?'

'I was thinking of how annoyingly silly some of the residents in that house are.'

'It would almost be acceptable if they were interesting or amusing, or half as eccentric as my uncle and your mother. But they're not. They're just your plain, average, middle-class man and woman in the street hoping to live out a quiet old age in a stately home. Nice enough people, who have given up their dreams and passions, in the hope that, having done so, they will earn a free ride to heaven. They're bitter and pompous, because it's all over for them, the life of taking chances, spontaneous living. They blame it on old age, and never consider that they have chosen to give up the big things in life for the little things, hard work for an easy life, for having arrived where they are intact and with nothing to do, except to create problems and projects to reassure themselves they are still alive. Lady Hardcastle and my uncle are the odd ones out. They are still remarkable, vital, independent spirits, not willing to conform, in spite of old age and their conservative, frightened neighbours.'

Here he hesitated. He was buttering a piece of brown bread and watching Arianne fork some of the cottage pie into her mouth. He liked her mouth. Found himself fixated by it. She caught him and he felt somehow foolish. 'Do you know about your mother and my uncle?'

'No.'

'Oh!'

'Just, oh?'

'Sorry, I assumed you knew. Now I find this embarrassing.'

'Please don't, not on my account. Artemis and I have never exchanged confidences. It's just the way we are. We have an odd mother-daughter relationship, always have had.'

'One would never guess that, the way you are with her.'

'How am I with her?'

'Incredibly kind, dutiful. She is, after all, not an easy woman. Mightily attractive as a woman and a charmer, and an interesting character, but not easy.'

'What about them, Ben – my mother and your uncle?'

'Well, for one thing they're off on their annual holiday together. You didn't know that?'

'No. But I guessed she was going off with a man.'

'You had no idea there was something between them?'

'That night when you gave me the lift back to London, for a fleeting moment I suspected something because of the way she ordered him to pay my taxi. I did know that they were close friends, she, Gerald, and Sir Anson, and for a very long time. She had told me that much. Now you must tell me more. She never will, you know. And I'm so happy she has someone in her old age. Men have always adored her. And she has always adored them adoring her.' Playing thus with words brought a smile to her lips. 'Do you think they love each other?' she asked, thrilled for Artemis that it might be so.

Ben hesitated for a minute. Arianne looked so genuinely happy for her mother. He felt it would be no betrayal on his part to tell Arianne what he knew. There was no question in his mind that she would be discreet about it, and would most probably never mention to Artemis that she had heard anything. She looked to Ben like that kind of a woman. He filled their glasses and they continued with their meal.

'Yes, I do think they love each other. They have for a very long time. They have been lovers for more than thirty years. Quite a romantic love affair. They have managed to go off together alone on a jaunt of one sort or another every year since the first time they met and fell in love.'

'And Gerald?'

'Gerald, Artemis and my uncle were friends and remained close friends until Gerald's death. If Gerald knew, he turned a blind eye. They were very discreet. Uncle Anson did tell me that several years after he had been with Artemis he asked her to marry him. She turned him down. Not because she didn't love him, she told him, but because she loved him too much to ruin his life. She was too selfish, she told him. She needed a man like Gerald who loved her beyond all else in life. She knew my uncle could never sustain a marriage with her. He had his work; he was passionately ambitious, a career diplomat; he had his hobbies, and many women; and she was clever enough to know that he would never be able to give those things up. Another thing: she liked a frivolous life. So did he, but for no more than an hour or two. So they remained friends and lovers.'

'She is a remarkable woman, my mother. She never stops surprising me. She does keep her secrets well.'

'I bet you do too.' The blush that came to her face told him that he had struck home on that assumption. 'It's not a bad thing, you know, to keep a part of your life secret. What law is there to say that you have to reveal yourself to the world? We all retain the right to keep our intimate life for ourselves. Some can, some can't. My uncle took me into his confidence about his affair with Artemis because I am the executor of his will and he wanted me to understand the reason for some aspects of his will pertaining to Artemis: that their thirty years together should not end with the death of either of them. He is in the end the ultimate gentleman and a grand romantic.'

The colour had not gone from Arianne's cheeks and because it had not, Ben was more certain than ever that this lovely lady sitting across from him had yet to reveal herself to him. And that he wanted her to, although there could possibly be more to an affair with Arianne Honey than he was prepared to take on. Love seemed to be stirring, feelings for her he had not anticipated when he had tapped at Artemis's kitchen window to gain her attention. Though to love her seemed both exciting and comforting, was he ready for love again – and what it might lead to? A question he did not care to probe. Once again he retreated, this time by looking at his watch.

Arianne saw a change in Ben's expression. She was enjoying being with him, so much so that the restless look that came into his face upset her. 'Do you have somewhere to go? Am I keeping you?'

Reaching across the table to take her hand in his was instinctive. A spontaneous gesture. He was quick to tell her, 'You're not keeping me. I should like nothing better than to linger over this lunch with you, but I do have to catch a ferry at

Dover this afternoon. You see, I only came over to collect some papers of my uncle's which he had forgotten to send on to the Home Office. His valet, Pandit, was not here to do it; he's with my uncle.'

Arianne covered her disappointment well, 'Ah, then fate and not Christmas has taken me out to lunch.'

'Yes, I suppose you could say that.'

'You'll be having Christmas Day dinner in France?' She was thinking of her goose – how she would have liked making Christmas goose with all the trimmings for him. How lovely it would have been to dine at a table in front of the fire in Artemis's beautiful drawing room, to drink champagne and get tipsy together. She stopped her day-dreaming there, before it went too far. Before she had to face the truth of it: she wanted to be held in Ben Johnson's arms, for him to bring to life those long-dormant sexual feelings she had so revelled in in the past.

'Yes. And where will you be having yours?' He was surprised when she told him.

'In Cairo.'

Chapter 11

There was something surreal about Heathrow on Christmas day:
the twinkling lights of Christmas decorations, the huge, beautiful
but somehow sad Christmas tree with its plastic decorations and
tinsel, its coloured lights and fake decoratively wrapped and
ribboned presents piled too high under it, in the near-deserted
terminal. Maybe because it was surrounded by black metal
bollards with a chain linking them together. Christmas, chained
in, protected against people?

Then there was the incredible emptiness, except for the
Salvation Army band playing Christmas carols sounding more
pathetic than jovial. A cluster of Hare Krishna people, shaking
their tambourines and doing their little dance and usually
boisterous and enthusiastic chant, lacked lustre. Even the irritating
sound, 'ping, ping, ping', which rang constantly on every other
day and night of the year rang out only occasionally over the
tannoy system to bring your attention to the departure board. The
'click, click, click' of the small, square, metal rotating letters and
numbers to announce flights and departure gates appeared to be
working in slow time. The urgency and bustle of mass tourism
and travellers in London's main terminal was gone, because
there was only a trickle of people working or travelling on
Christmas day. And they appeared to be, without that airport
frenzy, disorientated and lost.

Everyone looked as if they were moving in slow motion, as if
their energy had been drained from them: attendants at the check-
in counters leaning on their elbows, looking into space, dreaming
of a Christmas anywhere in the world but where they were;
passengers seemingly confused by the lack of queues, the
boredom of delayed departures. To hear your own heels clicking
on the hard surface of the floors was an eerie sound. Arianne liked
it. She felt adrift in an unreal world where most of the people had

already left for another planet. It was weird, a little frightening, and yet wonderful. An experience to savour. Like stepping into a Magritte painting.

The real world reappeared when Arianne was greeted by a clutch of stewards and stewardesses at the entrance to the plane, all smiles, all systems in place. Life was turned on again. She handed in her boarding pass, but that surrealistic excursion through the terminal still lingered. From Chessington Park and its own special kind of world to this surreal one in a single morning? And there was Cairo to come. Quite a Christmas day, she told herself as she smiled back at the steward and followed him to her seat.

The plane was half full and she had her seat next to the window just behind the first class section – exactly where she liked to be on commercial economy flights. She buckled herself in, and was just getting comfortable when a steward appeared and asked, 'Are you Mrs Honey?'

'Yes, I am,' she answered, surprised that he should know her name.

'We are nearly empty in first class. May we offer you a place there? More comfortable.' The rather senior steward did not miss her hesitation to take up his offer. He bent forward and removed her travelling bag, a large, soft Louis Vuitton weekend case, the only luggage she was travelling with. 'You would be doing us a favour. It would spread our work-load.'

Arianne unbuckled the belt and followed him through the curtains to take yet another window seat. 'Lots of leg-room.' The steward smiled, removed the arm of the seat next to hers and vanished. Once they were airborne, he returned, attached a table to the wall dividing the first-class passenger area from the pilot and his crew, and placed on it a tray with a glass vase and a red rose in it, and a Kir Royale in a large champagne flute, with a small white card placed underneath it. He vanished once again. Puzzled, Arianne looked around and saw the first-class steward and stewardess watching her. Smiles shone broadly on their faces.

She read the card. How did he do it? He was always taking care of her. First class had obviously been on his instructions, as were the Kir Royales and the pot of caviar that followed. The red rose?

142

That too, she thought as she removed it from the vase and sniffed its intoxicating scent. She pondered Ahmad and the network of people at his fingertips that kept his life rolling just the way he wanted it. That was one of the things about him that always intrigued her – his ability to live his life to the fullest with no emotional price-tags. It was one of the most attractive things about him. Now, more than ever, that was what she wanted – that living at the top of your life, as she had done when married to Jason, when she shared a bed with her husband and her lover. She sensed a determination in herself that she had never had before, to do just that. She would no longer wait for someone else to take her along on the joy-ride she knew living could be. She felt her heart thumping, the adrenaline to live rushing through her.

Too many Kir Royales did not mix well with the excitement of her living at the top of a life created by her alone. It sent her into a deep sleep. She came out of it reluctantly and only by the steward's gentle hand on her shoulder. 'Time to fasten your seat belt for landing,' he told her with a smile.

Still in a half sleep, her first thoughts were of Ben and how amusing he had been when, after the pub lunch, he took her back to Chessington House. He had insisted he return her through the kitchen window. 'This is madness,' she had told him while he had struggled to raise the window.

'You think so? Maybe you're right,' he had said as he turned from the now-open window to face her, scoop her off her feet and into his arms and hoist her to the window-ledge where she sat, legs dangling. She was looking at a man much amused by their situation. 'I choose to think of it as romantic. Certainly more fun than confronting raised eyebrows and maybe a directive of some sort. Or a barrage of questions about where my uncle is from one of the residents patrolling the courtyard or manning the front entrance. Will you concede romantic?'

'Churlish of me not to.'

'Good. Then may I call you in London, take you out for something grander than a cottage pie?'

He had memorised her telephone number and kissed her hand before she had swung around to stand up in the kitchen. A final wave and he had gone, before the window had even been closed.

She felt the wheels touch down on the runway with a decided

thump. The force of the brakes cutting speed made the plane shimmy and rattle. She felt herself being pulled forward against the belt holding her tight to her seat. She braced herself with her hands and closed her eyes. She wondered if Ben would remember her telephone number. Would he call her?

At last there was a slow taxi to the terminal and the crackling of the intercom announcing it was safe to release seat belts and passengers were to remain seated until further notice. Not for her it seemed. The steward was there again with her jacket over his arm. He picked up her case and suggested, 'Follow me, Mrs Honey.'

She did, to the first-class exit where the two stewardesses were already assembled. Arianne slipped into the fine-wool, navy-blue, fingertip-length jacket, one of Ralph Lauren's works of art. It looked like a naval attaché's jacket of a period from the past made for the now chic and stylish woman of the nineties, with its handsome gold needlework around the stiff collar and bands of the same gold-work on the cuffs. She was wearing it over wide, white flannel trousers and a white silk-knit pullover with a crew neck trimmed in navy blue grosgrain ribbon. While doing up the gold buttons she was thinking, In a few minutes this door will open and I will be back in my beloved Egypt, and with Ahmad. All else – her yearning for independence and the will to leap into life alone, even Ben – seemed suddenly pallid beside Egypt and Ahmad and a boat race on the Nile.

Locks were released, a wheel on the door spun round and the door was manhandled open. Warm air rushed in. Arianne sighed. She felt terribly happy. It was involuntary, the smile that came to her lips and brought a twinkle of delight to her eyes. The gangway of stairs was advancing towards the door. The crew were chatting, and then suddenly stopped as a black Rolls-Royce advanced slowly towards the aircraft.

'I hope you had a good flight?' asked the steward.

'Yes, very. I think a special thank you might be in order,' she answered.

The steward beamed. She had taken notice of the efforts he had made on her behalf. Knowing smiles appeared on the stewardesses's faces as well. She cynically wondered how often the steward was retained by Ahmad on passion missions. One of the things that had always kept her and her two lovers together was that none of them ever deluded themselves about each other.

The stairway was bumped and locked into place against the plane and a ground-crewman ran up the stairs to check them out and deliver a message. 'Mrs Honey?'

'Yes, I am Mrs Honey.'

The man waved to someone on the ground and the chauffeur alighted immediately from the car and opened the rear door. Then Arianne caught sight of one of Ahmad's personal assistants, Abdol. She knew him well. From the front passenger seat she saw the huge bulk of Muhammad unfold and walk towards the gangway. He was Ahmad's bodyguard-cum-valet and had been with Ahmad for more than twenty years – devoted to Ahmad, all secrets were safe with him. Arianne was happy to see him. He had cared for them all, and only he knew how intimate their lives had been with each other. For one moment Arianne half expected to turn around and find Jason standing behind her. *Déjà vu.* She shrugged off the strange sensation of having lived this moment once before. She told herself: No more of that nonsense. Jason is gone, and you know it. Nothing to be gained by living for a ghost. You're over that. There's no relapse here, only the appearance of Muhammad. A reminder of other times.

The tall, hugely muscular Egyptian had the face of a simple, kindly soul. Most men retreated from him in any confrontation because of the enormous strength and power of his physique. He had been devoted to her husband – maybe not so much as to Ahmad, but there did seem to have been a close bond of loyalty to Jason.

Arianne felt really happy to see him again. She waved to the two men, but not before, almost without realising it, she had turned around to look over her shoulder.

Abdol raced up the gangway, a broad smile on his face. He took her hand in his and kissed it. 'How very nice to see you in Egypt again.'

'It's been a long time, Abdol. I'm really pleased to be back. The race – am I in time for it?'

'In time to catch up with it,' he told her as they walked together down the steps to Muhammad waiting on the tarmac to greet her.

'Oh, damn. But nothing ever happens on time in Egypt. I banked on that.'

'Egypt is changing.'

'Surely not that much?'

'Well, if truth be told, not that much. Ahmad put the starting time forward by three hours, so they actually did leave at the old starting time. Well, two hours after that.'

They both began to laugh at Ahmad's wiliness and the impossibility of anything happening on time in Egypt. 'Never mind,' and a shrug of the shoulders. '*Malaish*,' he repeated in Arabic. That was always the password in Egypt when things went wrong: *malaish*, the perfect antidote to frustration.

Arianne stepped on to the tarmac and shook hands with Muhammad. His usually impassive face changed almost imperceptibly – Muhammad's version of a smile. They walked to the Rolls and there another old acquaintance, the chauffeur, removed his hat in greeting. During her many visits to the country these three men had always been in charge of Arianne when Jason and Ahmad were off doing something that did not include her – family retainers, ever kind and helpful for anything she wanted. Ahmad knew how to make a woman feel safe, cared for, even when he wasn't there.

She got into the back seat with Abdol, who asked for her passport. He handed it over to Muhammad, who was sitting in the front, and the car sped across the tarmac to a gate. Muhammad alighted from the car to stand next to a man in a small shed. They exchanged a few words. Arianne heard the sound of the stamp as it hit the passport. The entire operation took less than a minute. Once through the now-open gate, they sped recklessly through the traffic around the airport towards Cairo.

The windows were rolled down to admit the scent of Egypt, the unseasonable heat from a waning sun, the crazy horn-blowing traffic, the tinkling sound of harness bells, and the rhythmic clip-clop of hooves on tarmac of the occasional donkey and overloaded flat-cart, driven by the *galabiyah*'d and turbaned men. They drove past a group of women draped from head to toe in black cotton, not a hair showing from under tightly wrapped headscarves, with bangles on their wrists, and kohl accentuating their dark eyes, hands on ample hips, their sensuous bottoms wobbling fleshily as they took long strides, while balancing bundles on their heads. Those women and the children trailing behind, walking towards the metropolis, served as reminder to Arianne of how far removed she had been from life, and Egypt and Ahmad, for too long.

She made polite conversation with Abdol, but failed to ask him any of the things she really wanted to know. She was preoccupied with thoughts about the race and Ahmad, too excited to ask even about them, anxious only to get there and join it.

Several miles from the airport the car swerved off the main road to a secondary road that seemed to be cutting across country. Almost instantly everything appeared to be more rural. Strange, because she knew that this was still the outskirts of Cairo. But Cairo was like that: partly a metropolis, partly the largest, most over-populated village one could imagine; concrete and the Nile and its verdant banks; its smart and not-so-smart endless suburbs; and then the desert. Glorious Cairo. With the Cairenes the sweetest and least complex people of all the Arab world.

And now the Rolls took a sharp turn on to a dirt track. It slowed down: the motor purred. So soft was the ride over the bumpy road that it seemed there was a cushion of foam between the tyres and the dirt track. They passed through a poor village that appeared to be deserted. Arianne found that strange. It was difficult to find an empty village in Egypt – they seemed always to be filled with old men, women swathed in black cotton and happy, smiling children at play. They passed planted fields, bright green with a crop. She sensed they were near the river, in that strip of fertile soil between the Nile and the desert that produces four crops a year.

Another sharp turn and she saw it, the Nile. They were just on the edge of the city, where Cairo stretched back as far as one could see: a low, concrete jumble of buildings, shining white against the horizon and broken by minarets and the odd tower block against a still-bright blue sky. Arianne felt a surge of excitement at the sight. She should have thought it ugly from where she was viewing it, but that was impossible for anyone who knew the city that could capture the heart and never let it go. Beyond her vision she could see in her mind's eye, on the other side of Cairo, the

147

Sphinx and the three great pyramids of Egypt, and the desert further off; Egypt of the past through various of its glorious periods. The Mosques of Ahmed Ibn Tulun and Kalaun, the El-Azthar Mosque or Blue Mosque, the statue of Rameses II ... The flowering trees, parks and palm trees, some bursting with clumps of dates ... And could one forget the museums and their Pharaonic and Coptic treasures? The step pyramids of Saqqara?

All this was the background of the extraordinary sight of scores of feluccas a quarter of a mile or so down-river under a winter afternoon sun, gliding full sail south to Upper Egypt. They were spread out nearly the full width of the Nile, navigating the tricky currents, seeking stronger winds from a favourable direction. They seemed still to be jockeying for position. Arianne wondered where Ahmad's felucca was. There was a big entry, that was for sure. The Nile looked nearly solid with sail for some distance back towards Cairo. Arianne felt the thrill of the race, of being in Egypt, of being a part of it and Ahmad's life. She had that marvellous facility of being able to abandon herself to the moment, the experience and nothing else. She felt very alive and vital, incredibly excited and happy. She was right there in the moment.

They were on an even more narrow track now, running parallel with the river. On its banks were groups of people, jabbering excitedly. The missing villagers, thought Arianne. So that was where they had all gone, to wait for the race of the feluccas. Several hundred yards on the car stopped at a dangerously dilapidated dock that stretched out from the bank into the Nile. Tied to it was a large Chris Craft motor-boat, with two men standing at the wheel and another at the rear of the boat looking out for their arrival. He waved. And before the Rolls even cut its motor, the Chris Craft's burst into life.

The passengers were quickly out of the car and on the edge of the dock. There was a great deal of fussing as to whether the dock would hold the weight of them all, and then more fussing about how to get Arianne down into the Chris Craft. But once one of the men in the boat had made it clear they had to get a move on or they would miss their chance to get Arianne on the felucca, all safety was abandoned and they marched on to the rickety dock. The chauffeur tossed Arianne's travelling bag down the twelve feet to one of the men in the boat. He caught it and stowed it away.

'How am I going to get down there?' asked Arianne.

Abdol looked very concerned as he told her, 'Ahmad has worked it all out.'

Much shouting of instructions and arm-waving between the men in the boat and the men on the dock followed. It did little to put Arianne at ease. But she stood there patiently, leaving them to work it out, her eyes fixed on the fleet of sails coming up-river. The Chris Craft was disengaged from the dock and was manoeuvring into a new position. Finally Abdol approached her. 'OK.'

'OK what, Abdol?'

'Just relax. You don't have to do a thing. Muhammad is going to lift you up and lower you over the side. Then at just the right moment he'll drop you. Ali will catch you. You'll see.'

'What if he misses, Abdol?'

'That's not in the plan.'

'A ladder would be easier.'

Muhammad approached her. 'You trust me,' he told her. Then, he looked at her shoes, evidently seeing them as the only complication. She removed them. Before she realised it he had swept her off her feet with a vice-like grip around her waist, her back drawn in against him. He walked to the edge of the dock and lowered Arianne over the boat below, lower and lower as he went from standing to kneeling on the dock. Then, moving his hands to under her arms, he slowly lay flat out. She felt foolish dangling in mid-air with her shoes in her hand – foolish, but not unsafe. Ali in the bobbing boat, arms raised, awaited the right moment, found it and gave the shout. She dropped several feet. He made a perfect catch. It all happened so fast that Arianne barely had time to turn round to see Muhammad scrambling down the rotting wooden piles to grab Ali's outstretched arm and leap into the Chris Craft after her. Handshakes and smiles as the pilot revved its motors and shot out on to the river. Abdol and the chauffeur shrank to small figures in the distance in what seemed a matter of seconds.

To those on the banks of the river it must have seemed as if the speed-boat had been devoured by the feluccas. It vanished among the fleet of wooden boats and triangular sails in search of

Ahmad's felucca. Twice they circled crafts to ask where in the race Ahmad was lying and shot off again to find him in mid-fleet. She waved frantically to him and was thrilled by the look of pleasure on his face at seeing her. He was dressed in a pair of worn jeans and a denim shirt, with a red knitted sleeveless waistcoat over it. Around his neck a navy-blue cotton scarf with white dots was tied in a knot. He looked extremely handsome, very much the odd man out among the crew in their long white robes and turbans. But then again he seemed to belong, if not exactly where he was, most certainly in the exotic and privileged Egypt he was born to. His olive-coloured skin, black hair, sultry dark and sensuous eyes, all proclaimed unmistakably that he was Egyptian. Arianne felt not that she was seeing him for the first time, but that she was discovering him for the first time – a strange sensation for one who had once known him so intimately.

There were no greetings: haste forbade it. Everyone seemed bent on getting her on to the felucca. She assumed that the felucca was going to drop anchor and they would one way or another get her on board. No such thing. To bring her aboard the Chris Craft, there had been much chaos and shouting. There was none of that now. She knew the reason: it was Ahmad's presence. Silently he demanded with utter authority that the job be done, quickly and with exactness. Everyone moved into position. Scarcely a word passed between them. Arianne, guided by Muhammad's hand on her elbow, stood where he placed her. She and Ahmad engaged each other's eyes while the speed-boat pulled parallel to the felucca and a mere six inches away from it. Tension. A palpable fear in the men of failing in their task. The fear emanated from Ahmad's presence. Never before had she seen this hardness, such ruthlessness in him. But it was there, in his eyes. It gave her a fright, made her shiver. She grasped her hands and held them together to calm herself. Then it passed, this fear of Ahmad, as quickly as it had come. She saw in his gaze simply the smiling, sexy man who wanted her. She put the unpleasant flash of fear and mistrust out of her mind and attributed the experience to her own fear of being injured while boarding the felucca.

Success in the manoeuvre demanded that the pilot match the speed of the felucca and then maintain it exactly. No easy task when one vessel was under sail, the other powered by turbo engines. What seemed an age passed, though in reality the pilot's expertise quickly achieved the manoeuvre. Her hand luggage was tossed aboard the felucca, then her shoes. Two men stood next to one another on the felucca and leaned against the side of the boat, then Muhammad, without warning, hoisted her on to one shoulder and climbed on to the Chris Craft's rail. He found his balance and kept it steady against the light winds. There was no time for Arianne even to muster her courage against her fear. She gathered what little daring she had before she was grabbed by the two men on the felucca and swung on to the deck.

Ahmad loved it. He clapped his hands and shouted thanks to the men in the Chris Craft, who waved to them both. The men's expression declared their admiration for Arianne and how she had handled herself. That same admiration was evident in Ahmad's face when he pulled her into his arms and gave her a huge hug. Together they watched the speed-boat shoot away. They felt the swell of the waves slap against the side of the felucca, rocking it.

'You never let me down,' he told her.

'I think it's called trust; I always trust you to get it right for me,' she told him – hoping he was unaware that her knees were still shaking and her legs felt like over-cooked noodles.

'You're here and safe and we never lost speed. Quite an accomplishment. And . . .'

'*And,* what?'

He placed an arm round her and whispered in her ear while walking her the few paces to Muhammad, who had somehow scrambled on board behind her: '*And* we are going to discover each other as we have never done. Before this voyage is over you'll be mine as you have never been. I want to lay all this . . .' – he waved an arm and she followed it with her eyes. She took in, once again, the grandeur, beauty and passion of the Nile, the many felucca sails in the soft, warm wind, the banks of green and the desert emptiness beyond, the clear blue sky. She sensed the mystery and intrigue of Egypt, the present, the past. An Egypt of the gods of antiquity, where life and death were entwined and revered – ' . . . at your feet. So we can vanish together from the world and prying eyes. There's a special, secret world I have planned for you.'

Seductive words. The promise in them . . . Arianne felt herself being drawn into his desire for her. 'Is that where I want to be?' she might have asked. Was there no hint of the sinister in his whisperings? But the time, the place, the man, were too attractive. She heard only what she wanted to hear, innuendoes of sensual delight, the appeal of love.

Chapter 12

Arianne took a position in the bow of the felucca out of the crew's way. For the next few hours she and Ahmad put aside erotic yearnings while he and his crew jockeyed for position in the race. Periodically he would return to her, to place an arm around her shoulder and to point out their objectives, their rivals for a better position.

'You sail as if you were playing chess,' she told him, while she snuggled close into him, very happy to be in the race, but no less so to be in his arms.

'And like a warrior going into battle.'

'Yes, there's very much that side of you.'

'I always give everything – never less than my best shot. You know that, Arianne.'

'And the lengths to which you will go to win. I know that too.' She gave him a seductive smile. She had a frame of reference. Many times in the past, Arianne had seen him take extraordinary chances for something he wanted, or a prize he must win. Though he was a good loser, he was a much better winner.

The smile had been a flirtatious innuendo. She had been thinking of his erotic game-playing – the lengths she had seen him go to in winning a woman away from another man; the seemingly endless sensual pleasures he created for Arianne to keep her enthralled. He did not miss the allusion. It amused him that she thought she knew him well. And she did. Yet not so well as she believed. After all that had passed between them, she still had little idea of what he was capable of, when provoked. And she had provoked him once, by remaining in her deliriously happy marriage, despite learning that Jason had deceived her with another woman. In his heart Ahmad had hoped she would leave Jason for him; transfer to him such undying love and adoration.

153

Shortly before Jason's death, Ahmad had sensed a change in him. Arianne had been blinded to it. Whatever the problem was, Jason did not allow it to disturb his marriage, which remained as solid and happy as ever. But Ahmad knew Jason very well. The signs were there. Something decidedly shady was afoot and a sexual restlessness Ahmad had not seen in Jason since before he had met and fallen in love with Arianne. It disturbed Ahmad. It was threatening the sexual *ménage à trois*, and he had no intention of letting that happen. Ahmad was too deeply committed to the licentiousness the relationship produced. It made all the other women and whores, the orgies he frequented, pale beside the erotic excitement the sexual triangle sated themselves upon. It also endangered his love affair with Arianne, and his role in a marriage he had become part of – a marriage that in a bizarre way was just as much his as theirs.

The girl was an eighteen-year-old, half black American, half Mexican beauty: dark and exotic with long, straight black hair to her waist; tall and slender as a reed, with voluptuous breasts; an impressive triangle of black pubic hair between long, slender and shapely legs that enfolded a wildly seductive cunt. Ahmad, having discovered them together, had watched Jason in the grip of lust for the girl. He could understand it. She was young, breathtakingly beautiful, and lewd.

Jason penetrated her again and again ruthlessly. With violent passion he heard her plead for everything sexual to be done to her and performed accordingly. At her bidding he sodomised her, evoking cries of pleasure and protestations of love and passion for his sexual prowess. She knew what it took to excite sexual pleasure in a libertine such as Jason. She led him further and further into a maddened desire for the ultimate orgasm into oblivion. Arora Rivera moved over, around and under Jason like a large jungle cat, a sleek panther. Together they were rutting beasts. Ahmad had listened to her demands, and to Jason professing undying love for her – and promising to run away with her.

Ahmad, having watched them long enough from the shadows of the balcony, had walked in on them. He had removed his clothes and joined them. Jason was angry but unsurprised at the intrusion. Jason's and Ahmad's eyes had met. The protest was there in Jason's, but it found no words. It was the girl who objected. Jason talked the girl out of hysterics and into accepting them both. Then he held her in his arms. She took his erect penis whole in her mouth, while Ahmad mounted her and they fucked in a passion for sex and the intoxicating sensation of orgasm to the exclusion of all else. Ahmad knew very well what he was doing: destroying Jason's love for the dark temptress. There were no doubts in his mind that Jason, besotted by her, was crazed by a new love. But Ahmad was a devil in sex and knew well how to manipulate men's lust for it. Skilled at destroying love? None did it better.

Several hours later, Ahmad saw the change in Jason. Gone was the role of lover he had been playing: the libertine Ahmad knew him to be shone in Jason's face. 'She's not a whore, you know, Ahmad,' Jason had said, somewhat pathetically.

Ahmad had answered, 'She is now, Jason. Unless you're prepared to give up Arianne and a marriage that is rare and has given you happiness and stability – Arianne's kind of love that asks nothing and gives everything. That's something neither of us has ever seen, let alone experienced in any other woman. Have you considered the loss?' Clearly he hadn't. Ahmad could see in Jason's eyes that, confronted with the possibility of such a loss, there was no contest.

The two men used the girl for the next few hours. Then Ahmad charmed her into making a visit to a friend of his in Saudi Arabia, where, he assured her, she would be well cared for and happy. It took a great deal of talking by Jason to persuade the girl to go; promises, too, that only he and Ahmad knew Jason would never fulfil.

Ahmad thought about that incident now as he drank in Arianne's insinuating smile. That had been the first time in his life he had experienced real jealousy. He hadn't liked the feeling. It had also made him come to terms with the fact that he was not getting enough love from Arianne. He wanted more. Only his close relationship and love for his best friend had calmed him enough to accept happiness in what he could get from Arianne and the *ménage à trois*. However, somewhere deep in his psyche lurked an obsession to possess Arianne to an even greater degree than ever Jason had. He nurtured a plan. One way or another he would find a way to exchange places with Jason in her affections.

Ever since that breakfast at Claridge's he had known she would come to him. And when she did, it would be because the past was finally dead for them. She would be ready to live again and to want him more than any other man. Three years is a long time to starve a voracious libido. The sexual fire was raging in her, he had no doubt about that, nor about how much she wanted to give herself up to Ahmad and everything sexual. She was there in the bow of the felucca with him because she was ready to begin again. 'Dead is dead,' he wanted to shout. 'And when we reach Luxor you will give me that same love and devotion you gave Jason, which I have coveted for so long.'

He pulled Arianne into his arms; he studied her face and touched her lips with his finger, caressing her lower lip with its tip, until she slowly parted them and sucked his finger into her mouth. How warm, moist and silky smooth was the inside of her lips as she sucked and ran her tongue around his finger. That cool and quiet beauty of hers, clothed in her Ralph Lauren elegance, sucking him so sensually. He gazed into her large grey eyes and could see in them the glimmer of lust that had been absent from them for far too long. She was slipping into that special kind of sexiness he knew she was so capable of enjoying. That finger in her mouth was cock – they both knew it was what she wished. He hugged her closer into him. 'You feel so good in my arms,' he told her and pressed a light, affectionate kiss on her lips. He could feel the hunger in her kiss, how much more she wanted from him. He liked her most when she was sexually hungry. He wanted her much more hungry for him than she was now. He would bide his time. He would cunt-tease her, toy with her, prime her with his seductive ways, his masculine charm. He wanted their return to lust and love and depravity to be splendiferous, beyond anything they had experienced together before.

He slipped his fingers in between the stiff, high collar of her jacket and her neck and he ran them round her neck, a sensuous caress that made her close her eyes and sigh. He unhooked the collar and several buttons of her jacket to make it easy. Reaching inside the jacket, he caressed a naked breast under the silk-knit pullover. She felt so good in his hands.

It was dizzyingly exciting to be petted by him on deck in the light breeze, racing against the other sails; to feel the pitch and roll of the felucca, the buzz of the race; to hear the flapping of the sails, the shouts of excitement in that oh-so-seductive Arabic; to see the thrill of people rushing about on the other boats to manoeuvre and challenge, with their own crew too busy to take notice of any passion but that of sailing up the Nile.

'I promised myself I would not allow you to be a distraction. And I am already distracted.' He removed his hand and buttoned up her jacket, hooked the high collar and smiled at her. 'But tonight is different. Every night it will be different. We will sail only from sun-up to sundown and then . . .'

'And then?'

Arianne wanted reassurance. He had to want her as much as she wanted him. That was important for her. 'We'll begin a Nile odyssey that neither of us will ever forget. Isn't that why you're here?'

Arianne hardly knew how to answer that. It was of course true, although she hadn't thought about her visit to Ahmad exactly in those terms. A series of wanderings? A long, adventurous journey? That was what an odyssey was. And she had to face the truth: she was there because that was exactly what she wanted, a sexual odyssey with Ahmad as her Ulysses. She had thought she had come to Egypt to be with him, to find love again. She did so miss being in love and marriage. Could she have been so wrong about her intentions? Once again, without realising it, she had allowed Ahmad to take her over, seduce her into the erotic world she so craved. Love and marriage seemed suddenly not so important, because she knew they might follow. Certainly love with Ahmad had once before. She could happily settle for that if there was to be nothing else for them.

She gazed into Ahmad's eyes. They promised sexual ecstasy and excited her imagination as to what was to come. Arianne placed her arms around his neck, her lips upon his. She licked his lips with her tongue and then kissed them. Her own lips trembled with anticipation. He placed his hands on her waist and pulled her gently towards him, rubbing her sensually against himself. He handled her body as if she were clay to be moulded to his will. She adored being created by him.

She gently pushed him away. She was flushed, and when she spoke there was a tremor of passion in her voice. 'Yes, that's why I'm here.'

He caressed the shoulder-length, chestnut-coloured hair and smiled seductively at her. 'It's a long time since I've heard lust in your voice.' He stepped nearer to her. Gazing at her, he placed an arm around her shoulders. 'I actually feared I would never hear it again. How good it sounds. I've waited a long time for you to return to me.'

Arianne felt weak-kneed. She wanted to weep with joy from the sheer relief of no longer being alone, of feeling once again that rage to live, at no matter what price had to be paid to do so. 'You want me?' Her eyes sparkled with life; she felt so very much alive.

'I always want you. I can never get enough of you. But this time round I want all of you and just for me.' With that, he raised her hand and lowered his head to place a kiss on it, then he was gone, back to his crew and sailing his felucca.

Arianne turned away from him to face into the wind. She placed her outstretched fingers at the temples of her head and ran them through her hair, pressing hard against her head. It felt good to take hold of herself. She thought she might otherwise dissolve into a pool of lust for Ahmad. Her mind was filled with erotic fantasies of long, luxurious orgasms, repressed longings set free by Ahmad, things carnal that she had thought were behind her forever, ended by the death of Jason. She sighed, happy, excited that sexual adventure had re-entered her life: desire, passion, the waters of life.

She sat on a timber that protruded from the side of the felucca and lost herself, less in erotic thought than in the sensational sight of the lateen sails making headway up the Nile. The sun was low on the horizon and the desert had replaced Cairo and its suburbs. Ten days to two weeks to Luxor, that was what it would take to win the race. Ten glorious days of sailing on the Nile by day and slipping into an erotic world with Ahmad by night. The *Osiris*, Ahmad's felucca, was sailing all-out, surrounded by the other boats. Arianne made a full circle where she stood, wanting to absorb it all. Reality and the outside world were fast receding from her thoughts. They seemed so pale and distant, so empty and

158

loveless. What need had she for that world when she could feel as alive as she did at that moment in the bosom of Egypt, in the arms of Ahmad?

Her last thought of that empty world that had given her such a hard and lonely life these last few years, was not of anything or anyone that she was leaving behind. Or so she thought until sometime later, as dusk was closing in on the river, when Ahmad walked up behind her to wrap his arms around her waist. For a brief moment Ben Johnson's handsome face, the warmth and macho charm he exuded, flashed before her. The vision was dimmed by a kiss on the back of her neck, a lick of Ahmad's tongue on her ear-lobe, a whisper of love: 'I adore you. I have always adored you. But seeing you here, alone with me on the Nile, that adoration is different. It's more acute, if that is possible, more intense.'

He slipped a hand under her jacket and down beneath the waist-band of her trousers to caress naked flesh. Delighted that she was as he had always demanded of her in the past, naked, without undergarments, ready and waiting for him, he moved his hands down further to caress her voluptuous mound of dark, curly pubic hair. Fingers searched between her cunt lips and found her clitoris. He teased and tormented it with the thrill of masturbation. He felt his own excitement mounting. She could always do that for him when he had her in his power. How she loved being dominated by sex, in any form he could deliver. She embodied for him that lethal combination of a lady in the salon, a depraved whore in bed. How he loved her for that, and for knowing that there was always more that he could get from her. Arianne's kind of love and passion gave and gave, until the last. And that was what drove his desire to take her further and further into sexual depravity.

'I'm going to mark you for life with the sex and passion I feel for you. Bathe you in my come. Whip you raw with lust. Share you with no one. Make you my erotic slave, a prisoner of love': Ahmad's whispered words. Ben Johnson was gone, an apparition, a stranger, an interlude that now hardly seemed to have happened. He might never have existed.

Ahmad and Arianne remained locked together in their lust under the cover of dusk until it turned dark. Several times he

159

removed his arm from round her waist to place his hand over her mouth as he felt her body tense, and her cunt muscles contract, grip tight and moisten his always caressing, masturbating fingers with soft, warm orgasms. He quelled the cries of pleasure he sensed she would be unable to hold back. And he had been right. So powerful, and divine was the sensation of ecstasy, that she replaced her need to call out by biting hard into his hand. He didn't care. He hardly felt it; he was enjoying her too much. She was female lust that he could mould any way he liked for their mutual pleasure, and he adored having her that way. It fed his libido, his ego, his sexual fantasies, the dark side of his nature. He kissed her on the side of her neck, and whispered in her ear as he removed his hand from her mouth, never stopping for even a second his possession of her clitoris under the pad of his index finger:

'To all those eyes watching us, we look like sail-race aficionados standing together, enthralled by the event and nothing more. Again?'

She could hardly speak – she was that much out of control, her breathing erratic, a tremor in her voice: 'Not here, not now.'

He laughed. 'Oh, yes. Right here, and now,' he whispered in her ear. 'Don't be afraid, let go. I'll see your orgasms don't give us away, I promise. Now, once more I'll ask you. Again? Shall I bring you on again?'

All the while he was whispering in her ear. His cunt caresses never stopped, and when she answered breathlessly, 'Yes,' he knew he was in possession of her. That excited the situation for them both. He wanted more of her than he was getting. Without warning, he thrust all the digits of his hand except his thumb, which he now placed on her clitoris, as deeply inside Arianne as he could. He rubbed his cheek against hers, kissed her there and on the nape of her neck and once more cruelly demanded in a whisper now hungry with lust for her, 'Yes, what?'

His hand around her waist again, he pulled her hard against his chest. 'Yes, what?' he repeated.

'Yes, please.' She knew what he wanted to hear.

He wanted her to beg for his sexual favours – he loved it when Arianne begged. It was no game with her, as it was with most women. Genuine lust and desire for him and all the ways he knew

160

how to make her come was what motivated her. But this was not the time or the place. Later that night, when the men were sleeping on shore . . .

Ahmad was a hardened libertine. He was also a great lover. He pondered: had he ever known another woman to come in multiple orgasms both visual and sexual? For that was what it was like for Arianne – his possession of her while enthralled by the beauty of the feluccas all around her, the Nile, the desert stretching out seemingly to eternity, the falling of dusk, that eerie blueish-grey swallowed up by the blackness of night, a near-full silver moon, and a sky studded with stars.

Lanterns were lit. A boy stretched out across the rail at the bow of the *Osiris* and swung a lantern back and forth, looking for obstructions in the river. Only then did Ahmad release Arianne. One by one the feluccas had pulled in towards the banks of the Nile to drop anchor until the dawn light would allow them to sail. The *Osiris* sailed on in the dark for as long as the crew dared. They and their captain took chances that only daring and well-experienced Nile sailors could possibly attempt. Ahmad and his captain and crew conferred. Excitement on board mounted as they bettered their position when the other feluccas fell back to drop anchor for the night.

Arianne, alone at the rail where Ahmad had left her, felt as if she were floating through some wonderful dream. She was in that region of sexual bliss where only the present, the life in every moment, was to be lived and nothing more. Now she had the excitement, the pulse of danger in the adventure of sailing in the dark, to engage her passion. She watched the men and particularly Ahmad scuttling about the felucca, listened to orders she could not understand, and was caught up in the thrill that only sailing against the elements and in competition can engender. Quite suddenly it was over. The sail was dropped and they headed in towards the bank where they too dropped anchor.

A new kind of excitement enveloped the men: pride and pleasure in having accomplished their objectives for the first day on the river. She watched them in the lantern light as they slapped one another on the back, and chattered about the day's sailing. The glee in their faces was unmistakable. There was something extraordinarily sweet about the camaraderie among them, even in the rough way the men handled themselves.

Arianne had hardly realised how much the temperature had changed. Here was the real chill of a winter night on the Nile. The men had brought out a brazier. Flames leaped up in the dark. Ahmad returned to her to take her hand and lead her to warm herself. Then she became fully aware of the cold.

More lanterns were lit. The cook set up his pots around the brazier. Several men were raising a black bedouin tent at the stern of the felucca. A plank was laid at a steep angle from the rail of the felucca to the bank of the river. Up and down the river several bonfires were already lit. Arianne could imagine other crews cooking and sitting or sleeping around them, anxiously awaiting the dawn.

Muhammad joined Ahmad and Arianne to wrap around her a huge cashmere shawl delicately embroidered with flowers. It reached to the ground. Ahmad took over and draped her in it, tossing one end over her shoulder. The two men spoke, Ahmad looking very happy. Whatever was said had brought a smile to his lips.

'Something you can share with me?' she asked.

He kissed her on the cheek, and answered, 'Yes, look over there.' Just then, on the bank about a hundred yards up-river, yet another bonfire burst aflame. Shouts of approval from the crew.

'That means the crew can sleep on shore and I can have you all to myself. We can do all sorts of exciting things to each other in privacy.'

'You planned it, the bonfire.'

'I did,' he said proudly. 'But, I must admit, not just for you. One finds little driftwood on the Nile. I had a boat-load of firewood sent up-river to lay bonfires for the competitors in case they wanted some warmth to sleep by. All a captain has to do is to look at his map. The location of the fuel is marked on it.'

They were gazing at each other in the firelight and Arianne could not help feeling he had done this, yes, for the men in the race – but more for her. She would not let him off so easily. She needed him to know that she was aware how much he wanted her, the lengths he would go to so they could be alone together. 'I don't remember bonfires on shore in the other races.' A deliberate note of asperity was in her words.

'I'm always trying to improve the organisation of the race,' he told her.

It was such a little thing, the slight change in the tone of his voice. An inflection. The way he looked away from her when he said it. Annoyance? She was teasing, playing a game. He was not. She should have left it at that, but she didn't. Or she couldn't. Something made her press on. 'I have always admired the way you conspire for people's pleasure. Most especially *ours*, *yours* and mine.'

The flames in the brazier leaped into the darkness like red tongues. The wood crackled, spat, and sprayed showers of fire that were extinguished the moment they hit the cold air. Miniature fireworks. They made the moment maybe more dramatic than it was meant to be. But she had spoken a truth that she had always found exciting. She meant it to be a sexy compliment for him. She wanted him, too, to understand that she was aware of how much *he* as well as she enjoyed the erotic life he created for them. Wanting to feel the warmth of his body up against her, she slipped her arm through his and stepped in closer to him. She continued, 'There is a plot. I sense that and . . .'

He did not allow her to finish her sentence. He removed his arm from hers and stepped back a pace. His face was half in shadow, half in the firelight. He seemed surprised, shocked even. The way he looked at her took her aback momentarily. 'What exactly do you mean by that?' he asked.

What had she said to upset him? She felt confused by his reaction. His anger was like a slap across her face. Hers was at best a shy personality, a repressed one that only shone and became overt in the arms of a man who loved her, wanted her sexually. That somehow set her free to do and say everything her hidden passions desired. Jason and Ahmad had been the only two people who had ever allowed her that. She felt his disapproval, his retreat, instantly. All joy, all those lovely sensual feelings she was experiencing, were extinguished. Her answer was automatic. She finished the sentence she had begun. 'I sense that, and a plot full of surprises, twists and turns, to add to our adventure.'

Ahmad could see the hurt in her eyes. He wanted to bite his tongue. Had his brain stopped working? How could she possibly have discovered his secret plotting: what he had done, what he was now doing with Jim O'Connor to ensure that he would one day possess her as Jason had, a hundred per cent of herself to him, and for all the world to see? He had, of course, not been discovered. It had been nothing more than that stupid word, plot. He had not thought of it as part of Arianne's vocabulary. She was the least devious person in the world, and incapable of thinking of anyone else as devious, or involved in secret plotting. He had had her, sexually, was controlling her through passion and lust, and he had nearly blown it. All because it was still not enough for him – he wanted more from her, her very life.

He took possession of himself, and, filled with an overpowering desire to possess her once again, all he wanted was to make Arianne happy. He stepped in close to her and swept her off her feet into his arms. He shouted something to the men and then told her, 'I told them we'll be back to dine with them. I must, they would be offended if I didn't. They would never understand my passing up a meal for a mere woman I happen to be passionately devoted to. One I adore and yearn to make love to.' He was walking with her towards the black bedouin tent at the stern of the felucca. She was tense and withdrawn in his arms. He stopped. 'Put your arms around my neck,' he suggested. She did not move. 'Please.' There was a softness once again in his voice, a passionate glint in his eyes that was for her alone. She could see it in the light of the lantern hanging on a hook on the boat's mast. The handsome, seductive face so close to hers, his sensuous lips – they made her bite the corner of her own bottom lip, something she did when she was disturbed. She felt herself slipping under his spell. She held back as best she could.

'What happened to us back there? What did I do to upset you? Why did you abandon me?' she asked. Tears of anxiety mixed with passion brimmed in her eyes as she obeyed him and did place her arms around his neck.

'You did nothing, my dear heart. Nothing, I promise you. For a brief moment, I was distracted by something that crossed my mind – it came between us and is now gone. But it had nothing to do with us.' He didn't care that he was lying to her, not in the least, so long as he could get her back to where she had been, erotically charged and ready, wanting him to take her further into a sexual tryst with him.

164

He pulled her close into him and placed a kiss on her lips. She sensed his mouth trembling with need. She had experienced kisses like that from him before – times when he had wanted her so much that he found he could barely control himself. It reminded her, too, of other times, when they were so steeped in sexual depravity that they had lost themselves and he had given himself up to her, willingly become *her* sexual slave. He kissed her now on her cheeks, and when she closed her eyes, he kissed the lids, licked them with his tongue and then sought her lips again with a greater passion. Between kisses, he bit passionately into her lips until she relented and returned his kisses. A triumph to have broken down her defences, to feel her, at first hesitantly and then with that same old hunger for him, return his kisses. He licked the roof of her mouth. They sucked each other's tongues. All resistance gone, she went limp in his arms. He walked with her thus to the tent where Muhammad stood.

Arianne wanted to weep with joy – simply at being where she was, passionately involved and in his arms. For the way they wanted each other. For nothing having gone wrong between them. Muhammad raised the flap and Ahmad walked into the tent with Arianne still in his arms. Still kissing her.

He had had inklings of it before, the antipathy he sometimes felt about Arianne. The not-quite deep, abiding love, not-quite hate, to which his passion for her drove him. There was love in those kisses, animosity in the way his fingers pressed hard into her flesh. He loved her for the excitement she brought to their sex life, passion that knew no bounds. Yet he resented her because she had for years managed to hold him to her in love as no other woman had ever done. Because she had power over him. And because he still could not get from her the utter love and abandonment to him that she was capable of – that had been reserved for Jason. But that conflict of love he felt for Arianne was being dealt with by a master of manipulation. He converted it into lust and enjoyed, instead of anxiety for what he could not get from her, the sexual power that he did have over her. They were both enamoured of each other because of it.

Arianne heard the tent flap drop into place. He ravaged her with kisses as she lay in his arms, sucked in the flesh at the side of her neck. She found the buttons of his jeans, to feel his flesh

165

in her hands at last. She wrapped her fingers round his penis. Long and soft and thick, she kneaded it as delicately as if her fingers were feathers. With her other hand she reached down under it and cupped the soft sac containing his testicles. They filled the palm of her hand. She caressed them, toyed with them, rolled them gently between thumb and fingers. She bent her head down and slowly fed him into her mouth, savouring the taste of him, the sweetness of his flesh. She licked him lovingly and her heart raced as he swelled in her mouth, grew hard, throbbing with passion and life – so large now that she could keep him there only by swallowing him greedily, by moving him in and out of her warm, wet mouth, and then taking him deep into her throat again and again.

Glorious as she was, much as he wanted to come, to have her swallow every last drop of the copious orgasm he held back, he wanted more. Ahmad stopped her with protestations of love, erotic suggestions to excite her imagination. She submitted. Once more he was in command.

Chapter 13

Love did not govern Arianne's splendid days and magnificent nights. What she and Ahmad had together was primitive. Sexual licence was their aim, what they never wearied of. New and exotic fare was what satisfied their appetite for each other, not love. Basic instincts governed their closeness on their journey up the Nile. Arianne was too busy living every minute, experiencing the erotic life again, to analyse, rationalise or justify. She merely assumed her actions were governed by love.

By day they sailed, and when time and privacy permitted, they spent hours together talking. Out of respect for the crew, and not wanting to offend or to detract from the excitement on board for the race and their determination to win it, the lovers were discreet in exercising their daytime lust for each other.

Ahmad's talk was always informative and amusing. He could truly charm. Arianne listened and learned, was somehow mesmerised by it. Her own contributions were far from dull – they kept Ahmad's attention, incited in him an even greater interest to possess Arianne utterly. Conversation and affection, stolen kisses and caresses, filled their lazy days while they waited for night to fall and the bedouin tent to be raised. Within, an antique brass brazier, with its domed and spired lid topped by a plumed bird cast in brass, waited to be lit to warm their romantic haven. The lanterns spread a soft, warm glow over the period Persian carpets adorning the deck, and over the gold, silver, crimson and purple brocades woven in luscious patterns that covered the large cushions strewn about.

Periodically through the day, when Ahmad felt that Arianne might be slipping from the erotic spell he cast over her, he would whisper lewd and exciting things in her ear: promises of passion to come after dark; thoughts that both excited and frightened. But frightened not enough to calm desire or to cause her to forget what ecstasy, what bliss he could wring from her. He had only to say a word, to touch her in a certain way, for her to think of being enslaved to him in lust within the tent, where, from the small, many-drawered, inlaid chest of wood, ivory and gold, he would each night withdraw some new and exciting object made specifically to intensify a woman's sexual pleasure. Like the huge fresh-water pearls on a silk cord which she wore even now in her vagina. He had placed them there so that during the day at any given time, whether in front of people or alone, he could order her to indulge herself, to contract the muscles of her vagina and feel those lustrous pearls, until she drove herself, as he held her hand or caressed her hair, to come. It felt wickedly sexy.

After several days on the felucca she began to wonder if the erotic ointments that were housed in small porcelain pots in the chest were not addictive. He used them on the outer and inner labia, those most sensitive of lips, and massaged them inside her vagina. The ointments heightened her pleasure, made her voracious for a man's penis and crazy with desire. They did, too, inspire in her longer, stronger and more violently exciting orgasms, multiple orgasms that exhausted her to near fainting. But there were things from the box to sniff, to revive her. There was always something more to control her, to enslave her to him, to the Eros embodied in him. Once such scented salves had faded away, she missed those heightened moments, and yearned for Ahmad to appear with his tiny pots of female ecstasy. But there was always something more, ever varied, always exciting, to be discovered in Ahmad's box of sexual wonders. Ahmad could and did on many a night seduce her with the erotic contents from the inlaid box – something to make her beg to be transported to that wonderful realm of sexual oblivion . . .

After several days on the Nile, one day seemed to drift into another. Time lost its meaning. They might have been together a day, a month, a lifetime. They were living and loving in a time-warp, where there was no beginning, middle or end – just dawn and dusk to measure their life by.

The river and the scenery had now become more dynamic and romantic. It was a scene that had regressed through the centuries of time. For the desert was there stretching out from the narrow band of green on the banks of the Nile as far as the eye could see into an arid, stony silence. The feluccas were spread out on the Nile now. The triangular sails, both behind and in front of the *Osiris*, seen at a distance, were like giant, prehistoric wings fluttering whitely under an unusually warm winter sun as they skimmed low over the waters of the Nile.

Each morning just before dawn, Muhammad would light several lanterns and wake Arianne and Ahmad. He would prepare a huge pot of strong black coffee, bring from the stores one of the several cured hams they breakfasted on, with a bag of bread, baked hard in ovens in Cairo, bread whose savour was to be resurrected by dunking in their morning brew. Slabs of cheese, a dish of butter, a large pot of honey. Oranges from a basket. When Arianne and Ahmad surfaced from their tent, light would be just breaking through the darkness, the stars and moon fading from sight. Ahmad would extend the plank from the rail of the boat to the bank, cross it and call to the crew to board.

From the first morning they had awakened on the *Osiris*, the pattern was set. All ate their fill because no more food was served until dark. They gossiped to each other, mostly about politics, or discussed the day's sailing, checking on their immediate objectives, and ensuring that everyone knew the drill. They were invariably the first to weigh anchor, theirs was the first sail to catch the wind.

On board each had his chores, and must pull his weight. An erotic voyage it may have been for Arianne and Ahmad, but for the *Osiris* to win the race had always been the prime concern. And Arianne did her chores as well as the next man, which gained her the respect and admiration of the crew. She did the washing-up, kept the stores in order, cleaned the lanterns in the morning, then lazed about all day unless called to help with the sail, or – if no one else was available – to sit on the bow's rail and scan the river for obstructions, or a rogue current. Someone was always on watch for anything that might impede them.

Now their plan was entering its final stage. They were lying in third place. This was the stretch of the Nile they had been waiting for, here was where they had their chance to win. No one knew the Nile from this section of the river to Aswan better than Abdul Wassif, a captain of his own felucca, who now took over.

169

Every second would count. Nothing must be left to chance. He demanded of them, 'You must want to win so much you can taste success in your mouth. It's on your tongue, there is nothing more delicious in the world than the sweet taste of success.' He had charged them up, their adrenaline was running. Fresh energy and passion inspired them all. They set sail with new vigour.

All Abdul Wassif's commands were translated by Ahmad for Arianne. Even she was given a new job on the *Osiris*. 'You've brought in a ringer. Clever move,' she told Ahmad, adding gleefully, 'we're going to win the race.'

'Had you any doubts?'

'Frankly, yes.'

He began to laugh. It was a self-satisfied laugh. Sly? devious? She wasn't sure, but it did irritate her, and she didn't quite know why. 'You'll tell me anything goes when you're out to win, or something like that.'

'I wasn't going to tell you anything, but, yes, that's true.' Again the complacent look in his eyes as he added, 'In love or war. And have no doubt, my lovely Arianne, to win is always to wage war in one way or another.' His gaze seemed to burn into her soul. It excited nearly as much as it frightened her. But she had no time to think about it. He swept her off her feet and swung her round and round while kissing her crazily all over her face. Ahmad was happy and it was infectious. Happiness makes it so easy to forget the questions.

Arianne and Ahmad were sitting together in their favourite place, at the bow of the felucca, their feet dangling over the side. There was hardly a breeze. The heat felt good. A short time before, they had taken a shower together in the stern of the felucca, where a small dressing room had been built.

Arianne's hair was still damp. She shook it and ran her fingers through it. She caught sight of Ahmad watching her and recognised a look he sometimes had for her. It was not frequent, but when she did catch it, it touched her heart. It was a loving gaze, filled with contentment.

Both were dressed in jeans and white cotton shirts. They went barefoot. They looked and felt younger than their years. Both knew that they were not like adults playing serious sexual games, but young lovers. Arianne reached out to take Ahmad's hand in hers. He reached into his pocket and withdrew a ring: a large and beautiful cabochon ruby mounted on a ring of blue-white diamonds. He slipped it on her finger. A perfect fit. The gem sparkled in the sun. It was a voluptuous jewel that cast an erotic spell; a powerful gem, no doubt with an intriguing history attached to it. One sensed great loves and great tragedies within the ring.

Arianne said the first thing that came into her mind: 'It might have belonged to Catherine the Great of Russia.'

Ahmad threw back his head and laughed. 'It *did* indeed belong to Catherine, mistress of those she ruled and master of those she loved!'

Arianne hardly heard his words. She was mesmerised by the beauty and the magic of the ruby. It was an extraordinary gift, and she knew that she could not accept it. It frightened her. Ahmad had given her many valuable gifts, but none quite as startling as this one. Many times she had been overwhelmed by his generosity, the connotations of his extravagant gestures. They sometimes disturbed her. They were powerful statements of what she was to Ahmad. They caused her anxiety, conflict, because she was those things to him – mistress, his sexual slave – because he sometimes trod a sexually sinister edge, and she was not unwilling to match him there, step for step. At times Arianne even coveted his sexual corruption of her. His gifts were sometimes like labels she was meant to wear, messages declaring to the world the dark side of her own sexual nature. They spelled out – albeit à la Cartier and Van Cleef & Arpels – whore, mistress, erotic love. She detested labels, adored her secret life with her husband and lover. In days past, she had always accepted those special labelling gifts he had lavished on her because Jason had always been there to calm her unease. Her husband and her lover had always protected her from each other.

Arianne had been aware that behind Jason's and Ahmad's façade of intelligence, kindness and love there lay cunning and selfishness. It had never mattered to her: she was unconditionally in love with Jason. How easy it was to give herself up to his and Ahmad's sexual whims. She had made them her own. She revelled in sexual excess because love governed, love made the choices. When she married Jason she became an instrument of his will. It suddenly occurred to her, while looking at the magnificent ring on her finger, that that was exactly what Ahmad wanted. And here, with that blood-red ruby dancing fire and passion in the light, was the label to prove her right.

Arianne felt suddenly thrust into an awareness of Ahmad that she had hardly encountered before. She had held Ahmad in high esteem. He had seemed above other men. Was he merely mortal? Had she lain with him for so many years only to find suddenly that he was a stranger?

Such thoughts ran crazily in her mind as she gazed into the rare Burmese ruby. What magic powers lurked in the heart of that jewel to conjure such thoughts? Or, she had to ask herself, was it the label he pinned on her when he had presented her with that so-unsettling ring? There was no Jason any more to protect her. She was alone with Ahmad. Suddenly she understood that she hardly knew him, yet he had a most profound power over her. An insistent inner voice asked: Who is this man to whom I so willingly surrender my whole being every time lust takes over?

'You're dazzled. You're also speechless,' he told her, amused by her reaction to his gift.

His words seemed to recall her from her anxieties. 'I have never seen a piece of jewellery so grand, so exciting. It's true it has rendered me speechless. But now I have my voice back, I have to tell you that I adore it and always will. But I cannot accept it.'

Now he laughed at the very idea that she might return it to him. 'It doesn't suit you?' he teased.

'I have no place to wear it.'

'In bed with me is place enough.'

This relieved some of the anxiety she was feeling over the gift of the ring. Here was more familiar ground. He placed a finger under her chin, raised her head, and, gazing into her face, searched it as if he expected some revelation. Whatever it might be wasn't there, and that seemed to satisfy him. He placed his lips upon hers and kissed her. His hands roamed under her shirt and caressed her bare breasts. He rolled her nipples between his fingers and felt her squirm under his touch.

She felt calmer about him, even if not about the ring on her

172

finger. Was she being fanciful about Ahmad? Had their relationship been more complex than she had imagined for all those years the three of them had been together? Yes, she told herself, you were being just a bit foolish. Never one to read too much into situations, she was relieved to rid herself of her anxiety over Ahmad and his intentions.

They held hands again and sat in silence for some time just drinking in the landscape. Several women draped in black were walking along the bank. They had appeared as if from nowhere. A line of children trailing a donkey behind them soon caught up with the women. Arianne and Ahmad waved to the group on the bank. Ahmad called out to them in Arabic. When asked who they were and why all the boats were on the river, he told them. More waving until the felucca left them far behind – small black dots on the green bank. He placed an arm around her. 'Happy?'

'Very.' That was no lie. She had fallen once again under the spell of Egypt and her handsome Egyptian lover.

'Then come for me.' A sensual tone was in his voice. Lust for her was in his eyes. He didn't wait for an answer. He whispered in her ear how he would like to take her. He inflamed her with images she found irresistible. She wanted to come. She squeezed on the pearls again and again. How exquisite always to have something inside her to kiss with her cunt. He held her tight. When she came he felt her tremble in his arms, and he wanted to weep for the joy she gave him when she sighed and rested her head on his shoulder. He had sensed her slipping away from him. Now he had her back again. She was so deliciously easy to corrupt. But Ahmad was in no way a fool about women. He knew he did not yet have Arianne's unconditional love. Her love for him was still like quicksilver in the hand – tenuous, elusive. Time, it was only a matter of time, he told himself.

He stroked her hair and it took several minutes before he recovered himself to ask her, 'You will keep the ring?'

'Would you be so very offended if I didn't?'

'Yes.'

She nodded her head. He looked delighted. She swung her legs around to dangle them over the inside of the boat now, and then hopped down on to the deck. Ahmad followed. They faced each other. 'It's a magnificent gift. Thank you.'

173

He placed his arms around her and drew her tight up against him. 'Ahmad . . .' She was about to insist, 'No strings attached.' But somehow she didn't dare.

They were walking together now on the deck to the starboard side of the boat. 'I've waited a long time to give Catherine's ring to you.'

'Oh?' she asked, puzzled by that. 'How long?'

'More than two years. Since that night we tried to have sex together alone for the first time.'

'Why didn't you give it to me then, Ahmad?' she asked. This was curiosity more than anything.

'It wasn't working for us. We were both suffering from loss. Neither of us could cope with our sexual hunger for each other without Jason. He wasn't dead for us then.'

'And he is now,' she added for him. It was surprising how easily they were able to speak about Jason in the past tense, so separate now from their lives.

At that moment one of the crew called for him to assist in the rigging of the sail. Ahmad took her hands in his, raised them to his lips and, turning them over, kissed first one palm and then the other. They stared for several seconds into each other's eyes. Another time, another place, and they would have immediately been together to assuage the sexual hunger they were feeling once more for each other. He walked away from her, and she used herself with her unusual string of pearls. He had commanded it with his eyes. She had obeyed. They were sexually obsessed with each other, always had been, and they were both grateful for it. So, at least, they kept telling each other in their tent that night.

'Are you going to remain at Christie's?' he asked a few days later.

She surprised even herself when she answered, 'No. I intend to give notice on my return to London.'

'A sudden decision?'

'Yes, actually. I had no idea I wanted to do that until I said it.'

'It's not like you to make rash decisions.'

'No. But I want to change my life.'

'You usually wait for someone else to do that for you. Caution, you're new at this game.'

What Ahmad said was true, but there was a sting in the way

174

he said it. She surprised herself again when he asked, 'Do you have any plans?' and she found herself saying:

'No.'

'Money?'

She began to laugh. 'Money? I have had nothing but despair and unhappiness over money since Jason's death. Until then I never thought about money, and I was right not to. It's a loathsome commodity. I have no idea how to handle it. It can give and take ruthlessly. I should know.'

'Why didn't you come to me if you were in trouble for money?'

'I didn't say that I was in trouble for money.'

'But you were. Was it pride? You knew I would have come to your aid.'

He knew. All the time he had known about her husband's bad debts, how Jason had been ruined by them. He didn't have to spell it out. Something in his attitude did. She tried to block that out of her mind, still wanting to believe that Ahmad did not know about Jason's financial fall.

'I waited for you to come to me for help.'

Does a friend, a lover, not go to you with an offer of help if he knows you are bleeding to death? Does he wait for you to crawl to him? Arianne didn't like what she was feeling about this conversation.

'Jason would have come to me. He did come to me, many times. I saved him more often than he'd care to remember. It meant nothing to me. He was my friend, I loved him. You're my friend, I am passionately in love with you. You're a part of my life as Jason was. Would I have done less for you?'

She had suffered so many humiliations trying to save face for Jason. She had endured giving up, paring her life down until there was nothing more to excise. And what had he been doing? Waiting for her to go to him. Should she have? Had it been pride? What had inhibited her from seeking help from Ahmad? It was all too uncomfortable to contemplate. That was the past. Jason was dead. That part of her life was over. She would not dwell on it now.

She ignored his question. Instead she told him, 'I'll buy a book, sell a book. I will deal in a modest way in the rare-book world. It's something I know. Thanks to you, I have a roof over my head, a house that I love. I'll live frugally – I am quite used to that. I have become quite used to taking care of myself these last years without Jason. I'm here, aren't I? At my own instigation, no one else's. Maybe I'm just a late starter in the game of asserting oneself.'

One could rarely read anything in Ahmad's handsome, seductive face. It was a mask to disguise his feelings. Not this time. Arianne read it perfectly. She had surprised him. He thought he was still dealing with the Arianne of their *ménage à trois*. That was the woman he loved and wanted. Arianne was not a woman to fool herself: she knew very well that she was still that woman, still a lady who liked being taken over by a man. But time and circumstances had changed her; she was also something more now. Really, she had always been something more, and Ahmad and Jason had known that. Though they had tended to ignore the fact most of the time, had they not loved her even more because they knew she gave up herself, her very life, willingly to them? They had had control of her, because she had wanted them to have it. Her passive nature? Had they been tricked by that? She reminded herself that men can be just as foolish in love as women. That brought a smile to her lips. She tilted her head back, performed that often sexy movement of throwing one shoulder forward, and began to laugh.

She looked lovely, beautiful, serene and sexy. Happy, with laughter that had bells in it. She was enchanting, and clever. Though Ahmad tended to forget it, she still held his interest as no other woman was capable of doing. He loved her so much for managing to bring a smile to his lips and laughter to his heart. The wide, curved neckline of the white tee-shirt she was wearing slipped to show a shoulder smooth, naked and brown. She was irresistible. He caressed it and placed a fleeting kiss upon it.

She took him by the hand and led him away to the bow of the felucca. There she slipped the ruby ring from her finger and into the palm of his hand, closing his fingers over it. She held his fist in her hand, and told him, 'Please don't be offended. I am asking you only to keep it for me until the time comes when I feel I can ask you for it.'

'When will that be?'

'When I can give you what you want.'

He began to say something, but she stopped him with a finger on his lips. 'No, please. Let's leave it at that for now. I'm not ready for any more than what we already have together.'

That night he controlled her sexually at first with many tender acts of seduction. His mouth, his lips, his tongue searched out every erogenous area of her body and he made love to them. He made a meal of her cunt, until she could not bear a minute longer of not having him deep inside her in violent passion. He removed the pearls and dropped them into her mouth and watched her lick them. It was such a wildly sexy thing to watch, it drove him to take her breast in his mouth, suck on it in a desperate hunger for more, always more, of her. Then he took the pearls from her in a kiss. He plied her with the aphrodisiac ointments, and with silk cords around her wrists. He probed between her legs, after placing cushions beneath her, and entered her slowly – so slowly she thought she would scream, she was that desperate to be riven by him. Now all tenderness was gone; they were both past tenderness. He used his cock on her as if he were whipping her to frenzy. He had primed her for violent love-making, for rutting like beasts at the mercy of instinct. That was what they both wanted and what they both now had. He placed a silk handkerchief in her mouth to stifle the sounds of ecstasy.

They had lost themselves to lust. All caution had been cast off. They had been there before, many times, but never just the two of them, without Jason. Not a word had been said about his absence, but they did crave another man, Jason, to add to their sexual madness, to stop them from going far off the edge into a danger zone.

The following morning when they awakened they made love to each other once again with tenderness and affection. They confirmed their enthralled attraction for each other, even a new and different closeness now there for them. These days and nights on the Nile, isolated from the outside world, with their past relationship firmly in the past, had allowed them to discover each other anew.

But something had happened to them during those hours of sexual oblivion. They had at last sated their passion. There was no place to go. Just time to savour where they had been. Orgasm, the 'little death'. They had been there *and* been there. Nothing could be more exciting than their 'little deaths', but they were losing track of life in the wake of their sexual passion and dying to the world.

Both of them needed time and space to come to terms with who they really were, what they wanted, beyond a sexual life together. If anything. That was what Arianne was telling herself; what Ahmad knew, though he was telling himself nothing. His obsession lived. He was more certain than ever that he would one day have that unconditional love he secretly demanded of her. There was much to question about themselves and their relationship, but these were extremely sensitive questions that neither of them cared to express. They were too complex, a psychological minefield not to be entered casually. What they had always had together in the past, and on this trip up the Nile, thrived on spontaneity of emotion and attraction, and on Arianne's capacity to give herself completely, to die to all else in the world when in the arms of the men she loved. Answers could kill all that – the last thing either of them wanted.

There was something manic about the next two and a half days. Nothing mattered but winning the race. The crew had worked hard and with complete attention ever since they had left Cairo. But now it was somehow different: they were ten times as quick and sharp, or so it seemed. By day they sailed, catching the slightest breeze, the best wind almost before it arrived, using the currents with alacrity, sheer genius, and until well after dark. At night the bedouin tent was no longer raised, the plank no longer put on to the bank; the men no longer slept on shore. The cooking pots came out as soon as the anchor had been dropped. The clearing-up began while the men sat around the cooking fire and the brazier from the tent. For everyone on board, including Ahmad and Arianne, even sleep itself seemed directed only at waking to resume the morning ritual and set sail once again in the dark to meet the dawn.

The *Osiris* and its crew did not have it all their way. There were other captains in that race who were masters of the Nile, men who could handle their crafts as skilfully as Abdul Wassif. The *Osiris* took the lead on the river more than once, only to lose it, and at one point to drop back not just to third but to fifth place.

The challenge only incited the crew of the *Osiris* to work harder, to miss no chance of regaining the lead. They sailed like winners. Abdul Wassif, Ahmad at his side as his second-in-command, became more aggressive towards the challengers. Together they ruthlessly manoeuvred them into less favourable spots on the Nile, coming near to crashing into them, to gain a better position and race ahead. And then when it counted Ahmad had all the competitors where he wanted them, behind the *Osiris*. Abdul Wassif navigated the Nile with its tricky currents and slipstreams, the shifting winds coming off the desert and up from the south, to pull ahead at speed and retain the lead. That was only fifteen miles downstream from Luxor and the finish. By then hundreds of people were already lining the banks of the Nile, shouting and running alongside the feluccas in the final dash to win the race, urging on the other boats, now mere dots of white sail lying far down-river without a chance.

The *Osiris* was challenged once more by the felucca that had won the race twice before. But the sight of the temple of Karnak was enough to draw from Abdul Wassif a final reserve of cunning and energy. He cut across the river, forcing the felucca, *Nefertiti*, to swerve into an area of swirling water. All was lost for the *Nefertiti*. By the time she navigated herself out of it, her best hope was a sad second place.

Two days of celebration later, the last of the feluccas crossed the finish. A final party was held. Not at the Winter Palace Hotel where Ahmad and those of the entrants who could afford it were staying, but on the opposite side of the river to Luxor, in the desert, in the Valley of the Kings. At a series of tents there, guests arrived in horse-drawn carriages or on camels, or astride beautiful Arab stallions, by caravans of donkeys, even in the odd car that was housed on that side of the Nile. As a privilege, the tombs of the Kings and Queens of ancient Egypt were opened and lit – for the Nile sailors, who were mostly from the peasant class of Egypt, and who would never usually make the journey to see wonders to which the tourists of the world flocked.

Ahmad created a huge affair for the contenders, their families and friends, and dignitaries who flew in from Cairo and Alexandria or the towns of Upper Egypt for the event. They dined on whole

179

lambs roasted on dozens of open fires, and a costly array of delectable dishes from the Arab cuisine: *baba-ghanoug*–baked eggplant mashed and mixed with sesame paste, flavoured with lemon and garlic and olive oil; *taameyya* (felafel) – patties of mashed fool (fava beans) with finely chopped parsley, highly seasoned and fried in deep oil, and served by the thousand rather than the hundred; *waraq anab* – rolled vine leaves stuffed with rice and meat; and *moulukhiya* – a steamed green vegetable resembling spinach, which was served in a soup of strong chicken broth and garlic. Then there were vine leaves stuffed with lentils, piled in a vast cone on huge trays. And no party such as this would have been complete without serving Egypt's national dish: *Fool mudhammas* – fava beans cooked with spices and tomatoes (something like a chilli con carne without meat). Pigeons by the hundred were broiled over open pits. And then came the real treat – grilled shrimp, huge, succulent and delicious, from the Mediterranean, and fish from the Red Sea.

All was accompanied by trays proffering mountains of herb-scented, buttery rice, some laced with pine-nuts and sultanas, and pyramids of unleavened bread. The desert floor was covered with colourful kilims and cushions. Groups of instrumentalists played Arab music and singers alternated with dancers to entertain. Huge platters of fruit and sticky sweet cakes followed, and pots of coffee, whose aroma mingled with the roasting lamb and herbs to fill the night.

TV crews from Cairo, Paris, and London had accompanied the race from the start, sailing on one of the feluccas, though they had kept away from the *Osiris*. It was a grand spectacular, but for Arianne it paled beside her erotic journey up the Nile and the race of lateen sail-boats that had seemed somehow outside time and the real world. Neither Ahmad nor Arianne wanted that journey spoiled for her. They had agreed that she should leave on arrival in Luxor before the real world engulfed them again.

As soon as possible after their win they discreetly slipped away to drink champagne together in his suite of rooms in the Winter Palace Hotel, with its stunning view of the Nile, overlooking the finish. For the first time in days, they had time for themselves. They bathed together, caressed and kissed and incited each other to rekindle erotic feelings – feelings that still felt good, but were somehow different, wrong even. They were both vaguely aware of that. Ahmad told her, 'Second-best times have never been for us. It's not because we are over, but because the journey up the Nile is.' He said it with charm and affection.

'I know,' she told him with a sense of relief. He sat on the end of the bed and watched Arianne change into her Ralph Lauren clothes, the ones she had arrived in. Emotions were high for them. It was hard to tell what provoked them – the race? a parting? – and it didn't matter. Rather than have what they had shared on the Nile together spoiled by words and uncertain meanings, they preferred to remain silent about what had passed, their parting, and the future.

Arianne and Ahmad kissed each other goodbye in the rooms, and then one last time on the steps of the Winter Palace Hotel. They descended the few remaining stairs and walked together arm in arm past the waiting horse-drawn carriages that taxied to and from the temples. They crossed the road that separated the hotel from the bank of the Nile. A sea-plane was moored, waiting to fly Arianne back to Cairo, where she would board a flight to London that was being held for her arrival.

The sea-plane's motors spluttered into life. At the moment they were to part and Arianne was to climb on board, Ahmad pulled her back. 'It's been wonderful, you've been wonderful. I've missed you. For a time I thought this would never happen for us again.' He seemed almost embarrassed telling her those things.

'I didn't know what to expect. In fact I didn't think; I just wanted to come to you. And I'm happy I did. I'll never forget these last eleven days, not ever,' she told him.

'Arianne, maybe these are our beginnings. A favour?'

'Anything.'

'Keep the ring. You don't have to wear it. A keepsake, not a bond. A token of new beginnings, if that's possible for us. If not, a bauble from a grateful lover for an unforgettable interlude.' He slipped it on her finger for the second time. She threw her arms around his neck, and they hugged each other, remaining silent. A moment of deepest sadness came over Arianne. She had to force back tears. He was and would always be her sexual devil – she was as physically attracted to him as ever. Even at this last moment on the quay she still wanted him erotically. Just being in his arms and feeling the warmth of his body, the smoothness of his skin, his very scent, was enough to excite sexual longing in her. But where was love?

LONDON, GLOUCESTERSHIRE, OXFORDSHIRE

Chapter 14

Arianne brought the cup of hot black coffee to her lips. The Fortnum & Mason coffee shop was usually an exercise in Mayfair gentility, with a clientèle of upper-class London shoppers, county ladies, and Jermyn Street-tailored art dealers reading the *Financial Times*. It was West End theatre without a playwright. Its stock company was the crotchety near-pensioner waitresses. After decades of serving the upper-crust they were arbiters of good taste, and terrific social snobs. They had their pets: Terence Stamp now, Rex Harrison once. They had seen it all, over years of smoked salmon sandwiches, champagne, game pies, chicken and mushroom tarts, and all the other delicacies the kitchens could provide for its clientèle.

Sleet was tapping on the windows, swirling round the corner and all but knocking at the doors. Few people had braved the weather. There were whispers from staff huddled together behind the serving counter, but hardly a word from the few people scattered around the room tucking into their mid-morning repast. Arianne amused herself with the idea that they were all in a Terence Rattigan play, waiting for the lights to dim and the play to begin.

She was waiting for someone to come through the street door in a flap of wet Burberry and dripping umbrella, and an icy gust of cold air. Arianne imagined the sound of an audience clapping for that person – the lead actor claiming centre-stage. It was almost too perfect when Terence Stamp did arrive, not through the street door but through the entrance that led into the ground floor and its luxurious food hall. Staff sprang to life as he took his usual table. Arianne had to lower her eyes and concentrate on controlling her amusement. Was her play-script coming to life?

She was amused but didn't dare look up, frightened that the

185

other members of the audience might attribute her presence there to more than a need of coffee and escape from the cold, driving sleet of a grey morning. They must not detect that she was there for a slice of life as much as for a slice of lemon-mousse pie.

Her lowered eyes watched someone refill her cup with steaming black coffee. She heard him say, 'Does madam take cream or milk?'

His question, the tone in his voice, his playing the waiter in Fortnum's coffee shop: it brought a smile to her lips and she raised her eyes to gaze into his. The recognition between them was immediate. Unmistakable. Her immediate reaction was to feel lucky and very grateful. Her heart was beating out all sorts of messages. She listened to them and it was a joyful thing, a great feeling. A glow came to her cheeks and she gave him an utterly charming laugh, covered her mouth with her hand to still it and shyly lowered her eyes again to break their gaze.

He felt unimaginably happy, that it was a serendipitous meeting. Her kindness was perfect, her veracity perfect, her relaxation perfect. On meeting her again this time, he was overwhelmed by a sense of her exceptional pleasantness. It was all there, energy and intelligence, expressiveness, the best voice, the best body, the best face, an infectious smile and laugh – dazzling.

His face was handsome and made blank for his role as bored, subservient waiter. He hardly looked the part he was trying to play, even with his props: the silver coffee-pot in his hand, the large, white napkin neatly draped over his arm. The black sand-washed silk shirt, red-and-black check braces and grey flannel trousers gave him away. The sensual, yet loving kindness emanating like an aura from him, seemed magnetically charged. It was drawing her to him. She tried to suppress a giggle instigated by his continuing in his role. But she managed that only long enough to say, 'Just black, please.' Then it escaped.

He finally abandoned the part he was playing and smiled at her – a smile filled with affection. 'Hello.' That was all he could manage.

Yet it was an intimate greeting that went straight to her heart.

She didn't even try to hide the emotion in her own response. 'Hello, Ben Johnson.'

Beyond him she saw the group of tittering silver-haired ladies in their firm-fresh Fortnum's uniforms, men's eyes peering over the tops of newspapers, women's from under fashionable winter fur hats. Was it or wasn't it a score? she could almost hear them thinking. Not Terence Stamp; he was buttering his toast. Briefly he gazed her way and gave her an amused look. He knew it was a score. 'How did you persuade them to entrust you with that napkin and their precious coffee-pot?' A little more control was in her voice now.

'Years of generous tipping, and lots of charm.' He too had somewhat recovered himself.

He placed the coffee-pot on the table and removed the napkin from over his arm. Ben liked the way Arianne was looking at him. 'May I?' he asked, indicating with his eyes and a nod at the chair that he would like to join her.

'Oh, please. Please do.' She drew the chair back for him.

Their delight in each other was interrupted. 'I didn't say you could keep the pot, Mr Johnson, or the service cloth.' The waitress tried to act grumpy, but a twinkle in her eye gave her away. 'Your jacket, Mr Johnson.'

Ben stood up and the short, plump, elderly waitress, after draping his brown leather coat over the other empty chair at the table, insisted on helping him on with the rust and chocolate-brown cashmere, subtle but frightfully elegant, tartan jacket. Arianne and Ben seemed suddenly to have been taken over by his co-conspirators. Another waitress arrived with a cup and saucer and placed it in front of Ben, along with a pedestal dish offering croissants, and a small pot of whipped cream. The white-haired waitress was obviously smitten with her long-time customer. She poured coffee for him and spooned a large blob of cream on to the surface. Side plates arrived. As if by magic a pair of silver tongs appeared, and with a flourish she attended to the croissants. 'Our Mr Johnson does like his whipped cream.' Then she vanished to her post behind the counter.

'Alone at last,' he told her with a broad smile.

'Well, not quite.'

They looked around the room. People were pretending that

187

they were not interested in seeing what came next. 'I did make rather a spectacle of myself. But I wanted to surprise you with more than, "Well, hello there, fancy meeting you here." It just didn't seem enough. I wanted to impress you.'

'Well, you certainly have.'

He seemed delighted. As was usual with them, conversation then faltered. They were quiet and sipped from their cups. He broke off a piece of croissant and spooned some whipped cream from his cup into his mouth. Then he asked, 'Have I really?'

'Really what?' she asked, delighted to be sitting next to him, to watch him. She was, as she had been on other occasions, warmed by his presence.

'Impressed you with my performance.'

They were being flirtatious with each other. She kept thinking, Oh god, this feels so good; and he: The trick is knowing what's important and what's not. And she knows this is the most important meeting of our lives.

It was true, she did know that. Because she was a woman free of neuroses, anxiety, or the usual insecurities, she knew how important this reunion with Ben was. She accepted that, and that she had fallen in love. It made her feel quite giddy.

He reached down into her lap, took her hand and raised it, then lowered his head to kiss her hand. She closed her eyes. It was only for a second and a little sigh escaped her.

'When I woke up this morning, it never occurred to me that I might fall in love in Fortnum & Mason's. Why now?' They were gazing into each other's eyes as he said it. He still holding her hand.

'Because love comes when it chooses,' came the answer, and he was grateful he was in the right place at the right time to catch it.

The happiness in his face was a joy for her. She watched him throw his head back and laugh aloud, not raucously, but with a genuine glee that he was unable to repress. It drew the attention of his waitress, and he beckoned her to the table. 'Two bottles of champagne, Miss Dulcie. Krug, vintage. One for this table and one for you.'

'That's very generous, Mr Johnson, but not necessary.'

'Oh, yes it is, my dear Dulcie, yes it is.'

Suddenly it was all so easy for them. They wanted to talk and talk. Nothing was too important, too banal, too serious, too silly. 'How was your Christmas?' he asked Arianne.

'Splendid. And yours?'

'Really good.'

She told him about the Nile race. He told her about skiing in Aspen. Neither talked about Christmas lovers – not to be evasive, but because for the moment they didn't matter. Ben and Arianne were too busy getting into each other: that wonderful time when after falling in love you want to crawl into the other person's skin to find out who and what they are, and what and who – if anything – you can be to each other.

The champagne was followed by a second bottle and then smoked salmon sandwiches – many delectable smoked salmon sandwiches. Soon they were back on coffee, and tiny pots of chocolate mousse. Finally he asked her, 'What made you come out on a day like this?'

'Work.'

'The books?'

'You remembered.'

'Yes.' It surprised him that he did remember, not only her work but everything about her. She had registered with him every time he had seen her, but he had not taken her into account for love. Who had been looking for love? Certainly not he, neither those other times nor this morning when he had walked into Fortnum's. Who chooses the time or the place, the person to fall in love with? Love dictates. And all his adult life his ego had demanded that he believe he was the one to make the choices in love. How had he missed it, the one truth? Love chooses. You do with it what you can. All morning, ever since his appearance at her table and that immediate recognition between them, he had felt as if he had found the other half of himself, that he had become whole as never before in his life. It had all but overwhelmed him. He had not imagined that one half of himself had been missing.

They were doing it again, as they had done several times before: lapsing into silence, looking half-inanely at each other. She was less overwhelmed than surprised that love should choose to happen to her again, that she should feel from the depths of her soul, once again, a oneness with another human

189

being that nothing in the world could separate. Ben was real, he was there, he was alive – and he was hers. She had to touch him. Feel the warmth of his body. Usually a woman who showed only a fraction of what she was or had, what she could be; one who believed that for her it was better to do nothing than to show too much of herself, or make too much of herself, she was unable to resist. She reached out and took his hand. She caressed it, turned it over and covered her mouth with it, kissing the very centre of its palm. Her face turned rosy and she lowered her eyes as she replaced his hand on the table exactly where she had taken it from.

Ben had never experienced such a profound gesture of love from any of the women he had believed himself to be in love with. Certainly he had never received such passion or love from his wife Clarissa as Arianne had imparted to him in that kiss. He realised that Arianne was and always would be more than he would imagine her to be – that she was unpredictable in the best sense, yet ever consistent. He saw her as a cool woman, always in control of what she revealed of her character. He realised now how right he was about that, while the fires that smouldered within Arianne Honey had now been confirmed by that kiss. A pure, yet sensuous kiss that told him, 'Ben, I love you.' It was so much more profound than the mere words, for the time and place she had chosen to say it in. Was he being fanciful? A tiny sigh with a tremor of passion in it escaped her. It was followed by a smile that had been kissed by the angels. He gazed into her eyes and saw sweet contentment, and that nearly brought tears to his own. No, not fanciful, just a man in love. Where had she been all his life?

'What brought *you* out on a day like this?' she asked.

'A bottle of perfume. A friend's birthday.'

Of course, she thought, there had to be a woman in his life. But strangely it didn't matter to her; she knew it would be all right. He would make it all right.

He raised his arm and signalled for the bill, then abruptly stood up, taking her with him by the hand. 'Come with me.' He looked at the bill briefly, signed the tab and patted the waitress on the shoulder. With coats draped over their arms, they walked up the steps to the ground floor of the store and the bank of lifts.

In the perfumery Arianne discovered to her amusement that he was a man who liked to shop for women. He seemed to know a great deal about scent. He chose a large bottle of perfume, Patou's classic, Joy, and an equally large bottle of Jolie Madame. When he had signed the bill and they had been wrapped and placed in small, elegant shopping-bags, he handed one of them to Arianne.

'You really don't have to do this, you know.'

'I know,' he told her, and kissed her lightly on the lips. He slipped his arm through hers and they walked to the lifts where he helped her on with her coat and hat, then slipped into his own coat.

'Do you have to go back to work?' he asked.

She began to laugh, 'I haven't been *in* to work yet. I seem to have been derailed along the way.'

'Does it matter? Have I ruined something for you?' There was concern in his voice, and she liked that.

'Two weeks ago it might have been a problem. I had a boss to answer to then.'

'And now?'

'Now I come and go as I please, although I do work closely with my colleagues there. It was a sort of promotion. I tendered my resignation; they didn't want to lose me; and although I wanted a more independent role in my work, I didn't really want to leave and go on my own. You see, I am not very ambitious or aggressive. I am only just learning to be assertive. Artemis thinks I'm . . . well, it doesn't matter what Artemis thinks. Now I work there as if I am working on my own, and deal with my clients and my discoveries through Christie's. It suits me.' Slipping an arm through his, she studied his handsome, open face and asked, 'And you? Do you have to go back to work? What will your boss say?'

He smiled at her. 'I'm my boss, I'm my work, I'm the only one I have to answer to, thank god. But I do admit it hasn't always been this way. But,' looking at his watch, 'I did miss a luncheon date, and a dozen calls I should have made. They left my head completely, the moment you turned it.' She laughed softly and squeezed his arm, leaning into him more, delight visible in her face.

Outside it was growing dark. Piccadilly traffic was sparse, mostly buses lumbering by. It was cold and raw and the pavements were slippery, the tarmac glistening like black satin. Christmas lights and decorations were looking decidedly weary, as if longing to be dispensed with. The shop windows beckoned with the warmth of electric light. After the sleet and wind, the atmosphere hung heavy with wet. There was a bitterness about the weather that made them huddle closer together.

They walked along Piccadilly with no destination in mind. Bad as the weather was, it proved a stimulus. Just to be out of the coffee shop and into the world . . . Nothing, no matter how bad, could detract from their sudden sense of well-being. They walked through the Burlington Arcade and window-shopped, cocooned in their awareness of each other. They passed Hermès at the corner of Bruton Street and Old Bond Street and stopped at Berkeley Square. It was dark now. Cars were spinning around the square, headlights aglow, almost mesmerising. They stopped at the corner. He might have said 'My place or yours?' But instead, he asked her, 'Are you free to dine with me this evening?'

'Only if you leave me here, and go catch up on your day.'

'I'll see you home?'

'No.'

'Are you sure?'

'Very sure.'

He pulled her to him and gave her a lingering kiss. She felt so good in his arms. His kiss was exciting, filled with promise. She sensed hunger for her in that kiss. After releasing her, he asked, 'Are you still sure?' She found it impossible to speak. He was already so much a part of her life that not to be with him was now unthinkable. Arianne felt alive and happy deep within herself. She nodded her assurance, and, squeezing on his leather-gloved hand, turned to cross Bruton Street and hurry round the square to Davies Street. She walked a few steps, ran a few steps, wanting to put distance between them lest she change her mind and run back to him. No more than two minutes after they had parted, Ben was grabbing her arm. They laughed at themselves. He took her by the elbow and told her, 'Just to the top of the square, I promise.'

* * *

That evening he arrived at her door with flowers. Theatre and dinner followed. And after that they decided to have a nightcap at Annabel's. He was greeted with enthusiasm by the manager of the exclusive watering-hole for the rich and famous, the upper classes and reigning stars. There English and European minor royalty mingled in the privacy the management guaranteed for the celebrated at play.

Arianne had not been there since Jason's death. He had been a member – Ahmad still was – and they had liked to go there when in London. Everything about the place suited them: one of the most pleasantly chic clubs in the world, with its oil paintings and drawings and comfortable furnishings, its mirrored discothèque to dance in, and its very English clubby atmosphere, where even the food was excellent and the wine cellar a triumph.

Ben was welcomed by the maître d', and then by several other people. He made introductions between them and Arianne but always with one foot poised to whisk her away to a table in the shadows of the far corner of the room. When they bumped into two men talking at the bar who turned to face Arianne and Ben, a pleasant smile of recognition confronted them. 'It's too long since we've seen you here, Arianne. What a tragedy – I still often think about Jason and the trips we made together. And Ahmad? Seen him lately?'

'Yes, I was in Egypt at Christmas,' she answered, feeling comfortable at meeting the man again and even at talking about Jason and Ahmad in front of Ben. That she could do it and acknowledge to herself that they were there in her life but firmly in the past, was a revelation that only added to her current happiness. Ben did not seem at all surprised that she should be known there. Discreet murmurs of welcome from the staff on entering had alerted him.

And it was welcome back for Arianne. The club seemed to open its arms to her. She felt happy standing in the midst of a night-life again. Three months before, she would have found it impossible to be there without Jason. She was so relieved that happiness had happened to her again with Ben that she felt the need to squeeze his arm, as if to prove that he was real. He looked down at her. 'Ow,' he exclaimed, pretending that she was hurting him. 'What was that for?'

'Just checking that this is not some dream I conjured up.'

He could not have been more delighted. 'You are a funny old thing. But shouldn't you have pinched yourself?'

'You're right. I am a funny old thing, but not a masochist.'

Seated at last, with champagne ordered, they held hands. He asked her nothing. She volunteered, 'Ahmad and my husband and I used to come here whenever we were in London. We were an inseparable trio. My husband's death ended so many things for me.'

That was the first time she had mentioned her husband, or that she was a widow. And earlier she had mentioned that she had been in Egypt with a man. Incredibly none of that mattered. Not even in the way she looked at him as she told him, 'We were an inseparable trio.' She was telling him much more. He understood immediately that she wanted him to know it all, but to fill in the blanks himself. He did. Why wasn't he surprised? Perhaps because he had always sensed in Arianne a quiescent lust that had intrigued him, and that he now longed to reawaken in her.

At Annabel's, they laughed together a great deal and found that they had a similar sense of humour. Artemis and Uncle Anson and their eccentricities were discussed and accepted with approval. Their attraction to Chessington Park and disaffection with its bickering residents had become, they each admitted to the other, a *bête noire*. Then other things – likes and dislikes that they had in common – all small-talk compared to the larger subject that they skirted: love, the rich, deep love that had come to life less than fourteen hours before. They didn't remain long at Annabel's; they were suddenly ready to be alone.

Ben entered Arianne's house. He had never been inside before. The first time he had been there, when he had driven her down from Chessington Park, he had dropped her off and remained in the car. The second time, earlier that evening, he could only ring the door-bell and hand her several sprays of white moth orchids in a clear cellophane box. Traffic, a yard chock-a-block with cars, had demanded that he wait for Arianne in his 1953, black, 220 Cabriole Mercedes Benz. He had taken the black soft-top car out, one of his favourites, especially for Arianne's comfort. He loved the touring car and would confess to her that vintage cars were one of his vices.

He helped her off with the full-length, white cashmere coat with its narrow lapels, large, mother-of-pearl buttons, and slash pockets. He draped it over the balcony. The way she looked when she had stepped out from her house and into the waiting car earlier in the evening had nearly taken his breath away. She was so extremely glamorous, with the finely bobbed, chestnut-coloured hair that shone like silk, the fresh face combined with a subtle but seductive make-up that insinuated fire and ice. Angel and seductress. He had expected her to look beautiful, for she was very beautiful. But the glamour and chic, the now-obvious aura of sexuality – that *had* surprised him. When they had agreed to dress up for their evening together, she had told him, 'Your best evening-dress suit – I will settle for nothing less.'

He had demanded of her, 'A long and seductive gown.'

'Are we being poseurs?' she asked.

'Why not? So long as it's for us and no other reason.'

'Quite right,' she had told him.

The long dress she was wearing was of the same fabric as her coat, but of a lighter weight, with long sleeves that clung to her slender arms, and a neckline just low enough to show her collar-bone and accentuate her slender neck. Simplicity itself? Except for the tailoring, there was nothing simple about Saint Laurent. The dress clung to her body, accentuating her shoulders, and was backless nearly to the waist. It was cinched at the waist by a gold, kid-leather belt. She wore gold evening shoes, with no jewellery except the ruby ring Ahmad had given her.

'No, don't turn around,' he told her and placed a kiss high up on her bare back, then slipped his arms around her waist and locked his fingers together to hold her there, right where he wanted her. Then Ben stepped up tight against her. He placed his cheek against hers, and she covered his hands with hers.

'A nightcap?' she asked.

'No. I have to leave you. If I could have stayed, would you have allowed me to?'

'But you can't . . .'

'No.'

'Then the question is academic.'

He had wanted her to say yes. She was hedging, unsure about

them. He rationalised that it was because of the overwhelming attraction they had for each other, the swiftness with which it had occurred.

'All evening I've dreaded the idea that I have to leave you.' Then he spun her around to face him. 'I must be on the other side of the Channel by eight in the morning. Calais, then Deauville. Appointments impossible to break. I'll call you every day. Be back in three days' time.'

He still had his black overcoat on. She touched the black velvet collar, and smiled at him. There was about her smile now a wanness that tugged at his heart-strings. He slipped his arm through hers and they walked together into the sitting room. She switched on the lamps as they passed them. Ben and Arianne stood by the fireplace facing each other. They were holding hands. How easy it would have been to whisk her up the stairs to bed. He wanted sex with her. He knew she would not reject that idea. But he wanted more than a one-night stand. He wanted her.

'Will you go directly to sleep when I leave?' he asked. 'Shall I tuck you in?'

'There's no sleep in me just now. I'll stay here and read a little.'

'Then I'll light the fire for you.' He did, giving all his attention to the fire. When it flared, he turned back to look at her. As he did, his gaze fell on the silver-framed photograph of Jason, Arianne, and Ahmad on the beach by the Indian Ocean. What registered with Ben was how rapturously happy, so in love, the three of them were. One had to be blind to miss that.

Arianne followed his eyes. Then she turned Ben's head towards her and gazed up at him. She took his face in her hands and kissed him. It was a long, sensuous kiss and their bodies relaxed into it. Then, taking him by the elbow, she ushered him through the sitting room to the front door, never detaching her gaze from his face. 'We loved each other for a very long time. It was an extraordinarily happy marriage until he crashed his plane into the side of a mountain and vanished from my life. Ahmad is all that's left of him, of what we had together. That's part of my life, my history.'

They kissed once more, standing together in the open door. That kiss confirmed what he already knew: something wonderful had happened to them, they were in love, their lives were beginning afresh. He felt the luckiest man in the world. 'I'll call you in the morning,' he told her, and was gone.

Chapter 15

The bedroom door was ajar. Ben pushed it open. The bedside lamps were still on, casting light across the sleeping Simone. She looked beautiful and sexy lying there, her arms at strange angles to her body, the bed-covers flung aside to reveal a black-lace and flesh-coloured satin nightgown, one strap slipped off her shoulder, leaving one breast partially naked. He walked across the room quietly to stand over her. The black-lace top half of her nightgown had a mesmerising effect on him. It was his favourite nightgown. He had bought it for her in Rome. Even now he savoured her breasts, the narrow waist and the hint of hip seen through a veil of black. How it enticed, that margin where the lace met the smooth, flesh-coloured satin.

Her naked breast was irresistible. He lowered his head and kissed the side of it, licked it, then slipped the piece of lace covering her nipple down, covered the long nipple with his lips, and sucked it gently. She began to stir. He stopped immediately, draped her with the white sheet and soft cashmere blanket, then sat in the lounge chair close to the bed. Now he could watch her sleeping.

He did that for some minutes before he loosened his black-silk bow tie from his neck and placed it in his jacket pocket. He unbuttoned his collar and two more buttons, then removed his jacket and laid that over the arm of the chair. He crossed one leg over the other and was untying his shoe when Simone said, in a voice blurred with sleep, 'How was your dinner?'

'Fine.'

He was aware of her readjusting the bed linen, slipping her nightgown strap back on her shoulder, while he removed a shoe and placed it on the floor.

'A good time at your sister's?' he asked.

'She's blissfully happy; the children are charming. The dinner

199

party was frightfully grand. Very interesting people. You were missed. Michèle and her diplomat husband have a really happy marriage – they lead a sublime life.'

'Sorry I woke you.' He reached out to turn off the bedside lamp closest to him. His hand seemed to freeze in mid-air when she said:

'I'm beginning to think I'd like to be married. I'd make a good mother.'

She was still lying flat, her head resting on the pillow, still luxuriating in the comfort of a warm bed. She neither looked at him nor gave any hint in her voice that she was angry or aggressive towards him. She was merely making a statement of fact in that seductive French accent of hers. Simone was a woman who always got what she wanted. Soon she would be married, he was quite sure of that. He left the light on, slumped back into his chair and recrossed his legs to take off the other shoe.

'I've got bad news for you,' he heard himself say.

She said, 'More bad news. You won't be able to come to my birthday party at Régine's tomorrow night. And the promised dinner *à deux* at Laparousse is off.' She waited for him to say something. He remained silent. 'We won't be going to Paris together?' she asked. He would have to answer that.

'No.'

'I should have guessed when you gave me that impressive bottle of Joy, and cancelled this evening on me. Not to worry, *chéri*. You know I never count on you.' She was not trying to make him feel guilty, that wasn't her way. Again, she was merely stating a fact.

It was his silence that made Simone turn to look at him. This time she could not blame his wretched vineyard, which he watched over like a mother though it was run perfectly without him, as it had been doing for two hundred years before he bought the château and its cherished vines. Nor was it his string of pampered polo-ponies he spent more than half a year travelling the world to play the game with. Never one to skirt around things she said, 'You were at Tramps with a beautiful blonde a few nights ago. A girlfriend told me.'

'And this evening I was at Annabel's. The bad news is that

I met a girl in Fortnum's coffee shop this morning. We parted half an hour ago.'

'Why should you choose this girl to tell me about, not one of the others?'

'Because it's true, Simone. And she is more important than the others.'

'Not another word, Ben. Just remember, it's not over till it's over.' She reached up to switch off the bedside lamp and turned on her side with her back to him. He picked up his clothes and went to the wardrobe in the dressing room. This was her flat, the pied-à-terre he had bought for her. Now he changed into jeans and a polo sweater, boots and his battered leather jacket, took out a large, soft, leather travelling bag and tossed into it the clothes he was wearing that evening, plus the few things he kept in her flat.

He stood briefly at the foot of the bed. Simone never moved, said not a word. This was not the time or the place to talk to her. He knew her well. She would not suffer a broken heart, merely a broken affair that had worked very well for them. Affection, sexual passion had been there for them. But neither had ever pretended that it had been love. But then neither of them had been looking for love and commitment. They had left that behind them and that had been what had kept them together. They had been a comfortable, sexually exciting, handsome and socially acceptable unit. No more, no less. He knew his Simone well. She would take his falling in love as a betrayal, which acquiring other women for sex and fun had not been. He would call her from the château.

He walked to the opposite side of the bed to where she was pretending sleep, his side of the bed, and switched off the last of the lights. He made his way out by the dim light cast from the small sitting room off the bedroom. He had his hand on the doorknob, but before he opened the door to the hall, he hesitated, placed his bag on the floor. Should he leave her a note? He thought better of it. Hand on the knob again, he bent down to pick up his travel bag. The crystal bottle of Joy just missed his head and shattered against the door. The sweet, golden liquid Joy splashed everywhere and ran down the door. He turned the knob, pulled the door open and left without turning around.

201

He was exactly where he should be, at a shipping agent's office in Calais at ten o'clock in the morning, when he called Arianne.

'Did you sleep?' he asked.

'Fitfully. Where are you?'

'In France. Got a pencil? Write these numbers down. I'd like you to be able to reach me if you want me.' That done, they were suddenly lost for words.

'Did you sleep?' she asked.

'Not a wink. When I wasn't driving to catch the ferry, I was reliving our day together. I wish I hadn't had to leave you.'

'How long will you be away?'

'Three, four days. I'm not sure. Why couldn't you sleep?' He so wanted her to tell him it was because she loved him, had missed him, wanted him.

'I guess I simply didn't want the day to end,' she told him. There was a sweetness in the way she said it, but something seductive as well. Yet he sensed she had been almost afraid to tell him.

'I'm going to be at the Biblos in St Tropez for a meeting with my polo team, the day after tomorrow. We go over business and itineraries once a year. Do you think . . .' There was a severe disturbance on the line. He kept calling her name, 'Arianne, Arianne.' And then she was back again, her voice calm and cool.

'I'm still here, Ben. Have a successful few days and come home as soon as you can. I'll be here.'

'I'll call you tomorrow.'

'You don't have to, I'm fine.'

'But what if I want to?'

'Well, that makes all the difference in the world.' She began to laugh, and he did too. It broke the awkwardness in their first telephone conversation. She sounded very happy.

'Look, let's leave it. I'll call, and you can too. And if we keep missing each other, well, I'll be with you as soon as I can.' For some reason he thought better of asking her to join him, as he had been about to when the telephone line had cut out on them for a few seconds.

Several men entered the room and he was obliged to shake their hands. He turned his back to them and told her, 'I have to go. I'm no longer alone in the room, otherwise . . . there are so many things,' he lowered his voice to a near-whisper, 'I would like to tell you, about yesterday, and us, and how I feel. But not with an audience.' He waited for her to say some of the things she was feeling, but she remained silent. He was not disturbed by her silence; he understood it. It was after all no easy thing to pour one's heart out to someone, not least by telephone.

'Ben . . .' and suddenly she was at a loss for words yet again.

He came to her rescue. 'Look, I have to hang up now. I'll call soon, we'll make contact, but don't wait around for a call, or get concerned if we miss each other. I'm into some heavy business that really does need my undivided attention. Bye, my love.'

Arianne put the telephone down and castigated herself: Why wasn't I more forthcoming? How stupid to feel about him as I do and not be able to tell him. She despised her reticence in not declaring herself to Ben. She felt especially wimpish about it because she could not stop thinking of him. She had liked him since first seeing him at Chessington Park, but that was nothing to what she was feeling for him now. Being with him was so easy and exciting. Every time he touched her she belonged to him that little bit more. All night she had lain in her bed hungry for him, imagining what it would be like to lie naked in his arms, to feel the warmth of his body, to be made love to by him, to create together a new erotic world, exclusive to them, where they could wallow in sexual bliss, die a thousand little deaths in every orgasm, only to be born again in his arms, with his kisses. He made her feel alive: here was a man to strike out into the world with, a partner to hit the highs with in life. That happiness was there again. The brass ring was within her reach once more.

In the days that followed she was continually happy. She went to work, and to the corner coffee shop at Fortnum's and sat there smiling to herself because she sensed his presence; she knew he would never leave her. Theirs was a lifetime commitment. They made contact one more time, at eleven one evening: 'I'm calling on the run to catch a plane. I'll be home, knocking at your door, in three days' time. Put on your glad-rags – I'll pick you up at about ten.'

Arianne seemed unable to concentrate on her work and she

was restless working at home. She had some reading to do, an eighteenth-century book on travel in the Levant. The English edition was a rare find made at a sale in Wales that none of the other dealers considered to be of importance. She decided to take the train to Chessington Park and stay there until the day of his return. She left a note for Ida revealing where she was in case of any calls, and headed for Paddington Station.

It was cold and wet and grey when she arrived at the house. No need this time for the drill she had had to perform before with Clive to get into Artemis's flat. Cook had returned and was in residence. Arianne was made welcome and pampered as Cook would never have dared do if Artemis had been around. After hot tea, buttered toast and jam, and talk of what Cook should prepare for dinner, Arianne went out for a long walk with the dogs who were back and now in Cook's care. She was grateful that she did not come across any of the residents. She was too busy thinking about Ben, remembering how kind he was with people, and thinking too, for the first time, about that hint of pain that she had seen several times, in his eyes.

He had not said much about his marriage or his wife's suicide, but clearly he had been through a kind of hell. She had no need to know about it, only felt the hope that they would be so happy together that the pathos she had seen in his eyes would vanish from them and from his heart for ever. She had a compelling desire to care for him. To love him, to be *in love*. That was how she had felt about her father, then about Jason, and now Ben. He was in her thoughts all the time. She loved him and she wanted him to know it. He was at the Biblos, or would be sometime today. She was at the far side of the stables when she began to run back towards the house, the dogs bounding after her.

She was dashing across the marble-floored hall, the dogs slipping and sliding after her, with barks of joy for their game, when a voice from the balcony called down, 'Muddy paws, muddy paws, and too much noise. See that you mop up after yourself. When I'm chairman of the House Committee, we'll have silence here.' It was spoken in a strange foreign accent – could it be South African? It was ugly enough. Arianne ignored the voice. Artemis is always right, thought Arianne, any sign of life or joy and some fool-resident, miserable with his own life, will be there to put a damper on it. 'Not this time,' she wanted to shout.

Once in the flat, she went directly to the telephone, not even waiting to remove her hat and coat. She sent a cable to Ben. *Ben, I love you. Arianne.*

Then she sat quietly in the chair for a very long time. Never in these last few years had she dreamed that she could ever feel as happy as she did now. She had felt the beginning of happiness when Ben had snatched her from Artemis's kitchen through the window for that pub lunch. She had felt truly alive again on her erotic race up the Nile with Ahmad. But this – this was something else: an inexplicable joy fired by love and a rage to live, the same sort of happiness she had known in her married life with Jason, a merriment born of sharing your soul with another human being.

Ida heard the knocking at the door; the sound of the bell was incessant. She opened the door and told Ben, 'I'm not deaf, you know. And you nearly scared me half to death, besieging the house at this time of the morning.' She looked at her watch. 'Who comes to call at seven in the morning? Bad news, that's who! You aren't, are you . . .?'

'Aren't what?' asked Ben. He hadn't expected to eyeball Ida.

'Bringing bad news, that's what.'

'No, no. I'm bringing happy news, the best news: I'm bringing love,' he told her, a smile breaking across his face. 'Who are you?'

'I'm Ida, the woman that does. Who are you? Besides a fool in love.'

'I'm Ben Johnson, looking for Mrs Honey. Is she still asleep?'

'She wouldn't be, after all that racket you were making, if she was here.'

'Not here? Where is she?'

'Come in. Better that than let all the cold air in. Are you the bloke what was to call from France?'

'Yes.'

As soon as Ida told him where Arianne was, he was on his way. No time for coffee or even a glass of orange juice, though first he bound Ida not to tell Arianne he was on the way to her, should she call.

His disappointment at not finding Arianne at home was short-lived. He felt the stubble on his chin – back to his flat on Piccadilly to shave, bathe and change. Then he took the Porsche and headed for the M4 and Chessington Park.

An hour and twenty minutes later he used the key his uncle had left him to enter the house and hurried across the hall to ring the bell at Artemis's flat.

Arianne opened the door. They fell into each other's arms and sealed their reunion with a long, passionate kiss. And then they kissed again. 'I got your cable.' And they kissed yet once more. Finally he asked, 'You are going to let me in?'

'Yes, oh, yes. It's wonderful you're here. But how? I only sent the cable at five yesterday.'

Together, arms around each other, they walked into the sitting room. He was still kissing her face, her hands. 'It's good to have rich and crazy friends. One of the polo players had arrived in St Tropez in his four-seater jet. He flew me from the south of France at dawn this morning, dropped me off at Heathrow and is probably back at the Biblos by now, or close to it. Tell an Argentinean it's an affair of the heart and he understands, is only too willing to play cupid.'

'But your work?'

'Finished that. And I gave my proxy vote to Jaime, the winged polo-player. So now here I am.'

Intense feelings of togetherness appeared to envelope them and dictate their actions. Such powerful emotions made them cautious with even half-intimate words. That oneness with each other they were experiencing was too sensational, a feeling that words would only diminish. So they spoke about other things: his polo schedule, and how he longed for her to be at the next match to see him play. How thrilled he was that she was interested in the game. The book she had discovered and what a sensational find it was.

By this time they were in the Porsche, driving towards Oxfordshire. They had decided to take a leisurely drive through the countryside and return to London after a lunch at Raymond Blanc's Le Manoir Aux Quat' Saisons – Ben's favourite country house hotel, Arianne's favourite chef. The cold, crisp day was somehow too beautiful to miss. The sun radiated no warmth, but it made the day bright.

Arianne was waxing lyrical about books and collecting, telling him how it was her first rare-book purchase to trade with on her own behalf. She had had to use all her savings to buy it. But it had hardly been a calculated chance because she knew the value of the book the moment she held it open in her hands. She had been all enthusiasm in telling him about the book, and he was waiting to hear more, when Arianne went suddenly silent. He sensed something was wrong and turned his concentration from the road briefly to look at her. Their mutual gaze brought a smile to her lips. She leaned towards him and kissed him on the cheek, caressed his thigh with her hand and told him matter of factly:

'It's true, you know. That's all the money I had in the world. I have the trappings of wealth and the good life. But they are just trappings. My clothes, all that was left once the receivers came in and settled our business debts after Jason's death, the house in Three Kings Yard, my ruby ring and this book . . .' She patted the large, soft-leather handbag resting in her lap, wherein lay the book. 'All my assets. I have Ahmad to thank for the house and the ring. Christmas presents. One in November, when he discovered I was living in a bed-sit in Belsize Park, the other a few weeks ago. I don't know why I'm telling you all this. Yes I do. I don't want you to think I live an extravagant life and can't afford it. I have friends who can finance for me the sort of forays into extravagant living that I was once able to make, when my husband was alive. I have gone from that to not a penny in my pocket, no roof over my head and being a salesgirl in Macy's basement just to stay alive – something I'll never do again. I feel better now I've told you. I don't want ever to live beyond my means again. I had no idea that was the way it was when Jason was alive.'

She seemed to Ben to be calm, not at all pouring her heart out all over him, not at all revealing the pain she must have gone through in the past. Right from the first, Arianne inspired in Ben feelings of trust. He had recognised her enormous capacity for understanding. Now he could understand why: she had been through hell and yet she always radiated a feeling of happiness and well-being. In that she was not unlike Ben himself. It was another thing they had in common. He would see that she never suffered again if he had anything to do with it.

Arianne had picked up where she had left off about the rare book she had discovered. He listened for no more than a minute before he pulled off the road into a dirt path, engaged the handbrake and, leaving the motor running, pulled her into his arms as best he could with the seat-belt holding her firm. He kissed her and told her:

'You have nothing to worry about. I'm wealthy, and never live beyond my means. You and I, we'll make it with money, we'll have a wonderful time. But we would have made it without.' He squeezed her hand and kissed her head and told her as he turned away from her, 'Now tell me more about the Levant in the eighteenth century.'

They passed through the gates of the Manoir. Ben parked the car in an empty space in the courtyard. For some minutes they sat looking at the handsome stone manor house, the neatness of the garden, now a suffering beauty under the chill of a mid-winter day. If one needed a romantic setting, surely this would do. The ambience was perfect. There were many more beautiful places they could have gone to, but Le Manoir on the February day in England seemed the only place for them. The quiet, the scale of this particular country house hotel, the intimacy – all seemed just right. It was easy. It allowed their sensual delight in being together to come to the fore. Ben raised her skirt a few inches past her knee and lowered his head to place a kiss upon it. Arianne closed her eyes. It was a most erotic, passionate kiss. She trembled in anticipation.

Anyone who saw them walking across the courtyard and into the reception area of the hotel could not miss that lovers had come to dine. They had Kir Royales by an open fire in a small sitting room while they waited for their table to be made ready. They held hands, the electricity between them seemingly recharged all the time. Each used all the will power available to keep their passion under control. They were aware that what was happening was something bigger than both of them. Each revelled in knowing love on such a scale.

They agonized over the menu. So much to choose from. Such

208

wonderful gastronomic splendours to share. Several Kir Royales later they had made their choice, the Menu Gourmand, to give them a taste of many different dishes. Ben selected the wines. They were now at a table off in a corner of one of the dining rooms with a view of the garden. Each morsel was delicious.

When the last of the three tiny portions of pudding had been consumed and the table cleared, they remained seated. Alone now in the room, they lingered over coffee, savouring the unique well-being that follows a meal created by a master chef, accompanied by wines that the gods on Olympus might have deigned to sip. They were tipsy on wine and love.

'I don't see us driving to London this afternoon,' he told her.

'No.' Her heart was racing with anticipation.

He went around to stand behind her chair. Before pulling it from the table, he kissed her head, caressed her shoulders. She covered with her own the hand that lingered on her shoulder.

The bedroom had a fireplace, with a pair of wing chairs on either side. The four-poster bed was hung with curtains, full-blown roses on a cream-coloured ground. It was a pretty, country-house hotel bedroom with several old pieces of oak furniture. They hardly took it in. They had eyes only for each other. Dusk cast a soft light into the room. Ben placed their coats on the chaise at the foot of the bed. Arianne was standing in the middle of the room watching him. He turned to face her.

She watched him remove his jacket, loosen his tie, unbutton the first two buttons of his shirt. He never took his eyes from hers. She was wearing a white silk blouse with long, full sleeves and a full, grey-flannel skirt that hung to just above her ankles. Round her waist was a wide belt of terracotta-coloured lizard. She lowered her eyes to concentrate on the buttons on her wrist as she undid them. The sexual tension was building, even as he walked from the fireplace to stand in front of her. The first button freed, then another and another. He stopped long enough to kiss her gently. Her lips trembled. He continued to undo her buttons. Arianne loosened his tie, slipped it from around his neck and dropped it on the floor. She pulled his shirt from his trousers, slipped her hands under it and caressed his flesh. He felt warm, so sensual in her hands. She reached around him and caressed his back, working her hands around to his chest, felt the silky hair

209

there, caressed his nipples and felt them go immediately erect.

While she was still undoing his shirt, her blouse slipped from his hands on to the floor. Unclasping her belt, he dropped that too to the floor, lowering his head to her breast to suck nipple and nimbus into his mouth.

They learned more about each other that afternoon through caressing hands and hungry mouths, tongues and lips on naked flesh than most people discover in a lifetime. How sweet for them the carnal love. How delicious the erotic tasted. How sublime, for both of them to submit, submit that little bit more, always that little bit more.

Theirs was a powerful lust, enjoyed in a long and languorous savouring of every caress, every kiss. Ben was an unselfishly magnificent lover, with an obvious sexual adoration of women. The way he kissed and sucked and licked Arianne's cunt, took possession of it, played with it for her pleasure, not his alone, established that. To feel her outer and inner cunt lips in his mouth and his gentle, long, slow sucking of those soft, fleshy lips, was to kindle fire in her, and excite orgasms so exciting and repetitive that she imagined – or really felt – her moist, warm cunt throbbing gently with life for him, for his penis. And always beneath the surface of his lust for her lay deep caring for her, a desire to take her with him into a state of erotic bliss.

What stamina, control, love, he had for her, to delay, always delay, for long intervals of foreplay. The protestations of love by both reinvigorated their sexual lust. Each admitted in whispers thick with passion that the other was more thrilling as partner than either had imagined.

Ben slipped on top of Arianne. This time, between passionate kisses of her mouth and her breasts, he spread her legs wide. Taking her hand in his, he wrapped her fingers around his pulsating, erect penis, and directed her hand. It was Arianne who guided the large, handsome crown of his cock to between her moist cunt lips. She rubbed it back and forth across her slit several times before she parted those lips with it. Then together they plunged his needy penis in one long, hard thrust to take final possession of each other.

'How wonderful, how beautiful you are,' she told him. 'Oh, yes, please,' – as he slowly withdrew and entered her again and

210

again. How she loved being fucked. He adored her unashamed passion for sex. It made her an even greater joy to fuck. Arianne was surrendering herself to him with his every thrust. Loving him and their sex, with roving hands and busy kisses, her eyes closed, she whispered magnificently erotic things to him. It spurred him on to love her more, take her again. With no woman in his life had he been more close, more intimate, more at one. No woman had ever given herself up to him as Arianne was doing. He could hold back no longer. His rhythm changed. The beat of his fucking, like the beat of his heart, raced and carried Arianne with it, while he whispered beautiful things to her.

Arianne felt herself right there in the moment with Ben, this new, lovely and very sexy man. She was his, he hers. When he was about to come, he was not alone, she was there with him, ready to come herself in a crescendo of orgasm, and to sail out on oblivion with him. Suddenly words came flooding back from the recesses of her mind. 'For the sake of love, a taste of eternity.' Jason's words, Jason's voice. Vivid memories of them lying naked together in each other's arms. Jason kissing her, fucking her, roughly taking possession of her with hands that caressed lovingly and bruised from excess of passion, and a hungry mouth that bit into her flesh.

'In our love, in the shadow of our lives with many suns to warm our hearts, no shadows remain,' he sang to her from a French love-song. He pulled her head back by her hair and devoured her lips, her mouth, with deep kisses.

It was all there for them once more, their life of all sun, warmth and strength that scorched and devoured them over and over again. They were together, as real as if he had never died, living their life of love and folly, trust and courage. Their desires, Jason's, hers, the comeliness of their life, were still blooming.

He spoke to her again: 'When sad days come, think of the sun, those many suns that have warmed our lives and an unaltered love over and over again. Passion and ecstasy, tenderness and pride, freedom – that's our love, our life, and will be for eternity. I'll never let it die, and nor will you. We're for ever and for ever,' Jason whispered in her ear. To feel him inside her was to be alive again. To sense the lust he had for her in his dark eyes under his long, thick lashes, the scent of him in her nostrils again, was the

211

essence of her life. His smile, and the joy mixed with unleashed passion on his face with every lunge of his penis, burned into her soul. She loved him so.

They were coming in a rush of the warmest, most lush of orgasms. She was unable to hold back her joy. She gasped, and then called out in thralls of ecstasy while those vivid visions of their last night of sexual intercourse began to fade. Arianne tried hard to hold them in the forefront of her mind, but they were drifting away, and taking Arianne with them.

Ben was coming, his orgasm flowing into Arianne. His ardour was so great that he remained erect as he caressed her womb with his warm sperm, and kept moving in and out of her. Such bliss. And yet, while still in the act of flagrant passion, he felt her receding, drawing away from him. His seed finally spent, he relaxed on top of her, only to feel she was no longer with him. He could hardly believe it, until she opened her eyes.

They were cold and distant. He was stunned. Ben slid from her body to lie next to her on the bed. He asked her, 'Why?'

She was calm. There were no tears. She made no apology. But there were distress and sadness in her eyes enough to make one's heart break. 'Why? Because of my husband.'

'But your husband is dead.'

She shook her head, and it was over for them.

They dressed as if they were strangers. 'Our past is not our guide, Arianne,' he told her. 'You and I, we mustn't be careless. Our love is much stronger than us.'

'Please, Ben, this is terribly awkward for me. I need to be alone, quiet and alone. I want to go to London, away from here and you, to dwell in the past.'

'He's dead.'

'Not for me. I just thought he was. A car, a train. Please can you arrange it for me?'

His heart went out to her. He was still too stunned to know what to do, except what she wished. Walking down the stairs with him, she could not look at him. He stopped her at the foot of the stairs and told her, 'You're in a cage.'

'I thought I was free, Ben. But I'm not. Forgive me.'

'What are you saying, Arianne? No more love for us? Do you honestly think that will work? How foolish you are. Love is stronger than us. If you think our pasts guide us, you're wrong. Love chooses. That's something mere mortals have no control over. If that's not true, then why did you tell me your husband was dead?'

'He is dead.'

There was no one in the reception hall. The hotel was quiet. Ben left her there and looked in several rooms. No one. He returned to Arianne. 'Look, this is crazy. It's two-thirty in the morning. You stay here the night. You are in no condition to travel. Get a train in the morning. Get some fresh air now – walk me to my car.'

Ben unlocked the car after scraping frost from the windshield. From a lantern shone a dim light to cut the black of a starless night. He took her hand in his and told her, 'Just remember you cabled me you loved me. I don't think you did that lightly.' Then he turned her around to face the hotel. 'Try to get some sleep.' He drove away from the hotel and did not look back.

Chapter 16

Ben could not believe what had happened to them. That he was driving away from Le Manoir aux Quat' Saisons and Arianne. 'If I had another chance,' he asked himself, 'what would I do differently? How could I have kept her? Should I have said, "Come back to London with me, we'll be pals"? How could I? We didn't start as pals: we started as lovers and we'll end up as lovers. She cabled me, "I love you". She does love me. She forgot that. She was upset, surely, and just got mixed up about who she is in love with. Why didn't I suggest that to her? Tell her that I accept her husband might have been a clever man and very charming, but the way she was reacting to a new love, a new life, he must also have been a man with a compulsion to manipulate situations and control outcomes. And he was still doing it, years after he had been laid in his grave. Her husband? What if he had lived? Maybe he would have turned into an old fool. But as it is, he will always be a young, handsome hero to her. Who knows? Maybe, if he had not died, they would have been a wonderful couple. Or, maybe, a pair of old fools who just hated each other.'

There was no doubt about it, Ben wanted Jason firmly dead in her mind. In the same way that Clarissa was firmly dead in his. Not forgotten. Clarissa was etched deep in his memory; she would always be a part of his history, the good and the bad that had been their marriage. But she had nothing to do with his happiness now, his will to live and enjoy life and love again, to be a whole human being who walked upright and with dignity in the present. He suddenly loathed Jason, not because Jason had come between Arianne and himself, but because Jason had done so much damage to Arianne by the way he lived with her, treated her. He had never prepared her to be happy without him.

He thought of the beautiful Clarissa, what their life might have been had she not taken hers. Beautiful, complex, totally mad Clarissa. When told that he was in a critical condition after surgery for appendicitis, she had refused to believe the doctors. She had made up her mind that he was dying, would be dead before she could get to him, because in her sick mind that was what she wanted. She used him, as she had always used him, for her own voracious, destructive ego, right to the end. Clarissa, his wife, who left a note addressed, 'To whom it may concern'. It stated quite simply, 'I cannot live without my husband.' No more, no less, from the once-famous model who, dressed in her best Dior gown and her jewellery, coiffed and made up to perfection, went down to the garage, sealed the doors with rags and tape and then ran a hose-pipe from the exhaust into the car. After turning on the ignition, Clarissa sat in the back seat of his 1937 yellow Rolls-Royce, his newest and then favourite acquisition. There she waited peacefully for a merciful release from a life she really had no appetite for. They knew she had died peacefully because when she had been found she was beautiful and perfect, with no signs of agony on her face, and looking not unlike the store-window display mannequins fashioned after her. The press had somehow managed to get a shot of the macabre scene in the garage before her body had been removed.

It had been nearly a week before he had been well enough to be told the sad news. Weeks passed before the world's newspapers and magazines gave up on the tragic death of one of the world's best-loved models and her polo-playing husband. He thought about those terrible weeks now while speeding away from Arianne down the M40.

'Such a waste,' he said aloud. Once said, it acted as a tonic for Ben. It confirmed what he already knew in his heart: Arianne was a woman flexible in her principles, but at the same time she was quite normal, even with all the things she had going for her. 'It's her very normality that's so seductive.' And then he thought, And that normality would never allow her to waste life or love as Clarissa had. Clarissa was gone because she had nothing to live for, no resources or will without Ben. That was not Arianne.

Until Arianne, Ben's sense of guilt over Clarissa's suicide had made him resistant to love. Reason enough for no woman to have had a chance with him. Time, the great healer, had been slowly diminishing this sense of guilt. Meeting Arianne, a nongrasping, non-manipulative woman with so much substance to her, pushed guilt that little bit further away; falling in love with her freed him from it for ever. Stunning realisations.

Ben pulled the car over to the verge. He left the lights burning and sat back, trying to put together what had happened in the bedroom at Le Manoir.

Arianne went back to her room and lay down on the bed. No tears. No self-pity. Nor was there embarrassment over what had happened. She was still traumatised by what she had seen, what she had done. All she could think of was that Ben was gone. Then the memories flooded back: him knocking at Artemis's door, stepping into the hallway to throw his arms around her. His passionate kiss. How happy she had felt to see him. There had been so few words, so many right moves. How he had found her hat and her coat and sent her for her bag, and then whisked her away from Chessington Park. Alone now, she understood even more how happy she was with Ben. The chance she had had to be loved again in the present, and, indeed, to be able to love a man again.

In the car, driving through the English countryside, they had become more accustomed to being together and words came easier. She had liked so much the way he had included her in his future when he was telling her about his days away from her, his business dealings: 'At the next wine auction, I'll take you with me. You'll love the château and my colleagues there will love you.' Why was she remembering that now, when it was all over for them? She seemed unable to empty her mind of the enthusiasm in his voice when he had asked, 'Are you committed to England – to London, to Christie's? Or are you free?' Free, she had promised him, but then she hadn't known she was not.

She thought about all the places she would not watch him play polo: Deauville, Palm Beach, Los Angeles, in Argentina, and India. The house she would never occupy with him in New York that he wanted to buy for them because they both agreed that the call to go home, back to the States, was growing stronger, as it sometimes did for wandering expatriate Americans. She remembered vividly how she had laughed at him because he was so very excited about them, and full of ideas and adventures for

217

them. 'Yes. Yes, yes,' she had answered to everything he wanted. And would there ever be a more exciting moment for her again than when they had walked from that dining room, knowing they were going to make love for the first time?

The adventurous life had been there for her, offered to her by a man she could love. If only she had dared to surrender herself to him. God knows, she had wanted to, had been doing exactly that, slowly, with every kiss, every caress, surrendering inch by inch to him with every carnal embrace. Arianne placed her arm across her eyes and tried to block out her losses, tried to sleep.

Ben shook his head. It's not possible – we're too good, too right to be tossed away for something dead and gone for ever. For anything, period. Live or dead. He was emphatic about that, and he would do something. At last he was coming out of the shock of Arianne's retreat from him.

It was not even six o'clock in the morning when he swung the Porsche into Hyde Park. He felt somehow ridiculous. What was he doing there? Suddenly he was in control of his life again, and knew exactly what must be done. He made a fast and dangerous U-turn and sped away from London along the M40 towards his destination, Le Manoir. But several miles later he made an equally dangerous U-turn. He knew that he had to be there for her, but he also knew instinctively that he was wrong to go chasing after her. It was one thing to be selfless and kind to her during this terrible time she was putting herself through; quite another to be forceful, aggressive, to make her see the rightness of them. His own independent spirit demanded that he let her return to London alone as she had requested, to allow her the independence to do what she chose.

Arianne did not sleep. She had merely lain there, eyes closed, her mind wandering between the past and the present. And the past was getting harder and harder to see. It kept drifting away from her memory, her marvellous life with Jason, and with Jason and Ahmad. Even that *ménage à trois*, one of the happiest experiences of her life, was so firmly set in the past, it now seemed almost like a dream. Ben, just her and Ben, not even her alone seemed to be the only present she could envisage, but she knew that had to be a dream too. It was over, and in time what she had thrown away would be just another memory of what could have been. But for now there was no peace for her because she kept thinking about Ben and how her past had snatched him from her.

It had been light for some time. She rose from the bed and went into the pretty bathroom she and Ben had not even shared. There she washed her hands and face, and seeing in the mirror how distressed she looked gave her yet another shock, as if losing Ben had not been enough. She all but recoiled from the woman in the mirror, but then composed herself. She sat down at the dressing-table and made an effort to cover her distress by carefully applying her cosmetics. That accomplished, she hardly knew what to do next.

Memory can be a cruel master. She could not expunge the memory of Ben and herself, naked, entwined. Sitting on the edge of the bed now, she wondered how she could be so torn. Suddenly she felt a surge of courage, and at last could bring herself to ask the question: Is my heart really in two places? Even to form the question was to bring her closer to the reality of her conflict. The ringing of the telephone was a merciful momentary release from anxiety.

She had left a note at the reception desk the night before asking which was the first available train to London. Here was her morning call with the information and the message that breakfast was on the way up to her room. She could take it leisurely and still make her train.

That galvanised Arianne, but it did nothing for the sadness she felt, the pain of a love lost. A quiet breakfast, a train ride, and home. That, if nothing else, seemed to make sense.

She half expected him to knock at the bedroom door. But there was no knock.

The train was crowded, and she sat huddled against the window, feeling more isolated from people and the world than ever she did in her darkest moments after Jason's death. She watched the countryside roll by as the train rushed forward, and she felt sick, not with self-pity, but something much worse, loneliness.

The train slowed as it approached London. There was hustle and bustle for the passengers making ready to exit and hurry on to offices, houses and family, to people and work. And then, before she realised it, they were turtle-like inching their way into Paddington Station. The coach was nearly empty when she rose from her seat to leave and step into the crowd rushing towards the exits. What had she done? Not just to herself, but to Ben. Could she resign herself to living in the past, or what was left of it, to Ahmad in the present? She could have once, before Ben Johnson. Now?

She walked as in a daze through Paddington. People jostled her, and she kept saying, 'I'm sorry.' At one point she hardly knew where she was going and just let herself be carried along by the crowd, while she tried to work out her life. She stepped from the station into a blast of London air that served to slap her awake. She clasped her coat around her and stood for some minutes, amazed that she no longer felt torn between a dead love – still overpoweringly exciting, even if it had to be lived in memory alone – and the deep love and strong sexual attraction she felt for Ben.

It had been too good, the sensuality and sexual tenderness combined with animal lust and love she had had with Ben for a few moments. Those things had brought her alive erotically as she had never been before, not even with her husband, who had always dominated their lust for the erotic. At last she understood. She had found more, even more to love, to give herself to, in Ben. She had seen a glimpse of an even more exciting love than she had ever known – one that would oblige her to put her marriage into a proper perspective. And that was what had made her bolt. To live in the past with Jason, and in the present with Ahmad? That now began to seem a penance.

She walked from Paddington Station to Three Kings Yard. Calm and sanity prevailed. Her mind emptied and she felt peaceful, her naturally passive nature rising again. She also felt quite drained. It was a very exhausting thing burying at last a ghost that had nearly become a myth.

Arianne was walking down Davies Street from Oxford Street. She had just passed South Molton Street when she saw him. He was standing in front of the entrance to Three Kings Yard, the collar of his leather coat turned up against the chill wind. He was clapping his hands and stamping his feet to keep warm. Her heart began to race. She walked faster, squinting against the sun. She raised a hand to her forehead as a visor. She must make sure it was him. He was at a considerable distance. Her eyes might deceive, but not her heart. And then he turned to look up the street. There was no mistaking him.

Ben recognised her figure at once among the pedestrians coming and going on the pavement. He didn't hesitate. He started walking towards her. First slowly, then more rapidly. The closer they came to each other the faster they walked. Soon they were close enough to lock their gaze across the distance and people. How sad, tired and cold she looked, but also disarmingly beautiful, with that quality of fragile femininity allied to formidable maturity. The first look after their estrangement was enough to tell them they loved each other and must be together. It ensured that he stood still, if only to take her into himself and catch his breath, to calm himself amid the happiness that surged through him.

Not so Arianne. Her feet hardly felt the pavement, she was moving so urgently. Finally she could bear the distance separating them no longer. She broke into a run. He regained his composure, and waited for her to come to him. She almost fell into his arms.

'I've been a fool, such a fool.'

He stifled her protestations with a kiss. When he released her, tears brimmed in his eyes. 'Love chooses. I did tell you that.'

'Yes, you did.'

She rested her head against his shoulder, too moved to say any more. He stroked her hair. She was so cold. 'Where's your hat?' he asked.

For the first time she realised she didn't have it on. She had lost it somewhere en route. 'It doesn't matter.'

'It does.' He removed his cashmere scarf from his neck and tied it around her head.

A gesture so simple, so pure, so loving; she was moved yet again by him. She asked, 'Ben, please kiss me again.' He obliged. Then he took her arm in his and they walked together down the street.

He whispered in her ear, 'I promise you that I do understand that you need, still, for the moment, not to let go of the past.' He sensed her anxiety and tried to make it easier for her. He moved

221

his arm to around her shoulder and hugged her to him as they continued down the street. She turned to look at him. Their eyes met as he reassured her that all would go well for them: 'Shush, shush. There's nothing to be anxious about; we'll work it out. All we need is time, you and I. Time together, to allow *our* love, *our* passion, *our* erotic longings for each other, to flourish as they once did for you and your husband. Arianne, we nearly lost each other. That is never going to happen again. If it were going to happen, we wouldn't be here together now, acting like two lovesick puppies on a London street.' He made light of what he felt deeply. It was the tone that seemed best to correspond to the heavy commitment they had just made to each other. 'I am right about that, aren't I?' he asked.

He had said it all: all that would ever now be said about the past; all he could manage to say on a street in Mayfair. Arianne knew very well that the answer she would now give was a firm commitment to Ben – one he had been looking for at Le Manoir but hadn't insisted upon. He was giving her a choice even now to back out, but there was no longer a way of retreat open for Arianne. Love had made its choice. 'Yes, Ben, absolutely right.'

They arrived at Number 12, Three Kings Yard just as Ida was leaving. Proper introductions having been made this time, she opened the front door for them. With a wry smile she suggested, 'You look as if you should be carrying her over the threshold, Mr Johnson.'

Neither Ben nor Arianne could keep smiles from their faces, or laughter from their voices. 'Are we that obvious, Ida?' he asked, looking delighted.

'Pretty much,' she answered, really pleased with herself for guessing that at last her lady had found herself a man. Ida loved a good romance.

'Ida, don't be surprised to see Mr Johnson around when you next come in,' Arianne told her. It seemed the correct thing to do.

'Surprised! I'd be more surprised if he wasn't.' Then she set down one of her carrier bags, took a bag from the top and handed it to Arianne. 'Better have these. Danish pastries, from a food exhibition in Soho. Did you know it's Danish week? I'll be in day after tomorrow. You be good to her, Mister.' And Ida was gone towards the arch at the end of the courtyard.

'She's amazing,' said Arianne.

'You're amazing,' said Ben as he swept her off her feet and into his arms, carried her over the threshold of Number 12 and kicked the door closed.

Hours later the sitting room was bathed in the eerie light that comes with dusk, investing with mystery the last moments of the afternoon – a winter dusk with a hint of pink light that made it a mauvey grey. It suited the sitting room, and the two people seated nude on the carpet in front of the fireplace – Arianne, with knees drawn up, between Ben's legs, leaning against him, enfolded by his arms and caressing hands.

He lowered his head to kiss her lightly, gently, on the shoulder, to raise her hand and bring it to his lips. The fire reflected orange flames in a pattern across their bodies. The warmth felt good. They had bathed together and dried themselves off with luxurious towels, discarded now close to where they sat.

Arianne eased her head to one side and nuzzled it against Ben's collar-bone, found a niche for herself and cuddled him there. She lowered her eyes and looked at the hands cupping her breasts. Ben loved her breasts, the weight of them in his hands. Most women can tell when a man really loves her body as Ben loved Arianne's. It inspires a woman to surrender herself to a man, for hours, body and soul. Arianne lazily lowered her knees and leaned back even further into him. With one hand still cupped around her breast, he moved the other to fondle her flat tummy, to slip his fingers over her mound and caress affectionately the soft, fleshy lips, moist yet again. She sighed and relaxed against him.

'What bliss. How divine a lover you are,' she whispered. The sigh that followed was pure contentment. She took his hand away from her cunt, covered her mouth with it, kissed the palm and licked it with the tip of her tongue, then placed it under her breast. His fingers played with her long, erect nipples. How she adored being fondled by him, being set free sexually by their lust for each other. Nestling her head against him, she turned it just enough to place a kiss on his shoulder, his arm, to insert her tongue between his arm and his body and lick him there. He understood, she didn't have to say anything.

She liked sitting nude between his thighs, to feel his large, flaccid penis grow as it pressed against her, the strength of his strong arms around her, his broad chest against her back. They seemed mesmerised by the dancing flames in the fireplace and by the feeling of being so sexually fulfilled. The warmth of the open fire crept subtly into their bones. It was a heat like no other, deep and penetrating, an intrinsic glow like the love and affection these two new lovers had for each other.

Arianne disentangled herself from Ben's arms just long enough to stretch herself: arms raised high and wide, legs further apart as she pushed herself deeper against him. Then she folded his arms back around her the way they had been and placed his hands once more under her breasts; the same hands that could excite a passion in her and be at times so sexually untamed on her body. That excited them and took them further, always further, into orgasms that reached beyond reality into a private world of erotic bliss.

'Are you happy?' he asked her, kissing the side of her neck, licking the lobe of her ear.

She answered him with a kiss. 'Will you stay with me?' she asked.

'Now and for ever. I thought that had already been established. It goes without saying. Truly it does.' And he kissed her.

'No, I mean here. Or do we live in your place?'

'Whatever you want. Here is a more romantic and cosier place than mine. It's like playing grown-ups in a dolls' house. I'm happy to stay here for when we are in London.'

'Good, that's settled then. I love you, Ben.'

'I love you, Arianne.'

They were yet again moved by emotion and their passion for each other. He kissed her on the eyes, her lips; caressed her breasts, opened his mouth and placed it over her nipple. He licked and sucked it. He could feel her responding to him. She squirmed under his hungry mouth, deriving from it a delicate pleasure. He slipped his fingers between her cunt lips and inserted them as deeply as he could inside her. Caressing fingers. She squeezed on them with her cunt. Her breath grew heavy with passion. He used his teeth to bite into the shaded nimbus of her breasts.

224

Arianne thought that she had been through, had come to the point of exhaustion, and there was nothing left, orgasm impossible, sexual exhaustion having taken over. But she had been wrong. She came with a tremendous orgasm that surprised even Ben. It flowed over his fingers, and he used them as he might his penis to penetrate her as deeply as he could. Her body grew tense in his arms and she held herself that way while she came. When it was over for her, she relaxed and went limp against his body. Only then did he remove his mouth from her breast to kiss her lips with affection, with a deep abiding love. She gazed at his erect penis, throbbing with life, and experienced the strangeness and beauty of it.

Ben picked Arianne up off the floor as he rose, and walked her to the sofa. He sat down with her on his lap. Turning her around in his arms to face him, he lowered his hands and spread wide her cunt lips. He played with them thus for several minutes before raising her by the waist. Bringing her down as hard as he could, he impaled her on his cock and pressed her to him, while gazing admiringly at her. He rocked her thus, slowly, lovingly, as one would a child. He caressed her hair, gently kissed her lips, and then raised her by her hips and eased her down again on him several times. He could feel the grip of her cunt kissing his cock. What pleasure, what bliss she was. And then, with her still impaled upon him, he gently manoeuvred them both to lie on their sides together on the sofa, watching the fire.

'Let's make our real home in the States. Begin a new life together there.'

She ran her fingers through his hair and touched his cheek with the back of her hand. He remained still rigid inside her. They were sexually quiescent, enjoying the affection they felt for each other, the feel of penis and cunt locked together.

'I think I'd like to go home with you,' she told him.

Arianne felt Ben stir inside her. He had been shrinking back. After several gentle thrusts she could feel him grow larger, rigid inside her again. The delight she felt at being riven by him showed in her eyes; he could feel it in the way her body moved. Her enjcyment of cock was something he understood. Arianne found it exciting to have sex with him because he appreciated how much some women love to be riven by an erect penis; how intercourse calms their wombs and fills their hearts with joy; how they derive the same pleasure as a man in a sexual abandonment that has nothing to do with responsibility or relationships, and is centred entirely on sexual bliss.

'Arianne?'

'Yes.'

'Will you marry me?' There was a certain formality in the way he proposed to her, the more so considering the way they were with each other. She somehow appreciated that, and his proposal went straight to her heart. It touched her in her soul.

'Yes, Ben, I will, when and wherever you like.' Then she clasped Ben in her arms, placed her lips on his and opened them with her tongue to search out rich kisses from the depths of his soul. What followed – her kisses on his face, on his cock, his to her cunt – excited him to roll them gently from the sofa on to the carpet in front of the fire, Arianne on her back. He straddled her and raised her legs on to his shoulders, then placed cushions under her and fucked her with passionate lust until they came together one more time.

They lay silent in each other's arms for some time, replete with sex and love. Once composed again, Ben kissed her lightly on the lips and inquired, 'Tea or champagne?'

'Oh, I think champagne.' Their life together began.

They were blissfully happy tucked away in the house in Three Kings Yard. Having found love, the lovers were now discovering each other, and were thrilled with their findings. This was that special romantic time in lovers' lives that can never be repeated, never forgotten, and Arianne and Ben were making the most of it. It was patently obvious to them that they were laying the foundation, as solid as bedrock, on which to build a marriage. They peeled away the layers of silence, broke down protective walls they had built around themselves, and gave themselves up to each other. And every day fell in love that little bit more.

One morning after a particularly passionate and profoundly erotic sexual coming together, Ben suggested, 'How would you like to repeat this tomorrow morning in my big four-poster bed in the château in France?'

'I think I'd like that fine,' was her reply.

'Great.' He kissed her and bounded out of bed to make arrangements.

It was not only Arianne who felt a tremendous excitement about their first visit to the château. Ben loved his eighteenth-century house in the Médoc and took pride and joy in the accompanying vineyard. He sensed that, at last, it was to have a mistress who would love it as he did. Together he and Arianne would turn it from a magnificent house into a happy, loving home. It suddenly felt to him that the years of restoration, collecting antiques and paintings, tapestries, eighteenth-century *objets d'art*, and re-creating the once famous gardens, had all been in preparation for this first visit.

'The thing about being a poor boy and having wealthy friends is that they can't stand their friends being poor. The wealthy feel more secure with their own – I owe most of my success to that fact. I have had a few good breaks in my life from wealthy friends, a tip here and there on the world's stock markets, a prime job offered through connections, old school ties and all that. I worked hard and I played hard and had some luck, and I wasn't greedy. I gave back to my friends, shared my luck with them and it made me wealthy and secure in myself. Now I'm one of them. And that short sharp business biography explains how we are able to drive through my neighbours' vineyards here in the Haut Médoc, Margaux country: Soussans, Contenac, Labard, to our own vineyard and house. That house over there.'

Arianne had until now found the Médoc in winter to be a strange landscape. Hectares and hectares of stubbly, pruned vines set out in neat rows, broken only by the occasional impressive château, under a white, white sun shining as bright haze through a grey clouded sky on this bitter cold day. Ben's vineyard ran from the tarmacked road close to the river Gironde. When they turned off it on to his land and drove through his vineyard on to a rise and she saw for the first time the magnificent ornamental iron gates and the château beyond, she had to catch her breath at the impressive beauty and charm of the place.

They sped through the gates, past gardens braving the winter cold and the chill wind coming off the river, and up the gravel avenue lined with trees past huge clipped shrubs now hidden under their winter canvas covers as protection against the frost.

Ben brought the car to a halt with a screech of tyres at the entrance of the eighteenth-century stone château, impressive not only for its age and beauty but for its inexplicable warmth and charm. This was the house where Ben hoped they would marry.

Soft yellow light from the lamps within the house shone through the many windows. Warmth seemed to be seeping out from it into the grey cold afternoon. Arianne began to laugh with delight. Ben found the joy in her laughter charismatic. It held his attention until he finally broke its spell to say, 'That's some reaction.'

'Ben, I love it. It's fantastic. A fairy-tale castle. I feel like Cinderella going to the ball.'

His turn to laugh. He grabbed her hand and pulled her across the seat past the steering wheel and out through the car door. Together they ran away out of the cold and up the steps through the dark walnut carved front doors into the house. They could hear a clatter of running feet somewhere in the distance as they crossed the black and white marble floor to stand and warm themselves in front of a roaring fire in the massive stone fireplace.

The housekeeper, a maid, a cleaner, Ben's personal assistant, a secretary and the head gardener arrived in the hall from all directions. They were set upon with congratulations, good wishes, kisses, the French way; first one cheek, then the other, and once again. Hugs, the shaking of hands, genuine affection, pleasure for Ben's happiness and delight in his chosen partner.

Arianne, overwhelmed by their generosity of spirit, was relieved to see there was nothing formal or grand about the way Ben ran his household. The staff appeared to be happy in their work and informal, though respectful and willing to please. She had only to look round the great hall to see that, casual as Ben's staff appeared, they were hard workers. It was impeccably clean and kept up to a high aesthetic standard: the fresh flowers arranged in eighteenth-century Chinese porcelain vases, logs in the basket, a fire laid and blazing – these were signs of a staff that served their master well.

Coats were removed and whisked away. From a marble console against a wall, a Baroque silver tray laden with crystal champagne flutes was picked up by the only Englishman in the household staff, Ben's butler-cum-valet-cum-major domo. Timmins passed the glasses among them while others followed, charging them with vintage champagne. Up from the kitchen in the lower level of the château came the cook's assistant and two under-gardeners carrying silver trays of beautifully arranged hot, bite-sized nibbles to go with the wine: chicken croquettes, foie gras topped with black truffle and wrapped in filo pastry, wild mushrooms stuffed with crab meat. Everyone seemed to be talking at once, the local gossip, questions: where, when, what kind of wedding would it be.

Someone pushed open the pair of doors to the drawing room and they all drifted in there, where there were two roaring fires at opposite ends of the handsome room. They were impressive for their size and the quality of the carving in their *fleur de pêche* marble surrounds. For all its elegance, grandeur, even, the room had a certain warmth and charm. It was a homely room, one to be lived in and enjoyed.

A room of elegant furniture, high-backed chairs covered in Aubusson tapestries, others in sixteenth- and seventeenth-century needlework, hunting scenes: unicorns and boars, stags, hunters on charging horses out for the kill, lords and ladies on fiery steeds galloping across landscapes of rolling hills, a wood, rushing streams, towards castles in the distance.

Precious Persian carpets worn with age covered the walnut-planked waxed floors and were impressively beautiful. On the walls: Old Master drawings in gilded and carved frames. An enormous David that dominated one end of the room, a battle scene with magnificently painted horses, handsome brave generals in the saddle commanding the troops. One could almost smell the cannon smoke. And there were women in the room, and what women! Odalisques, nude and magnificent Eastern female slaves and concubines painted by Ingres.

Vases of white lilacs, bowls of tulips, Han bronze pots of bright yellow daffodils, branches of spiral eucalyptus shared a Lalique crystal vase with white tulips, and large cymbidium orchid plants were in full bloom in the room. The four arch-topped windows whose doors led on to the terrace were draped in yellow silk damask – worn from more than a century of use,

229

they were frayed but still bright in colour. Books were stacked on tables and a cat, Persian, a smoky grey with dramatic green eyes, was curled up in a wing chair in front of one of the fires. Three period bird cages sat on a table at the far end of the room, and their residents, orange singing canaries, were in full song. The cat and the canaries miraculously shared this room, such was the tranquillity between them.

Arianne took it all in, and once she was over her initial surprise at the beauty and elegance of the life Ben lived, she relaxed and felt quite at home, comfortable, as if she belonged there with Ben and his things.

Several glasses of champagne later, quite discreetly, staff and the champagne flutes, the empty silver trays vanished from the room and Arianne and Ben were left alone. They sat silent in front of the fire for some time. Just being together seemed to say it all for them. Finally Arianne kissed Ben on the cheek and said, 'I think I'm ready to see more.'

It was a tour of the house, but not all forty rooms of the château. The kitchen, the hub of the house, was splendid and with a massive round country dining table in front of an open fire where Arianne learned Ben liked to dine with his friends most of the time, leaving the dining room for the most grand occasions. A smaller circular dining room overlooking the garden was used for intimate yet formal meals. 'And here is where you and I will dine when we want to be alone, away from cook and staff.' They viewed half-dozen or more rooms until Ben became bored with giving the tour and told her, 'There's plenty of time to see the rest.' He pulled her into the master suite of rooms he used. 'My bedroom,' he told her. 'Now our bedroom.'

'It's marvellous. I don't know what I expected, but whatever it was, the château, this room, it's all much more.'

'You can change anything you want to in the house. Is there anything you don't like? All you have to do is tell me.'

'I don't want to change a thing. I only want to become part of it, share it with you.'

Ben took Arianne in his arms and hugged her to him. He felt tremendously emotional at her response. So uncomplicated, so easy, and genuine, but then he should have expected that. That was Arianne. He needed a moment to compose himself. He released her and walked to the window to watch the river flowing swiftly past the château.

Arianne, sensitive to every nuance of Ben's feelings, went to him and took his hand in hers. They remained there very much together, the room silent except for the crackling sound of the open fire. Several minutes passed by, and he was in control of himself again. He turned away from the window to kiss her on the cheek, to smile at her. 'This is a wonderful room,' she told him, as he picked her up in his arms and carried her to the four-poster, canopied bed, elaborately draped in white silk and lined in grey and white silk-taffeta stripes, that had once belonged to a king.

Ben laid Arianne gently on the bed against the cream and white and beige silk damask pillows. He removed her suede boots and placed them neatly to one side on the floor. Then he raised her dark brown suede skirt up around her waist. He was deliberately slow, savouring every moment as he eased the black silk and lace half-slip she was wearing down off her hips, her legs, to drop it on the floor. After removing her silk panties, he placed two of the silk damask pillows under her bottom. To be undressed by Ben was sexy, to be thus exposed to the man she loved and yearned for was very sexy; the sensuous feel of the silk damask against her naked bottom was to render her hungry for sexual delights.

Ben removed his jacket and placed it on a chair, then returned to Arianne to sit on the bed. He caressed her mound, her thighs, to the top of her black silk stockings. He stood up and spread her legs wide apart and then climbed on the bed to sit in between them. He lowered his head and sighed, 'Ah, the glorious mound of Venus.' He ran his fingers through the pubic hair covering it, then placed a kiss upon it. Arianne watched him, and to watch him making love to her was yet another erotic excitement for her.

With deft fingers he opened her cunt lips and began to lick her. To suck tenderly on her labia, to place his pointed tongue at the opening of her vagina, to lick it, circle it again and again. He searched out her clitoris and teased it. How he loved her, adored her for loving him, for wanting him, for the delight she took in giving herself up to him in all things sexual, beyond body, beyond soul.

231

His kisses told Arianne everything. Revelling in them, she whispered, in a voice husky with passion, 'I love you so much, Ben. I've loved before, but what I feel for you is something so special, what we are together so right, all other loves pale before it.'

Here were words that rang true for Ben as well. Words he had waited to hear all his adult life.

She came, and he tasted her on his tongue. He filled his mouth with her and then he quite gently placed her legs together and slid himself up the bed to lie next to her. Taking her in his arms, he kissed her deeply and they fell asleep spent by love for each other.

When they rose from their dreamless sleep neither of them could remember that moment when kissing had stopped and deep dark sleep had taken them over.

PARIS, GLOUCESTERSHIRE, LONDON

Chapter 17

'The thing about being in the detective business is that it can be incredibly boring. You know – long, tedious surveillance stuff, dull people living dull lives, trying to escape a dull existence. It gets to be hectic when you have to travel – airport hassle, visas, foreign cops. But the work itself is still routine. The same dull guys sinning in the same dull ways. Only the scenery alters. Till you get into the high-flying stuff: intrigue, dirty dealings, power politics. You know – "Murder Incorporated" sorta stuff. Missing persons, we get a lot of those, and missing bodies, not so many of those. But always, whatever the case, big or small, it's always dealing with the human element. That's what keeps a detective hooked. That and a good mystery to solve, the ultimate.' At this point Jim O'Connor attracted the attention of the waiter and glasses were instantly refilled. In acceptable French he ordered another bottle of 1978 Montrachet, and told the waiter, 'I think another plate of frogs' legs.'

They were in a bistro in one of the back streets of Montparnasse, famous for its wine cellar and two dishes, the only ones this bistro served: deep-fried frogs' legs in an especially delicious light batter, and *escargots* served straight from the oven, in garlic butter, the snails sizzling in their shells.

It was Jim who had called the meeting, Jim who had selected the bistro. Ahmad sensed he was going to hear more about the detective business. Not interested, he cut Jim off before he could resume his dissertation. 'You've got a lot of style, Jim. This is a great place. The food, the wine, can't be bettered. Small, intimate, yet rough-and-tumble. Quite an atmosphere.'

'You might add, off the beaten track. Nice sorta place for a quiet meeting.'

'We could have had that in my rooms at the Plaza Athénée.'

'Not really. I promised to keep your name out of this

investigation you wanted me to take on.'

'Ah!' Ahmad was beginning to understand: Jim was relishing some sort of success.

Jim chose to ignore the exclamation. He wasn't ready to give anything away. Instead he said, 'Glad you like my discovery, Ahmad. Been coming here for years.'

'You're an unusual man. Many-sided, I'd say, Jim. It's one of the things I like about you.'

'Next you'll be telling me I've got some taste. Well, Ahmad, one frog's leg doesn't make a gourmet. Nor does a preference for great white burgundy that's strong and perfumed and suits my palate make me a wine-buff.'

Ahmad transferred the last frog's leg from the platter to his plate, took a swallow of his wine and then, while raising the succulent piece of meat to his mouth, gazed across the table directly into Jim's eyes. 'I think you're playing with me, Jim.'

'Not exactly playing.'

'What then?'

'I don't rightly know.'

That was honest, thought Ahmad. 'You have some news for me?'

'Yes.'

Ahmad's heart was racing. This was the news he had been patiently awaiting for months. He wished Jim would get on with it, and was about to order him to do so when the waiter arrived with the platter of frogs' legs. 'You're keeping me in suspense, Jim.'

Just then the door opened. The small bell on a spring at the top of it vibrated and rang out, as it had rung every time anyone used the door. Jim O'Connor recognised the man entering the restaurant and said, 'Ah, here comes Mike. Ahmad, he doesn't know who you are, or even that you are the client. Thinks you're just a guy I'm having lunch with. Keep it that way.'

Jim rose from his chair, stuck his arm out and shook the hand of the tall, slender American while giving him a pat on the back. There was a look of disapproval on Ahmad's face. But Jim was having none of it. This was his show and he would conduct it as he chose.

'How you doing, Mike?'

'OK. Yeah, OK.'

Jim knew the young man was slightly overwhelmed at giving his report directly to the big boss. That rarely happened. The field operatives usually went to their direct superiors who handled the cases.

'Glass of wine, Mike?'

'Great.'

A glass was summoned and brought to the table and filled for Mike. As soon as the waiter had made his retreat, Jim said, 'Mike, this is a friend of mine.' The two men barely had a chance to acknowledge the introduction with a nod before Jim fired an instruction, 'OK. Let's hear it. I know you have a plane to catch. You can talk in front of my friend.'

Mike hesitated. Jim didn't shout, but he did crack out an order: 'Tell it the way it is, boy. Just the way it is. Give me the bottom line first.'

Mike Chambers all but snapped to attention. The twenty-eight year old ran his fingers through his hair and told the two men at the table. 'He's alive. Just about. At least he was three weeks ago when I left him.'

'Are you sure it's Jason Honey?'

'Yes.'

Jim looked across the table to Ahmad, expecting some sort of reaction. Nothing. So he concluded that what he had suspected in Cairo was true: Ahmad had not been altogether straight with him. Not ever – even at the time of his first investigation of the accident. He turned his attention away from Ahmad and back to Mike. 'How are you sure?'

'My instructions were to find the guy without letting on we were searching for him, get proof of identity, and report back.' From the inside pocket of his jacket, Mike produced a small white card with a fingerprint photocopied on to it encased in a clear plastic coating. 'This is the right-hand index-finger print of Jason Honey. I gave him a shot of whisky from my own stainless steel cup, and Larry and I lifted the print from it once we were back in Islamabad. I faxed it to our New York office for confirmation. There's no doubt about it: that man is Jason Honey. I also managed to get these.' Mike handed Jim an envelope containing photographs. Jim slipped them in his jacket pocket.

'Why was he flying over the Himalayas?'

'A million-dollar wager – a fucking bet – with his best friend.'

'There has to be more to it than that.'

'A gold run?'

'Did he tell you that?'

'Hell, no. He didn't even tell me he was Jason Honey.'

'How do you know, then? OK, forget that, it's all in your report.'

'You've read my report?'

'Yeah, you've done a terrific job.'

'I'd like to be one of the guys going back to bring him out, Mr O'Connor.'

Jim O'Connor ignored the request and instead asked, 'One more question, Mike. What kind of physical condition is he in?'

'He's paralysed down one side, and dying a slow death from his injuries; a broken back, internal problems, malnutrition. And he's an addict. Heroin.'

Jim looked at his watch. 'You'll just make your plane.' The three men stood up and shook hands, and Mike Chambers left.

Ahmad and Jim gazed across the table at one another before they sat down. There was plenty to read in Ahmad's face now. He was visibly shaken. Jim reached for his glass; the wine felt good in his mouth. Ahmad stood up, 'I need something stronger.' He walked to the bar and ordered a double Calvados, drank half while standing at the bar and then had it topped up and another poured for Jim.

Returning to the table, he placed the glass in front of Jim. The two men remained seated and silent for several minutes, contemplative. Finally Jim spoke. 'Look, Ahmad, you don't owe me an explanation.'

'That's right, I don't.'

'But I'd like you to tell me why you did it, anyway.'

'Why must you know?'

'Because you have to go and get the poor bastard out of there and to some medics. Because you can't leave him to suffer in a remote village on the side of a Himalayan mountain now we know the facts. I'm the only one who can organise it for you on the quiet, and I'm not going to do that unless you level with me, something you should have done right from the start.'

'Maybe so.'

For the first time since Jim had had dealings with Ahmad, he sensed a note of regret in the man's voice. 'There's no maybes about it.'

'Jim, don't push this. I can pay you off right now, and walk away from this.'

'You can, but you won't.'

'What makes you so sure?'

'You may be a decadent hedonist, but you're no murderer. A selfish, greedy prick who always gets what he wants, somebody who plays with the dark side of people's natures, but you haven't got the killer-instinct. Not like me. You're too much of a gent. Murder is never beautiful, and you like beautiful. With men like you, sexual violence to the edge is as close to death as you ever go. But the final plunge you never take.'

'You always talk to your clients this way?'

'No, but I would to any of them who had led me up the garden path the way you have, Ahmad. You used my firm – and that's me – to investigate the crash and then lied about our findings. You claimed we found the remains of Jason Honey scattered all around the impact point. You buried a corpse that never was, and closed the investigation after a three-week search. For whose sake? His wife's? Yours? Jason Honey's? I didn't think anything of it until nearly three years later, when you called me to Cairo and I saw the false death-certificate. And you reopened the case. I've been curious about your motives ever since.'

Jim downed his Calvados in one gulp. Then he removed the photographs of Jason Honey that Mike had taken secretly with a mini-camera from their envelope and slid them across the table. Ahmad did not touch them. He merely studied them as they lay fanned out in front of him. 'How soon can you get him out, Jim?'

'Ah, not so fast, Ahmad. It's going to take more than money to bail this guy out. But before we get into that, I want some answers, or you get a new boy for this one.'

Ahmad left the table without a reply, to return to the bar with the empty glasses. Jim watched him standing there, doing his cigarette ritual with the amber holder. Jim had to admire a man

239

who was handling himself so well under the circumstances. He returned to the table with the bottle of Calvados this time. After filling the two glasses he sat down opposite Jim. Ahmad picked up the photographs and looked at each of them briefly, then placed them in the ashtray and set them alight. 'Jason is a very vain man. He would never want anyone who knew and loved him to see him in that condition. He'd rather be dead.'

A waiter arrived and unloaded from a tray a pot of hot, black coffee and two demi-tasse cups, a glass bowl of cherries with their stones and stems preserved in cognac, and two small ladles carved from olive wood. He picked up the ashtray that now held a miniature inferno, and carried it away from the table without a word. His grimace was eloquent.

'He's still handsome. Extraordinary, after all he's been through. His face, a bit haggard, yes. A slight twist to one side – I imagine that's his paralysed side. His hair's gone very grey. A jagged scar on his forehead. But there are signs still of that outrageous handsomeness of his. Oh, yes, you get him out, and I'll see that he gets the best medical care on offer.'

Ahmad raised his glass and touched the rim of Jim's on the table in front of him. Jim raised it to return the silent toast that sealed yet another business transaction between the two men. And then they downed the amber liquid. What choice did he have? Jim had read Mike's report. But then Ahmad began to speak.

'About Jason. To meet him was to fall for him. Everyone found him irresistible. He was a winning combination – all the best and worst that make a man. A good intellect, relentless charm. A compulsion to manipulate situations and control outcomes. He could be as hard as nails, or as soft and vulnerable as a child. That was the way he was. That's the way he lived. He was a great pilot, an adventurer, a bad businessman, a lover of luxury, a fighter for lost causes. An anything-goes man in sex, drugs and drink when he indulged. He had a rage to live. He had a dark side to his nature, like all of us, and that's the side that gave him his greatest personal pleasure. I knew that side of him as no other person did. We have been great friends for more than fifteen years.

'We got along so well because we were a lot alike. We could

240

have been brothers. We were both terrific womanisers. Sexual hedonists on a grand scale. The decadent, the depraved, has always been something we shared. We were romantics, who loved women, but used them more than loved them. The thrill was in the chase, the conquest, the corruption of them. Always the adoring lover – till we became bored. Heartless, amoral, existential in our thinking would be not a bad description of either of us. And then he fell in love and married Arianne.

'I never thought it possible that he would find love, but he did. Loving Arianne became the most important thing in his life, but it never really changed him. Love and marriage merely added to his life. I have never seen a happier marriage, but then you have to know Arianne. I knew Jason too well. He would only stay in that marriage for as long as he was sexually interested and he saw to it that she learned well how to keep him on heat. Two months after they were married, he gave her to me. Literally rolled her naked into my arms. The three of us became lovers. The years that followed until that crash were the happiest years of our lives. You'd never see three more successful pleasure-seekers. We were in love, all three of us, with each other. We had our separate lives – they as a couple, me as the hedonist bachelor – and we had our sexual *ménage à trois*. That was what fuelled our lives. In time we all understood that, without it, Jason would destroy Arianne and abandon love, marriage, a happiness that was the foundation of his life.

'During those years he put together a successful aviation corporation, but periodically I was bailing him out with funds. I never minded. I'm a very wealthy man. I know how to keep my wealth and make it work for me. If I couldn't bail out a man who had become so much a part of my life, who would I do it for?

'The thing about a *ménage à trois*, sexual or otherwise, is that you are inextricably involved with each other. The love is shared equally. Sure, Jason loved me as much as his wife. Differently maybe, but to the same degree. It was the same for me. Arianne – she loved us both equally when we were together. Then as the years rolled by, I came to realise that two problems were looming: the darker side of Jason was showing itself in strange ways. He was undergoing some kind of personality change. Only I could see it, though. And Arianne? When the three of us were together, she loved me as she did Jason. Unconditionally. Ready to lay down her life for me. We'd only to ask, either Jason or myself. No questions. It was total submission to our will. Her sexual passion for me was boundless, but her love was not. Although she did very well hiding it, there was a fraction of love she held back. That was reserved for Jason. Just for him. The rest is quite simple. I wanted that fraction.'

'Then it is in fact what you told me: all for the love and possession of a woman.' Jim was astounded.

'That's right. I very nearly did become a murderer. Jealousy, even more than love, had taken me over.'

So, thought Jim, Ahmad was not telling him his story because Jim had demanded it but because Ahmad had been shocked. For not only had Jason survived, but he had been dying a slow death for years. The life of Ahmad's friend, a great love and partner, had been destroyed. The dispassionate way Ahmad was telling his story suggested to Jim that Ahmad considered Jason, dead or alive, quite out of his life. But his feelings of responsibility for Jason were very much alive. He wanted his friend to stop hurting, and to live again, if that was what Jason wanted. Jim thought to himself, This is real macho friendship, real macho love. He was even quite moved by it, yet more so when Ahmad continued and revealed:

'Whatever you may think, it was not premeditated, what happened next. It was chance. Men playing the big gamble. Mike was right. I bet him a million dollars that he could not fly his vintage aircraft – a Hawker Civil Hunter, a supersonic, single-seat plane – against the clock from the Rockies to the Himalayas. He needed the money; he wanted the challenge, the adventure. And he goaded me into taking the bet. He wins, he gets the million. I win, he gives me Arianne – "But not just on permanent loan. Permanently." That was exactly how he put it. It was a mad bet, but we were both out of control, each sure he would win. We agreed it was to be a secret between us. With him out of the picture, I was sure I could win that small vestige of love she held back from me. It was all I really wanted. Arianne as my sexual slave – I already had that. As permanent fixture in my life? Well, I already had that, too. Arianne without Jason? I wasn't sure how that would work. But it was too good a prospect to resist.

'I took the wager. He took a shallow dive into a Himalayan mountain. It hadn't once crossed my mind that he might crash. He was the best of the best of pilots. I was shattered when the news came. There was no information, no investigation. I couldn't live with that. I found it impossible, not having any answers. That was why I hired you in the first place. Arianne and I clung to each other like lost souls those first weeks after the crash. It was a miracle that the crash had been sighted at all.'

'Why did you tamper with my report? Why claim that parts of the body had been found? Why fly a coffin of rubble back to the States and bury it in a grave after a funeral that you knew was a mockery? Why not tell the truth – that no body nor even any part of Jason had been found?'

'He was gone. He'd vanished. And he took part of our life, Arianne's and mine, with him. He broke the *ménage à trois* that had become a linchpin to my happiness. Not just mine, but Arianne's as well. I hated him for leaving us, and I loved him for giving Arianne to me. We needed something to mourn. Who, in the end, knows what my motives were?'

'And you and Arianne?'

'Ah, a case of crime and punishment, of sorts. In the first weeks after the accident we were together in grief, and I mean real grief. But then, as time wore on, we missed him so terribly it became impossible to be together. It only increased our pain. It was easier to stay in touch by telephone, letter, gifts. To see each other was to be reminded of when he was alive and we were as one.

'Then once, months after the burial, we agreed to meet and try to have sex together. The attraction for each other was still there, and we were hungry for each other, but his absence was profound – it ruined it for us. As three we were sex at its best, and it worked for us. As two, impossible. We never tried again. We rarely saw each other, but kept in communication. She was a lost soul without him, living with his ghost – she loved him so much that was enough for her. It was nearly three years before we could fully exorcise the ghost of him. I wanted her back. She wanted me, I knew that when I saw her in November in London, but I waited for her to come back to me.

'When she called to ask if she could come on Christmas day to Cairo, I knew an erotic life for us was on again. It suddenly occurred to me that, if I wanted her in the same way Jason had had her, I might have to marry her. The more I thought about it, the more it became a possibility. That was when I called you to Cairo. It was what made me make one more attempt to find absolute proof that he was dead. My happiness with Arianne depended on it. I wanted him never to rise between us again. Never in my wildest dreams did I believe you would find him alive.'

Jim wanted to say to Ahmad, 'You're a couple of depraved, evil, self-serving bastards underneath all that rage to live and charm.' But he had met enough people in his business to know that Ahmad and Jason were not unique. He had dealt with much worse, men far more evil than the man sitting across from him. Jim was not a judgemental man. He could rarely be that in the business he was in. He had no doubt that Ahmad had spilled out that story not because Jim insisted on the truth, but because he was shocked by the news that Jason was alive. Ahmad was re-evaluating the past in order to be able to deal with the problem facing him. Jim had heard other men's secrets come tumbling out under similar circumstances. He had to admire Ahmad – he knew himself well and liked himself. Why wouldn't he? He always paid the tariff to live the life that suited him, emotionally and otherwise. He was a man honest to himself in his depravity. There was not a hint of false sentimentality in all that Ahmad had said. Jim saw that the man in front of him was feeling honour-bound to save Jason's life, if that was possible; if not, at least to make him more comfortable in his dying.

Jim took one of the cherries from the bowl on the table by its stem and popped it in his mouth, then another, and another. He spat the stones into his hand. After several more, he placed the stones and stems in a small white saucer on the table. 'Delicious.' Ahmad ladled out cherries and their liqueur into two bowl-shaped, long-stemmed glasses. He passed one across the table to Jim. He sipped the drink and ate several cherries himself. Jim reached for his briefcase, removed Mike's report on Jason Honey and placed it on the table next to him, then broke the silence between them.

'We answered your brief and have treated it as highly confidential, as you requested.'

'I'd like you to keep it that way.'

'Then you expect the report to go the way of the photographs – up in flames?'

Jim placed a hand on the sheaf of papers and was about to push them across the table to Ahmad. 'Presumably you would like to read them first?'

Ahmad raised his hand in dismissal. 'No. Just give me the facts relative to finding him, and the hows and whys of what has happened to him.'

'Let's get some fresh air,' suggested Jim. He rose from his chair and went to the bar to settle the bill.

In the street, Ahmad ordered his car and driver to follow the two men through the streets of Montparnasse a few hundred feet behind them. It was April and the sun was warm. The trees were in full bud and the Parisians were once again savouring the apéritifs and coffee in the street cafés.

Jim began his report: 'I'll start from the beginning. After I left you in Cairo on Christmas Eve, I went over the original investigation with the men who had run it. It had been a tough job because of several factors, the first being the location of the crash: halfway up a mountain in one of the most remote places on earth, with no local authority of any force to help. Their inability to locate any traces of a corpse led them to search a fifty-mile radius, looking for any inhabitants who might have rescued the pilot. In three weeks they found one small village, where nobody had seen or heard anything. Then they met a single witness who had seen the plane "fall out of the sky". It was that man, and two others who were trekking down to the valley and to Islamabad, who had reported a crash. They supplied an approximate location. They stated that no one parachuted from the plane. I don't want to make this any more ghoulish than I have to, Ahmad. But, by the time the local authorities in the district located the site, three weeks had passed. The authorities and later my men agreed that no one could have survived that crash. No remains were found, and the only explanation came from the local militia who were doing the rescue operation. They believed that animals had gotten there first. Scavengers had picked the wide area of debris clear of any remains. Hence our report to you that no body was ever found.

'I assembled the same men who had worked on the investigation. After going over every detail I called in two more men to join the new search for Jason Honey. New blood on an old case is always a good thing. We were three solid days going over every detail of what we knew about the accident, pin-pointing on the map every location they had been in search of evidence. Then Mike, the guy you just met, came out with, "You were looking in the wrong place. The pilot never crash-landed with his plane. You were looking for him on the right mountain range, but on the wrong mountain."

'The protests lasted for several minutes until I insisted we listen to Mike's theory: "The plane was sighted as it was diving out of the sky and no parachute was seen. Look at this." He held up a photo of a Hawker Civil Hunter, then he continued, "I bet that after Jason Honey had bought this supersonic fighter plane to add to his collection of vintage aircraft, he reconditioned it and kept the original ejector-seat. That plane came out of the sky and into view empty. The villager who spotted the incident could not have been close enough to see a man at the controls. He only assumed that a pilot was still in that plane. Jason Honey ejected high above the Himalayas, and we'll find him or his remains as much as a hundred miles from the scene of the crash. Certainly on the far side of the mountain from where the search was made. Or on a different mountain altogether."

'Mike was absolutely right. Jason was found more than a hundred miles and two mountains away from his plane. Mike and his team had a lot of good breaks once they had plotted with a crack team of sherpas where to climb. We could have mounted a helicopter search but no permissions were forthcoming for the air-space. So the search-team were dependent on the goodwill and gossip of the people they came across for information which would have been otherwise unobtainable except by means of a trek. They never aroused any hostility. Quite the contrary. They brought out the hospitality in the people. Finally they got wind of a foreigner who was being kept alive by villagers and the travelling doctor, who went through the district once a year.

'They found him. Still keeping to the brief you gave, they

never let on they'd come in search of him. He had become an oddity in the village, a precious visitor whom the villagers cared for in turn. He had been found in a deep coma and remained in a persistent vegetative state for nearly a year, kept alive by some fairly primitive feeding-methods. His injuries, well, I've already told you about them – and his addiction. They don't believe he can survive being moved, so they insist on keeping him there and caring for him. The way they look after him and the amount of heroin he uses cost money. He's supplied well. He told my men he had stuffed two six-pound gold bars in his jacket before he ejected from the plane and that was enough gold to see him out. Mike told Jason they would try to get him out by helicopter as soon as possible. Mission of mercy and all that.'

'Did he agree to that?' Jim noticed that Ahmad's question was delivered in an icy, matter-of-fact manner, as if his interest was charitable rather than personal.

'It was hard to tell.'

'What do you mean, it was hard to tell?'

'He laughed. Told the men it was too late. Then he drifted away on them. He used to do that several times a day. Just drift off and not speak. Mike was sure he heard everything, but he was just too pained out. He had too little energy to reply. Jason Honey must have an incredible will to live. He's just not ready to die. He's fighting the final goodbye, but he's hung on to life and hope too long. It's worn him out.'

'I want him out of there, and as soon as possible. For the moment I don't want my name or his wife's – or, for that matter, his – mentioned. A mercy mission by some vague organisation will do. You have to be very careful. I don't know why he would be carrying two gold bars. But I do know a gold run is a serious offence. Nor do we know what happened to his plane. What made him abandon it? Until we have him safe in a hospital in Paris or London or New York, you go along with whatever he tells you. If he wants to see me, he'll ask. He's a broken man – I doubt he will ever want to see anyone he loved again. But that has nothing to do with you. Your job? Get him out of there. Alive if you can, dead if that's the way it has to be.'

'A corpse at any price – is that it?' (A cheap shot, thought Jim, but the wily bastard deserves it.)

247

'Crudely put, Jim.'

Ahmad did have a way of making Jim feel like a lout. He couldn't but smile to himself when it popped into his mind, How is it I'm holding all the cards but he's winning the game? Jim could understand why men and women were devoted to Ahmad: he had a lethal charm, was a devil incarnate – and who didn't fancy dancing with the devil? He knew that, long after this business was over, he and Ahmad would keep their acquaintance going. But, for the moment, what bound them together was business as usual.

'Even if we do get him out alive – you realise he is likely to spend the rest of his life in a hospital?'

Ahmad ignored the question. Instead he stopped walking and signalled for the Rolls following them to pull forward. 'After you, Jim.' Once the two men were seated and Jim had told Ahmad where he wanted to be dropped, Ahmad opened a compartment mounted in the back of the front seat of the car and produced a brown manila envelope. 'Two hundred and fifty thousand dollars on account. Will that do for the moment?'

Jim placed the envelope in his briefcase. 'For the moment.'

'What is the tariff so far? How much will bring my account up to date? Do you want some working money?'

Once Jim had answered all the financial questions and Ahmad had established an arrangement for future funds, Ahmad surprised Jim. 'Companionship is obviously the other thing I must supply for Jason. I can't merely put him in a hospital without someone to stimulate his interest in life. I'd like Mike to be his minder, his friend. I also want you to keep me abreast of things as they happen. You, Jim. Not one of your operatives. Not even Mike. Jason's to have anything he wants. And if he wants to get in touch with me or his wife, you let me know immediately. Mike is to make no direct contact with Arianne Honey.'

'The media? What if they should get hold of this?'

'It's up to you to see that they don't. Remember I don't want him identified. Not for the moment. The world believes he was dead and buried years ago. You use any false name he gives, and get him travel documents, a passport, under it.'

'How are you so sure he won't give his own name?'

'Pretty certain. He didn't give it to Mike.'

248

'Good point. You think he wants to be left as missing or dead?'

'Yes.'

'And you'll allow that?'

'For the moment.'

The Rolls was just circling the Place de la Concorde. The men were silent, their business concluded. Ahmad placed a cigarette in his holder and Jim gave him a light. He offered Jim a cigar from a box he took from a compartment next to the one he had withdrawn the money from. A cigar-cutter appeared from his waistcoat pocket. When they pulled up to the Crillon, where Jim had asked to be dropped off, Ahmad asked, 'Are you staying here, Jim?'

'Yes.'

'How long will you be in Paris?'

'Not sure. A couple of days anyway.'

Jim got out of the car. Leaning on the door, he eyed Ahmad through the open window. 'I'll be in touch.' Jim shoved a hand through the window and the two men shook hands.

'Your firm has done a remarkable job for me, Jim. I am very grateful to you. Most especially for keeping the entire investigation secret and my part in it confidential. I am not unappreciative. I did promise you a bonus – I would like to have it delivered to you. Shall we say this evening?'

The seductive charm in the man's eyes held Jim. Subtle, exciting corruption titillated. 'What time?' Ahmad asked.

The sweet smell of success permeated Jim's soul. To tip-toe through the tulips with the devil in Paris in the Spring – who would want to pass up that? The libido sang a happy tune. Jim told him the time.

Chapter 18

Ben stopped the car. He and Arianne got out to watch Artemis cantering across the fields towards the lake, Anson keeping up right next to her. They were a handsome sight astride two magnificent stallions with the parkland as backdrop.

Arianne had known, since a child, that Artemis, rotten mother as she was, was also something special. Today, in the May sunshine with the park bursting with new life, seeing those two elderly people still with a grip on life and ready to run with it, Arianne realised how grateful she was to a mother who had never pretended to be anything other than what she was. Suppose she had not left her husband and child, but had remained with them, a miserable creature imparting to them guilt and remorse for tying her to a family ethic she despised: Arianne would have suffered for it.

This was the first time she would be seeing Artemis since before Christmas. No phone calls, no letters or cards had come from her mother. But Arianne had expected none. Ben had his arm around Arianne's shoulder. She leaned in to him, their eyes still following his uncle and her mother, and said, 'Ben, I don't want to tell Artemis about us. Not until after we're married.'

They had come to Chessington Park to see their respective relatives and to tell them their happy news. They would ask Artemis and Anson to be best man and matron of honour at their wedding, which was to be at Ben's château in France. They had been talking about it for weeks.

'That does rather change our plans.'

'Do you mind?'

'No.'

'Don't you want an explanation?'

'I'm sure you have good reason.'

By now they were looking at each other. There was no sadness

251

in her eyes, no emotion in her voice. That was good enough for Ben: just so long as Arianne was not upset about anything, and life was still sweet for them. Arianne put her arms around his neck and reached up to place a seductive kiss upon his lips. With his hands on her waist, he slowly raised her from the ground. He liked the feel of Arianne against his body. He bit passionately into her lips; her lips parted and she licked the roof of his mouth with her tongue. Her kisses were electric. He slipped his hands under her knitted jumper and held her that way against him; hands caressing her naked back.

In the weeks that had passed since the first night they had had sex, Ben had become erotically besotted with Arianne. They were creating an erotic life together he had never imagined possible with one woman. They had become sexual adventurers. They had fallen in love, had wanted to be together, before they discovered what a powerful lust drew them to each other. Love and a mutual passion for unbridled sex made their relationship one of complete trust in one another. Their togetherness was always new, fresh and exciting. Utterly stable. What need had he for an explanation? If that was what Arianne wanted – not to tell Artemis about them or their plans – it had to be right for all concerned.

Arianne withdrew her lips from his and began kissing him crazily all over his face. She bit Ben on his ear so hard that he winced and put her down. Artemis, wedding plans, all else vanished from their minds. Desire was taking over. The passion of love, sexual hunger. Taking her by the hand, he pulled Arianne from the drive several feet into the wood. Then, leaning her against a huge and very old chestnut tree in full bloom, he raised her jumper to expose her breasts to his mouth. He sucked on her nipples while he caressed them. She squirmed with pleasure, and was unable to restrain her sighs of satisfaction or to hold back anything from Ben. She raised her skirt. 'If anyone from the house sees us . . .' he said, obviously not caring in the least: he was pushing his penis slowly into her yearning cunt, and relishing the woman he loved. Arianne wrapped her legs around him and he stepped back from the tree. His kisses resumed an urgency and passion that kindled a fire in them. Arianne was doing the thrusting, moving on and off Ben's cock, an act of

252

intercourse that drove them into orgasm.

Arianne could hardly calm her breathing after he had laid her down in the grass under the tree and was caressing her hair, her face, whispering, 'I love you. I never knew I had so much love in me, that I could love you so much.' His words could have been hers; she could have echoed them. Those were her feelings too. Lying together in each other's arms, recovering from a breathlessly exciting intercourse, she listened to him tell her, 'No woman has ever given herself so completely to me. Have you any idea what that means to a man, to have a woman just give her whole being up to him? Every fuck with you is like the first time. Always when it's over, it's not over. My body, my heart, my head is always telling me there's more, always more. We've yet to begin. All this and love, deep and abiding . . .'

Arianne stopped Ben by placing a hand across his mouth. She smiled at him. 'I love you, Ben. These last few weeks together have been a revelation for me. I loved Jason, and we had a marvellous marriage, but I feel a different person with you. The love I have for you is different. Without betraying his memory, I must admit that our love is more profound. There are things about you that bring out similar things in myself. Things that have been lying dormant. Things that add strength to my character. These last years of widowhood have taught me to be my own woman, an independent creature. Meeting and falling in love with you has altered my feelings about being a woman. I think of being your wife, and of the life we're going to create together, and it seems to have to do with having children, being there for them, being flexible and supporting you and loving you well. But loving you has also taught me to keep my experience, my own separateness alive. I should have learned those things from Artemis. She practised them, and still does. She has showed me those things all my life. I simply never got the message. I did from loving you. I love you, Ben. I love you. And I feel so lucky to be marrying you.'

They were somehow embarrassed by their emotional outbursts and covered it by silence and merely sitting together, holding hands, under the chestnut tree. Occasionally Ben would reach out to remove a blossom from Arianne's hair. It was some time before he asked, 'Shall we walk together? The wood is so lovely.

253

Look at the sunlight filtering down through the branches.'

He helped Arianne up and they adjusted each other's clothing, making themselves presentable for Chessington Park and anyone they might come across. 'Think of the scandal if someone saw us in the throes of lust. Do you think they would ban us from visiting the house, walking the grounds?' Ben teased.

'They'd probably call a general meeting of the house to vote on it.'

Ben began to laugh. 'No, they would wait for an AGM and make it mandatory that no one fucks in the park. A house rule, citing us as an example.'

'But,' a now-amused Arianne added, 'Beryl Quilty would have called an emergency meeting of the Executive House Committee, to see that we were put on remand forthwith, issued with a formal letter, until an AGM decided what to do about lust and love in the park.'

They were still laughing when they returned to where the car was parked in a bay on the drive. They leaned against the car, still holding hands, somehow reluctant now to approach the house. Arianne said, 'About Artemis?'

'What about Artemis, Arianne?'

'Artemis and I, we love each other, but it's a strange kind of love. Not at all your average mother-daughter relationship. Strangely, it might be something very much closer than that. I don't know, and I doubt that Artemis does. And it doesn't matter. You see, we never get involved with each other's lives. When I was a child we did superficially, for those Christmas, Easter or summer holidays. They were my annual pilgrimage to Artemis. But when we were apart, nothing. And that's the way it is with us now. Artemis is uninterested in my life or what I do. When I make these visits here, she never asks about it – no more than I ask about hers. It's strange, but it's that lack of interest that binds us together. You see, we have never impinged on each other's lives. Artemis would hate to be involved with our wedding plans. I got swept away on the idea that she would, because I was so happy, and the château is so beautiful – she would like the château and vineyard. You mustn't think that she would not be happy for my happiness, because she would. She would merely not express it. I am no different with her. Ours is a cold kind of love. But it has worked for us.'

'How about we call off the big wedding at the château that we were planning?'

'Oh, Ben. Would you mind?'

'Not if that's what you want.'

'We could still have a huge and very grand party there sometime after we've been married.'

'Yes, that might be better. A party not fraught with emotion, the inevitable at large weddings. We can have an intimate, romantic wedding, just you and I. Would you like that?' he asked, kissing Arianne affectionately on the lips.

'Yes. Very much.' The relief Arianne felt was enormous. Being swept up in love and their plans for a future together, she had not realised how much anxiety she had about a large wedding. She had not been aware until now when it was cancelled that she had actually felt an irrational fear about it – that the past would suddenly loom up and ruin her wedding day. The very thought of it sent a shiver through her.

'What's wrong?' Ben asked.

'Nothing, just a chill, no more than that.'

At the front door Arianne and Ben parted company. He went to his uncle's, Arianne to Artemis's door. Arianne could hear the faint sound of a piano. Artemis. She rang the bell and the door swung open. Hadley greeted her.

'Good to see you, Hadley.'

'It's good to see you, madam.'

'Did my mother have a good holiday?'

'Yes, she seemed to enjoy herself.'

'And her health?'

'Now or then, madam?'

'Both, I think.'

'You will find her as usual, in good form. We had a rather "off" period of about two weeks, but she rallied and came back to us, good as a shiny penny, madam.' All this was in whispers in the small hall that was closed off from the drawing room. Butler and daughter understood these clandestine conversations were necessary if Arianne were to know anything about her mother's mental health. He opened the door to the drawing room. Arianne entered the room.

Artemis was looking marvellous, still dressed in her riding clothes and playing beautifully. Schubert. Arianne leaned against the piano and smiled at her mother. Artemis smiled back. 'Well, you look jolly nice. Happy.'

'You too, Artemis.'

Artemis continued playing. She looked up from the keyboard to gaze at Arianne. 'I do like to look at you when you're well turned out and happy.'

Then it was back to concentrating on her playing. When she stopped, concentration focused on a Kir Royale that Hadley had brought on a silver salver. She remained seated on the piano bench. 'Had a really good ride this morning. Enjoyed myself thoroughly and so did the dogs.'

'Where are the dogs?'

'Getting some of the mud off them.' Just then, on cue and unmuddied, they came bounding into the room. They were all over Arianne and Artemis with paws and wet tongues. The two women laughed, then with several sharp words settled them down. 'We were going to have lunch in the summerhouse, but frankly, the wind has the tiniest of a nip to it. So I changed plans. We'll lunch in my dining room: I have invited Sir Anson and his nephew to join us.'

Did she know? How did she guess? Coincidence? went through Arianne's mind. Of course she didn't know that Ben and she were together. And did it matter, anyway? Arianne nearly told Artemis about herself and Ben right then and there. She was stopped by Artemis speaking first.

'Anson had asked us to dine in the members' dining room, but frankly I was in no mood today to share the premises with any of the residents. They are as silly as ever. Downright stupid sometimes.'

'I'm beginning to understand them, Artemis – how they can be annoying with their petty possessiveness about this place.'

'Well, if truth be told, I am pretty possessive about it myself. The place does get to one.'

'But never petty, Artemis. No one could call you petty. Nor an interfering woman.'

'I should hope not. I take it you have been here while I was away and crossed swords with them?' The mischievous in

Artemis came to the fore. She seemed to delight in the idea. She all but giggled. 'Ghastly lot.'

'Maybe you should move rather than put up with them and their interminable committees and vain attempts to make a community of themselves.'

'No. I'm here till the end. No more moves for me. They will simply have to tolerate me.'

'Why?'

Artemis walked to the fireplace and leaned against it. 'Old age. Security. I feel secure here from burglars, the world in general. I'm fighting the good fight against old age and the winding down, just like they are. That's about the only thing I have in common with them. And, believe me, that's a great deal. I like Chessington Park, I can afford it financially and emotionally. I have the horses and the parkland, the great hall when I want to give a mini-opera or a concert for my friends. There's a restaurant to entertain in, room for staff, and I can live in a style that has always been my custom and not be diminished by time. It's a hell of a thing to admit, but I'm better off here than anywhere else.'

'Does Sir Anson feel the same?'

'You'll have to ask him.'

Clearly Artemis had gone off the subject. Arianne felt disturbed that Artemis's life should be winding down when hers was just beginning all over again. But that was a fact. If Artemis could face the facts of her life, so would Arianne. It was what was happening to her mother and the other residents at Chessington House. Each was handling it as best they could. Declining years were bringing out the best and the worst in them all. Old age, the great revealer of character. Artemis was right – she generally was on her own interests. Chessington Park and the house were a relatively safe haven for her. Arianne cheered herself up with the knowledge that the park and the Tudor stately home and Artemis would always rise above the mundane in life. It wasn't so much that the others in the house appeared to be the dross, but that Artemis was the gold.

Sir Anson and Ben entered the room. Arianne watched Sir Anson go to Artemis and present her with several dozen long-stemmed white roses. The pleasure she found in the presence of the men and in the scent of the roses, the flirtation with life that

Artemis indulged, were all there in every word, every gesture. She enslaved her guests with her charm. They obeyed her by basking in her light. Never had Arianne loved her mother more, never been more proud to be her daughter. She knew now why she had always loved Artemis. She had within her, even now, in her declining years, that rage to live. Life was still an adventure for her.

All through lunch – lobster tails in a thermidor sauce, roasted wild duck breasts on a bed of sliced white peaches, wild mushrooms and rice, a purée of fresh fine beans, and most especially over the pudding, a plum tart with a light custard sauce – Artemis wooed Ben, to the delight of everyone around the table.

Fortified by several fine wines drunk with their meal – a white, Corton-Charlemagne 1980, a Margaux 1976, and a Sauternes with the pudding – they were now, over snifters of Calvados, quite tipsy with well-being.

'What a marvellous lunch, Artemis. What a wonderful woman you are. Thank you.' With elaborate chivalry, Ben placed the perfect continental kiss upon her hand.

'Charming of you to say so, Ben.' She hesitated, then added, 'There was a time when I would have run away with a young man like you.'

Arianne rose from her chair and went to stand next to Ben, to place an arm around his shoulder. 'Like mother like daughter, Artemis. I already have. He's taken.'

Everyone in the room was astounded. It was so unlike Arianne to take such a forceful action. No one was more surprised than Arianne that she should give away her precious secret. Her public declaration of love for Ben nearly overwhelmed him. He knew she hadn't intended to make it. He removed her arm from around his shoulder and kissed her hand in another calculated display of gallantry.

'How nice, Arianne, that we have, at least, kept him in the family,' Artemis announced to her daughter, a knowing smile crossing her lips. 'Now, how about a rubber of bridge?' Artemis had absorbed their news as she did all good news, with momentary delight and a practised indifference.

The day with Artemis was one of the most agreeable Arianne had ever spent with her mother. When Artemis, Anson and the dogs walked the couple to Ben's car, she adjusted a strand of Arianne's hair that had fallen out of place and brushed a bit of lint from her shoulder. Then, turning to Ben, she said, 'What a lucky man you are, Ben. Arianne is more like me than I ever imagined she could be. Now run along, you two. There is a big wide world beyond Chessington Park to be wickedly happy in, and you're young and able enough to do it.'

Halfway down the drive, Ben said, 'You have a remarkable mother.'

'Yes, I do.'

'That was a seal of approval being stamped on us – or am I wrong?'

'Not wrong. She has conferred her approval.'

'And that's it?'

'That's it. We are expected to be happy and live our lives to the full for us and us alone, as she has always done. Still does.'

'She won't want to be involved with our lives?' asked Ben.

'She would hate that.'

'Nor interfere with the way we want to live?'

'She never has in the past.'

'All Artemis will want is to have a good time when we meet, which will be at her convenience?' A note of incredulity shaped Ben's question.

'That's just about it.'

'Arianne, she sounds the perfect mother-in-law.'

The two began to laugh and then Ben teased, 'We mustn't laugh, that would be tempting fate. A non-critical mother-in-law, what a blessing.'

'I never promised she wouldn't be critical.'

'Oh.' The laughter evaporated from Ben's voice.

Arianne leaned over and kissed him on the cheek. 'It's not so bad. Artemis's criticisms are always sharp and to the point. Always delivered on the spot, directly at me. And only when I am standing in front of her. She is no telephone nag. Not one of those mothers who send lethal letters of disapproval. Her aloofness doesn't allow it.'

'What a relief.'

'She detested Jason. She had a basic instinct that he was the wrong man for me, no matter how happy we had been together.

She never changed her mind about that. But she never interfered in our life. She merely stated an opinion – and only to me.'

Ben was surprised by that. Why should Artemis feel that way about her daughter's husband when Arianne had been nothing but happy in her marriage with him? Ben felt no jealousy about Jason. Nor about Ahmad, who seemed still to figure in Arianne's life. She and Ben had no ban on their dead spouses or past loves being mentioned. Very occasionally those past loves drifted into their conversation but that was all. It was as if their own love had put the past in a proper perspective to the present and left them with no emotional hang-ups about relationships that were dead or out of their lives.

More than once during these last weeks while Ben had been living with Arianne in the house in Three Kings Yard, he had marvelled at the silver-framed photograph in the sitting room of Jason, Arianne and Ahmad lying on a beach, the waves rolling over their bodies. The happiness, sensuality, love, of the *ménage à trois* seemed to leap from the figures frozen in time at the click of a camera's shutter. Under a pane of glass and imprisoned by a silver frame they were captured for posterity. Ben doubted that Arianne realised how revealing the photograph was. His first instinct on seeing it was that the three were lovers. Only after his own sex with Arianne revealed to him her exquisite passion for all things sexual was it confirmed.

Trust. That was implicit in their relationship. That trust that allowed them to understand the sexual truth about each other without having to discuss it. There was no doubt in Ben's mind that Arianne knew he was aware of the sexual life she had led with the two men. Every night they made love he became more aware of her rapacious libido. It suited his own to perfection. What need had they to talk of other erotic liaisons that had only added positive experience to the sexual freedom and pleasures they now shared?

Thoughts about Arianne and the two men who had made up her marriage were triggered by Arianne's declaration that Artemis had never approved of Jason. Those thoughts vanished from Ben's mind as he turned his attention back to his future wife.

'Arianne, let's start from the beginning. Go back to the States, get married there.'

'In the next few weeks,' she added, as if reading his mind.

'We'll buy a town house in Manhattan and get married there, in our own place.'

Palm Beach, a tropical island, even Las Vegas, and Aspen, Colorado were the other suggestions. There were too many options, and they wanted to get married in them all. 'Never mind that now, let's think of the present.' And Ben headed the car in the direction of Le Manoir, where it had all begun for them, albeit disastrously. This time the memory of Jason did not surface for Arianne. They remained there for three days, playing truant from the world and their business affairs. Theirs was a love affair of the heart and the soul, which they did not take for granted, but felt humbled by. And it was there that they finally settled their arrangements of how and where to become man and wife.

In London they got on with their lives, lives that seemed richer, more wondrous and exciting now that they had each other. They took a week in New York to look for a town house in the upper East Side. Manhattan swept them up into its very special orbit. The buzz of the city, the adrenaline high of the people they met, the fun of rekindling old friendships, revisiting old haunts, only confirmed to them that it was time to go home, to make New York and the States their base, the château their second home and the world their playground. Europe would be another workplace.

For Arianne it was a bonus that Ben discussed his work with her, that he sought her opinions and respected them, that he wanted her to be a part of everything he was involved with. When they were apart, he would call her several times a day to tell her how his meetings were going. She found it easy to respond with constructive suggestions when he posed questions to her about his business affairs. His willingness to take her into every aspect of his life seemed to build her confidence to go forward on her own projects. They were exciting, but the more so for Arianne because she had Ben to talk to about them now. She was delighted when he asked to attend a viewing or a sale with her. This was a new kind of togetherness that she had never experienced with a lover before. Her life was new and exhilarating.

In the weeks that followed they made two more visits to New York, flying in by Concorde, to see houses. Finally they found

261

one they both fell in love with. It had been the library, a magnificent room, where Ben suggested Arianne could bring her clients once she had a stock of rare books to offer, that had convinced them this was the house for them.

There, sitting on the floor in the empty library, with not a scrap of paper in the room, not a book on the shelves, Arianne broke down. The tears were streaming down her cheeks. Ben placed an arm around her shoulders and hugged her to him. He tried to make a joke of her tears simply to ease the pain he saw in her eyes. 'I said we'd buy the house, not that you couldn't have it, Arianne.' He kissed her wet cheeks.

'Are you sure we can afford it, Ben?' Even his answer did not seem enough for Arianne. It was then that her story came tumbling out: Her father's library that had had to be sold for debts; her own collection, everything that she had ever owned and cherished, put on the block. A lifetime of dreams and memories swept away to leave her in near-poverty for nearly three years. The humiliation of being poor, living poor, without hope, of walking the streets of the big cities alone, with a fancy wardrobe but no place to go. The people cheated of their money because she had to go into liquidation for Jason. The burden of protecting Jason, because, had he been alive he would have made it all right.

'It's the empty shelves and our spending the rest of our lives collecting and filling them. I don't think I can bear to do it and have it all snatched away from me again.'

'I want to tell you a story.' And it was in that exquisite, walnut-panelled library, in that turn-of-the-century, limestone-fronted town house on East Seventy-Ninth Street just off Park Avenue, that Ben told her about being born into genteel poverty, of being made a victim of keeping up with the Joneses. A child having to live off scraps from the butcher, of having worked a paper-round as soon as he had been old enough to cope. A boy working his way through school from the age of eight until he graduated at university. 'Even in those hard times, Arianne, my mother and my father taught me that it was just as important to know how to play with your life as it was to make a success of it. I may have been the poor man on the block but we lived on the right block. I may have been the most financially deprived of all my friends but I made it not matter. Because of that my friends rallied around me, and the connections I made among the wealthy boys I played with gave me my first breaks. I don't think you should be frightened of filling these shelves. We are mature, responsible people, you and I. We will know when we have to curtail any extravagant living, because we have licked the other side of the coin. Don't be afraid. Don't deprive yourself or me of one moment of happiness in our new house.'

It was on the tip of his tongue to say, 'It was Jason's failure, not yours, that sent you down the tube.' But that seemed too cruel and unnecessary, and Ben had no intention of speaking ill of a man Arianne had loved for so long and so well.

They were back in London in Number 12, Three Kings Yard, having just returned from a trip to Paris, where Arianne had ordered her wedding dress from Yves Saint Laurent. Ben went with her because he knew the *vendeuse*. He had met her many times while married to Clarissa. The dress was one of his wedding-gifts to Arianne. He insisted she accept it, since she had so little money of her own.

They hadn't as yet got around to such things as engagement or wedding rings. They were so completely together and happy they felt several steps past all that. Moreover, friends of Ben, once they had met Arianne and understood that the couple would be marrying in the near future, were now constantly dropping in on them or inviting them. Here were a jet-set, sporting sort of crowd that were amusing and adventurous. It was evident in the way Ben looked at her that he was pleased she would get on with his friends. Now he had only to get on with hers. That was why, when the first phone call came from Ahmad to Arianne, Ben was delighted for her and showed it. Since he had met none of Arianne's friends, Ben was sensitive to the idea that she might feel he was forcing his own crowd on her. They were, after all, not a couple in their first flush of youth, and friends and the compatibility between them and new spouses could sometimes threaten lovers or the newly married trying to blend their old lives in a shiny new life. It never entered Ben's mind that Arianne should do anything but keep Ahmad as her closest friend. He was aware that, whether either man liked it or not, for Arianne's sake they would have to accept each other as friends.

The first call from Ahmad had come soon after Ben had moved in with Arianne. She never told him much about the call except to say that Ahmad was well and happy and he hoped to see her soon. A second call followed, much the same, except that he had asked her to join him in Paris for a long weekend. She declined, telling him the truth: she was going to New York with a friend. But not who the friend was. Arianne had been honest with Ben. She told him, 'I don't think I can tell Ahmad about us on the telephone. I think face to face would be better.'

'I'm not so sure about that. When I told Simone about us, she nearly took me out with a flying bottle of Joy.'

They had been together for months now, and still Ahmad and Arianne had not met. Only a few days before, Arianne had remarked that she felt that, if Ahmad did not turn up in London or New York in the next few weeks, she would have to go to see him wherever he was, to tell him about her and Ben's impending wedding.

Ben was sitting in a chair next to the telephone, discussing with Arianne when she should do that, when it rang. Ben picked it up. Almost at once he realised that it was Ahmad. When Ahmad asked who was on the line, Ben answered, 'Benjamin Johnson.' Ben did not ask who was calling, he merely added, 'I believe you would like to speak to Arianne. If you will hold the line I'll go and get her.'

Chapter 19

'Hello, Ahmad.'

He hadn't seen her crossing the room because he was behind the *Financial Times*. Engrossed in an article, he had been too distracted to hear her arrival. Somehow, when he lowered the newspaper, he was not surprised to see that she had arrived for lunch with a male friend. Ahmad rose from the settee to greet Arianne and her companion. He stretched his hands out to take hers, leaned forward and kissed her. Claridge's musicians were playing soothingly, and the large, elegant, comfortable room was busy with expensively turned-out men and women having pre-luncheon drinks. Ahmad extended his hand again, this time to shake Ben's.

'Hello.' The big charming smile, the direct look into Ben's eyes, a gesture: fingers to his temple, as if calling on his mind for an answer, 'Ah, the man who answered the telephone yesterday morning?'

'Quite right,' Ben's reply.

'Arianne, how lovely you look.'

Arianne's pleasure at seeing Ahmad was evident. She was beaming when she made introductions between the two men.

All three sat down and the waiter arrived with fresh glasses for Ahmad's guests. He poured champagne. 'You will, of course, stay to lunch with us, Ben,' Ahmad offered graciously.

'No, I won't, actually. I have just enough time for a quick hello and a glass of wine, then I must be off to catch a plane. Another time. I hope there will be many other times for the three of us to dine together.'

Well, he's quick to be staking his claim. Now this is interesting, thought Ahmad. Arianne has a lover, and a handsome, sexy one at that. He was actually amused, pleased that she had been audacious enough to bring him around for Ahmad to check out. A candidate for a new *ménage à trois*? She never ceased to amaze him. It also excited Ahmad. This was the first man other than Jason and himself that Arianne had had since he had known her, if you excluded the men he or Jason had introduced into their orgies to amuse the three of them. He liked the look of Ben; to think of him sexually with Arianne was to imagine the three of them in sexual ecstasy.

He turned his attention back to Arianne. 'I've brought you a memento.'

She accepted it with obvious delight. While she fussed with the silver wrapping-paper and red and purple, shiny silk ribbons, the two men talked about the business article Ahmad had been reading when they arrived – the beginning of a City scandal. Anyone in the room watching them might have noted that both men were busy sizing each other up.

The parcel, when unwrapped, revealed a large photograph of Ahmad and Arianne in a stunningly beautiful Fabergé picture-frame, taken on the *Osiris* sometime during the Nile race. The two were looking at each other. In the background, a line of lateen sails was billowing in the wind as they raced past them. They looked a happy and handsome couple. It wasn't nearly as revealing as the other photographs in Arianne's house, but there was something sensuous, romantic, erotic even, about the picture. Arianne showed only delight at having the picture 'as a record of the thrilling, two-week race up the Nile'.

The three chatted amiably for several minutes. Ben found Ahmad attractive, an interesting man. 'I take it you two have not seen each other since Christmas? That's a lot of catching-up to do. Thanks for the drink, Ahmad. I'm really pleased to meet you.' Ben rose from his chair and shook Ahmad's hand. He kissed Arianne on the cheek, and then took his leave of them.

Ben had been curious about Ahmad – not overly, but definitely curious about the man whom he had seen in the photograph at Number 12, Three Kings Yard. He had not expected the charisma of the man, the seductive charm that emanated from him. He was something special. Ben could understand women finding him irresistible. But he did not feel threatened by Ahmad. Ben was so secure in Arianne's love for him that he felt, if anything, sorry for Ahmad Salah Ali. The man had lost the most divine of women to Ben. Ben guessed he would not take it very well. He had just had a drink with a man who was many things, but certainly not one of the world's great losers.

When the call had come through from Ahmad that he was going to be in London and wanted to take Arianne to lunch, both Ben and Arianne were relieved that Ahmad had surfaced at last. Arianne wanted very much that Ahmad should know she was marrying again, and how happy she was. Ben and she had actually made plans for Arianne to go to see Ahmad sometime in the very week he had called. Ben and his polo team were flying off to a sale of polo ponies. Arianne would have been at a loose end without him for a few days. They had agreed that would be the perfect time for her to spend with Ahmad. Now, as Ben walked from Claridge's, he was pleased that the timing had worked out for them. But, having met the man, he doubted that Arianne would have her few days with him. He might have played second best once, but was Ahmad going to assume an even lesser role second time around? And anyway, that was not an option open to him. But friendship was. That was between Arianne and Ahmad. He had every faith in Arianne that she would work things out.

'He's very pleasant,' Ahmad told Arianne as they watched Ben walking away.

'Yes, he is. I feel very lucky to have him.'

'As a friend?'

'Yes, as a friend.'

'And a lover . . .'

Arianne took a long drink of champagne from the glass that had now been refilled for the third time since she had sat down. Ahmad ordered another bottle. 'Yes, as a lover,' she answered.

'Is he a good lover, Arianne? He looks like he could be.' Arianne should have expected a question like that from Ahmad. But somehow she hadn't. She felt very private about her intimate life with Ben. But she knew Ahmad. The easiest way out would be to answer him truthfully.

'Yes, a very good lover. He makes me happy, Ahmad.'

'Good. That's all that matters.' He raised her hand to his lips and kissed it. He held on to it and stroked it.

'I'm so glad you feel that way,' she told him. Arianne was not just saying that; she really meant it. On hearing that he was pleased for her, she gave an inward sigh of relief, and relaxed. It was only then that she realised she had been anxious about this meeting and how Ahmad would take to Ben, and his seeing her with another man.

Arianne hadn't realised how difficult it was going to be to tell him she was remarrying. She had not reckoned that she would still be so physically attracted to Ahmad now that Ben had come into her life and she had fallen in love. But she was. That old erotic magic was still very much there. There it might be, but she felt no conflict in giving up erotic love and sex with Ahmad. Love had chosen for her, and that had sealed Ahmad's and Arianne's fate. It was as simple as that. That was the moment she chose to tell Ahmad about her impending marriage. But she was not quick enough. Ahmad snatched the moment from her when he suggested:

'I've booked a table in the dining room. But I have a better idea. Why don't we have lunch in my suite? I have the Art Deco one. Remember? The one with the massive bathroom that you like so much and that lovely, large sitting room. I have had it filled with vases of spring flowers and orchids. We can have a nice leisurely lunch there at a table set in front of the fireplace, and I can catch up on all your news.'

'Oh, yes, a lovely idea. You always have lovely ideas, Ahmad.' Arianne was very pleased at the change of plan. It seemed far more natural to her to be alone with Ahmad in a more intimate place than Claridge's dining room to talk about the monumental changes she was making in her life.

Ahmad watched her while she was studying the menu. She looked different, completely happy and stunningly sensuous in the Jean Muir dress she was wearing. The black silk jersey liked her body: it wrapped itself around her and showed her off to best advantage. The silk jersey plunged dangerously loose between her breasts to form a V-neckline that went nearly to her waist, yet it hugged the full, rounded breasts and showed the faintest shadow of nipple. She knew how much he liked that dress. She wore very high-heeled black crocodile shoes and cream-coloured stockings so sheer as to seem almost not there at all. She wore also the ruby ring he had given her on their trip up the Nile. She had dressed to please him. And she was right to do so: it made him happy that she could still obey her instincts towards him, new lover or not.

They lingered over the bottle of champagne. Ahmad charmed Arianne with risqué stories of his escapades with the women he had been involved with since they had been together. There was nothing unusual about that: sex and women had always been the first equation in his life. He had a Don Juanesque way of telling his stories. It could excite women to want to be part of this erotic world he dwelt in. Slowly he was drawing her back into his world, a world she had lived in and enjoyed to the full. Here was familiar ground she was treading with an unimaginably exciting, handsome man, a lover few women could resist.

He gathered up her handbag and the short, enchanting jacket of rag – strips of black silk of various weights, tattered and knotted – then the framed photograph. Taking her by the elbow, he escorted her from the room to the lift.

Arianne was just that little bit light-headed from an excess of wine, being too much in love, and feeling happy at being with Ahmad again. It felt so good, being back in the world again and feeling so intense about life. She found it quite extraordinary that, when she and Ahmad were apart, she hardly ever missed him. But once with him, she became instantly aware that she had. In his presence she was always made to feel that he was sweeping her into his life, that she belonged, and could breathe better there than anywhere else in the world.

In the lift she giggled to herself: how many women, had, over the years, come to her in tears to tell her those exact same things? He had the ability to make all women feel they were vital to his life. She turned to face Ahmad. As they were alone in the lift, she leaned against him and kissed him briefly on the lips.

'Ah, and why do I deserve that?'

'Because I love you so much and I'm so happy to see you.' A reply to please any man.

He found her very sexy, extremely provocative – more like his Arianne than she had been since Jason had vanished from her life. He sensed it there in the lift. Ben was no mere sexual interlude. She loved him, and exactly as she had loved Jason. He wasn't having that. He dismissed the thought before he allowed it to take hold. He had not come this far with Arianne not to win her undivided love. He would see to it that, whatever Ben was beyond a sexual interlude, he would be it no longer before this day ended.

Ahmad placed an arm around Arianne's waist as they walked from the lift down the corridor towards the suite of rooms she had known so well in the past. To see the wide, handsome corridor with its tables adorned, some with beautiful, period Chinese ceramics, others with vases of fresh flowers; the cosy seating-area, settees and tapestry-covered French chairs; and the soft light cast from under silk shades on to opulent lamp-bases of stunningly beautiful Chinese Imari porcelain; was to remember some of the best days of her life when Ahmad, Jason and she had walked down that same corridor together. How the three of them had relished their jaunts to London. The Art Deco suite at Claridge's had always been one of their homes from home. To walk the corridor now with Ahmad was to step back in time for a moment, and to be grateful for the exciting life she had had when she had been married to Jason.

She felt Ahmad slide his hand from her waist to the side of her breast. His caress was light and teasing. He well knew how sensitive she was to being caressed there – the motion of his hands cupping the side, jiggling her breast ever so lightly in his palm, the scarcely perceptible pressure circling the sensitive nimbus through her dress. It all felt so good, so natural and right: his touch, the familiar corridor, her being there.

Ahmad rang the bell of the suite. In the few seconds before it was answered, she looked up and gazed into his eyes. His lust for her shone in them. She was naked to them. He was imagining the carnal ravaging of her. He moved his hand from her breast to around her slender neck, and ran a feathery touch up and down, using occasionally some pressure of his fingers. Slipping his hand beneath the black silk jersey of her dress, he squeezed her shoulder and smiled at her before removing his hand and taking her hand in his.

It was going to be far more difficult than she had imagined to tell him that it was over for them. Not so much because she was still reacting to him sexually as she always had since he had first taken possession of her, but because there was something more

270

than lust in his eyes, something dangerous, inexplicable. It was not the first time she had seen that look, but never before had she sensed that, whatever it meant, it was directed at her. Strangely, she was not frightened, merely uncomfortable with that realisation. And, as was usual with Arianne, to be uncomfortable made her act very calm.

Muhammad opened the door, and Ahmad and Arianne handed her things over to him, after a friendly greeting between Arianne and Ahmad's man. They walked from the entrance hall of the suite into the drawing room. Arianne smiled. She did so like this room. She turned to face Ahmad. 'I always imagine Noel Coward walking in here from the bedroom. In my mind I keep hearing his songs, and Gertrude Lawrence singing them.'

Ahmad laughed. 'You always say that, every time we come here.'

'Yes, I guess I do. Though it has changed through the years, it has not changed all that much. I always like the crisp whiteness of this room, broken by the Art Deco curves and angles,' said Arianne, then adding, 'look at those orchids in that vase. Perfectly wonderful. And the Casablanca lilies – my favourites, yours too.' She left his side to go and sit on the sofa and rub her hands across the hammered silk covering on it. 'How very in keeping with the period this pale amethyst fabric is.' Then, showing an even greater delight, she said wistfully, 'It's still here, the nude ivory figure on its bronze base with its scarf of bronze held above the head. The prancing, dancing lady.' She ran her fingers over one of the sculpture's raised legs, caressed the breast, its tiny but perfectly formed, seductive nipple. Ahmad watched her, never took his eyes from her. He sat down next to her and passed his hand up her own leg, caressingly, eased it towards the inner side of her thigh. She felt so warm and soft and good in his hands.

Arianne leaned back against the cushions, hardly even aware of his hand. She was lost for a brief moment in the past, thinking of the first time she had caressed the lovely Art Deco ivory lady. They had at that time been a sexual trio, her husband and Ahmad and herself, for a mere three months. Even now she felt the same sexual excitement she had then when she had given herself up sexually to them to do with her what they wanted. Jason and later

271

Ahmad had taught her the ways of erotic love that few women would know. Would she ever have learned them without those two lovers who had honed her sexual drives to match their own? And now there was Ben. Thanks to them she was a sexual being that Ben not only appreciated but loved and adored for being the woman they had helped to make.

She broke her concentration to look at Ahmad. Her skirt had parted and he was still caressing her thighs. She looked down at herself and thought, How raunchy to see oneself being made love to like this, as he bent his head down to place a kiss just above the edge of her lace-topped stocking, to further part her skirt, to place a kiss upon her triangle of silky-soft pubic hair. She could see the passion for her on his face, his delight that she continued still to wear no panties, wanting to remain naked and free, always ready to receive an instant caress, a kiss, to be penetrated by cock on demand. Little had husband or lover realised that her obedience had come to dominate them, these men who thought that they had enslaved her. Her readiness for them, wherever she was, whatever she was doing, was so seductive. They were indeed each other's sexual slaves. Only now, in this lovely Art Deco room, had Ahmad come to realise that. Was it possible that he hated her as much as he loved her, and that was the reason?

'They were some of the best days of my life,' she told him, her voice heavy with the sound that women sometimes produce when sexually stimulated, thinking of orgasm. 'I don't regret one minute of them. I will always love you for them.'

Ahmad covered her nakedness neatly with the skirt of her wrap-around dress. 'I should hope so. And now, there is now.'

'Yes, there is now.'

Arianne was thinking, there is no other way but to just tell him. 'Ahmad, I'm in love with Ben.'

'You mean you have fallen in love with Ben, too?'

'Too?'

'Yes, too. You told me only minutes ago that you love me.'

'I do, very much.' She was about to elaborate on that. To add, 'But in a different way.' And then to tell him she was going to be Mrs Johnson in a matter of weeks. But she was, yet again, too slow.

272

He was already telling her, 'Then Ben and I, we're both lucky men.'

They were interrupted by the doorbell. Ahmad rose from the settee to answer it. Room service arrived with their lunch – two tables on wheels resplendent with crisp, white damask and flowers: one, a serving table, the other set for luncheon for two with beautiful Art Deco silver and dinner-service, and crystal of the same period. A chef and two waiters were in attendance. Muhammad supervised where things were to be set up. Ahmad took Arianne by the hand and led her to a small sitting room off the drawing room. There he poured her a glass of champagne, and told her, 'I have something to show you.'

Arianne was completely captivated by his latest acquisition: *A Traveller's Tale of Egypt*, an Italian edition with fifteen plates, printed in 1696. He sat down in a wing chair and opened the book. She sat on the arm so that they looked at it together. It was a thrilling book to own. He thought she looked uncomfortable, and he manoeuvred her from the arm of the chair to sit on his lap, she holding the book. They looked at it together until they went in to dine.

Arianne was ravenous. She ate her meal with gusto. A mound of long, plump, fresh asparagus, cooked to perfection, and served with a light hollandaise sauce, formed the first course. That was followed by quail's eggs dipped in celery salt and eaten with hot toasted brown bread cut in slender strips and rolled in melted butter. For their main course, they had pan-fried Dover sole in a champagne sauce served with succulent white grapes, and paper-thin slices of potato baked in cream, which had gone all crisp and crunchy on the top layer. Then came a salad of endive. After tiny pots of rich, dark, chocolate mousse and Cornish double cream, dribbled thickly over it from individual jugs, they retreated to the settee while the remnants of their meal were cleared away.

The food and marvellous wines, the service and the ambience might in themselves have made an especially good luncheon date, but there had been more. Arianne's sense of being so very much alive again, so full of happiness. Her feeling that the bad and lonely times were over for her. Ahmad's enchanting good company and reminiscences of their voyage up the Nile. Sensuous innuendoes that were imperceptibly drawing them closer together, and held in check only by the presence of waiters and chef.

At last they were gone. Everyone, even Muhammad, had been sent away. Sitting next to Ahmad on the settee, Arianne was feeling utterly relaxed, seduced by his warmth, charm and generosity, and by his erotic presence. She was silent, savouring a certain togetherness that was familiar and important to both of them. The world outside that room vanished. Ahmad enfolded her with his arm and his powerful gaze. He grazed her lips with his fingers. He could sense ease, that the mind and heart were quiescent, and that her body was open and ready for him. The woman next to him was no more than a sensual being, holding back nothing of herself, a woman making a gift to him of her complete trust.

'A little music.' He removed his arm, kissed her on the top of her head, and left her. When he returned it was to the sound of Verdi's *La Traviata* playing softly in the background. After placing her legs up on the settee, he sat down next to her again, and laid her down in his lap, her head crooked in his arm. They let the music confirm their togetherness in its own way.

Ahmad petted her as one would a favourite cat, kissed her as one might a quiet, half-sleeping child. He knew his Arianne well – how easily he could release in her the exciting sexual animal she was beneath that calm beauty of hers. He cautiously untied the soft bow that held her wrap-around dress, not wanting to jolt her out of her dreamy meditations. She was naked to the waist, wearing only a black half-slip of open-work lace. With equal caution, he slipped her arms from the long sleeves of her dress and, holding her away from him, drew it off her shoulders. She shifted in his arms, and resting on one hip placed her arms around his neck and kissed him sensuously with open lips and a tongue moist and warm that licked his lips. Then she slid back to where she had been in his arms.

He knew that she was half there, in that state where her libido was taking over, that he could have been himself, or Jason, and now even Ben for that matter, until she came out of the reverie she was for the moment indulging. Arianne in that state was always an exciting prospect for Ahmad. She was putty in his hands. He could mould their fucking any way he chose. That was

274

part of the excitement of Arianne's sexuality. Along with her passivity came also that moment when her sexually aggressive side took over, and she became as exciting a female libertine as he would ever know. He and Jason had been responsible for that.

He lowered his mouth to her breast and, cradling it in the palm of his hands, took the nipple and the soft dark area around it wholly in his mouth. He knew well how to suck and lick her to excite sexual passion. First one breast, then the other, again and again. She began to squirm in his arms. She raised her knees and placed her feet flat on the sofa, then opened her legs wide. Her lace slip fell back. There she lay naked except for the diaphanous lace lying askew around her waist. It was sheer provocation. His lips never left her breasts, while his hand found its way between her legs, and, his thumb on her clitoris, his fingers parted the soft, voluptuous cunt lips. He inserted caressing fingers there at the very opening of her vagina and along the channel between her vaginal lips. It gave her immense pleasure. The teasing of those outer and inner cunt lips between his fingers, and the toying with the soft, sweet flesh of the slit beneath, made her ready for his easing them slowly into her cunt. It was already moist and warm in that place where he so wanted to be, and softer and more silky than the finest velvet or satin. Ahmad excited her with his fingers and watched her.

He was moved by the serene beauty of her face, the way she bit into her lower lip, trying to hold back lust just a little bit longer. She opened her eyes and the trust was there as clear as could be. She sighed, reached up and placed her arms around his neck yet again. Her head resting on his chest, she clung on to him. He felt the tiny movements she was making with her pelvis, a gentle rocking. He knew that motion: it was Arianne yearning for a man's penis to penetrate her, to move in and out of her. He revelled in her need.

Ahmad had something for her. As he had put on the music, he had removed her gift from a velvet box and slipped it down the side of the settee where he was sitting. He had been waiting for a moment like this. He had commissioned it to be made to his specifications for Arianne. No vulgar plastic vibrator for her, but one encased in amber and carved by a Japanese sculptor: a penis

275

with a large circumcised head, of a semi-precious material, and just the right size. He withdrew his fingers, and finally his mouth from her breast. Deftly using both hands now, he stretched open her cunt lips as wide as he could to insert slowly the magnificent, translucent, honey-coloured dildo. A gasp of pleasure escaped her and she fell back in his arms. He turned the switch, increasing the power for her pleasure.

How exciting it was for him to control her like this, to watch the vibrating amber dildo drive her further and further towards sexual ecstasy. He used it on her now as he would his own penis, virtually fucked her with it. How exciting to see it vanish inside her, to taunt her by withdrawing it. Then in again, creating a rhythm to excite her need for more, always more. The crazed excitement and hunger for whatever was sexual, whether base or exalted, was there in her eyes. The way she held her breath, the way her body tensed for him, caused him to seize her roughly by the hair, pull her head back and impose his wildest kisses. Gazing into her eyes, his kisses became more urgent as did his need to hear her call out for him to stop this rapid and now rough penetration by the amber.

He saw tears brimming in her eyes. They meant nothing to him. He stopped his kisses only long enough to ask her, 'How does it feel, my darling, my love, my whore? It was made just for you. Because I love your hunger for cock.'

'Wonderful, an incredible sensation, sublime! Have you had it, have you felt it? I want you to. It's the most amazing sensation. You've set me alight; you're torching me with an erotic flame, Ahmad, Ahmad, help me!' All this between gasps, reaching for a moment of calm while lost in lust.

He lowered his head to her mound and bit hard into it, then pinched her nipple, rolled it between his fingers and pulled it. He wanted her to feel controlled by him, to realise how alive he and only he could make her feel, and for her to know that he was ready for her.

She pulled his hand away from her breast and stiffened in his arms, and in a husky whisper told him, 'Please, don't. No more. I didn't mean this to happen.' He had heard those protests before from her and other women. Such words and sentiments only drove him on to possess them. He withdrew the amber halfway,

276

then gave it a violent thrust. She let out a cry, and he continued fucking her with the amber-covered vibrator, that long, thick shaft sculpted with tiny raised flowers. It was a fine piece of pornographic art. He turned it, twisted it from side to side inside her now with every penetration. He knew well what he was doing to her, how he was rubbing her vagina raw with passion, pressing as hard as he could against the opening of her cervix, how this artificial penis throbbing inside her filled her more tightly than she had ever been filled. The exquisite pain and pleasure she was experiencing was only the beginning for her this afternoon. There was copious sex to come for them.

Ahmad watched her bite her knuckles, close her eyes. He withdrew the amber one more time, then with one last deep thrust, he left it there and closed her legs together. He picked her up in his arms. He could feel just slightly the vibrator inside her doing its work. He was carrying her now to the bedroom. She was behaving as if drugged by sex. He kicked the pair of doors open and walked, with her still in a half-world of sexual ecstasy, to the bed.

The covers had been turned down. The bedside lamps were on. She recognised the pots of salve, the small bottles of aromatic oils, the silk cords he liked, on occasion, to tie her up with. The ice-bucket containing a bottle of champagne was there to quench their thirst, and so was the box he kept his cocaine in, the phials and poppers he liked to break for them both to take when they were coming together. The chemical played tricks on the blood and the mind and the nervous system. An orgasm endured an eternity.

A glimpse of those things on the bedside table instantly sobered Arianne. He had planned it. And why not? Any other time it would have been the norm for them. But this was not the norm. Much as she wanted him, wanted to experience anything and everything sexual with him as she had been doing for so many years, and despite the strong attraction and love she still felt for him, it had already gone much too far. There was Ben. Being in love again. She wanted nothing that was not a part of his life, their life together. She had relapsed dangerously into the past. Had caught herself only just in time. This was not what she wanted – fantastic sex but no feeling beyond an erotic love. That was all that was happening here, what she had always had with Ahmad. Good as it still was, as it could always be, it was simply no longer enough.

'Put me down, Ahmad. It's over.'

Chapter 20

Ahmad smiled down at her. It was a wicked smile, amused at her resistance. A smile that told her he didn't for one minute believe her. He intended to take possession of her in as many sexual ways as he pleased, even against her will.

'Don't do this. *Please*, don't do this, Ahmad,' she begged. 'Listen to me, Ahmad. This part of our life together is over.'

'Over'. That word rang hollow in his hearing. With Arianne still in his arms, he turned from the bed to walk to a chest of drawers standing against a wall of Art Deco mirror. 'Over.' His voice was icy cool. 'Open your eyes,' he commanded, a sharpness in his tone that made her obey instantly. 'Just look at yourself, just feel your own lust at work, those little orgasms coming still, with the aid of a piece of amber filling your cunt, vibrating pleasure even now as you tell me, "over". All that and your reflection. A magnificent lasciviousness there, wouldn't you say?'

The way he mocked her word sent a shiver of fear through Arianne. His grip tightened. He was holding her to him with one arm now, using the other to sweep everything on top of the chest of drawers angrily off it. Sounds of splintering glass. Flowers and water, chocolates and books, a decanter of brandy and glasses, tumbled everywhere.

He sat her on the top of the chest of drawers, facing the mirror, but still held her in his grip. 'Tell me, does this look to you like a woman who believes it's over?'

Arianne averted her eyes, not wanting even a glimpse of their reflection. It was quick and it was sharp, the slap across her face. She caught her breath, it was nearly a sob. She obeyed him, and looked in the mirror. 'And what do you see?' he asked, one arm still holding her prisoner by the waist. She squirmed, hardly knowing what to do with her legs as he pushed her closer to the mirrored wall. She was obliged to open them, spread them wide. She could feel his heart pounding against her naked back. 'Relax,' he told her, in a whisper to her ear. He kissed the side of her cheek. She covered her eyes with her hand. He was so very gentle with her now as he took her by the wrist and removed her hand from her eyes. 'Look, how magnificently sexy you are. I love looking at your cunt,' his voice syrup-smooth. He held her captive now, not with his hands, but with his body. She was trapped between him and the mirror. His hands between her thighs were caressing the soft, succulent flesh, her mound of Venus, and pulling back the lips that hugged tight the amber vibrator that was still in place, and was felt even more deeply because of her sitting position, the angle of her legs. She was fearful of denying what he knew to be true: he was still able to do things to her that were unimaginably erotic. Unwilling to lead him on more than she already had, she kept silent.

Raunchy, base, but also voluptuous and exciting: all that she saw reflected in the mirror. It was mesmerising, the sight of her naked but for the slim strip of black lace rolled up around her waist. Breasts tender and pink from his sucking, nipples erect, a tiny bead of blood on the nimbus of one where his teeth had broken the skin. Her genitals, open and exposed from her clitoris to her anus, being caressed by fingers intended to excite. Several inches of the golden amber protruded. She watched as he now wrapped his fingers around it to twist and turn it for her pleasure, while he kissed her passionately on the side of her neck, her shoulders, her back.

She watched the movement of the amber penis, riveted by the sight of the alluring object vanishing again and again inside her. It was as if her cunt were swallowing this honey-golden penis. She caught a glimpse of Ahmad's handsome, decadent face, the eyes brimming with erotic hunger for her, the lips she knew so well yearning to devour her. She was seduced by the aroma of his skin, fresh as if he had sprung from the sea, with still a hint of sandalwood as if he had passed through a forest of it. He continued his attempt to take possession of her. 'Does this look like a woman,' he asked her again, 'who believes our sexual life together is over?'

He was not waiting for an answer. He inserted the amber deep

280

inside her for one last time and turned the power down. Now she felt only a faint tremor, the merest shiver. Ahmad turned her around to face him and then raised her from the commode into his arms. There he cradled her for several minutes, kissing her lips and her breasts, and carried her thus to lay her gently on the bed.

He was removing his clothes now. She watched him, wondering what she could do or say to make him understand that she had meant it. It was over for them. She wanted him to let her go, but for them to remain friends. She knew now that this was a naive dream. But she had not realised that when she had made their lunch date, nor when she had entered the suite, nor even when she had allowed herself to slip under his charismatic charm, nor when he had trapped her in the erotic web he spun around her. She bit the side of her lip. She would try one more time to make him understand. She simply could not bear to see all those happy years end like this, for him, too, to vanish as Jason had from her life.

He was naked now, erect, and exuding a powerful sexuality. He would have her, and they both knew it. He bent over her and placed a tender kiss on her lips. He licked them with his tongue, and touched the deep, pink marks on her breasts. He licked the now dried droplet of blood from her nimbus and opened her legs, slowly removed the amber and placed it on the bedside table. Sitting on the edge of the bed next to her, he filled the two bowl-shaped champagne glasses with the chilled Bollinger. She sat up against the pillows and drank from the glass he held to her lips.

Her mouth was dry with a fearful determination. She drank the glass empty. She watched Ahmad open the silver lid of one of the small crystal pots on the table. She knew from experience what that ointment would do when he rubbed it on her clitoris and applied it to her cunt lips, and the rift between them. She closed her eyes and a tear appeared from beneath her long, dark lashes to moisten them. 'Don't do this, I beg you, Ahmad. You must listen to me. In spite of what you may want, it is over. That's what I came here today to tell you.'

He replaced the pot on the table and turned to gaze into her eyes. 'But you couldn't.' He refilled their glasses, drank his own dry in one swallow and set it down once more on the table. His gaze was steady.

'My feelings got all mixed up.'

'Shouldn't that tell you something? At the very least that our sex life is still driven by love, a love you are unable to give up.' He went on his knees next to her. She sensed his next step would be to caress her lips with his rampant penis, to drape his balls over her lips. He wanted her to take him in her mouth, something she had always enjoyed in the past. But now, tempting as it might be, it seemed out of the question. She held up her hands, palms outward, to stop him before he made his move. 'I'm going to marry Ben some time in the next few weeks. I know a new kind of happiness, different from any I have ever felt before. It doesn't deny how I feel about you. It just puts it firmly in the past.'

He sat back on his haunches to listen to her; then he rose from the bed. If he had heard her, it seemingly meant nothing to him. He was going to fuck her whether she wanted it or not. 'Mark my words,' he was very calm, quiet even, very steady, as he told her, 'you are not going to marry Ben Johnson. You can be sure that I am right about that.'

If his voice and demeanour were calm, the look in his eye was certainly not – hard, nasty. He gripped her by the arm and pulled her to the edge of the mattress, turned her around with her back to him, and forced her down on her knees. She felt the hardness of his penis, the softness of its skin, between the cheeks of her bottom. At this she began to fight back. She scrambled away from him. Still on her knees, she turned to confront him. 'Oh no, Ahmad, you'll not do this to me. Never once did you or Jason ever force me to have sex when I didn't want it. It was always when I was open and ready and hungry for you. I am not any longer there for you like that now. So, please don't do this to us. I would never be able to see you again. I couldn't remember you with love. I couldn't bear that. Rape me now and you'll destroy all those good years. No, not rape at this time of our lives. I gave you everything of myself, I trusted you to use me sexually for our pleasures. I died hundreds of little deaths in orgasm with you, denied you nothing to slake our thirst for sexual oblivion. Is rape going to be my reward?'

Brave words. Formidable implications. Arianne had no idea

how long they faced each other. She had never been so frightened of anyone in her life as she was of Ahmad during that time. The spasm of hatred for her in his eyes shocked her. She gasped, 'You hate me.'

'Yes. I do. Nearly as much as I love you.' Was that sadness in his voice, or resignation? He froze her with the ice in his tone.

She raised her hand to her mouth, curled it into a fist and bit into it. He reached out to her; she shied away from him. But he had her and pulled her forward on her knees towards him, unrolled the black lace slip from around her waist and covered her nakedness with it. A dry sob escaped her lips, she was trembling. He poured her a glass of champagne and ordered, 'Drink this, you'll feel better for it.' Then he turned his back to her, walked to the chaise longue and picked up his black silk damask dressing-gown and put it on. He left the room momentarily, only to return with her dress. He threw it at her, sat on the end of the bed and watched her put it on.

'Please, don't be angry – be happy for me. Life goes on.' She spoke hardly above a whisper.

'Nothing stays the same, that's quite true. You wanted me in the beginning, and then always while Jason was alive. You do remember that?'

'Yes, of course I do.'

'Whenever I was in the same room with you, or came near you, whenever I touched you, it was more important than anything else in the world, wasn't it?' He raised his voice when her answer didn't come quick enough. '*Wasn't it?*'

She felt fright in the pit of her stomach. But answered at once, 'Yes, yes, it was.'

'We planned it that way, Jason and I – right from the beginning when he fell in love with you – that you should become as debauched and depraved a libertine as we were. We made a bet that within three months we would be sharing you. We chained you to us with sex, erotic love.'

'I don't think I want to hear any more of what you're telling me, Ahmad.'

'Ah, but why not? It's very interesting. Love. You were in love with Jason, and then me, and now Ben.'

'Let's just leave Ben out of this, Ahmad.'

'All right, we'll leave Ben out of it for the moment. We'll get back to erotic love and the eternal triangle. You loved me then, and now you don't any more.'

'Oh, Ahmad, what's the use?'

'Answer me. Before Ben came along, did you still love me as much as you did when Jason, you and I were a marriage? You cannot deny we were a marriage?' She acknowledged it with a nod of her head. 'Ah, now we are getting somewhere. Then, answer me, when we made our journey up the Nile, did you still love me as you had before Jason's death?'

'No.'

'At last.' He all but spat the words: they seemed full of venom. Bitterness.

'That's what you wanted, isn't it? The truth. Well that's the truth, Ahmad.'

'Then you have been lying. All those days on the river. And for nearly three years after Jason vanished – you didn't love me then as you did when he was alive? Well, never mind, I knew that. I waited, bided my time, stayed away from you and waited for the day that was bound to come when you would love me as you once loved Jason, utterly and completely – that day when you would give me that last fraction of love that you had always withheld from me. I knew what you were going through, the humiliations, poverty, your aloneness. And still you preferred living and making love to the ghost of Jason to giving yourself up to me. How could you lie to me on that voyage?'

'I did love you then, Ahmad, but not the way you wanted me to. I wanted to love you, more than anything in the world; I wanted to love you as I had once loved Jason. But it didn't happen.'

'Why, Arianne? Why didn't it happen?'

'Because it simply wasn't there to happen. I cannot control love. Love chooses. I follow.'

'Then love chose Jason?'

'Yes.'

'So our love, yours and mine, was a frayed sort of love. When did it die, this poor, shabby love of yours for me?'

'Stop.' Now there was anger in Arianne's voice. 'What I felt for you was never poor or shabby. I won't let you denigrate something as special as what we once had. I loved you from the first time you took me on that beach by the Indian Ocean, and I loved you as well as I could. The same way you loved me. Not wholly or completely, because neither of us was capable of that. It wasn't because of Jason. It was because of you, because of your voracious appetite for other women. Because love for you is always a game. Because you never wanted the real thing, and you don't now. If you did, I would have sensed it. It might have made all the difference in the world to us. I was an erotic game for you, and – you would have me believe – for Jason. When did my love for you die? A long time ago with Jason's death. And now here you are killing whatever love still lingers with your insane jealousies and childish cruelties. After today I won't even be able to relive my memories of us without finding you there shutting them off for me.' Arianne stopped there. So many home truths had come tumbling out with her anger, fear and anguish, she could face no more.

'A wounded look does not become you, Arianne. You swim with the sharks. You're bound sooner or later to get bitten.'

'I think I was swallowed up whole.'

Arianne was appalled when Ahmad raised an eyebrow and gave her a look that confirmed to her that that was exactly what she had allowed to happen to her. She had been devoured by her marriage, by the *ménage à trois*. Till now she had not fully known it. All the anger she had felt was suddenly gone. Sheer exhaustion took over, as if she was emerging from the worst beating of her life.

'Then what if Jason were still alive?'

'But he isn't, and therefore we aren't.' Her answer was spontaneous. It did manage to revive her. She rose from the bed. Picking up her handbag, which he had brought in with her dress, she walked into the bathroom and closed the door.

When Arianne opened it again and stepped into the room Ahmad was already dressed.

'I'll see you home.'

'That's not necessary.'

'I insist.'

Her home, his gift to her, was no more than fifteen minutes away from that room. It seemed a million miles from Claridge's to Number 12, Three Kings Yard. They stood on the doorstep and Ahmad handed Arianne the Fabergé framed photograph he had been carrying for her. She took it and they gazed long and hard at one another for some time in silence.

She looked at the photograph, the happiness that shone on their faces. 'They were the best of times, weren't they?' The question hung heavy between them.

'Were they?' He threw the question back at her.

'We can at least part as friends,' she suggested.

'No. I don't think so.'

'Don't say that. Maybe in time, we will be able to see each other again.'

'No. We'll never see each other again.'

'Can you be so sure?'

'Absolutely.'

'Then this is it. You having nothing else to say to me?'

'Only that you are not free to marry Ben, and never will be.' And with those words Ahmad turned his back on Arianne and walked away.

Chapter 21

'You are not free to marry Ben. You never will be.' Those words kept ringing in her ears. The hatred in Ahmad's eyes, where once there had been passion and love, made Arianne tremble. It shattered her. She had stood up bravely to his abominable behaviour in the suite at Claridge's. But now this. Was it true? Was she not free to marry Ben and leave the past thoroughly in the past? And what about all those other horrid things he had said to her, about herself and Jason, their marriage and the *ménage à trois*?

Her hands were shaking so badly it took her several minutes to place the key in the lock. At last she managed it and was inside the house. She closed the door and leaned against it, trying to suppress panic. She took several deep breaths. She must compose herself. A feeble attempt. She was unable to control the shaking. To hold her nerves in check as she had while avoiding rape and attempting to keep her illusions about the two men she had loved for so long and so well, was no longer possible. How cruel and vengeful of Ahmad to destroy all those happy years for her. To tear away the veil and expose his and Jason's black core, their damaged souls. To leave her only hard and ugly accusations that she would never be able to confirm or deny about her husband and her marriage.

She walked to the dining room, turned on the light and placed her handbag and the framed photograph face down on the dining table. She could not bear to look at it. A deep and troubled sigh escaped her. She covered her mouth with her hand, trying to suppress another. It worked, and she walked to the console from where she took the cut-glass decanter of brandy and poured herself a large measure. Arianne had to hold the snifter with both her trembling hands to control the glass. She lifted it to her mouth and drank. The bite of the brandy felt good in her mouth; the

287

warmth seemed to calm her. She walked from the dining room through the hall and into the sitting room and sat on the sofa. She felt terribly cold – the sort of cold that comes with shock. Not even the cashmere and fur car-rug seemed able to warm her. She lit the fire and then sat shivering in the darkened sitting room. She had to put her life together, to understand just where she was, who she was. It was like running a motion picture, *The Story Of A Marriage*, backwards, and viewing it without rose-coloured glasses. Not a good idea. It raised too many questions that could not be answered without Jason and Ahmad. And that meant questions that would never be answered because Jason was dead and she would never see Ahmad again. It left her alone to face herself without them as props and with all her flaws showing.

Several hours later she was still in the dark, watching the flames leaping in the fireplace and casting dancing shadows in the sitting room. She felt her self-esteem had been seriously damaged by Ahmad and his warning. She suddenly rallied. Ben. To lose Ben, never to experience the new kind of love and hope and happiness they wanted to share with each other, was too much even to contemplate. She rose from the sofa and placed two more logs on the fire. She would fight for Ben. Love had chosen. Nothing Ahmad might say or do could change that. She sat on the sofa once again, huddled under the car-rug, and tried to think constructively about her horrid experience with Ahmad.

There had been no surprises for Ben when he met Ahmad at Claridge's. He had known what the man looked like from the framed photographs at Number 12, Three Kings Yard. He expected an urbane man, a charmer, an Arab Don Juan. He felt no jealousy when he saw the joy in Arianne's eyes at meeting Ahmad, nor at her enthusiasm for him when she introduced the two men. He was not even surprised at the intimacy and attachment so obviously displayed by them both. Arianne had not concealed from him the importance of her friendship with Ahmad. Ben had needed no intimate details of their past relationship, nor did he want any. He had realised what their relationship had been by merely listening to Arianne when she spoke about her husband, her marriage, and their relationship with Ahmad Salah Ali. He also understood that Ahmad was history, part of her past, but that she wanted him as a friend and part of their future.

Ben saw Ahmad as a quite remarkable and interesting man, certainly someone worth knowing. A man of substance, but a rather dangerous womaniser, a devil in Savile Row clothes, who played with evil and people, a dilettante. But on first impression he was a man more complex than he ever let on, a man who wore his charm to mask his emotions. Here, thought Ben, is a man who could be as formidable an enemy as a friend, and far more ruinous than Arianne ever realised.

But Ben had liked them together. Theirs was an immensely close relationship. One with great depth, loving even. An enduring friendship. Why then, when Ben walked away from them and into the spring sunshine, did he have an impulse to turn back and rejoin them? Fear of losing her? No. There was no danger of ever losing Arianne. During the several minutes he waited at the entrance to Claridge's for the black Bentley to arrive, he sensed that something was very wrong. Not between him and Arianne, or even between Arianne and Ahmad. It was much bigger and more complex, his sense of foreboding.

The open door to the Bentley and his colleagues was a distraction. He joined his friends and would-be partners and was swept into their company. It was not until they were on the private jet, having smoked-salmon sandwiches and champagne while flying to Dublin, that that sense of foreboding returned. But not for long: conversation and high spirits suppressed it. He and his friends had formed a consortium. The object of this trip to Ireland was to buy a stud farm. These days had been set aside for viewing the country, investigating several prospects, visiting going studs, and looking over stock. It was an exciting project. All the men, veterans in the horse business in one way or another, were seriously interested in making a good purchase during the next few days. Millions of pounds were involved. They had been a long time getting the whole project together. Hopes and ambitions were soaring. But, interested as Ben was, he found himself drifting away from the business at hand.

His distraction was annoying to him because he found no basis for concern. It did not arise from any doubt of Arianne's ability to handle her meeting with Ahmad, or the next few days she had expected to be seeing him. Nor was he concerned about her breaking the news of their coming marriage. Ahmad had had years to offer her marriage, if that was what he had wanted. It seemed irrational to him that he should feel Arianne needed him, that he should be there at her side.

All through the day and into early evening, Ben was haunted by an inexplicable unease. It was at the Shelbourne Hotel in Dublin during an alcoholic dinner with his colleagues and his Irish hosts that he suddenly felt threatened – but not by them, nor by anything to do with the business in hand. Ben was not a man to entertain imaginings. He was, nevertheless, convinced that he was in the wrong place at the wrong time. That he was unprotected. That he and Arianne were vulnerable to some dangerous force. Once that thought took hold, he knew he had to return to London and Arianne.

Ben boarded the plane. His sense of something ominous engulfing them did not vanish, but his unease did, because instinct approved his decision. He would be close to the problem, if indeed there was a problem, and ready to confront any harmful force that might threaten him or Arianne. All the way in from Heathrow airport, calm and control of his imaginings prevailed. The closer the taxi came to Three Kings Yard the happier he was for having acted upon his impulse.

In Dublin, it had crossed Ben's mind that he might be over-reacting to an irrational fantasy. He had even questioned whether he was conjuring up this sense of something menacing because he was a man in love who had left his lady with a formidable Don Juan. Those doubts once formed were immediately discarded, never to return. Ben knew himself to be secure and emotionally stable. Hence it was easy to eliminate such thoughts.

The taxi pulled into Three Kings Yard. If there had been any doubts about his breaking away from his deal in Ireland to return to Arianne, one look at Number 12 would have dispensed with them. There was only one light on in the house, the dining room light. The draperies were open and no one was in the room. It was well after midnight. Was Arianne upstairs asleep? If she were, she would not have left the dining room light on.

Ben opened the front door. He was as quiet as he could be in closing it behind him. Standing in the small front hall, he was able to look into both the dining room and the sitting room. The dining room was empty, the sitting room in darkness; a fire burned in the hearth. Odd to have a fire on such a warm spring evening. He took several steps into the sitting room. In the firelight, he saw the silhouette of Arianne sitting on the sofa, wrapped in the car-rug. She was staring into the flames. 'Arianne,' he called, as he walked towards her.

She did not turn to look at him. She hadn't heard him. 'Arianne, it's me. Ben. I'm home.'

She turned to look at him. 'Ben?'

He sat down next to her. She took his hand. 'Why are you sitting in the dark?'

'I didn't expect you. I expected a call. You said you would be two or three days. Oh, I'm so happy to see you.' She placed her arms around his neck and, pressing her lips to his, she kissed him. Ben thought he would never forget that kiss. It was filled with love, affection, and there was about it a sense of gratefulness, sublime togetherness. He stroked her hair and kissed her on the cheek, then on one hand and afterwards on the other, before he rose from the sofa to switch on a lamp. Turning to look at her now, he smiled. She returned his smile, and he was aware in her eyes of the love she felt for him.

He placed a log on the fire, not because the room was cold – it was in fact very warm – but because it was obvious that that was what Arianne wanted. He removed his jacket, his tie and opened the first two buttons of his shirt. Then once more he sat down next to Arianne. He took her hands into his and rubbed them warm. 'Are you so cold? It's quite warm in here. Do you want to tell me about it? Why you're sitting in the dark? Why you're so cold when it's such a warm and balmy night?'

A wan smile. But a smile it was nonetheless. Ben was glad of that. Arianne rose from the sofa and removed the cashmere rug from her shoulders and draped it over the arm of the sofa. She sat down next to him. 'I'm feeling less cold,' she told him. She leaned into Ben. His arm around her warmed her now and he rocked her gently. They remained like that in silence for several minutes. He sensed their togetherness had taken them over: Arianne seemed comfortable enough now to talk about what was troubling her.

'How long have you been sitting here in the dark?'

'I don't know. Hours? Yes, hours.'

'Why?'

'A bad day. No, much worse, a horrid, upsetting day. Things did not go well with Ahmad. He quite shocked me. He never wants to see me again, and I certainly never want to see him again.'

'Oh! I'm sorry. I know how much he meant to you, how much a part of your life he was. Is it because of us?'

'Yes. He was mean and cruel to me once I told him we were going to marry. He behaved like a madman. Not at all like the Ahmad I have known.' Arianne released herself from Ben's arms. Turning to face him, she added, 'I handled him the best way I could because I wanted to save our friendship. But that was impossible. I realised that only when I was made to listen to the things he had to say about us, you and me, and my marriage, about Jason. He was hardest on me, painting a picture that tore my self-esteem to shreds. The abuse and vile behaviour continued. I was actually scared he would hurt me. I fought against him until he released me. But I was never safe from him until I was here at my own front door and he walked away from me. And he went only after one parting shot. The one that devastated me. I have been sitting in the dark trying to work out what he meant by it. "You are not free to marry Ben. You never will be."

'At first I thought he had said it for spite, or maybe to frighten me. I guess he had a sense of rejection, because he refused to accept that the past really was just history for me. Or maybe he couldn't handle my being in love with you and wanting to be your wife. But he sure looked like he knew he was right. When he spat out that declaration he sounded sinister. And, Ben, it was a declaration, nothing less. He frightened me with those words, shattered me. I was no longer afraid of Ahmad. The shock that *we* might not ever be together, that all our dreams of a shared life might never happen, took over. I felt cold as death. Hence the brandy and the fire and sitting in the dark.'

'Try and put him, this day, the things he said, his need to hurt you, out of your mind. I wish I could have saved you from this. But I felt like an intruder at that meeting between you. I did believe that, as your greatest friend, he would be happy for you.'

'Put the things he said about me out of my mind? Not easy. Some of them were very cruel, Ben. That I have been nothing but an instrument of his and Jason's will. That they had deliberately used my love to corrupt me. And that I had obeyed their every wish, their every command and loved every minute of it, revelled in the erotic world they created for me. That their greatest joy was to see what a magnificent sexual animal they had turned me into, that that was what kept my marriage together.

'I had to work that through. And moments of truth, the sort that burn deep, and open your eyes. Truths I had never faced before confronted me. Truths I could no longer ignore. Suddenly I saw things in a new light and very clearly. The reality of my life was spread out in front of me as I have never seen it before. Not the pretty picture I thought I was.'

'The bastard, the fucking bastard.'

'Yes, he certainly is that. How did I not know he was a cruel devil of a man? Why didn't I see it? Or did I see it, know it all along, but blind myself to it, out of obsession with Jason and my marriage? Or was it because of the pleasure I discovered in the erotic, anything sexual?'

'Never mind. It hardly matters. It's over; it's all behind you.'

'Ben, he thought I was still the plaything of his will. He didn't understand. He couldn't see that, if I had been that, I was no longer. I'm not the same person that I was before Jason's death. Ahmad frightened me into questioning whether I am emotionally and psychologically free to marry you. He is such a Svengali, I almost believed that I was not free, not even worthy of marrying you. He made me so insecure about myself it took hours of rehashing who and what I am before I realised that he had only given my self-esteem a pounding. He hadn't destroyed it. Ahmad is wrong about me, about us. There is nothing he can say or do that would make me run away from you. And in my heart I know you will never abandon me.'

'I'm glad you understand that.'

'OK, so now we know he cannot separate us, nor stop our plans. But, Ben, that look in his eyes, that certainty that I am not free to marry you . . . That evil, self-satisfied expression on his face – what did he mean with a statement like that? If we ourselves are not the reason we will never marry, then what is?

That was what I was pondering when you arrived. What does he mean, Ben? We can't take lightly anything Ahmad says. I know him well enough to be sure of that.'

'I'll go and see him in the morning. Maybe I can find out what this is all about.'

'Then you think there *is* something in what he said?'

'Not necessarily. In fact it doesn't matter what he meant. We will marry, and be happy, I can promise you that.'

'Then there is no need for you to go and see him.'

'No, I suppose not,' he told Arianne, without conviction.

For Arianne the world seemed right again. She smiled at Ben. 'My goodness, it's warm in here.'

He returned her smile. She was just fine, recovering from a traumatic meeting as a lesser woman might not have done. There would be no scars. He loved her just a little bit more for that and for her courage. Heroic. Yes. He was about to marry a lady who was beautiful, heroic.

The aura of the admiration Ben felt for Arianne was so strong it drew her to him. She reached out and caressed his cheek, took his hand, and said, 'Thank you.'

'It's hard to hide love,' he told her.

'By God, I'm happy you're here.'

'It seems I could be nowhere else.'

That provoked her to ask, 'What happened? How is it you are here? The consortium, your deal? Oh dear.' She looked upset for him.

'No. No. Everything's all right. I must return to Ireland in the morning.'

'You flew back for me.'

'Yes.'

'Why?'

Ben knew there was no point in hiding the truth. 'I had a terrible sense of menace and foreboding, something ominous, around me. I had hardly walked away from you and Ahmad before I wanted to return. I thought myself silly. I put the idea firmly out of mind. All day I was suppressing a feeling of unease. In Dublin I realised I was not concentrating as well as I should be on the business in hand. I felt I must be here for you. For us. *For me.*'

Arianne grew pale. There was something very wrong. And only Ahmad knew what it was. She knew Ben to be one of the most stable, secure men she had ever known. If Ben sensed something ominous stalking them, it had to exist. It suddenly loomed as a fact more than a threat. They were together. Together they would take whatever it was in their stride. They would deal with it. 'You came back for me because you sensed I was in danger.'

'For us, I told you.'

'But what about Ireland?'

'You're coming with me in the morning. We have to make the first flight out.'

Life seemed to be running again for Arianne. She nodded assent, and gave him a more open and happier smile than he had seen since his return. 'I'm ravenous. Will you make me an omelette? One of your big, delicious, fluffy omelettes. I want to shower. To wash away Ahmad and this awful day. I'll be down in twenty minutes.'

Arianne had sprung to life again. She was right there living in the present with him. All else seemed irrelevant. 'An omelette it is,' he proclaimed. Arm in arm they walked to the foot of the stairs. She went up and he went into the kitchen.

The long shadow of Ahmad still obscured their future.

LONDON,
FRANCE

Chapter 22

Marguerite Wrightsman was the woman you went to for people, gossip, good food, the right wines, and to find an amusing party when in London. She ran a salon hardly less impressive than Madame de Stael's in Paris had been in another age. Her salon boasted a cross-section of interesting people: writers, painters, musicians, the aristocracy, a smattering of industrialists, the high-fliers in politics, handsome men and distinguished ladies. She knew how to mix and match people so as to bring out the best in them. She was a woman of a certain age, well past her prime, much loved and admired, and powerful because of her connections that spanned several continents. A woman of infinite charm and intelligence, her wit was almost legendary.

Marguerite knew almost everyone that a man like Ahmad might want to know about. When he walked away from Arianne and Three Kings Yard, it was to her that he went, to Marguerite and her town house in Belgravia. Marguerite was that rare thing, an international English aristocrat. Her first husband had been a French cabinet minister, her second an American millionaire, a Washington power-broker, a Chief Justice of the United States Supreme Court, and adviser to several presidents. Her years in France and Washington had honed her into the high-society hostess that she continued to be. Widowed for the second time by the death of Mark Wrightsman, she returned to make her home in London, the city of her youth. And it was in Belgravia that she held court.

Ahmad liked Marguerite Wrightsman. She was everyone's friend and no man's fool. He had no qualms about arriving at her door unannounced. He was shown into the handsome library on the ground floor overlooking the garden by Marguerite's black American butler, impeccable in black trousers and a white cotton jacket. Marguerite never merely entered a room. A diminutive, elegant woman, still a great beauty who looked many years younger than she was, she simply materialised, was just suddenly there. She left it to others to make an entrance. She held out her arms now, offering both her hands to Ahmad as she walked towards him. He took them in his and pressed them.

'A surprise, Ahmad, a very nice one. You will of course stay to dinner. I have people upstairs in the drawing room.'

She was – as he had expected her to be at his bursting in on her evening – hospitable, kindness itself. Marguerite had known Ahmad Salah Ali for years, yet this was the first time he had ever come to her house unannounced. She led him to one of the pair of Queen Anne settees covered in a luscious terracotta and silver Fortuny fabric. They sat together on the same settee, he still holding her hands, caressing her jewel-encrusted fingers.

'I must apologise for this intrusion, Marguerite.'

'I think not, Ahmad. It's always a treat to see you.'

'You look marvellous – as you always do,' he told her. This was mere conversational foreplay. She cut into it.

'How can I help?'

'Do I look as if I need help?'

'No. But at this hour – and you arrive without notice. Must we pretend you have come without reason?'

Ahmad smiled at Marguerite. He had always liked her directness. She usually chose carefully her moment to employ it. 'I had lunch today with a long-time friend. A very dear old girlfriend. She was accompanied by a man, someone she wanted me to meet. I think she was seeking approval. She is rather a naive woman, who has lived an interesting but really quite sheltered life. It appears this man has charmed her and, though she knows very little about him, she has accepted his proposal of marriage. He only stayed long enough for a drink. That's not long enough to find out much about a man. The woman's husband was one of my best friends. I feel an obligation to make certain we are dealing here with a good man. His name is Johnson, Ben Johnson. Now I told myself that if Marguerite knows him or has even heard of him, he may not be all bad. You are my first stop in finding out something about this man. I would like to know my friend is safe with this Ben Johnson.'

The butler arrived with two crystal glasses and a bottle of

300

champagne opened and resting in a silver cooler, and a silver salver offering freshly made cheese straws. They were placed on a table and glasses were filled.

'I don't know him well. Not at all well, but yes, I know something about him. He is the nephew of a very good friend of mine, Sir Anson Bathurst Belleville, one of England's respected senior diplomats. Ben Johnson is one of those continental Americans – well, half-American. He is Anson's sister's child. A handsome man. You have nothing to fear for your friend, he's no fortune-hunter. He's selective, doesn't run with the Euro-trash types, or the fast American nouveau riche jet-set, though he is always on the fringes of the Cotswold polo cliques. He is a top polo player. Ben had a very beautiful, extremely difficult and neurotic wife – a tragic marriage that ended with her suicide. She was neurotically possessive. It was a difficult and unhappy marriage. Her death was a severe blow to him. You see, he loved her, worked like a demon on his marriage and did everything to help her.'

'How long has he been a widower?'

'Years, I don't really know how many. But for the last year he has been seriously involved with someone I do know very well. Simone Carrier. I think she thought she was going to marry him. He has been very generous to her. And she very liberal with him. That's how she kept him. Simone always gives her lovers a long leash. A few months ago, he broke off the affair. I had lunch with Simone and her sister shortly after the break-up. She was – still is – angry, very bitter. She expected marriage, or, at the very least, a permanent relationship. Ben Johnson suited Simone. He had all the things she likes in a man: wealth, good looks, an adventurous attitude towards life. He liked to live well. Simone flits between lives in London and Paris. She has a flat here; he bought it for her. They spent a great deal of time together, but he always shied away from a permanent arrangement. She is stunningly attractive. I thought he was besotted with her, as did everyone else. He seemed that way whenever they were out together. I think everyone expected what Simone did: that they would eventually marry. They made a dazzlingly attractive couple.'

The more Ahmad learned about Simone Carrier and Ben

Johnson, the more interested he became in Simone. She seemed to be just the person he needed. 'I was right to come to see you, Marguerite. I feel better knowing something about the man. Would I find Simone attractive?'

'Oh, I think so. She is extremely chic and clever. Flirtatious. The sort of woman you like. Always amusing, somewhat of a *femme fatale* with the men. Your type of woman, Ahmad, a challenge.' It amused her, the twinkle she saw in Ahmad's eye. How he had perked up at the idea of a new woman – another seduction to add to the long list of women he had had and discarded. She knew he would ask for an introduction. Marguerite was not disappointed.

'Why don't we have lunch together?'

This little piece of intrigue delighted Marguerite. She was a woman not easily fooled. There was more to all this than Ahmad was letting on. A mystery to be unravelled. 'I'll call her in the morning. If she is in London, I'll arrange it.'

Ahmad touched the rim of his glass to Marguerite's. The ring of crystal. Round one, Ahmad thought.

Marguerite had no illusions about Ahmad. She had known more than one woman who had had an affair with him – women who had talked. She knew what he was: the ultimate charmer, seducer, a libertine in the bedroom, an eligible bachelor unlikely ever to be caught. Simone would enjoy him. She would give him a run for his money. Simone never did come cheap. They would be good together for a short time. She was tough. She would not walk away hurt, confused, damaged as most of his women did. And just to make sure, Marguerite would warn Simone to have a great time but to be cautious.

Ahmad was waiting for Simone in the back seat of the black Rolls-Royce. He was taking her to Paris. They had been seeing each other nearly every day since they had been introduced several days before. She was not at all the sort of woman he really enjoyed. Simone was too hard, too avaricious for Ahmad. He liked women he could corrupt; Simone was already corrupt. They were having a good time together, but neither of them had any illusions about the other.

Simone Carrier was perfect for what Ahmad wanted. She was

the best ambassadress he would ever find to deliver the *coup de grâce*. It was almost too easy.

He had not approached her about it as yet. The time had not been right. It was a bonus enjoying her handsome, sensuous good looks, her company. And she was good company, with her brilliantly cultivated, seductive femininity. And the sex? Exciting. She was a whore in bed, more than value for money. But Simone did cost. She enjoyed enormously those after-lunch shopping trips to Bond Street. Yes, she was perfect and might just relish the job he had in mind for her.

Simone rushed down the stairs and out through the front door. She was late as usual, keeping a man waiting as usual. Ahmad opened the door and leaned forward. He smiled. She liked his smile: sexy, full of danger and mystery. She was not fooled by his attentions, and knew they would not last. He would keep her only until he got what he wanted. She still hadn't figured out what that might be. It didn't matter to her: she was having a great time playing along with his game of seduction.

'You look beautiful,' he told her.

'Very beautiful?'

'Oh yes, very.'

'Thank you sir, kind sir, generous sir.'

There was something in her smile, a facetiousness in her tone that was saying, 'I'm on to you, Ahmad. You're not fooling me one bit.' He liked that. She was playing the game, but that smile told him the game was nearly over. It was time to advance with his plan.

'Do you like surprises?' he asked.

'Love them.'

'Good.'

At the airport he made several phone calls. They cleared customs and he flew them across the Channel to land in Brittany at a private grass airstrip cut through fields of green crops.

It was a very warm spring morning. The sun was bright in a cloudless sky. They were greeted by an old, battered touring car, its soft top rolled back, the driver a Breton, who seemed pleased to see Ahmad. They drove over a rutted, potholed road and then on to a dirt track and entered a wood dappled with sunlight. Wild daffodils, narcissi, and dwarf tulips were scattered beneath the ancient trees crowned by fresh, bright green leaves. It seemed to Simone a magical place, breathtakingly beautiful. When the wood thinned out the land rose gently into a blanket of bluebells for as far as one could see. Simone gasped at the dazzling opulence of nature.

The dirt track wound through the bluebells to a water-mill on a bluff overlooking the crashing waves of the Atlantic Ocean, which had been converted to an inn. In the courtyard they drank chilled champagne with their hosts and left the innkeeper and his wife with the picnic basket prepared for them. It was Ahmad who drove them back along the dirt track. When he found his favourite place among the blanket of bluebells they parked the car. Taking the picnic basket between them, they walked through the blue flowers for a breakfast picnic of more champagne, exquisite *oeufs en gêlée*, *foie gras*, brioche and butter. Hot black coffee was poured into pretty pottery cups from a silver thermos.

'I like your surprises, if they are all as good as this one, Ahmad.'

'They get better even than this.'

'You're full of surprises. I like the grasp you have on life. The effort you make for your pleasures. A pleasure-seeker *par excellence*, I think.'

Simone knew how to flatter, how to gratify a man. How she must have wound Ben Johnson around her little finger! Yes, all the while that Ahmad had been executing his seduction of Simone, Ben had been on his mind, not Arianne. For it would be Simone and Ben who would deliver the blow to Arianne that would end her dreams of making a new life with Ben. He watched Simone gather the remnants of the picnic together and pack them in the basket. How extraordinary it was, he mused, that when he had walked away from Arianne and Three Kings Yard she was dead for him. Years of sexual delights, happy times, passion, love, all dead and gone for ever. It was almost as if they had never existed. Revenge, no matter how sweet, was a killer.

Simone and Ahmad lay on their backs under the hot sun. Their skin tingled; the heat ate into their bones. Life felt warm and awfully good to them. Ahmad had removed his jacket and now he removed his shirt. Simone turned on her side and watched him with admiration. He was excitingly sexy. He had such erotic charisma as few men possessed, because they never made the erotic the centre of their lives as Ahmad did. 'Don't stop there,' Simone suggested. His response contained a suggestion of his own in his eyes. She unbuckled his belt. He unzipped. She watched his every move as he stripped. Then he helped her off with her clothes. They lay down together naked under the sun, silent, holding hands and letting the sun do its work. Ahmad dozed off. When he awakened he plucked enough flowers to make a crown of them. Waking Simone with a kiss, he raised her up to place the wreath of bluebells in her hair. 'We have to go. More surprises ahead.'

'Not just yet.' She guided his hands to her breasts.

He enjoyed the hunger for him in her eyes. Her need to have him caress her. He placed his mouth over her nipple and sucked and licked. She wriggled under his love-making with need and pleasure, and the excitement of what was to come.

Ahmad savoured Simone's breasts. They were magnificently raunchy; they provoked in him a need both to make love to them and punish them for enticing him to sexual excesses with her that he enjoyed far too much, and knew he would soon have to abandon. It was not sex and orgasms he wanted from her: they were a by-product of his greater need for Simone.

It was not only Simone's breasts that excited him. He liked her hands that could so tease a man. She bent her knees and placed her feet flat on the ground. She relished the feel of the grass on the soles of her feet, the scent of the bluebells, the sweet smell of the earth. The heat of the sun and the scent of their bodies was an aphrodisiac to Simone. She spread her legs wide. Ahmad slipped in between them and covered her body with his.

He wanted the tight grip of her cunt on his penis. And he had it, after one swift, forceful thrust. He enjoyed his every entry, his every retreat. Her cunt took him over and he looked away from her up to the sky and then through the wood and the carpet of blue flowers, and he listened to her moans of pleasure. He added to them when he slapped the sides of her breasts and sucked passionately on her nipples, using his teeth. Her moans grew louder and she raised her arms to the sky and called his name. She told him how magnificent he was, begged for more and more. She was bliss to fuck, offering the joy of fucking without the pressure of love, without passion – just the animal pleasure of sexual release.

He had no idea what triggered it, the interference in his joyous coupling with Simone. But it was there: the realisation that he would never again take Arianne like this. He would never know her on a bed of bluebells, or anywhere else for that matter. Never again feel the kiss of her cunt on his penis. Never manipulate her into the erotic bliss made familiar over so many years. Their orgasms would never flow together. The taste of Arianne was already no more than a memory. The libertine that he and Jason had created was gone from his life.

Anger seized him. He looked into Simone's face and saw the look of sexual ecstasy there. He slipped his arms under hers, gripped her by the shoulders and pulled her up against his chest. This fucking of her turned into something nasty, something more like rape. Miraculously Simone's ordeal only lasted a few seconds, because Ahmad came to his senses when he looked away from her and saw the beautiful woodland and the miracle of nature. He heard her shouts of protest, felt her long, red-lacquered nails digging into his flesh. 'It's over, Simone, it's over, we're all right. Don't leave me, stay with it.' He kissed her with tenderness and asked forgiveness: she was won over by the charm and his determination to please her. Their intercourse ended with them coming together in a long, exquisite, madly exciting orgasm.

Chapter 23

Walking through the wood to the car, Ahmad took Simone's hand and squeezed it. The way he looked at her told her he was profoundly sorry for that terrifying moment he had put her through. He did not drive back to the inn but through the wood to the airfield and his plane. There they left the car to be picked up by the innkeeper and boarded Ahmad's plane. There had always been a distance between Ahmad and Simone, disguised, but nevertheless a distance cultivated by them both. Now, Simone felt distanced even further from this attractive and exciting, somewhat mysterious lover. He switched on the motors.

Ahmad turned to Simone and told her, 'I'm going to show you France – some of the finest châteaux as you have never seen them before.' Then he bent close to her and kissed her gently on the cheek.

He was as good as his promise. He flew them from the coast of France across the country to Paris. Much of the time they flew low, several hundred feet above the top of the trees, giving them a bird's eye view of some of the great palaces of France, cathedrals, churches, beautiful villages, and magnificent landscapes. They did, however, make one more landing before Paris, on another grass landing-field. This time they were picked up by a more impressive car and driver that drove them the several miles to Vienne and the restaurant La Pyramide, there to dine on a sumptuous lunch prepared especially for them. It was late for lunch. It didn't matter: they were expected. There were few diners left, a table of lingering chic Parisians.

Simone and Ahmad entered the famous and much-loved restaurant. Ahmad didn't miss the enquiring glances. He knew he and Simone made a handsome couple. He looked at her now and appreciated once again how appealingly beautiful and chic she was. She carried herself like a ballerina: chin high, head just that little bit thrown back. She moved in a sensuous walk that accentuated her figure. Today she was dressed in a Christian Dior black linen jacket over a dress of black-and-white printed silk, with large, splendid black roses on a white background. The skirt of the dress had been cut on the bias and its hem bound in an inch-wide ribbon of black linen. It flared out sensuously with every step of her long, shapely legs.

The mâitre d' led them to their table. Ahmad, just that little bit behind Simone, leaned forward and whispered in her ear, 'I bet every man at that table wishes he had been where I was in that wood of bluebells. You were magnificent; you are magnificent.'

Simone turned her head and smiled. In many ways a dose of Ahmad Salah Ali's flattery and attentions had been just what she had needed. She was not ungrateful for his attentions, whatever the reason. Now more than ever she believed there were ulterior motives behind this casual affair they were having.

At the table, as usual at La Pyramide, the cuisine demanded attention, making conversation between them easier. In fact Ahmad seemed nearly as charming and amusing as he always was, a perfect Don Juan, persuading Simone that she was the only woman in the world. While they dined on truffles wrapped in a puff pastry and drank a memorable white burgundy, that unpleasant lapse of Ahmad's in a Breton wood began to fade. During their second course, a *coquille St Jacques* with lobster in a champagne and cream sauce fit to make any woman's heart sing, it was almost forgotten. With *Côtelette de pigeon Pompadour*: the bird split in half and boned, dipped in egg and breadcrumbs and fried in butter, garnished with artichoke bottoms filled with lentil purée, a truffle slice on top, and tiny round potato croquettes, a truffle sauce served separately in a silver sauce boat, they drank an impeccable Margaux, the colour of garnets, that had the scent of sunshine, oak, the grape. Blended together they made a perfume such as only a superb wine could boast.

Looking up from her plate, Simone caught Ahmad off guard for just a second. It was enough to see that all his bonhomie was just that little bit forced. Here was a complex man. It was at moments like this, when she recognised the complexity and secrecy in Ahmad, that she appreciated Ben even more. Simone suffered yet again the tremendous sense of loss that came often since Ben had abandoned her for love. Her anger, her bitterness had not diminished in the least since the night he had walked away from her. How many times had she reproached herself for letting him get away? Not again, she vowed to herself, and pushed him out of her mind and forked yet another mouthful of delectable meat. She savoured the taste and gave her attention back to Ahmad. Ben was relegated to the category of 'bad mistake' in the recesses of her mind. She got on with enjoying her meal and Ahmad.

The cheese board arrived – a rich selection of ripe cheeses to tease the palate. She chose, then sat back and gazed over the table at Ahmad. Though she said nothing, he saw it in her face, the question. He remained silent, but he knew this was his moment. They were alone in the dining room, waiters hovering at the far side of the room. Replete with good food, fine wine and, in her mind, questions – oh yes, they were there, showing in her eyes. He sensed the timing to be perfect.

Ahmad cut a piece of Brie, and waited. Simone was studying his face. She had known many men. Few had ever had such exotic beauty, been true libertines, or worn a sensual soul so proudly. For most women, merely to look into such a face was dangerous. It could be the beginning of seduction. How many had fallen for the excitement of playing with danger, the possibility of surrendering your life to sexual bliss? Simone thought she must be the rare exception. She placed the cheese knife on her plate. Here was the moment of truth. She sensed his readiness to be honest with her.

'Would you like to tell me what that was all about, back there in the bluebells? The anger, the hatred, your wanting to hurt me . . . It wasn't directed at me. You were fucking me, but raping someone else. What was that all about?'

Perfect: he couldn't have choreographed a better opening himself to press forward with his plan. He knew Simone would not fail him. He felt grateful to her for it. He was really pleased with himself.

It was that self-satisfied look on Ahmad's face that made her think, I'm clutching at straws. He'll never tell me what we are all about. But then, Ahmad often has a self-satisfied look on his face. This intrigued her, because she never found him pompous: his charm precluded that. Now that she knew him, she could understand that self-satisfied look of his. He was a man truly pleased with himself. She leaned back in her chair and told Ahmad, 'You're a terrific poker player.'

'How did you know that?'

'Takes one to know one. Don't tell me you hadn't guessed? So am I.'

He smiled at her and raised an eyebrow. 'Ah, then, if it's poker we've been playing, I'm calling the cards.'

'Good, I think it's time for cards on the table, Ahmad.'

'Are you saying the game is over, Simone?'

'Let's just say, this hand is, Ahmad. But, before you toss in your cards, you haven't answered my question. I'm curious about that sudden flare of anger. I don't think that was part of this game you and I seem to be playing. Back in the bluebells you gave me a nasty moment that might have turned into something very ugly, where I might have come to great harm in your hands. I think at the very least you owe me an explanation.'

'Simone, I'm dreadfully sorry about that. I'll make it up to you. I had intended to buy you something lovely and send a note of apology with it. I'm terribly embarrassed about the incident.'

'It had nothing to do with me, did it? You were raping someone else. I just happened to be there taking the punishment.'

'Something like that. Please can we leave it at that? There really is no more to it than that where you're concerned.'

'Isn't there?' she asked. 'Good. I'll let you off the hook on that one. But cards on the table: what am I doing here? Not that it hasn't been wonderful. You've given me a good time, Ahmad, but I know it will never go any further.'

'You've never been fooled then?'

'Not for a minute. Flattered, yes, but fooled, no. Smitten, yes, just as you have been smitten with me. I watched your interest in me grow but I also saw you constantly putting the brakes on. I saw a man seducing me for a reason other than love and great sex.'

'How are you so wise about men, and so bitter?'

'Do I look bitter?' She seemed genuinely surprised.

'No, but at times you sound it.' Ahmad could not but feel a

surge of excitement. The thrill of winning was near; he had all the pieces in place. Now he thought of revenge. He could taste the sweetness of it.

'Ben Johnson. This game I am playing with you is about Ben Johnson. Your bitterness, that's about Ben Johnson too.'

Ahmad had to admire Simone. She had not flinched, her face remained passive, she appeared to be in complete control. He knew she was surprised, maybe even stunned, but she never showed it, except in her eyes. It was the anger in her eyes that gave her away. Ahmad sensed animosity, not only for him, but for Ben Johnson too. She started to say something. But he raised his hand to stop her. 'It would not be a clever move to attack me. I might be about to do you the biggest favour of your life – and then again, I might not.'

She calmed herself and asked, 'What has he to do with us?'

'But for him we wouldn't be sitting here now. He has everything to do with us.'

'You're a deceptive bastard.' Simone stood up and scraped the chair back, after flinging her napkin on the table.

'It would be stupid to walk out on me now,' he told her, grabbing her wrist as she attempted to walk away from the table. 'If you want a second chance with Ben Johnson, or merely sweet revenge, then return to your chair, because I can give it to you. If you don't, you have every right to walk out.'

Ahmad held Simone's wrist in a tight grip for some time before he slowly released the pressure and removed his hand. After several minutes she moved away from him. She took a deep breath, and looked at him once, briefly, before she returned to her chair. Seated once more, she placed her napkin across her knees and took a sip of wine. Looking squarely at him she told him, 'This had better be good.'

'It's as good as it can get for you, Simone. Arianne Honey can marry no one. Not Ben Johnson, nor anyone else. She is not a widow. Is that interesting to you, Simone?'

'She'll get a divorce.'

'Never.'

'You seem very sure of that.'

'I am. You see, I know the circumstances. She will leave Ben Johnson and return to her husband.'

'How can you know that?'

'It doesn't matter how. I can assure you that's the way it's going to be.'

'I can't simply go to Ben and tell him a story like that. He would never believe me.'

'He would if you gave him proof.'

'What sort of proof?'

'Jason Honey's whereabouts. An address where he can find him. Detailed information of what happened to him when he vanished three years ago. Would you consider that proof enough?'

'Why are you doing this?'

'In the first instance, sweet revenge.'

'Then surely you should deliver the news to them yourself.'

'Impossible. I told you that was in the first instance. My role in the lives of Jason and Arianne Honey is far more complex than mere revenge. And that's all you need to know. Why are you considering delivering this *coup de grâce*, Simone?'

'More's the pity that we sometimes don't realise that we love someone until after they've left. A gamble? A gamble on getting a second chance to show it.'

'If that's the case, Simone, you will have to be clever in your approach. I won't deceive you. I've done that enough. This is going to ruin their lives. Ben may not forgive you for playing the dark messenger, not even give you the chance you want to show him you love him.'

'You leave that to me. Something puzzles me. Why? Just why have you chosen to give me this chance? There are so many ways you could have taken to blast their lives apart without me and without involving yourself. So why this way, and why me?'

'Poetic justice? Can we just leave it at that?'

'We can, but I don't for a minute believe it.'

'Fair enough, Simone.'

'Are there any invisible strings attached to this affair between us that I should know about? If so, please come clean about them now. I think you owe me that.'

'No. No strings, only some conditions that we must both abide by. The first one will be quite sad for me because I like you – you're a great gal – but it's a necessary requirement. Once I deliver the information to you, we will never see each other again.

We will make no contact of any kind. You see, once Ben Johnson and Arianne receive the news about Jason, I am through with the Honeys. Ergo, I am through with you. You will all be firmly put in the past so far as I am concerned. I am interested in the present and the future.'

'God, you are a cruel, manipulative, loveless creature, Ahmad.'

'Yes, I am. But I am also other things as well. Surely these last ten days together must have shown you that?'

Simone chose to ignore that question. She did not feel at all generous towards Ahmad, even though he was quite right: she had seen some remarkably good things about the man. 'You said, conditions, plural. Let's not be shy about them, Ahmad.'

'Just two other conditions for you to abide by. You will never reveal this conversation to anyone. Nor will you ever reveal who you received the information from. I must have your word on that. You need fear nothing. I have worked out how to cover you so you are not put on the spot about it.'

'How do you know you can trust me?'

'What do you think I have been doing these last ten days with you? Do you think I would have stayed with you had I not liked and trusted you? And besides, you're a woman in love.'

'You forgot to add, hungry enough for another chance at the man she loves to make a pact with the devil.'

'Ah, then we understand each other.'

'Perfectly, Ahmad.'

The hub of Ben's business was the office at the château in France, the same office that had called Arianne's house to say that Simone Carrier had left a message: could Ben contact Simone as soon as possible? Arianne, efficient as ever, had marked the time, 11 a.m.

Ben found the message on the pad next to the telephone. He looked at his watch. It was now three o'clock. Arianne was out: no chance of further information from her. This was the first he had heard from Simone since he had walked out on her. He had tried to make contact on several occasions: letters were returned unopened, phone calls were rejected with the slam of a receiver. Now, all these months later, here was a message of some urgency. He knew Simone well. Urgent. That was a word alien to her vocabulary. Simone took all things lazily, in her own time, never anyone else's. She would not use that word lightly. He rang her at once. Her voice came on the line.

It surprised him, how pleased he was to hear it. He had after all had a year of very good times with her. He had always liked her voice, its soft seductive quality, the French accent. 'Hello, Simone, it's Ben.'

A moment of hesitation before she spoke. 'Thanks for returning my call. I'd like to see you.'

'I'm glad about that. I have tried so many times to make contact with you.'

'I know. I wasn't ready to see you. I'm not even sure I am now. But I need to see you.'

'Simone, I can't blame you for not wanting to talk with me. That night, I could have broken it to you more gently. I am sorry about the way I handled things with you.'

'It's best we don't talk about that now. I do really need to see you today or I would never have called and intruded into your life. I had intended never to do that, not ever. But now I find we must meet. We can talk then.'

'OK. Simone, is something wrong? Are you in trouble?'

'We'll talk.'

'Shall I come to you?'

'No. I don't think I could bear to have you here. Too many memories. How about five o'clock at the bar at the Connaught? It's always quiet and we can talk.'

'Fine. Five o'clock then.'

'What a relief!'

'Something is wrong. Why relief?'

'I was afraid you might not want to meet me, and it's so important that you do. Goodbye, Ben.'

Perhaps Simone was not in trouble, but it certainly sounded as if she was. Ben found it difficult to concentrate on Simone. The year they had spent together had turned out to be a catalyst of some sort that had transported him into the condition of happiness he now shared with Arianne. Every day he loved Arianne that little bit more. Days and nights with her created something never achieved with any other woman. She, not Simone, was in Ben's thoughts when he turned the corner from Mount Street into

Carlos Place, crossed the street and greeted the doorman at the Connaught Hotel.

The hotel had its own quiet elegance. It reminded him of a private club rather than a chic hotel. He walked through the hall, which suggested some stately home in the country, and was greeted by the concierge. In the bar, silence. Not a soul except the bartender, quietly preparing for the cosmopolitan Americans, upper-class Englishmen, French publishers, and Italian movie directors who sought this haven of peaceful elegance away from all things commercial. For those who frequented the Connaught bar, it was a private club with a patronage that filled the hotel year in and year out, and kept newcomers at bay.

Ben stopped at the bar. The bartender recognised him at once. After a greeting he presented Ben with a bowl of succulent home-made potato crisps – always irresistible to Ben. 'You never forget anything. You always recognise your man, don't you?' He accorded the bartender a smile and ordered a martini, very dry, with a twist of lemon.

Ben chose a table in a corner of the room and sat on a comfortable velvet chair. She would be late – Simone was always late. Only as he was sipping his second martini did he remember how volatile she could be. He was thinking, she might still be angry, violent even. He looked up: she was striding towards him. She was extremely elegant in a white Chanel suit, its jacket dotted with gold buttons and trimmed with black silk braid around the bottom, the cuffs, the neck, and down the front. The jacket was open. Showing through it, was a gold, semi-transparent silk gossamer blouse, with frills that stood up around the neck. Her high-heeled shoes of gold kid, and a Chanel bag with a gold chain over her shoulder finished her outfit to perfection.

Ben stood up to greet her. He suddenly felt vulnerable.

'I'm thinking of the scent of Joy. I've never been able to take it, not since you flung that bottle at me and it splattered the stuff every-which-way. No repeat performance with your champagne cocktail, I trust?'

'I could have killed you with that bottle. I meant to, you know. You can feel safe. If I couldn't kill you then, I won't try now. Difficult, anyway, with a few bubbles of champagne cocktail.'

He smiled at her, feeling safer, took her hand and kissed her cheek. She sat down next to him. A champagne cocktail arrived and was placed on the table in front of Simone. The waiter, pleased with himself for remembering what she drank, smiled at Simone, then vanished.

'They know us too well here. I was handed crisps before I even said hello, and you have your favourite drink. They were good times then.'

'Yes, very good times.'

'I wanted to tell you that, Simone, and a great many other things, but you never gave me the chance.'

'I don't want to hear about that. Just tell me how you are. Well? Happy?'

'Yes, very.'

'Still in love?'

'Will I offend you if I tell you, more than ever?'

'No, it won't offend me, but it will hurt.'

'Why hurt, Simone? We made no promises to each other, no commitment, just mistakes.'

'Sometimes you have to lose someone, Ben, to realise how much you love them, deeply love them. We were too clever, you and I, in keeping love out of our life together. We pretended abiding affection was enough. A big mistake, on my part, anyway. I fell in love, too late. And you fell in love elsewhere.'

'Simone, I had no idea.'

'How could you know? I didn't know I loved you myself until you walked out on me. Then it was too late to tell you, let alone show you.'

'Simone, I don't know what to say.'

'Don't say anything. You found someone else. That says it all, Ben.'

'And you, Simone, did you find someone else?'

'No, but I will, when I stop loving you.'

She smiled at him and took his hand.

'Ben, don't look embarrassed. That's about the best thing that's come out of our year together. I learned about love, unfortunately too late.'

'What can I say?'

'There isn't anything to say. I've put it down to "one of life's cruel tricks". I hated you when you walked out on me for another woman. I could have killed you. For a long time I wished I had, until I realised why. It was because I really loved you, and you were as blind to that as I was. I never thought I would see you again, let alone ask you to meet me. But it's because I do still love you that we're here. Love has changed me, taught me that, even if it is unrequited, if you love someone, in times of crisis you don't abandon them.'

'Are you in some sort of trouble, Simone?'

'No, *I'm* not. It's you, my dear heart, my friend, who is in trouble. Can I have another?' She held up her empty glass.

'What's this about?' he asked her, feeling very concerned.

'Ben, are you married?'

'I will be soon. We're returning to the States. I've bought a wonderful New York town house on the upper East Side. It's in the process of being redone. When it's ready, Arianne and I will be married there. But, Simone, you don't want to hear all this.'

'No, I don't actually. I'm no masochist in love. But I had to ask that, Ben. Although we can never be lovers, we certainly can't be enemies. And that's why I'm here, in spite of not wanting to be. Something has happened, Ben. Something that might harm you. If I can prevent that, then I think I must. You see, if you really love someone and you can't have them, difficult as it may be, you can't deny them.'

At this point Simone covered her eyes with her hand. Her words were strained with emotion and somewhat muffled when she told him, 'I don't even know how to tell you this. The last thing I want to be is the bearer of such bad news.' She removed her hand from her eyes and bit her upper lip. 'You must believe that I have had nothing to do with this cruel joke. I don't understand any of it, or why this information should have come to me. At first I thought it was the work of some jealous bitch trying to get back at me for something – one of my so-called friends, whom I might have offended, who wanted to put the knife in and turn it. A little torture for Simone. I am afraid I have made myself vulnerable because I haven't been too clever in hiding my anger over having lost you. People have used it as a weapon against me. Or so it seems. But you must understand, the anger I once had is gone and I have accepted that I learned to love too late for us. I didn't give you what you wanted or what you needed. I take that now fully on myself.'

Simone actually wiped a tear from the corner of her eye and cleared her throat. Then, reaching for her handbag, she removed a cream-coloured envelope bordered with a thin line of grey. Written on the front in a neat hand, were her name and address. 'Three days ago, this arrived at my Paris flat. I thought after first reading it that it was a prank someone was playing on me. Then, as it kept eating away at me, I thought there was something more sinister behind that letter being sent to me – that it was sent to me by someone who wanted that information passed on to you. I had no idea what to do. I almost tore it up. You were out of my life, I didn't want to care one way or another about you and your happiness. I even said to myself, "Tough luck on Ben if it's true." I felt a moment of sweet revenge that you can't have the woman you love, just as I can't have the man I love. But revenge wasn't sweet enough. It troubled me all that day and the following day that you might be unaware of someone looking to make trouble for you. That the contents of the letter might be true. I finally came to the conclusion that that letter had nothing to do with me and everything to do with you. Someone was trying to get at not me but you and your fiancée.'

Simone was putting on the best performance of her life. Her hand even trembled as she passed the envelope into Ben's hands. The letter was short and to the point.

Madame Simone Carrier,

> *Ben Johnson's fiancée, Arianne Honey, is not a widow. Her husband, Jason Honey, is alive and can be found in a monastery in the old souk in Tangier. Get in line for a second try. Arianne Honey will return to her husband, she will never marry Ben Johnson. Maybe you'll be lucky second time around.*

At the bottom of the page was a telephone number: presumably that of the monastery in Tangier.

Simone spoke again. 'I'm a friend. You have to believe I'm not here for a second time around, Ben, or for revenge. I couldn't bear you to think that. Whoever sent this note is a nasty piece of work if he thinks that's what I might want. I'm here because I realise this is not to do with me, it has to do with you, and that woman who I don't even know. How cruel to involve me in it. The person who sent this wants to hurt me through you, to drag me into this so as to raise hopes in me only to dash them. I'll not fall for that and be hurt again. One-sided love affairs are not for either of us. And that's what we will always be, whether that man Jason Honey is alive or dead.'

Ben had not said a word. He had grown pale and silent. It was Ahmad's threat come true. That ominous warning had been hovering in the background of their lives, for all their trying these past few weeks to forget it.

What an evil bastard, was all he could think to say and that was to himself. Handsome. Charming. And rotten right through.

'Please don't hate me, I couldn't bear that, Ben. Don't take it out on me for bringing the bad news. I promise you, I feel no relish in delivering this blow. For God's sake, say you don't hate me.'

Ben finally stirred himself to speak. 'No, I don't hate you, Simone.'

'I didn't know what to do.'

'You did exactly what you should have done. You will understand that I must leave. I must go to Arianne. There were things I wanted to say to you, but they've gone right out of my head. Another time. I'll call you or send you a note. If ever you need anything, you have only to call the château and leave a message. They always know where to find me.'

He touched her shoulder. It was a gesture of warmth and affection. Then he walked away from her to place a bank note on the bar. He left the room.

Simone ordered another champagne cocktail. She took a compact from her handbag and powdered her nose, dabbing the powder puff at the corner of her eyes.

LONDON, TANGIER, GLOUCESTERSHIRE

Chapter 24

Ben's first inclination was not to tell Arianne. He would go directly to Ahmad Salah Ali and demand an explanation. He was not fooled by the elaborate way Ahmad had relayed his message of intent to destroy Ben's and Arianne's life. That letter had originated with Ahmad.

All the way home Ben could think only of Arianne, how this news was going to affect her. The fifteen-minute walk through Mayfair was hardly time enough to work out how to break it to her. But that only occurred to him too late, as he was placing the key in the lock of the front door of Number 12. For a brief moment, while pushing the door open and stepping into the hall, he tricked himself into thinking it was a hoax. There was no proof in that envelope that Jason Honey was alive.

He heard voices and Arianne's laughter. It was Jaime. 'Ben, we're in the kitchen,' called Arianne.

Ben found a smiling Jaime – and thought to himself, When is Jaime not smiling? – and a happy Arianne.

'Look,' she said, 'who I found on our doorstep.'

The two men greeted each other with a handshake and a slap on the back, an elaborate manly hug.

'He's taking us to dinner at Le Gavroche.' She held up a serving dish, a silver bowl with a moat of crushed ice surrounding a smaller crystal bowl heaped with caviar. 'You know Jaime never arrives empty-handed. Open the champagne, Ben.' Jaime brought party-time to London with him.

They filed through the hall and into the sitting room to drink champagne and eat caviar on triangles of hot, buttered toast. Ben tried to put out of his mind the contents of the envelope in his inside jacket pocket. Jaime was a *bon vivant*, a first-class polo player, gourmet and master chef, amusing and clever. He and Arianne were talking food, and what they would order at Le

Gavroche. That gave Ben time to deliberate exactly how to play that letter. His preoccupation was apparent to his companions.

Jaime turned from talking with Arianne. He snapped his fingers, 'Come back, Ben, back from wherever you are. Ah, Arianne, he's sulking because he doesn't want to dine with the Roux brothers. Pierre Koffmann – I'll settle for that, we'll go to Tante Claire. It's not too late to cancel our booking.'

It was no use, Ben knew he would never be able to carry off the evening. There had to be a limit to evasion. He must talk to Arianne alone. 'Jaime, much as I'd like to, much as we'd like to, we can't make dinner.'

Arianne knew they were free. Jaime was possibly Ben's best friend, there was no other man whose company he liked more. Something was definitely wrong. Why else decline an evening out with him? Jaime too sensed calamity behind the refusal. He said, 'Of course, Ben. Is there something I can do?'

'No, Arianne and I will work it out.'

Suddenly the life seemed to go out of Arianne. She said, only just above a whisper, 'Sorry, Jaime.'

'Ben, I think maybe I should leave.'

'Sorry about this, Jaime, do you mind?'

'No. Something is clearly wrong, I'm here for you if you need me, Ben. I'm staying at the Ritz. Anything. You call me. I'll check in with you tomorrow.' He kissed Arianne.

Ben placed an arm around his friend's shoulder and told him, 'I'll see you out.'

'OK.'

'Look, I'm sorry about tonight and Le Gavroche, we would have loved it. But Arianne and I have to talk.'

'Listen, I understand. I don't need explanations, we're old friends. Call on me if I can help.' And Jaime was gone.

Arianne formed a fist, put it to her lips and bit into her flesh. It was not mere distress she saw in Ben's face. A hitch of some sort perhaps. He had blown it up out of all proportion, she told herself, all the time her heart sinking: she knew Ben never dramatised anything. She tried to calm her anxiety, to make light of the moment.

'You're going to leave me. Going to leave me for Simone. You met her and fell in love with her again. She worked her

French charm on you. She stole . . .'

'Stop, Arianne.'

But Arianne wouldn't stop. She was smiling at him, teasing him, poking his arm with her finger. 'You did see her, didn't you?'

'Yes.'

'Has she stolen you from me?'

'No.'

'But she wanted to. Well, fat chance. I'll fight her for you.' She placed her arms around Ben's neck and told him, 'I'll never let you go.'

'Thank God for that,' he told her. 'Now stop fooling around and come and sit down. We have a problem – we're in trouble. I did see Simone and she was not the bearer of good news, although she could not have been nicer considering the impossible position she'd been put in.'

'What's this all about, Ben? You're frightening me.'

He took her hands in his. 'There's no easy way to tell you this.'

'Then just tell me.'

'There is a possibility that your husband is still alive.'

Arianne began to laugh. 'That's ridiculous, Ben, it's not at all possible.' She pulled her hands away from Ben's and stood up. 'What a cruel joke, where did you get that from? Impossible. How many times have I prayed for that to be true, that Jason was alive somewhere and hurt, and that he would mend and come back to me. That was my fantasy for years. We buried him, Ahmad and I, we buried Jason. We buried him and we mourned him. Did you get that from your friend, Simone? What could she possibly gain by telling you a story like that?'

'Nothing. And she didn't tell me the story.'

He reached in his pocket and withdrew the envelope and handed it to Arianne. 'Simone received this two days ago in Paris.'

'I don't want to read it. It's a lie.'

'Read it. We can't ignore this, Arianne.'

She sat down, opened the envelope and read the letter. Ben stood by the window, staring at the sea of cars parked in the yard. He remained standing there with his back to Arianne as he told her almost exactly what had happened at the meeting between Simone and himself.

There was silence in the sitting room for several minutes. Then Arianne spoke. 'I must find Ahmad, I must talk to him.'

'Then you believe it's true?' Ben turned to face Arianne. She was ashen.

'I don't know what to believe, I can only think of Ahmad's last words to me. This is what he meant. I am not free to marry you. Why would he say that unless it was true? He knew it, Ben. He knew all along that Jason was alive. He would never have told me if you hadn't come into the picture – had we not fallen in love and wanted to marry. Why would he have done that to me – known all these years and kept it from me? I'm jumping to conclusions. I must call Ahmad, I must see him.'

'Whoah, stop. He may have nothing to do with this.'

'Oh, he has to do with this. You don't know him as I do. He's playing with us, playing with our lives, yours and mine. And Jason's. He's toying with us. He sent that letter to Simone. Clever. Cruel. He placed her in your life again, another form of torture for me, giving you to someone you can make a life with.'

'Then you believe this is true?' he asked, taking the letter from her.

'Of course it's true. I see Ahmad's hand in this. He owes me an explanation, I must go to him.'

'Maybe it's not true. Maybe he's just playing with us.'

'No, it's true, and he *is* playing with us. This is his *coup de grâce*. What are we going to do, Ben? What are we going to do? Jason is alive and he abandoned me. Why? Was it a plot between them?'

'Arianne, you're out of control. Hysterical. And you're grasping at straws. Stop it. We have to get control of ourselves, Arianne. I don't give a shit about Ahmad Salah Ali or what he did or didn't do. There's no point in going to him. I doubt if he'd even see us. We've got to handle this rationally. We have now been dragged into playing games of power, seduction, the twisting and turning around of people's lives. To hell with that. If we go to see him, we'll get nothing. We'll deal with this ourselves, with the information we have.'

'Oh, Ben, what's going to happen to us if Jason is alive?'

She walked into his arms and he held her close. Now at last, he too wondered what was going to happen to them if Jason was alive.

Together they walked to the sofa and sat down together to read the sheet of paper that threatened to play havoc with their lives.

Arianne began to cry. Tears streamed down her cheeks. She closed her eyes in an attempt to control emotions both high and confused. What if Jason were alive? And those years of love and happy times, passion, adventure, were offered to her again from him? Her years of deprivation after he vanished came flooding back to her. They mingled with her present happiness and the passionate love she felt for Ben, the excitement of genuine togetherness she felt with him. Her past was tearing apart her present. She could hardly bear it.

Ben thought his heart would break just looking at her. She was traumatised, severely shaking; her trembling hands gave her away. Ben folded the letter. As he tried to take the envelope still clutched in Arianne's hand, it fluttered to the floor. A small white calling-card slipped from it.

'What's that?' asked Arianne through her tears.

'I don't know. I missed it. I didn't look in the envelope.'

Retrieving it from the carpet together, they read: *For further information contact Mike Chambers: 0101212 6660524.*

'That's a New York telephone number.' Ben rose from the sofa.

'Where are you going?'

'To call this number.'

'Why don't we just call the number in Tangier and ask if Jason is there? They might say he is dead. And this entire nightmare will be over. Ben, if Jason was alive, he would have made contact. This whole thing is some sick joke.'

'What if he'd been unable to make contact?'

'Oh, God, it just can't be. It's all too fantastic. We buried my husband, Ahmad was there with me. He did everything, organised an investigation. He had detectives working round the clock. It's thanks to him we were able to bring Jason's remains home for a proper burial. Oh no, it's all some sick hoax. Just call Tangier – they'll tell you they never heard of a Jason Honey, and it'll all be over with. We'll be all right again.'

'Arianne, I'm calling New York. You must trust me in this. Instinct tells me we'll find out more by going the route that's been laid out for us. Someone, probably Ahmad, plotted this very carefully, I suspect, for the sole purpose of destroying your happiness.'

She had quite worn herself out. So Arianne relented. She nodded her head in assent. 'You're right, of course.'

Ben called New York. Mike Chambers was not available. That was all he could learn from the contact number. Ben replaced the receiver, more puzzled than ever. He returned to Arianne.

'What happened?' she asked.

'A man answered the phone. I asked for Mike Chambers. He asked who I was. When I told him, he said, "Mr Chambers is expecting your call. He is not here but will make contact as soon as possible. Your telephone number, please." So I gave him my number.'

'Call Tangier.'

'No, I don't think so, Arianne. I don't think we should do anything rash. Let's wait for the call from Mike Chambers. I'm going to follow intuition in this.'

The hours slipped by. Nothing happened. Arianne was far enough gone in anxiety and confusion to be able to block it out of her mind. This was an act of survival. Together she and Ben made supper. They talked about his drink with Simone, and then later about Simone herself, something they had never done before. The one thing they didn't do was talk about Jason or Ahmad.

By midnight they realised Mike Chambers was not going to call back. They bathed together and made love, which somehow distanced the immediate problem that was haunting them. For Arianne, the scent of his flesh, the feel of his skin, the taste of him in her mouth, was reality. Coming together in exquisite sexual union was her joy. They dispelled every thought of Jason alive, made the past taking over the present an improbability. For Ben the sexual excitement, the passion, the love experienced with Arianne that night confirmed their togetherness. They could face whatever was challenging their future. They had each other. After sleeping fitfully in each other's arms, they were awakened by the incessant ringing of the telephone.

'Will you get it or shall I?' said Ben. Neither doubted the source of this call.

Arianne said nothing. The ringing seemed to compel her into silence. He placed a reassuring hand on her shoulder, kissed her forehead and told her, 'Don't worry, you're not alone. We're in this together.'

She closed her eyes and took a deep breath. It might control the anguish she was feeling. Ben rolled over on his side and pulled himself up against the pillows. He took the call. Arianne could bear it no longer. She slid from the bed. She was naked still under her silk dressing-gown. She tied the sash and walked from the room. Now they would know for certain if Jason was alive. Waiting to hear had become unbearable. The very idea that he had survived that crash was drawing her closer and closer to him. He was coming alive for her. Certainty seemed superfluous. What power did Jason still have over her to be drawing her away from Ben whom she loved and wanted to be with for the remainder of her life? The mind playing tricks, she told herself.

She brushed her teeth, drew a bath, dropped her dressing-gown on the floor and stepped into the jasmine-scented water. She lay back in the bath. She must stifle the memories of life with Jason that intruded. Once she had done everything to retain those memories. No more. She had finally given them up, accepted Jason's death and the love of another man. And now this. The damage was done, whether Jason was in fact dead or alive. He was back in her life again. He was competing with Ben for her love.

She had no idea how long Ben had been standing at the bathroom door, leaning against the jamb, watching her.

'Hi,' she said, half pathetically.

Ben walked over to the bath and sat on the edge. He placed his hand in the water – it had gone cold. He pulled the plug and turned the hot water tap on. The cold water swirled away as the hot steamed in. Neither Ben nor Arianne seemed able to break the silence. Arianne reached for the crystal bottle of scented liquid soap and added more to the bath. She dipped her hands into the newly warm water. It was liquid satin, with a crust of foamy bubbles. Ben replaced the bath plug. He and Arianne seemed mesmerised by the sound of the water flowing from the tap, a distraction they were both grateful for. Ben sensed that Arianne was distancing herself from him, possibly even in spite of not wanting to do so. He felt compelled to stop it.

'It's not like you to sit in a cold bath.'

'My mind was drifting.'

'I thought as much.'

Ben opened his robe, draped it over the chaise longue and returned to Arianne. Pulling her forward by her hands, he stepped into the bath behind her and lowered himself into the water. Spreading his legs far apart he placed his hands around Arianne's waist and drew her against him. He kissed her back. Then, taking the sponge, he lathered it up with the bar of Guerlain soap and began washing her back. 'About my conversation with Mike Chambers . . .'

Arianne grew tense. She leaned back, rested herself against Ben's chest and removed the sponge from his hands. She made herself busy, lifting his arm out of the water and starting to wash it. Ben removed the sponge from her hands. 'This is not going to go away, Arianne.'

She slipped down in the water. Turning on her side, she pulled herself up on to her knees to face him. Still between his legs, she sat on her haunches, the water covering her breasts. Ignoring his words, she retrieved the sponge and resumed washing his shoulders.

Bathing together was one of their great pleasures. He caressed her breasts, so slippery and sensual in the soapy water. The dark nimbus around her erect nipples was puckered. She looked sexy. Hungry for her, he raised her by the waist from the water and buried his face between her breasts, moving his head from side to side. Lost in their voluptuousness, he took first one nipple in his mouth and then the other. He sucked hard and held it between teeth that teased and taunted. He covered her breasts now with loving, urgent kisses. When he saw in her eyes that she was right there with him, not drifting somewhere else, he could have wept with joy. She was back.

Arianne did nothing to hide the pleasure he was giving her. She had been calmed by his love for her. She could face anything now. They smiled at each other, understanding through sensual delight rather than words, that with him she could face the crisis confronting them. He lowered her gently back into the water.

Her hands had not been idle. They had closed on his penis, been fondling his scrotum. He had grown long and thick and hard there; life and love were pulsating. To be handled thus in the silky hot water was exciting, sensuous. Only one thing could be better. Hands on her waist, he raised her once more, but this time high up out of the water, only to pull her down again, impaled upon him. Now their pleasure with each other was complete. To be filled so by Ben in one slow, exquisite thrust was nearly to take Arianne's breath away. Involuntarily she threw her head back and let out a sigh. It was of more than pleasure. Relief? Release from anxiety? She intoned to the heavens, 'Oh God, what joy, what bliss.'

She placed her hands on the edge of the bath and leaning on them, moved herself languidly on and off his penis. His kisses were deep and filled with passion; he licked her lips. Finally, still impaled upon Ben, she leaned against his chest, resting her head upon his shoulder. He sponged them with streams of the hot steamy water, and said, 'That phone call.'

No, she didn't want to hear about his conversation with Mike Chambers. Ben eased her from his shoulder to lay her on top of him. Arianne was careful to straighten her legs over his without disengaging. She liked having him erect and yet quiescent inside her. They lay in the water, bodies touching. He enveloped her in his arms. Lying there, up to her chin in the warm water, she felt safe and cocooned in a sensuous world of passion and love. He caressed her back and bottom and felt her yielding in to him with a warm and gentle orgasm. For some time they lay together, silent and contemplative. Then Ben kissed her lips once more, her cheek, her eyes, before he slid from beneath her on to his side and held her for several minutes. Now it was he who gave a sigh. At last he rose from the bath, taking her with him.

He held the pale grey, terry-cloth robe, trimmed in plum-coloured grosgrain ribbon for Arianne. She stepped into it. The large mother-of-pearl buttons shone as if newly prised from the sea. He watched her do them up as he dried himself with a bath sheet and wrapped a smaller towel around his waist.

She was at the dressing-table brushing her hair. He went to

her and took the brush from her, and then her hand in his and led her to the chaise. They sat down and stretched their legs out. He eased an arm around Arianne and said, 'You look absolutely beautiful. To me you are the most thrilling and clever woman. I think we love each other very much. You're going to have to remember that.'

Ben was taking advantage of the calm and collected Arianne now before him. He wanted to make what he had to tell as easy for her to accept as possible. 'Mike Chambers.'

'You were a long time on the telephone with him.'

'Yes.'

'Jason is alive, isn't he?'

'Yes. And he is in Tangier, just where that letter said he was.'

'It seems incredible that we could have called that place and asked for Jason and, just like that, have heard his voice. And he would be alive for me again.'

'Well, it might not have worked in exactly that way. More likely, we'd have asked for him and they would have said, "No such person here." Jason is living under an assumed name: Edmund Waverly. The monastery is a hospital and a hospice run by monks. It boasts the finest medical attention in Tangier. A team of French doctors. They dedicate themselves to the terminally sick.' Ben saw the anguish suddenly return to Arianne. 'Jason is in no immediate danger of dying, but he has been critically ill for a very long time. That's all Mike Chambers would tell me – except that he is Jason's friend and companion. And we are flying to Tangier, day after tomorrow, to meet Mike.'

'Did Mike send that note to Simone?'

'No, I asked him that.'

'Then it has to have been Ahmad. I think we should call him, Ben.'

'I don't think that's a good idea.'

'He was our best friend. He loved Jason as much as I did. Jason was as much his life as he was mine. He knows Jason is alive. I must talk to him, ask him why.'

'Leave Ahmad out of this, Arianne. This is something we are going to deal with without Ahmad. He is no friend. Forget what he has been to you and Jason in the past.'

Ben was taken by surprise when Arianne turned on him. 'How

can you say that? You weren't there. You never saw how he loved Jason and mourned him. You have no idea what a loss he was to our lives. How can we leave him out of this? You are unfair to Ahmad.'

'I doubt that. Arianne, have you such a short memory? And why are you so angry with me? Are you afraid I might be right? You are your own woman, now – remember? You don't need to be propped up by anyone. Let alone a bastard like Ahmad Salah Ali.'

The reprimand realerted Arianne to the reality of her situation. She placed her hands over her face. 'Oh God, Ben, I'm sorry. You're right.' She removed her hands from her face.

'Look, I know this is a shock for you, a shock for both of us. That's why we must think rationally, face realities and deal with them. You don't have to defend these men or what they have done to you. They are not defensible. Mike Chambers skirted around nearly every one of my questions. The few he did answer, and the hints that he dropped, lead me to believe we are about to hear an unsavoury, probably dishonourable story. One we should not become embroiled in. I am not passing judgement. All I am saying is, we should prepare ourselves, and most especially you should prepare yourself, to face the day after tomorrow. Your husband may not want to see you. He has, after all, made no contact with you for years. And if he does see you, what then?'

'I don't know.'

'Arianne, you know, maybe we can deal with Jason through Mike Chambers.'

'You mean not see Jason? Ben, I have to see him. I have to know what happened. I have to know . . .' She hesitated, reluctant to finish the sentence. Instead she said, 'Surely you can understand that?'

'Yes, I can understand that.' But Ben understood more than Arianne thought he did. He understood that, in spite of her wishes, hour by hour, he was losing her. That she was slipping away from him into the arms of a dead man come back to life, and there wasn't anything he could do about it, except put up the best fight he could for the woman he loved.

Chapter 25

Arianne was angry. Angry with Jason and Ahmad, but mostly enraged at herself. A pawn in some game? Not likely! What she needed was a good lawyer, not a trip to Morocco. But here she was, swaying down the aisle, clinging to the top of one seat and another for balance as the plane made its descent towards a landing in Tangier.

She was surrounded by noise: the hum of the motors, chatter in several languages, the hustle and bustle of polyglot people making ready for a fast exit from the plane. Arianne asked herself what she was doing there. It was difficult to tell when she had finally put emotions aside and returned to the reality of her life: love with a good man; the future where games were restricted to polo matches, tennis, and board games. And the fact that her husband, dead or alive, no longer existed for her. Arianne felt an enormous weight had been taken off her shoulders. Her mind had been set free and her heart could flutter again at the sight of the smallest flower or the largest expression of life. She was in control of herself, her emotions.

Ben's eyes were closed; how handsome he looked; good and kind. Her mind recalled the first time she had seen him. Chessington Park. She thought of her mother, Artemis, and Ben's Uncle Anson, the parkland and the house – a world away from the madness of this flight to Morocco to confront the past. She smiled, thinking of Beryl Quilty and her pathological need to control life in Chessington House. Another kind of madness, another slice of life. Something between a laugh and giggle slipped from between her lips. She placed her hand on Ben's shoulder. He covered it with his, opened his eyes and stood up, then stepped in to the aisle, allowing her to take the seat next to the window.

'I was in a half-sleep, a doze really, but I thought I heard you laughing.'

'I was having a little giggle about the madness of life.' She turned to face Ben. 'We should be on a plane about to land in New York, not in Tangier.'

'I'll buy that.'

Ben noted the change of tone in her voice, the sparkle in her eye: Arianne in control. The Arianne he fell in love with, no pawn in any man's life. Arianne had come out of her shock. He had never doubted that she would.

'How stupid I've been. Here I am looking for explanations, when all I really need to look for is a divorce.'

That word, divorce, was music to Ben's ears. When they left London he had still been concerned that Arianne might be returning to her husband. Now, minutes from landing in Tangier, they were there because she was seeking a divorce. Everything he had hoped for. Arianne knew what she wanted. It had somehow become clear to her that, however much she had loved Jason, happy as she had been with him, there could be no return.

Mike Chambers watched the airplane door open. A ground steward tapped him on the shoulder. 'OK, Mike, that's us.'

The steward took the steps two at a time: his way of testing them before any of the passengers descended from the aircraft. On the stair landing he stopped to speak to the first-class cabin steward. The passengers were held back until Arianne and Ben were found. The steward spoke to Ben and pointed Mike Chambers out to him.

Ben and Arianne descended the stairs. This tall, handsome, well-built man, dressed in a putty-coloured linen suit, and an elegant woman dressed in cream linen, high-heeled, cream lizard shoes and wearing a large-brimmed hat of straw, turned out to be the people Mike was waiting for. He was impressed. He gave the lady all his attention. She was carrying a large, cream-coloured lizard bag. It hung from her shoulder by a gold chain. She had a beautiful face, serene even, with kindness in the eyes. It was a face with an angelic quality about it. She was not the woman he had expected Jason Honey to be married to. But then what had he expected? He had had no clue. Jason Honey had never mentioned a wife. Hell! He hadn't even mentioned that he was Jason Honey yet! Mike Chambers stepped forward, his hand out to Ben's. Ben introduced himself and then said, 'This is Arianne Honey, Mr Chambers.'

'Mike. Please call me Mike.'

Mike Chambers was the consummate diplomat. A clever young detective, he knew how to keep on the good side of his connections. He introduced Arianne and Ben first to the airport official standing with him and then to his two colleagues.

'We have to thank these two men for taking the sting out of your landing in Tangier. If you give your passports to Mr Hussein, he will get them stamped and meet us at the car.'

Thanks followed from both Arianne and Ben as Mr Hussein walked off in one direction, while they walked in another across the tarmac to a waiting car. 'You seem to be a man of influence, Mr Chambers.'

'No, just a detective with friends. We do a lot of security work here in Morocco. Did you have a good flight?'

Banal conversation. Arianne knew it was what was expected, and therefore duly delivered until they got down to the real reason they were there. Arianne was just a bit flustered by Mike Chambers. She had expected an older man, not a tall, handsome fellow who could be no more than in his mid-twenties. But he was American, open-faced, bright, obviously very confident in whatever he did.

The small group stood next to a large black Mercedes parked on the edge of the tarmac near an exit gate from the airfield. They made chit-chat about Tangier, questions – had either of them been there before? – declarations of admiration for Morocco.

It was the first day of July; the heat was oppressive. 'You'll be cooler without your jacket,' suggested Ben and helped her off with it. The linen dress worn beneath it had wide shoulder straps that crossed over her bare back. Mike mused to himself, She may have the face of an angel, but that body belongs on earth. For him Jason was a mystery, but his desertion of this woman standing before him was an even greater mystery. 'The car is air-conditioned. We can wait for the passports just as well sitting comfortably.'

Mr Hussein returned with them before they had a chance to

sample the air-conditioning – profuse thanks and handshakes all round again. He gallantly handed Arianne a bunch of deep purple, pansy-like flowers, with a long pin stuck through the string binding them. 'May your stay in Tangier be all flowers and joy.' In the car Ben pinned them to her dress. 'May it just, God willing,' he whispered in her ear.

'Do you mind, Mike? I really hate being sealed in an air-conditioned car,' Arianne asked. The windows were immediately rolled down. All the way in from the airport the scent of Morocco, its colour, its rhythm, the excitement of North Africa, impinged on them. The women, draped and masked, walked along the roadside together in groups of two and three, or zoomed past in powerful limos, on the saddles of bikes, or slowly on flat carts drawn by donkeys. Then there were the men in robes and turbans, others in jeans and brightly coloured shirts. Children, loud laughter, push-carts with fruits and vegetables being hawked by boys who dashed in front of cars to wave them down to shop. Transistor radios blaring Moroccan music, the whine of oboes and high-pitched stringed instruments, thumping drums. Arianne was entranced. She was far more interested in Tangier than she had thought she would be. Ben knew Tangier, though not as well as Casablanca or Agadir. He had hoped one day to take Arianne and show her Morocco, to explore it more deeply himself. But now was not the moment.

'I've booked you into a hotel. Your luggage will be delivered directly there from the airport. But, for the moment, I thought I would take you to a garden where we can have lunch and talk.'

Mike was sitting in the front seat of the car with the chauffeur. He had been turned around facing Arianne and Ben, telling them the plan. Now he placed an index finger to his lips, as if to say, 'Be silent. Don't say anything about your mission to Tangier until we are there.'

Ben indicated to Mike that they understood. Arianne found the secrecy a little annoying. She wanted to get on with it. She was almost uninterested now by what Mike had to say about Jason. She had even reached the point where she wished she hadn't come to meet either Mike or Jason. She no longer felt she had to see them. She could get a lawyer and send him to settle it all.

338

A welcome thought, but Arianne knew that was impossible. The ghost had to be laid – if not for her sake, then for Ben's, and for their future. She distracted herself with Tangier. The sights were enhanced by its being a port city, an Arab city on a bay of the Strait of Gibraltar that had for years been held successfully by various powers. Having been established as an international city in 1923, it had never lost that international chic that mingled with the Arab Morocco. Now a city that had abolished that international status and assumed independence, it was its own special place. It made for a mélange of architectural styles, yet each was subservient to that of the country's own.

Driving through the city, Arianne was impressed with the sunny disposition, the smiles, the charm of the people gathered in groups in the squares and market places. It retained too its lingering Gallic chic. Arianne was captivated by Tangier even before the Mercedes pulled up in front of a magnificent Moroccan house.

They walked through rooms resplendent with tiles, marble floors, and complex fretwork, and were greeted by turbaned servants and maître d'. The owner of the establishment, a handsome Moroccan of considerable age, dressed in splendid robes and turban, saw them into a courtyard where a fountain tinkled. Wooden bird-cages hung in the shade, bird-song filled the quadrangle. They went through more rooms to another courtyard, this one smaller, with another fountain, and clay pots of flowers in abundance – a riot of colour and an overpowering sweet scent. Here was a place Matisse might have painted or de Nerval surrendered his sanity to.

In the rooms and courtyards Arianne saw attractive, dark-skinned men with bright eyes and Arab features, wearing white turbans and dark blue robes trimmed in white silk braid; servants drifting silently through the rooms carrying trays proffering delicacies from the Moroccan cuisine enticingly presented. Sitting on divans resplendent in Moroccan dress and bulky, exquisite jewellery, beautiful women covered their faces as Mike and his party passed them. They were attended by men in western dress, elegant and chic, who accorded the foreigners a friendly smile.

Arianne was enchanted. They were shown to a table in a far

corner of the splendid garden of palm and date trees, hibiscus in full bloom on bushes taller than a man, flowering lemon and orange trees, green lawns, and an endless display of flowers. Here were more fountains to cool the air, a small pond of golden fish, another covered with water lilies, and at its edges clumps of irises and flowering papyrus. From other tables dotted around the garden came the sound of laughter, the sight of smiling faces, happy diners. People acknowledged Mike's table as they passed by. Ben was no less impressed, even though he had been there before, dining with Simone and a contingent of French friends. 'You certainly have found your Tangier, Mike. This is one of the hidden wonders of the city.'

'You've been here before, Ben?' asked a surprised Arianne.

'Yes, I even have a friend who lives here, a French friend. He has a marvellous house.'

'You didn't say.'

'It didn't seem relevant, but now I think it might be.'

Long, cool fruit drinks were brought to the table, with mint leaves and slices of orange. 'I was somehow not prepared for this. It never occurred to me that I might take to Tangier,' Arianne announced.

'It's easy,' said Mike. 'There's a large expatriate community to prove it, and others in Casablanca, Agadir and Fez. Many successful westerners, some celebrated writers, people from all over the artistic and social world, are here, enjoying an exotic lifestyle in handsome Moroccan palaces or lesser, but still enchanting houses.'

'And you're one of them?' asked Arianne.

'No, I'm here strictly for business. But I manage to enjoy it.'

'And what is your business?' asked Arianne.

'I am a private detective working for a very respectable agency. Your husband doesn't know that.'

'But you told Mr Johnson here that you were a friend, a close friend, and his companion.'

'That's true. It's rather complicated. I have become very attached to him. It's hard not to, he's such a charmer. But I am doing a job as well.'

'Don't tell me any more. I think I'd rather not know. You say my husband is alive?'

'Yes.'

'You understand what a shock that is to me? He vanished from my life, then we buried him. I mourned for years, and now I find it's all been a sham. I need only know one thing. Is my husband capable of making contact with me?'

'Yes.'

'But he hasn't. Now I really don't think I want to know any more. That one thing was important. The rest is irrelevant, except that I am still married to Jason Honey. Had some malicious person not notified us that my husband was still alive, I would soon have been a bigamist. And he would have allowed that. I thought I wanted explanations from him. I don't. I only want a divorce.' There was a firmness, a definite hardness about Arianne that both men began to admire and respect.

'Mrs Honey, it would be better for you to hear me out. There's no elaborate deception here on my part, or my firm's. I have instructions to tell you certain facts. If you don't want to hear them, don't. But I think you would be wise to do so, because you are going to be hard-pressed to get a divorce from Jason Honey. You see, to all intents and purposes he has had himself wiped off the face of this earth. I know he is Jason Honey, I have proof. But he doesn't acknowledge that. And the proof I have cannot be used on your behalf. It's confidential to my firm's client, who is not Jason Honey. His passport doesn't say that he is. And he doesn't acknowledge you.'

'Where does that leave me?'

Ben saw the flash of vulnerability in Arianne. Emotions taking hold. He came to her rescue. 'Arianne, painful as this may be, you are going to have to hear Mike out. Otherwise there is no way we can deal with this problem.'

Arianne nodded agreement.

'Good.' Ben reached under the table to take her hand in his, raised it to his mouth and kissed it tenderly. Then, placing it on the table, he held it tight. He asked, 'Mike, who do you get your instructions from?'

'My boss, Jim O'Connor, the Managing Director and owner of the company I work for. He must be getting his instructions from somebody pretty important, certainly very wealthy. Jim O'Connor doesn't fuss with little things or deal with men way down the ladder like me. Not ordinarily, anyway.'

'And he is giving you instructions as to what you are to tell us?'

'That's about it.'

'Arianne, I think we'd better hear him out.'

Fresh drinks were brought to the table, and a platter of tiny filo pastry squares stuffed with rice, slivers of pigeon, currants and pine-nuts, for them to nibble on. No one touched them. Once the servant had disappeared, Mike began.

'I got involved with this case because I was instructed to find Jason Honey, keep it a secret and report back when I did. I found him on a mountain in the Himalayas. My instructions were to locate him and not to let on that we were a search party.

'He was in bad shape at that point, dying a slow death from his injuries. He had been rudimentarily taken care of. The villagers and one doctor had done their best for him, saved his life. Your husband couldn't have made contact with you for a year after his crash. He was in a comatose state. Then he came out of it, miraculously without any brain damage. I didn't know that then, but I know it now because the doctors treating him here have discussed it with me. When I found him, and that was only several months ago, he was paralysed down one side. He had what we thought was a broken back and all sorts of internal injuries, and he was and is a serious heroin addict.'

Ben squeezed Arianne's hand, a gesture of reassurance that he was there for her and concerned about her. 'I'm all right, Ben. Go on, Mr Chambers.'

'The next instruction from my boss was to bring him out, get him the best medical care possible, give him what he wanted, anything at any price. A simple enough order, but hard to accomplish. It wasn't easy to persuade him to leave the village. He was living in that great, heroin-induced twilight zone, floating in and out of pain and consciousness, with no interest in life. He had everything he wanted in that village. It took time to get through to him, to convince him to leave for a more comfortable life. It was he who chose Tangier, he who chose the hospice he is in. We got him a false passport in what he claimed was his name. It was a chancy thing to do, to bring him out of there – an 80:20 chance he would survive the trip. My instructions were to stay with him and play his game, and at any cost give him what he wanted.'

'That has to be Ahmad, Ben. Only he would do that for Jason. Only he has the money to finance such an undertaking.'

Ben chose to ignore Arianne's comments. She made it sound as if Ahmad was acting from a sense of love and generosity. Ben didn't believe that for a minute, though he did believe Ahmad was behind the rescue operation, and for many an ulterior motive. 'Go on, Mike. Let's hear it all.'

'Your husband knows Tangier well. He knew the hospice. Your husband is hiding in that monastery under an assumed name, the name he used whenever he was in Tangier before. He is never going to come out. He has money; he has made a miraculous recovery; he doesn't want to see anyone; he doesn't care about anyone. He has a friend, a young woman – she is the only visitor except for a couple of men he does some sort of sneaky business with. I am never allowed in the room when they are there, so I can't tell you anything about that, and frankly I don't want to know.

'Your husband is never going to walk again – or so the doctor said. I wouldn't bet on that, though. They said he would remain paralysed for the remainder of his life, and he is no longer paralysed. I needn't tell you about your husband, Mrs Honey. He is an extraordinary man, one of the smartest men I have ever met, but he is also a wilful, dangerous man. A man of extraordinary charm – that is all still there. There is also something else, a darkness. A lovelessness. He won't be generous about you or your showing up there.

'I had a new set of instructions sent a week ago that Mr Johnson would make contact. I was to tell you what I have just told you, no more, no less. I am to deliver Mrs Honey and you, Mr Johnson, to her husband. I suggest you be very careful about approaching him for a divorce. Don't raise any hopes. He's not going to let you go. I don't think he can. Your husband has to stay dead; he has to stay in hiding, which is what he is doing in the monastery, in the middle of that souk in Tangier. I think he has done some very bad things to some very bad people. You would have to expose him to get a divorce. Do that and you might be responsible for killing him. I have been on this case for a very long time and I've been putting pieces together. He's a charmer, but he's one very bad guy, and bad guys come to bad ends an awful lot of times.

'Look, when we spoke on the telephone, Mr Johnson, I had my instructions to get you here and tell you what I just have. It's my job. To bring you to him, that's my job too. I may be stepping out of line here, but you seem like nice people, so for what it's worth, go away. If you see him, he will only hurt you. He may not even want to, but he is a heroin addict, living in a world of dreams and fantasies, and unfortunately, he plays games. He likes to play with the darker side of people's lives. I'm a strong guy, I can fight him off, but he is a charmer with the devil in him, and he knows how to get to people and hurt them.'

All the while Mike Chambers was speaking, Arianne kept thinking, That's the man I lived with, loved, was obsessed with. Jason made me the woman I am now. Mike's not telling me something I never knew or closed my eyes to. She looked at Ben and felt appalled that he should be hearing this, that he should know that this was the man she mourned, who was still controlling their lives. What life could she and Ben have, unless she found a way to dissolve her marriage legally?

'I don't want you to see him, Arianne. Let's get on the next plane back to London. We can still go to New York and get on with our lives.'

Mike stood up. 'I'll go see about lunch and give you some time to talk this over.'

'Arianne, come away with me now. We'll make a life and make believe he's dead. He is dead to you, isn't he?'

'Emotionally, yes. But I am tied to him by a wedding licence and I want it dissolved.'

'You're playing with fire here.'

'We're playing with fire, anyway. We're here. Let me see him and try to get a divorce.'

'It'll take years.'

'No, months maybe, but not years. I'll make him give me a divorce. He's so crooked, he'll find a way to get us a divorce. He owes me that. We have to see him, Ben.'

'Who are you doing this for?'

'For us. For the children we're going to have. So that he or

Ahmad can never come back at us in the future. I don't want to be punished any more. The weakness! The mistakes I made loving them! Allowing myself to be so dependent on their pleasure, their adoration of me! God, it makes me sick! I'm so happy you found me now that I'm a complete person, myself unto myself. Think about it, Ben – in a few months, we can get round him. And then be free to marry. You can see what he's done to me. How can he deny me a divorce? I love you, Ben. I can't bring this to you. It'll hover over us for the rest of our lives.'

'We'll go and see him,' Ben told her in a near-whisper.

She closed her eyes. A sigh of relief, and then she said, 'Thank God, you understand.'

He did understand. He understood that she was naive, no more able to swim with the sharks than she had ever been. What could he do? Her mind was made up. He would give her her chance to prove him wrong.

'Oh, I love you, I love you so much, Ben.'

'And I love you, and it will all work out.'

Chapter 26

Jason felt himself pulling out of a dreamless sleep into the state that Mike Chambers called his twilight zone. There was no place lovelier in the world than that twilight zone. All things came together for Jason in that hazy world of no pain. He drifted for several more minutes into sleep and out again. He did that often. It helped him gather energy to turn his brain on. How delicious. He wanted to be nowhere but where the needle was king.

He opened his eyes, only just. He liked this room: the white stone walls and floor; the white semi-transparent cotton curtains that swayed with the slightest movement of air; the misty view through them on to the balcony that overlooked the roof-tops of the souk. Often he pretended that he could see a ribbon of blue sea beyond them. The bright blue sky, and under it, the narrow streets, crooked houses, the bougainvillaea, the potted flowers, the colour of Morocco: it all came alive in his imagination.

Nature within the hubbub of people living and laughing, scheming and cheating and dealing in secrets . . . The mysteries . . . He liked the poverty, the strength of character to be found in the souk-dwellers. The wily merchants, even the ugly tourists who swarmed the streets. It was here he lived without having to leave his room.

He opened his eyes just that little bit more. Jason savoured the silence of the monastery, his aloneness, the swishing of the monks' habits, the clicking wooden beads and crosses as the monks moved silently through the cloisters. Most of all he liked the barrier: the high vaulted ceilings and the narrow slit-windows of the stone halls that ringed the hospice rooms, once monks' cells, now enlarged to accommodate the terminally ill and dying, the famous in retreat. They kept the outside firmly where it belonged, outside his life, and let him control when to admit it.

The mosquito netting that hung from a rosette on the ceiling had been draped around the bed. To look through it now was to see everything as if shot in soft focus. Jason smiled – that was his life, a world in soft focus. Brother François had closed the shutters. The afternoon sun, still bright, slid into the room in slits of light. The room was hot and the air, what there was of it, was being moved lazily by the blades of the ceiling fan. He liked that fan, so reminiscent of a fine old wooden propeller.

In the shadows of the room, he saw a lovely creature dressed in white, a beautiful woman, romantically ethereal through the netting. She had a strong back, bare, crossed by white straps, slender naked arms and long, luscious legs. Who was this woman? A vision in his twilight zone? Or a visitor? A man . . . Jason drifted off again into a half-sleep. When he opened his eyes again she was still there. Only now she had turned around. It was Arianne.

The man was still there too, and looking at Arianne in the same way that he, Jason, used to look at her. He was handsome: sexy bastard, fucking my Arianne. He approved of that: he had always liked other men fucking his wife. It was a turn-on for him because he knew that she never gave everything to them as she did to him. She always held back that little bit for Jason. He smiled and feigned sleep while he listened to the man and his wife. They were talking in whispers. He lowered his eyelids to slits, just enough to watch them. He found it strange to have them there in this half-world of his. She was still beautiful, but was she still vulnerable? That had always been her best quality, her vulnerability. The thing he liked to play with.

'Yes, that's Jason. How handsome he still is. I once loved that handsome man. How like him to discover Tangier and hide here. I thought he would look worse for all he has been through, but he doesn't. Except for that scar, he looks exactly the same – older, maybe, a little grey in his hair, thinner, and he's a little more haggard-looking.'

'The man has been through a lot, Arianne.'

'Ben, hold me.'

Jason watched the man put his arms around her, kiss her, fondle her shoulders, place his hand on her breast, and then Jason slipped back into sleep.

Time was irrelevant for Jason. He had lost track of it. It had no meaning for him. Now was just now – later, earlier no longer mattered. It was blissful to live in a void.

She was there again, with Brother François. Whispering – he liked it when people thought he couldn't hear them because he had slipped into his private twilight. They whispered and were usually indiscreet. He learned more by pretending to drift into a heroin-heavy coma. He played games with whisperers, though they never knew it.

Jason heard them leave the room. Awake now, he was beginning to feel some pain. Clarity of mind, too much clarity. But he sometimes liked that too, especially today. He rang the bell next to his bed. Brother Vincent glided silently into the room and raised the netting from around the bed.

'We are awake?'

'Yes, Brother Vincent. Up with the shutter. Awake enough to want some fresh air and to look through the balcony.'

'And the pain?'

'There's always the pain, Brother Vincent. It's a constant companion. We're like Siamese twins.' And Brother Vincent ministered the immediate nursing that Jason needed.

On the third visit, Arianne was more bold, bold and beautiful. This time she was dressed in yellow. The man stood next to her holding her hand. She spoke, 'Jason.' The man moved away from her. 'Too sensitive', Jason labelled Ben, unable to tell the difference between kindness and sensitivity.

'Jason! Can you hear me?' Jason opened his eyes and looked directly at Arianne. The room was filled with sunshine. The balcony curtains were open and a light, hot breeze was ruffling the curtain.

'That was very bad of Mike Chambers, bringing you here. Very bad indeed.'

'That's as maybe, but I'm here, Jason, and you're alive.'

'Not for you or anyone else, Arianne. What brings you here?'

'Is that all you have to say to me?'

'I think that it was a good question. You've intruded on my privacy.'

'Now see here . . .' said Ben.

349

Arianne grabbed Ben's hand and squeezed it. 'Jason, this is my friend Ben Johnson.'

'Hello, Ben. Look, why don't you two go out and see the city? It's an exciting, thrilling city. Go and have a good time.'

'Look here, we're not in Tangier to play the tourist.'

'What are you here for, Ben?'

'I am here to ask you for a divorce, Jason.' Jason began to laugh. 'Why are you laughing?'

'There is no Jason. He's dead. Dead men can't give divorces, Arianne. Go away, forget me. Forget you found me, ever saw me. I gave you away once, I don't intend to give you away again. Maybe I should have said, I gambled you away once.'

Ben had a sinking feeling. This was too unsavoury. He didn't think it was good for him, still less Arianne, to hear it. He took her hand. She pulled it away.

'What do you mean, "gambled me away once"?'

'Ask Ahmad.'

'I'm asking you, Jason.'

'Go away, Arianne. You're a complication I can no longer handle. And this is becoming tedious.' The door opened and Brother François entered with a doctor in a white coat, pulling a trolley, from which was suspended a clear plastic bag of fresh blood. An orderly, in a long white robe and white turban, rolled in an oxygen tank.

'I did tell you it was time to leave!' Jason spat out.

Arianne was stunned. Asleep, he had seemed so much the Jason she had once loved. Awake, he was a Jason he had never shown her. The sight of the medical team and their equipment shocked Arianne. It was a reality of Jason's condition that she had not quite taken in. Without another word, she and Ben walked from the room.

Arianne had to lean against the stone wall in the corridor. Ben placed an arm around her and she leaned her head on his shoulder. It was silent and peaceful in the long, narrow hall. She closed her eyes; tears stained her lashes. She took a deep breath, and when she felt more composed they walked slowly down the long hall. The only sound was Arianne's high heels echoing off the stone floor. From there they walked down the spiral stone staircase, through a cloister and across a courtyard paved in

350

stone, in its centre a well of marble worn by centuries of use, the angels and flowers carved in it impressively beautiful still. There was silence, except for a bird perched on the rim of the well, singing. The fluttering of wings – several white doves sitting on the cloister roof – ruffled the peace of this haven of quiet hidden behind walls in the midst of the teeming souk. From the cloister they entered another wing of the sixteenth-century monastery – the hospital wing, crowded with people, the poor people of Tangier.

It was a free hospital for the needy. People were everywhere. On chairs, sitting on the floor, leaning against the walls. Crying children and adults, white-coated doctors, nursing monks. Some Catholic sisters in their nun's habits, wearing huge wimples reminiscent of enormous white butterflies, flitted through the halls. It smelled of disinfectant and unwashed bodies, garlic, stale urine. Arianne and Ben elbowed their way through noisy crowds to burst out into the street where unruly lines of people formed to enter. They made their way through the narrow street of the souk to a café. Here they were to meet Mike Chambers.

Seeing the young man sitting at a table under an awning, Arianne halted and, placing a hand on Ben's arm, stopped him. In the midst of the crowds on the move they were jostled but Arianne stood firm, holding on to Ben. 'Ben, I want you to go, return to England. You've got to leave me here.'

'Impossible. I want you to come home with me today. We'll get a lawyer and let him handle it. It doesn't matter how long it takes, I want you out of here.'

'Don't do this, Ben. I honestly don't think you should insist upon that.'

'That's a sick man in there, not just because he needs blood transfusions or because he's bedridden, but because he's sick in mind. He's a lost soul, because he's a drug addict living in a half-world. Because he doesn't love you. He loves no one. He's a loveless creature and he's going to hurt you. He's hurting us now. You've seen him, he's alive. So what? You cannot deal with this. I can't deal with this. That boy sitting at the table over there, he'll tell you that. He's already told you that. We're leaving, even if I have to charter a plane.' He took her hand and pulled her along.

Arianne stopped him once more, just a few feet from the table.

'Everything you say is probably true, Ben, but I can't leave him now. I need some time with him. Even if I come back to you empty-handed, I need some time with him. I didn't think I did, until I saw those men come in. He's alone, utterly alone. He's getting the best medical care, I believe that, but he has no one to love him.'

'You love him?'

'Not in the way you mean. The sick need all the love they can get, and there is no love for him. The sick and the dying need love. Unconditional love. I've got to give him a little of that. I spent years loving that man. He was the biggest part of my life until you came along. I cannot leave him just now. Please understand that.'

'Ahmad understood that, Arianne. He knew you could never leave Jason, that you would go back to him. That son of a bitch, he knows you better than I do. How clever he was to plot all this – he knew it would separate us, bring you back into the fold.'

'It won't!'

'You don't think it will, but you're wrong.'

'A month, give me a month, not a day.'

'A month. And what after that? Another month, and another? Arianne, think well about this. I know this is hard for you. And if I could make it easier for you I would, but I can't, no one can. This is no overreaction to what I saw today. This is trying to avoid a tragedy.'

'Two more days,' she begged.

Ben hesitated. They remained for a time gazing intently at one another. 'I'm booking a reservation for the day after tomorrow, for two. The rest is up to you.' He walked away from her to join Mike. Arianne was appalled. Ben had never walked away from her before. Not since that day he served her coffee at Fortnum & Mason's.

At the table Mike asked, 'How is he?'

'I would say he was in cracking form.'

'Oh.'

'Precisely. Arianne wants to stay with him.'

'Oh, Arianne – you don't know what you're taking on.'

'Oh, but I do!'

'You've only seen him a few times and he was asleep most of the time.'

352

'She thinks he needs love and she's the one to give it to him. "Unconditional love", isn't that what you said, Arianne?'

'Yes. I do think that's what he wants, what he needs, and I can't walk away from that. Just a month, just to stay here in Tangier, and visit him, care for him, love him . . . Not the way I love you, Ben, this is something else. I will give him that and I know Jason: he'll give me a divorce. I can't just walk away from him.'

'You've never been able to walk away from him.' Mike Chambers discreetly vanished from the table. 'The first time I made love to you he was there. You gave me up for him then, and he was dead. At least, that's what you thought. And you couldn't give him up. If you stay now, what's going to happen to us?'

'I'll come back to you. I can never love anyone, Ben, not as I love you. And I don't think you can love anyone the way you love me. I'll come back to you.'

'And what if I'm not there? What if I won't wait? I ran after you once and won you back, but I'll not run after you a second time. I'm warning you now, Arianne, you risk losing me.'

'Then I'll find you when I've done what I have to do. When I'm really free. I'll take my chances that you'll wait for me. I believe we feel so deeply, so profoundly for one another, that time and distance are irrelevant. You'll be there for me – I have to believe that or I could never do what I feel compelled to do.'

'And how will you know when it's time to leave him?'

'I'll know.'

'That's not an answer. And did it ever occur to you that he might not let you go?'

'He will, because I'll tell him that I'm just visiting, staying with him. But you're my life, my future, my happiness.'

'Your mind is made up, isn't it?'

'Yes.'

'No matter what I say?'

'You wouldn't want it any other way. You'd always be wondering whether I should have stayed. Please indulge me in this.'

'Indulge you?'

'The wrong word.'

'Yes, Arianne, most certainly the wrong word.'

'Ben, I love you.'

'I know: more's the pity, but I think we're star-crossed lovers.'

'Don't say that.'

'Well, it certainly looks that way.' Together they walked through the café, his arm around her waist. 'We're gambling with our lives, Arianne.'

They found Mike at the end of the souk, waiting in the Mercedes for them. They drove through the traffic, horns blaring, crowds of people dispersing to let the car go through.

'We missed our drink. I know a nice place, are you game?' suggested Mike.

'Yes. My last night in Tangier – we should have a drink together. I'm taking the first flight out of here in the morning. I'd be grateful if you could get me that VIP treatment we had when we arrived.'

'No problem.'

It was several minutes before Mike turned around and said, 'Ben, I'm glad you managed to talk Arianne into leaving.'

'I guess I didn't. I'm taking that flight out of here alone. Arianne will be staying on and I'd be very grateful and indebted to you, if you could keep an eye out for her. I think she's going to need it.'

'Sorry, Arianne, but I wish you'd change your mind,' Mike said, looking concerned. Arianne bit the side of her lip and turned away from the two men, tears brimming in her eyes as she looked out of the window.

In the hotel Ben and Arianne ordered dinner to be served on the balcony of their room, but found they had no appetite. Instead they went to bed and made love: sweet, gentle love. As the night wore on that love turned to passion and later to lust, and then their thirst for each other was impossible to slake. Sleep was banished on their last night together. Jason's name was never mentioned again.

The sun was bright in the sky when Ben untied the silk scarves that bound Arianne to the bed posts. He had lashed her to them in his passionate desire to fuck her into sexual oblivion. Exhausted by then from her many orgasms, she wanted only to give him as much pleasure as she had had. She was over him with hands and mouth and searching fingers that only incited his ardour for her more, triggered his sexual fantasies.

The scarves had been found, Arianne tied down and she was his. At the mercy of his lust. She came and came, in a stream of orgasms she could no longer control. To swallow his seed, to feel him come inside her, to feel the exquisite gentleness he used to ease himself into that place between the cheeks of her bottom until she was so relaxed and open that he could move in and out of her, giving her incredible fucking. Then to feel the warmth of his sperm there. It was to submit to Ben and her orgasms with boundless joy. She was there where he wanted her to be, where he knew she loved to be, in that distant, mysterious place, sexual oblivion. A place of bliss like no other for a woman.

Mike was as good as his word. He was waiting for them in the lobby. The three walked to the waiting Mercedes. Ben was on the first flight to Paris. Hardly a word was spoken on the way to the airport. On arrival, the Mercedes went through the side gate, on to the tarmac and stopped where the men were standing. Handshakes all round for the same men who had met them only four days before. Ben thought about that: only four days, it seemed a lifetime. His loss was incalculable.

Ben and Arianne left the men standing near the car and crossed the tarmac together. They saw the stewardess wave from the top of the stairs. He was the last passenger to board and they were running late. The plane had been held for him. They hurried their steps.

'You won't change your mind?' he asked her, the pleading there in his eyes.

'I can't. Wait for me, Ben?'

'I can't promise that. Goodbye, Arianne.'

'That sounds so final, Ben.'

'It has to be.'

'It doesn't, you know. I'll call you. I'll call you tomorrow,' Arianne told him somewhat nervously.

'No, don't do that. You've made your decision, Arianne, I've made mine. I'll be moving out of Three Kings Yard. Don't make contact. I don't want to see you, hear from you, until you're really ready to come back once and for all.'

'Then you will wait?'

'No. I won't. I meant that goodbye. You'll have to take your chances just as I'm taking mine now.'

The stewardess ran halfway down the stairs of the plane's landing stage. She was shouting, 'Mr Johnson, please! Mr Johnson!' Ben pulled Arianne into his arms and he kissed her deeply, with great passion, and then ran for his plane, never once looking back.

Chapter 27

She was there again, standing on the balcony in a haze of bright sunlight, dressed in something white. He could see the outline of her body, sexy and provocative, the shadow of long legs, thighs, and when she turned around, as she did at that moment, just a hint of pussy. She looked at him and, seeing he was awake, stepped from the sunshine, into the room. The shadow of her body vanished under the cotton dress. He could imagine men's hungry eyes, heads turning, hands reaching into long robes to cop a feel. He laughed and reached under the crisp white sheet to do the same thing. But to Jason it meant nothing. He couldn't be bothered. Sex for him was more exciting in the mind, less demanding than in the act. At least that was the way it was now. These days, heroin was sexier than cunt.

Miraculous, his doctors termed his recovery, that he could move again – even achieve erection – was nearly whole, and in time... He laughed again, aloud this time, and smiled at Arianne. Life and sex were more sensual, more exciting, a hell of a lot more erotic than physical sex, when you lived in the twilight world. But then, he thought, who knows? Orgasm, like everything else, was available to him, but called up no emotion in Jason. Desire was only faintly there. His only real passion was the needle now, and that packet of pure white heroin and its accoutrements he kept taped to the underside of the table next to his bed.

'What are you doing here?' he asked her, not unkindly, 'and where's your friend?'

'In Paris.'

'You should have gone with him.'

'That's what he said.'

'Go away, Arianne, you're not going to get what you want here. No divorce, no answers.'

'What if I told you I'm not looking for answers? I've given up the idea of even forming any questions.'

'I'd say that was good. Good for you and very good for me. Now go away.'

A gentle knock at the door, perfect timing, and Brother François entered the room with a white enamel tray. On it were a syringe and a length of rubber tubing. 'Oh!' – his reaction on seeing Arianne there. 'I'll come back later.'

'No! I can't wait, you're late now, François. Go away, Arianne. I promise you you don't want to see this. Go away. If you're waxing sentimental about happy times, forget it. The happy times were over long ago. That tray, what's on that tray, is happy times now, and all I care about. Go home. Brother François, come on, we're wasting time. Nirvana calls.'

Arianne grabbed her handbag. She was biting back tears. The meanness, the anger in his voice – never in their life together had it been directed to her, but it was now. What had happened to him? She fled the room and ran down the empty corridor, her steps echoing behind her. Only in the sunshine of the courtyard, when she leaned against one of the pillars, was she able to breathe again. What was she doing there? Why hadn't she left with Ben? It was impossible, yet she felt compelled even now to stay, to try again to reach Jason. She hurried from the courtyard, elbowed her way through the mob of patients in the hospital corridor and into the street. The crowds gave her some comfort. Even the merchants hawking their wares as she pushed her way through the narrow streets were a welcome distraction.

In the square she found a taxi and fled back to her hotel. Arianne sat for a long time thinking about Jason, the Jason she had known and loved: the laughter, the smile in the eyes, how he had once loved her, cared for her, coddled her. His sexual ardour and prowess, how he had taught her the glories of sexual pleasure, created in her a sexual animal to satisfy him. She saw a vestige of that man in the Jason lying in that hospital bed in the hospice. How she had loved that other man. How easy it had been to give herself up to him and Ahmad. But that was then.

She looked at her watch: Mike Chambers was taking her to dinner. She changed into a black linen dress and clasped a choker of pearls around her neck. The dress, an off-the-shoulder affair, that fell softly to the waist, was cinched by a black belt, solid with black glass bugle-beads. Arianne draped a black silk shawl over her arm, not for warmth – it was hot, even late at night – but to cover herself in the streets.

Mike took her home to a small house he rented in the souk. It was behind a whitewashed wall with a crude wood door painted bright blue set into it. A fuchsia-coloured bougainvillaea dense with flowers lolled over the wall. They stepped into a small courtyard resplendent with more bougainvillaea and pots of flowering bushes. Lanterns and fat white candles cast a soft, warm glow into the garden – hanging on the wall, down on the tiles, strung up in the bushes, two on the stairs.

Mike called for the servants, a lady cook and a man, who came out and greeted him with happy smiles. Then he gave Arianne a tour of the sparsely furnished, immaculately clean, comfortable, but far from impressive house. One flight of stairs led to the bedroom, with a balcony overlooking the crooked streets in the souk. They took another, steeper flight up to the flat roof of the house to see the lights of Tangier spread out before them, and roof-tops of people catching a breath of air, dining, sleeping. Mike pointed out the monastery, surrounded by houses and shops and hidden in the maze of streets. There they remained to drink gin and talk about the wonders of Morocco. They returned to the garden for dinner, a *couscous aux poissons* and a tagine of lamb with olives and potatoes.

'You know I'm not always here for your husband. I'm sometimes reassigned for a few days to other jobs, but he is my main assignment.'

'Then he has no one when you're not there?'

'He does know a couple of people in Tangier, and they visit him. I never ask about it, it's not my business. I think they keep him supplied with more than company.'

'I don't understand.'

'The hospice, they keep his habit going because they have to. If Jason were to quit heroin, it could kill him – he is too far gone. So they are obliged to keep him supplied but controlled. But I've seen him at times when he seemed more out of it than usual. I know he's getting more from some place.'

'Shouldn't you do something about it?'

'No, and neither should you. I made a pact with your husband.

Anything he wants, remember. We brought him here to Tangier on the condition that it's his life and he'll do with it what he wants. Those were the conditions that even the hospice had to accept. The hospice is quite remarkable. They give him everything to keep him comfortable, and ask nothing.'

'There are no conditions?'

'None.'

'And who pays for all this?'

'Ah, I don't know, but it is paid for and handsomely. Your husband has everything he wants, that's why you should go home. He's got his life worked out for him, even his death.'

'I'm not going home, Mike, not just now. I want to stay in Tangier for a few weeks, a month. Can you find me a room somewhere? Something cheap. You see, I don't have much money and the hotel is too expensive. A room near here, even closer to the hospice.'

'Are you sure?'

'I'm sure.'

Every day she made a visit to Jason and almost every day he said barely a word to her. Arianne was in Jason's room again. This time she had brought flowers, long-stemmed miniature sunflowers. She arranged them in a clear glass vase – she had brought that too – and placed them on a table near the only chair in the room and where he had a good view of them. He was reading *Napoleon at Waterloo*. He ignored her for some time, then looked up. She was fanning herself with her hand. 'It's so hot,' she told him.

'It can never get hot enough for me. I'm always cold. Even on a day like this I'm just warm. You know I can give instructions for you not to be allowed in this room and they'll obey them?'

'But you won't do that.'

'Are you so sure?'

'No.'

He went back to his book and then drifted off to sleep.

The following day she arrived with Mike. Mike and Jason played chess. Jason won. Arianne had been in Morocco nearly three weeks. She spent her days discovering Tangier and visiting the hospice. Jason allowed her there – or more accurately, tolerated her presence. Most of the time he ignored her. Occasionally he would ask her about something in the city. 'Is Pépé's Café still in the square? Get Mike to take you to the marriage market. I always used to like going to the marriage market.'

'I never knew you'd come to Tangier.'

'You never knew a lot of things. End of conversation.' He was bored, uninterested.

One day she found him not in bed but sitting in a chair in the sun on the balcony, with a blanket over his knees. 'That's wonderful! You're up and sitting in a chair!' She was genuinely happy about his progress.

'Why don't you go away and take your enthusiasm with you?'

'Do I disturb you so much?'

'You don't disturb me at all. I merely asked why you don't go away.'

'I don't think you understand anything about what I'm doing here, Jason.'

'Oh, don't I? Go away, Arianne, and take your love with you.'

'You once liked my love, adored me for it.'

'That was a long time ago, and it was over a long time ago. It's a faint memory for me and one I don't even think about. I don't want to hurt you, but I don't want you to kill me with love either.'

'Then why do you let me come here?'

'Because I don't care enough even to stop you. I don't care much about anything any more. Only the needle and anybody that takes the pain away for even a minute.'

Arianne made ready to leave the room: she had had enough for that day. Brother François entered with an orderly carrying two plastic bags, one filled with clear liquid, and a syringe. Arianne rushed past him, appalled yet again that his condition demanded such medical care. It finally dawned on her how truly dependent he was on the good brothers of the monastery and the nursing sisters at the hospice, his doctors, and the needles. He hid it so well, his dependency. But hadn't she realised what he was still going through? He could move his arms, his legs, maybe he could even function sexually, but the rest – all those internal injuries, not being able to walk . . . He would never leave that room even if he could. She knew that she hadn't really understood it before now. That was his world; the room, the people who cared for him – they were his family, they were his lovers, they gave him all he cared about, all he wanted. Arianne began to cry. She could only stop when she realised she was crying for herself, not for Jason.

Mike had found a room for Arianne only a few houses from his – a small room at the top of a house, and she had the roof garden as well. The Moroccan family that lived below her room cooked meals for her. She was quite happy living there in that small room.

Mike was often away on other cases, but never for long. When he was in Tangier and free he would take Arianne out to dine. She was aware of Mike's attraction to her. Several times he had made a discreet pass at her. She was grateful for his company, and, though she did find him attractive, she side-stepped his advances. At least once in every ten times they met she would tell him, 'I will be leaving quite soon.' But Arianne did not leave Tangier. It had seduced her, and Jason was still accepting her visits. He seemed to rally; his humour improved. He never quite lost the Jason charm. It could still attract anyone to do anything for him.

He had even, on occasion, showed kindness, a begrudging admiration for Arianne. Once they even laughed together. Arianne found herself in a strange situation. It was inexplicable to her. She was there for him. Not loving him, but giving him all the attention and love she had within her that he would accept. Unconditional love, the sort she had always given him. Yet there was a tremendous void between them, an emptiness, a lack of emotion.

Arianne discovered the book markets, the booksellers. She found treasures, rare books, and bought them, packaged them and sent them, some to Christie's, others on approval to a client in New York. Jason, Tangier, became her life and yet strangely they were not her life at all. They were something transient. She knew she would one day have to leave.

She met several expatriates, and then stayed away from them. She wanted not to be a part of their world. She almost never thought of Ben. He was relegated to some safe place in the back of her mind, though she loved him not one bit less. Several times she told herself, I hope he'll still be there.

It was nearly three months since she had arrived in Tangier. Now it was she who could take Mike to places where real travellers, not tourists or the expatriates, went. One night in a small restaurant on the outskirts of the city where she and Mike were dining, she told him, 'Several times I've been to the hospice, knocked on Jason's door but could not enter. It had been locked from the inside. I would wait around for as much as half an hour and would leave having not seen him. I never mentioned it before because I always thought the doctors or some medical emergency demanded privacy. But the other day when I was there, the door was again locked and I passed the doctors and Brother François in the hall.'

'Jason sometimes locks the door when he has special visitors.' Mike looked embarrassed by his specious explanation.

Arianne felt numb, she hardly knew why. A woman, why should that affect her? Had she in her subconscious possibly hoped there could be something more for them than indifference? Platonic love? Was that what she was waiting for? Or the passionate love for her he had once been capable of? 'Oh!' she said.

'Sorry,' said Mike.

'You don't have to be.'

They talked of other things and then, apropos of nothing, she said, 'If only you had known us before the crash – we were something special together. He was a terrific person, a wonderful man. Oh, why did he ever make that trip? Whatever possessed him to fly over the Himalayas? With Jason it was always another adventure, another challenge. When I thought he was in the Rocky Mountains, he was flying halfway around the world. Why, Mike, why? To play the daredevil yet again?'

'I asked him once, when I first met him in that village in the Himalayas, what he was doing there, flying in that area. He told me he did it for a bet. He was flying against the clock from the Rockies to the Himalayas and back. A million-dollar bet. His best friend put up the million, and if he lost . . .' Mike stopped in the middle of his sentence and closed his eyes. He couldn't believe it: he hadn't realised what he was saying, who he was talking to. He had stopped thinking of Arianne as being Jason

Honey's wife. He thought of her as a beautiful, loving woman, in love with a guy called Ben Johnson, when he wasn't thinking of her as a woman he would like to make love to, hold in a passionate embrace. He couldn't very well tell her that Jason Honey had gambled his wife for a million dollars – and lost.

Arianne had a sinking feeling the moment Mike said, 'A million-dollar bet, his best friend put up the million.' It was impossible to fathom. Or was it? Arianne hesitated long enough to compose herself, then asked, 'Mike, what did Jason put up against the million? What was he going to give his best friend if he lost?'

Mike could see it in her eyes. She knew. She had somehow managed to figure it out. 'I didn't mean to tell you, I never meant you to know. I'm sorry. God, I'm sorry.'

'It doesn't matter. You don't have to say any more. It was me. He gambled me. He'd have given me up to win the bet. It all makes sense now. He crashed into the side of a mountain and lost the wager. He never made contact with me because he'd given me away to Ahmad, his best friend. He bartered me for a million dollars. He was through with me – he sold me on as if I were a slave. Oh, am I dumb! God, have I been stupid!'

'Arianne, you've got to put this out of your mind. It's bad, it couldn't be worse, the guy is warped. A rotter with a great cover. Forget him. You've got a great guy in Ben Johnson. Mark Jason off. You had the better side of him for a while, and then it went bad. That's how you have to think about your marriage to Jason. Forget the details. They could just drive you crazy.'

'Knowing hardly hurts. It shocks me more than pains me. I suppose that proves that I'm as finished with him as he is with me. I think I'd like to go home now.'

As they approached the house where Arianne was living Mike stopped her. 'Look, I could bite my tongue for what I let slip back there in the restaurant, but now you know, you have to take into account that Jason's got a dark side, darker than most of us. He's always had a dark side, you just never saw it. Don't reproach yourself for that.'

'I don't anymore.'

The following day Arianne returned to the hospice. She entered the room and sensed immediately that Jason was in one of his blacker moods. She had bought some sweet cakes and fried doughnut-like pastries that she knew he liked. On her way in, she had ordered some tea from one of the sisters. Arianne had moved the table close to his bed, and arranged the pastries on a plate. She drew a chair up to it. Jason watched her every move and when the tea arrived he was charming to Sister Marie-Pierre. As soon as the sister was out of the door, he told Arianne, 'I really hate it when you play the Good Samaritan.'

'But you like the tea and cakes?'

'Yes, that's true.'

'There is no pleasing you, Jason.'

'At last you understand.'

Arianne had learned over the last few months when Jason was in need of his fix. He became jumpy, as nasty as he was charming, vicious and clever. She had learned to let it wash over her. She ignored his remark and poured the tea.

Jason thought she was looking especially sexy in her simple thin cotton dress with its round neck and great balloon sleeves tight at the wrist. 'Go and lock the door,' he told her.

'Why?'

'Just do as you're told, go and lock the door.'

She locked the door. Returning to her chair, she sat down to drink her tea. Jason ate one of the doughnuts and smiled at her.

'You're really a good woman, Arianne. You've always been a good woman, that's why it was so much fun corrupting you. That was the best time of our life, the best part of our marriage, the sex. You know what made you so good? There was always that little bit more to get out of you, the little bit that you held back. You could always be pushed further, further into depravity. That was the most exciting thing about your love. That and your loving me unconditionally. There were times I could have fucked you to death. Nearly did. That was what made you so dangerous. Interesting but dangerous. You would have drowned in orgasms for me. For Ahmad, almost. He and I, we never had that with any other woman, I'll give you that.' This was the first personal conversation he had had with Arianne since her arrival. He could see how uncomfortable it was for her. He didn't care. 'You haven't changed.'

'I have, you know. You just don't want to see it.'

'Well, if you have . . .' And he did know that she had. There had been so many signs that he could hardly have missed. 'You haven't in one thing – you still know how to love.'

Arianne was surprised that he gave her that. She could not help wondering if she was after all reaching him. That was what she had been doing there: trying to give a sick man some love and attention. Compassion.

'You never mention Ahmad, Jason, why?'

'Indifference, even for old friends. Especially for old friends.' He drank some tea and ate another cake. 'Who did you find to replace me, Arianne?'

'You were never replaced, Jason.'

'That surprises me.'

'I'm sure it does. Could you have been thinking it was Ahmad?'

Jason chose not to answer her. Instead he asked, 'Did he get it off you, Arianne?'

'Did who get what off me?'

He leaned forward, a nasty look in his eye. 'Ben Johnson. That last vestige of love you held back from everyone but me. I bet he didn't,' and Jason began to laugh. 'Jesus, you're a bitch. You're a man-killer. You always hold out. I grant you, you enslaved yourself to me and I loved it, till I got bored. Do you know when it went wrong? Is that what you're doing here, come to find out when it went wrong? When it was over? That time in New York at the Plaza, remember?'

'Don't, stop. I don't want to remember.'

'Afraid?' he asked, a snigger in his voice.

'If I wasn't afraid then, I certainly am not now. Listen, Jason, if it was over for you that night, believe me that that sort of life I lived with you is over for me now. Those erotic games, those men. What were thrilling sexual games then are unthinkable obscenities to me now. I did them for love, damned right. But that's the past and dead. Why are you suddenly thinking about it now? So you were finished with me way back then. Bored and pretending, was that what you were? There's Jason at his best, always making capital out of his leftovers. You gambled me away.'

366

He began to laugh. When the laughter died, he told her, 'You've changed. I don't think I like you this way. I liked you better when you kept your mouth shut. I had complete control over you.'

'Well, you don't now.'

'I know, that's why you're boring. But you bring good cakes.'

'Why did you make me lock the door?'

'I wanted to see your tits again. For a brief moment I wanted to know once more how they felt. But the moment passed and I lost interest. You can unlock the door.'

'I'm leaving Tangier.'

'Without your divorce?'

'Yes, unless of course you can find some crooked way of getting one for me without revealing that you're not dead but very much alive.'

'I'll think about it. Put off leaving.'

'Why?'

'You've got no place to go anyway. You like Tangier. You give good cake.'

'I don't think so.'

The following morning, after several months of living in Tangier, Arianne left. She made a trip to Fez. It was a week before she returned to the hospice. She found Jason charming, if anything, over-excited at seeing her. She watched him talking to Mike, and listened to him giving a perceptive dissertation on Napoleon. How handsome he looked; the old charisma seemed to shine. But it was dulled for her. In the months that she had stayed with him he had got the last vestige of her that he had always wanted.

Mike was leaving. Jason and the young detective shook hands. 'Come here, you young stud,' ordered Jason. He reached his arms out and the two men hugged each other.

'See you when I get back,' Mike told him. He said goodbye to Arianne, then he left.

Jason dozed off. Arianne sat looking at him. She lost track of time. Her mind was for the first time in a long while quite empty of any thought of Jason. When he awoke, Jason was quite sombre.

'You're leaving me.'

'How can you tell? I've been leaving every day since I arrived months ago.'

'But today is different, you're really leaving me. You're dressed in the same outfit you wore when you arrived, looking very smart and chic. You came to say goodbye that first time. I think it was "Hello, give me a divorce, and goodbye", but you couldn't do it.'

'Well, I can do it now. Do I get my divorce?'

'Yes. You've earned it. You're five minutes away, ten at most, from freedom. If you come back in fifteen minutes the papers will be here.'

'Jason.'

'No, we don't want to talk now. You come back in fifteen minutes.'

Arianne did as she was told. She was smiling, looking beautiful and very happy when she walked from his room down the corridor, the same corridor she had walked a hundred times since the day she had found the hospice. She all but skipped down the flight of stairs to the inner courtyard and leaned against a pillar. Happy, so very happy it was over. She somehow felt she had escaped near-death, had come out of some dark and lonely place. She felt reborn, and able at last to think about Ben. He had waited, he could do nothing else. She had to believe that. There was so much to live together for.

Arianne looked at her watch. Five minutes, ten minutes away from freedom. Her airplane ticket was in her handbag, the last flight to Paris. Mike would drive her. She would never see Jason again. He had come through for her, and just when she had given up. She felt joyful. They were living in different worlds now, Jason and she. He was as happy as he would ever be in his. Now so would she be in hers. What more could she ask? She could always remember they had done their best for each other, all that they were capable of doing.

She looked at her watch again. A few minutes. Just enough time to walk that corridor and enter that room for the last time. Had he done it, what he had promised? Could he do it? Of course, he could do anything he wanted to. How clever he could be.

Arianne walked from the courtyard through the cloister and took the first few stairs of the spiral stone staircase. She felt suddenly and inexplicably strange, a hollowness in her stomach, a dryness in her mouth. She began running up the last few stairs to burst into the long hall. She stopped and tried to calm herself, took several deep breaths, while looking up at the vaulted ceiling. It stared back at her. Arianne braced herself and took several steps down the hall. Soon she was walking faster, then faster. She was whispering, 'Of course he can't do it. There will be no papers. But he promised me freedom.'

She began to run as fast as she could. She pushed past a sister in black robes and white wimple, who stumbled, pitching an enamel tray and its contents on the stone floor, but then caught herself and started running after Arianne. Brother François was coming out of another room having heard the quiet of the corridor shattered by clatter and running feet. He followed them. Arianne burst into Jason's room. She screamed, 'No! God, no!' and fell across his body, weeping. He looked handsome, at peace with the world. His arm hung limp, the needle still embedded in it, the syringe dangling from it.

They buried Jason Honey in Tangier. At his graveside were Mike Chambers, Arianne and Brother François. Arianne left the city the same night.

Epilogue

It was the end of the polo season, when Arianne returned to England and to Number 12, Three Kings Yard. The day she returned, she called Artemis and invited herself to lunch.

She stepped from the train on to the Chipping Wynchwood station platform. The station-master greeted her as if she had been gone for only a few days. The taxi driver chattered on about the weather, about not having seen her for so long. They went through the Chessington Park gates and up the winding drive towards the house. Everything looked perfect, clipped and green and fresh, the house a fairy castle, a children's dream-house. A wonder. Arianne, until her return, had hardly realised how much she loved it. Chessington Park, Chessington House – a safe haven from the real world.

It was a glorious day, warm, the sun bright in the sky. Beryl Quilty appeared as if from nowhere. She greeted Arianne briefly with a smile and reprimanded the driver. He had sped far too fast up the drive. Arianne laughed. It was really nice to be back and to know nothing had changed: not Chessington Park, nor Chessington House, nothing: neither time nor life had changed them. Reassuringly, Beryl Quilty was still on her beat.

Arianne rang the bell and entered the building. She crossed the glorious hall, and on entering Artemis's flat found Artemis at the piano playing Chopin amid the leaping and barking dogs. She leaned on the concert grand and smiled at her mother.

'How very nice you look, Arianne,' Artemis, visibly pleased, told her daughter.

'Mother, would you know where I can find Ben Johnson?'

'He's playing polo at Cirencester. I suggest after lunch would be a perfect time. It's cup day. A nice surprise for him if you appeared there.'

'Do you think so, Artemis?'

'Oh yes. Most acceptable. I'll ask Anson to join us for lunch. Then we can get him to drive us to Cirencester polo field in his Nazimobile.'

Lunch was delicious, a great success, with Artemis at her most charming and flirtatious with Anson, and Arianne entertaining them with a travelogue of her many months on the road: India, Pakistan, her trek across the Himalayas. The beauty of China and Japan. Those months that it had taken to put time and distance between herself and the tragedy that had been Jason. Artemis, in full control, like some benevolent general, ordered their departure from the table to the polo field. Her timing was impeccable: they arrived for the last chukka.

He looked so handsome, rode so well, played like a champion. It had been more than a year, and yet, seeing him again, time vanished and she felt as if they had hardly been parted at all. They watched the ponies leave the field and line up, waiting for the presentations. The riders dismounted to stand next to their ponies. She recognised Jaime talking and laughing with Ben. She had always believed it would be all right for her and Ben, but seeing their friend Jaime gave that extra tinge of certainty.

The silver cups and salvers were carried out to the field and placed on a green-baize-covered table that had preceded the trophies. Arianne, Anson and Artemis walked slowly round the edge of the crowd, seeking a better view of the event. An announcement came through a loudspeaker: 'Player of the Year . . . Ben Johnson.' Applause.

Arianne watched the Duke pick up the cup, and walk towards the line of ponies, their riders now standing at attention next to them.

'Thanks, Artemis.' Arianne kissed her mother on the cheek and left her standing with Anson. With her head held high, Arianne strode on to the field. She quickened her steps as she approached the Duke. Tapping him on the shoulder she asked, 'Do you mind, Your Grace?' With a dazzling smile, she removed the cup from his hands.

Arianne walked swiftly away from the Duke to Ben. She placed the silver trophy in his hands and said, 'We could drink champagne from it together at Le Manoir. I've made a reservation. What do you think?'

Ben closed his eyes. He took a deep breath; a slow, emotionally charged, tremulous sigh escaped him as he opened them again and a smile of exquisite delight appeared on his handsome face. Handing the trophy over to Jaime, he enfolded Arianne in his arms and told her, 'I think it's about time.' Then he kissed her deeply and with great passion, for all to see, many to envy.

ROBERTA LATOW

Her Hungry Heart

THE NEW NOVEL OF UNASHAMED SEXUALITY FROM THE AUTHOR OF *CANNONBERRY CHASE*

'A sunshine sizzler, packed with non-stop sex'.
People magazine

He was handsome, tall and slender, with bedroom eyes that devoured women. She was a tall willowy blonde with the looks of a showgirl, wealthy, cultivated and intelligent, an enchantress who knew how to tame men and, once they were tamed, clever enough to keep them. They met on New Year's Eve 1943 at a chic party in New York's fashionable Stork Club. Their erotic attraction was immediate and mutual. Their love affair would last a lifetime. But Karel Stefanik was not free to love Barbara Dunmellyn. He had Mimi, whom he had abandoned in the cruel chaos of war, a child whose fate becomes inextricably entangled with that of her father and the woman he loves.

This, then, is the story of their hungry hearts, the lovers that fuel their lives; and finally of their own all-encompassing love.

Don't miss Roberta Latow's seductive sagas *Three Rivers*, *Cheyney Fox* and *Cannonberry Chase*, also from Headline.
'The first lady of hanky panky. Her books are solidly about sex...it adds a frisson. It sets a hell of a standard'
The Sunday Times
'Naughty, certainly...the sex is larded with dollops of exoticism and luxury' *Observer*

FICTION/GENERAL   0 7472 3884 7

A selection of bestsellers from Headline

THE GIRL FROM COTTON LANE	Harry Bowling	£5.99 ☐
MAYFIELD	Joy Chambers	£5.99 ☐
DANGEROUS LADY	Martina Cole	£4.99 ☐
DON'T CRY ALONE	Josephine Cox	£5.99 ☐
DIAMONDS IN DANBY WALK	Pamela Evans	£4.99 ☐
STARS	Kathryn Harvey	£5.99 ☐
THIS TIME NEXT YEAR	Evelyn Hood	£4.99 ☐
LOVE, COME NO MORE	Adam Kennedy	£5.99 ☐
AN IMPOSSIBLE WOMAN	James Mitchell	£5.99 ☐
FORBIDDEN FEELINGS	Una-Mary Parker	£5.99 ☐
A WOMAN POSSESSED	Malcolm Ross	£5.99 ☐
THE FEATHER AND THE STONE	Patricia Shaw	£4.99 ☐
WYCHWOOD	E V Thompson	£4.99 ☐
ADAM'S DAUGHTERS	Elizabeth Villars	£4.99 ☐

All Headline books are available at your local bookshop or newsagent, or can be ordered direct from the publisher. Just tick the titles you want and fill in the form below. Prices and availability subject to change without notice.

Headline Book Publishing PLC, Cash Sales Department, Bookpoint, 39 Milton Park, Abingdon, OXON, OX14 4TD, UK. If you have a credit card you may order by telephone — 0235 831700.

Please enclose a cheque or postal order made payable to Bookpoint Ltd to the value of the cover price and allow the following for postage and packing:
UK & BFPO: £1.00 for the first book, 50p for the second book and 30p for each additional book ordered up to a maximum charge of £3.00.
OVERSEAS & EIRE: £2.00 for the first book, £1.00 for the second book and 50p for each additional book.

Name ....

Address ....

....

....

If you would prefer to pay by credit card, please complete:
Please debit my Visa/Access/Diner's Card/American Express (delete as applicable) card no:

Signature ....Expiry Date ....